1636
THE KREMLIN
GAMES

1636
THE KREMLIN GAMES

ERIC FLINT
GORG HUFF
PAULA GOODLETT

To science and technology,
which changes our lives, improves our lives, and often saves our lives.
And pfui to the nay-sayers.

1636: THE KREMLIN GAMES

A Baen Books Original

Baen Publishing Enterprises
P.O. Box 1403
Riverdale, NY 10471
www.baen.com

ISBN: 978-1-4516-3776-2

Cover art by Tom Kidd
Maps by Gorg Huff

First printing, June 2012

Distributed by Simon & Schuster
1230 Avenue of the Americas
New York, NY 10020

Library of Congress Cataloging-in-Publication Data

Flint, Eric.
  1636 : the Kremlin games / Eric Flint, Gorg Huff, Paula Goodlett.
     p. cm. — (Ring of fire ; 14)
  ISBN 978-1-4516-3776-2 (hc)
  1. Time travel—Fiction. 2. Seventeenth century—Fiction. 3. West Virginia—History—Fiction. 4. Russia—History—Fiction. I. Huff, Gorg. II. Goodlett, Paula. III. Title. IV. Title: Sixteen thirty-six.
  PS3556.L548A61867 2012
  813'.54—dc23

                                        2012003330

10 9 8 7 6 5 4 3 2 1

Pages by Joy Freeman (www.pagesbyjoy.com)
Printed in the United States of America

Contents

Maps   vii

1636: The Kremlin Games   1

Cast of Characters   407

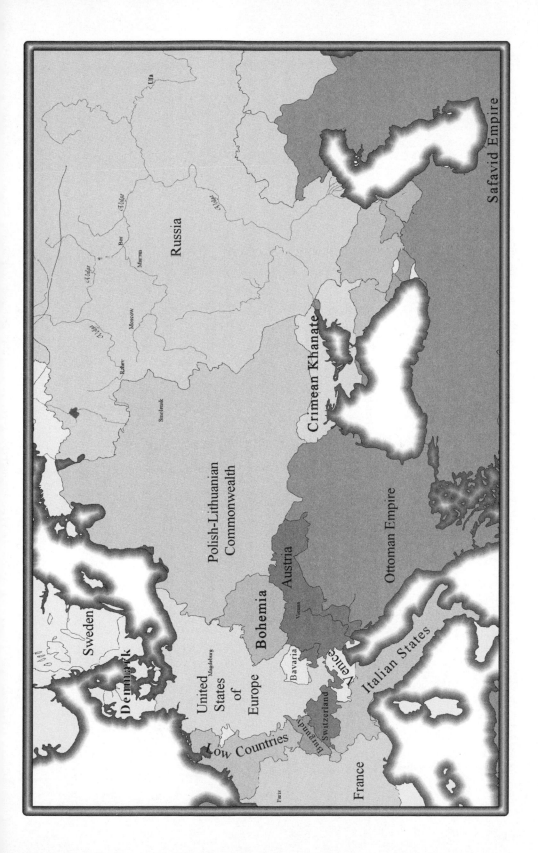

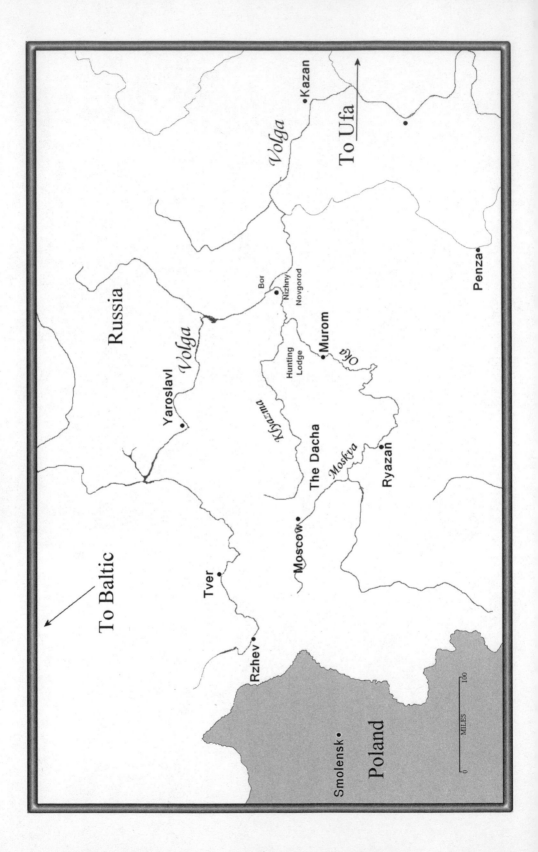

Part One

The year 1631

Chapter 1

Grantville
October 1631

Vladimir Gorchakov pulled his horse up as he saw Boris Ivanovich Petrov stopping to look around. "Apparently Tilly's tercio commander wasn't the liar we thought he was."

"This place is worth the trip," Boris said. "See the cuts in the earth where the land was changed? Look at these hills. The structure is different from those outside the ring. Everything inside this Ring of Fire is different."

Most of their entourage was still on its way from Jena, but neither he nor Boris had wanted to delay long enough to sell all their trade goods or drag what was left along with them. They had left the matter in the hands of Fedor Ivanovich and ridden on ahead, with just two attendants.

"I was convinced it was a fraud of some sort." Boris was shaking his head in wonder. "But anyone who could fake this kind of thing would have too much power to need to fake anything."

Vladimir nodded to the bureau man and patted his horse. "I believed it was a preposterous lie right up until we got to Jena. It was the up-timer and that APC that made me start to suspect it might not be. Once you've seen one of those 'cars,' well, you must believe that something has happened."

"For me it was the view from Rudolstadt." Boris grinned. "But I am a cynic. Cars can be made by men. Not this!" He waved at the circle of inward- and outward-facing cliffs.

Vladimir remembered his first sight of over a mile of mirror-smooth cliffs. It had been beyond impressive. It was as though God had taken a scoop out of the earth and replaced it with a scoop of something else. He could see Boris' point.

Vladimir looked over at Boris. Boris Ivanovich was an unassuming little man, the sort of man who could blend in anywhere and not be noticed. He didn't look at all impressive. Appearances lied. Boris was a bureaucrat of Russia, specifically of the *Posol'sky Prikaz*, the Embassy Bureau or State Department. He was an experienced spy and a well-traveled agent. He spoke, read, and wrote Russian, Polish, Danish, German, English, and, of course, Latin and Greek. He had been assigned to accompany Vladimir Petrovich on this "fool's errand" by the czar's father in an attempt to keep the czar from looking any more foolish than could be avoided. *And probably*, Vladimir acknowledged, *to keep me out of trouble.*

Vladimir was sure Boris had his own thoughts about the situation. He could even make a good guess about what Boris was thinking. Not that any of it showed on Boris' face. Boris, at the moment, was wearing his I'm-too-dumb-to-pound-sand look. No, it was the situation; any bureau man would be thinking the same thing. Boris' rank in the bureaucracy that ran Russia was higher than Vladimir's, or had been. He had been demoted without prejudice for this mission since Vladimir was a *kniaz,* a prince. Vladimir, as a prince with almost independent lands—combined with his friendship with the czar—was almost certain to end up as a boyar of the cabinet. It would be totally inappropriate to have him under the orders of someone with Boris' lack of pedigree. But without prejudice or not, it was still a demotion. And if things went wrong it would be really easy to leave Boris demoted. That had been a major concern on their way here, Vladimir knew.

The fact that Grantville wasn't a hoax presented Boris with both problems and opportunities. Powerful people didn't like to be proven wrong, and there was more than a little bit of a tendency to kill the messenger in the Russian government. On the other hand, the fact that Grantville was not a hoax meant that keeping the czar from looking foolish in sending the mission became much easier. Certain people at court were not going to like that, either.

Moreover, since Grantville did exist, a network of spies would have to be put in place to watch it. Boris was in an excellent position to end up an important figure in that network. And the politics of the situation meant the Grantville Office in Moscow would be an important one. Poland was Russia's great enemy at the moment and Germany was just the other side of it. Now a section of Germany was peaceful and relatively prosperous instead of being torn up by war. The up-timers, as the locals called them, had to be encouraged to take Sweden's side. So far they had friendly relations with the Swedish king but nothing more than that.

"It is not such a large place," Vladimir said, looking around as they rode, and patting the horse's neck now and then. "And there are not so many up-timers as I had thought."

"A small place, yes, but it will play a large role," Boris said. "The cars, APC's—or whatever their proper name—the improved roads, that device we saw in the fields outside Rudolstadt..." Vladimir knew what Boris was talking about though he didn't know the name either. Whatever they called it, it did the work of a village of serfs faster and possibly cheaper.

"In a way, more important is that scraping bucket that was pulled by a team of horse," Boris continued. "I would imagine that the cars and that thing in the field are hard to make but the scraping bucket...that any Russian smith could build given the idea and a bit of time. This place will change the world. We will need to find any centers of learning they have. Gather quickly the information they give freely. If they really do give it freely."

"Yes, Boris. Look into that as soon as we find a place to stay," Vladimir said.

Chapter 2

"I would like some information," Boris said to the woman behind the desk.

"Your name is?"

"Boris Ivanovich Petrov, of Muscovy."

"Ah." The woman smiled. "Russian, then. I wondered about your accent. All I could really tell was eastern European. I'm Cecelia Calafano."

"*Da*, Russia. That is what we have called the motherland for some time now. It is the rest of Europe that still calls us Muscovy. That has changed in the future?"

"Yes, it has," the woman Cecelia confirmed. "How can I help you?"

Boris smiled at her. "We've been sent to determine if this place is real."

Cecelia laughed. "I've lived here all my life. Trust me, it's real. What did you want to know?"

The man behind Boris was clearing his throat, as though Boris were taking too much time. Boris was much too much of a professional to turn and pound the oaf into the floor. Not too much to want to, though.

It was a moot point. Cecelia gave the oaf a look that melted him on the spot. Apparently, librarian was a post of some importance here. Boris gave her a list he had written in consultation with young Vladimir. Cecelia took a quick look. It was in English,

6

carefully written. She sighed and Boris wondered why. Consistent spelling was some time in the future; it wasn't something that Boris had ever known so wasn't something he missed. It was, to Boris' eye, a perfectly legible list.

She began to read aloud carefully. "How to make telephones. A history of the Romanov family. How to make cars. A history of Muscovy, or Russia. I think you're probably in the wrong place."

Boris looked at the woman. Here it came the runaround. *Yes, we give such knowledge away, but not here* was what he was expecting to hear.

What heard instead was, "Never mind," followed by another sigh. The meaning of this one was clear. She had seen his response before. "Some of this you will be able to find here. Like the history of Russia or part of it. I'll get you some books."

Boris examined the books. *Russia Under the Old Regime* by someone with the very non-Russian name of Pipes. He looked at the table of contents. *Chapter 4: The Anatomy of the Patrimonial Regime.* Boris tried to translate the words to Russian. The body parts of the fatherhood rulers? That sounded positively obscene. Boris worked it out. Anatomy meant the structure of a body . . . perhaps it was used here to represent the structure of the government. Patrimonial regime . . . might mean inherited rule or it might mean government by the church. Was Russia going to be ruled by the priesthood? Considering the relative political strengths of the patriarch and the czar, it could happen. This would be monstrously time-consuming. He looked at the other book. Perhaps it would be clearer. What was the USSR? What was the revolution of 1917? For that matter, what was St. Petersburg? At least, that's what he thought it said. There was no St. Petersburg in his Russia.

He read through the books as well as he could for several hours, making notes. Some things were clear enough. The year of birth and death of the czar and his son and his grandson. Others weren't. The analysis was just weird. It was all there, Boris thought, but looked at as though through a prism. The light split into the spectra and the image was lost. Was this Pipes an idiot? Upon considering the matter, Boris didn't think so. So might a citizen of Caesar's Rome respond to a history of Rome written by a modern scholar who had never seen the Coliseum or been present at a triumph.

The woman stopped by a time or two. Handed him what she called a magazine. "Here," she'd said. "You might find something in this."

It was an old, fragile thing, this magazine. And what did *perestroika* mean? Boris knew what "restructuring" meant, but the word seemed to be used a bit differently here.

Much befuddled, Boris gave up for now. It was getting late and he needed to get back to the room they had rented. He wasn't going to figure it all out in a day.

It was as he was putting things away that the librarian came and sat down at the table. "Can I give you some advice?"

Boris nodded cautiously.

"If what you wanted was a nice place to come and read an occasional book, this would be the place for you and I encourage you to do that. However, this isn't the place for what you're after. The Grantville Public Library was never intended to be a center of research. It was designed to be a small-town library at the tail end of the twentieth century. We had interlibrary loans and the Internet. Before the Ring of Fire, if we didn't have the book someone wanted, we could get it in a few weeks through interlibrary loans. What we had on the shelves were the books most likely to be wanted in a small town. A small town that didn't need to make telephones or automobiles. We could buy them. We have books on how to fix an automobile. Those books usually tell the reader how to install a new part that they are expected to buy from an automobile parts supply store that got its parts from a manufacturer in another state. What I mean is, they tell you how to fix a car, not how to make one from scratch."

Boris nodded politely, but he was wondering if this was perhaps how they were hiding the important information. That concern decreased as she continued.

"Shortly after the Ring of Fire, it was decided to use the library at the high school as our national library, our Library of Alexandria." The woman gave him a questioning look and he nodded his understanding.

She continued. "In it, we have at least one copy of almost all the books that came through the Ring of Fire. In those books there is enough information to tell you how to make an automobile, at least most of it. Even there, it's not all in one book. It's scattered around in books designed to teach children the basics of how things work, in biographies of the people involved in the inventing of the automobile and its mass production and so on." The woman took a deep breath. "That makes it a treasure hunt. It's hard even for a professional to know which book to look in to find the thing you're after. Trying to do it on your own..." She shrugged. "I recommend you hire a professional researcher. If you don't have the money for that, you can put in information requests and the library researchers will get around to it as they have time. Your other option is to take the library science basic course at the high school and pay the usage fees."

Boris considered. The little talk she had given him was well-rehearsed. "How often do you give that little speech?"

She smiled. "About twice a week."

"About the usage fees you mentioned...you don't have them here. Why not?"

"We're funded by the national library. We have been since a few months after the Ring of Fire. There was a minor fight in the emergency committee about that, but public libraries being free for public use is a long standing tradition up-time. There was a bigger fight about having fees to use the national library." She laughed. "By the time that fight got going there were already millions of dollars worth of products coming out of the library. People were wondering why the cash-strapped government should pay to make a bunch of people rich. A compromise was worked out. You can get anything you want out of the national library and research center free, if you're willing to wait your turn. And it can be a long wait. You can also pay to get it faster. Quite a lot of people pay either by paying a professional licensed researcher or by taking the course and paying the usage fees."

Boris had a lot to think about as he walked back to the room they had rented.

"So, Boris how did it go?" Vladimir asked as Boris looked for a place to sit. The difficulty had to do with the size of the room. Grantville's population growth had far outstripped new construction. Even their small room was expensive.

The lodgings were fantastically well appointed but horribly cramped. The four of them shared a single bedroom with its own "half bath," an indoor toilet and sink with "faucets" that provided hot and cold water. They had access—from two to four in the afternoon—to the main bath, where they could take hot showers.

"Confusingly, Prince Vladimir," Boris said as he sat on the bed. He shook his head. "It's early yet to tell, but I don't think they are lying about it. Understanding the information is a problem. The English language...it has changed. Very much. The woman at their public library freely gave me books to look at. Books that will need to be looked at again. I've made notes." Boris waved a sheaf of papers in the air. "Pages and pages of notes, but very few of them make sense."

Vladimir started going through the notes. "This is clear." Vladimir pointed at a line. "Czar Mikhail will...have only a few more years. The patriarch...much less."

"Perhaps not." Boris' face showed very little. "I asked about that. These up-timers...they do not understand what has happened. But their arrival changed many things. The librarian said that those changes will—already have—changed history. In ways not imagined. When I saw that place in the book, I, too, was shocked. The woman was very kind. She asked what was wrong, and then saw the page I looked at. She said that there were things we could do. 'Send the aspirin,' which they have here. It might help or it might not."

Vladimir nodded. "We shall, with the first courier."

Boris waved the notes aside. "That is not what I wished to discuss. We can use the public library with no trouble but the real wealth of knowledge is in the national library. From what the woman said, using the national library will entail some cost..." He shrugged. "...or unacceptable delay. I am not that concerned about the fees to hire a researcher.

"I am concerned about two things," Boris continued. "First that the researcher might edit the reports and second that he might sell reports on what we were looking into to agents from other lands. I think we need someone to take the library science course and, at the very least, watch any researcher we hire. For some questions we will want to do the research ourselves."

"That sounds like a job for me," Vladimir said. "I speak the language and am less experienced in some of the other work we will need to do here." *In other words, I'm not a very good spy.*

Boris was nodding. "That was my thought." He smiled. "That will leave the rest of us time to learn how the rest of Europe is responding to this place. Also if you would write the letter to Patriarch Filaret, I would be grateful. That is an area where I suspect you have more skill than the rest of us combined."

Most esteemed Patriarch,

This is not what you expected to read in my report. Nor is it what I expected to write. Tilly's officer was neither insane nor a liar. No one knows the why of it but the Lord God has seen fit to do something remarkable here. I am sitting in a room that has a window covered with a large, flat piece of glass. It lets in the sunlight and the scene outside with no noticeable distortion. In the next room you can turn a knob and have hot water. These things could be the work of skilled artisans. However, they are not all we have seen. There are works of man that could not have been done by the men of our time.

The Ring of Fire itself could not have been made by men of any age. I do not believe that it could have been made by any power short of the infinite power of God. What they call the Ring of Fire is a circle, as near as anyone can tell a perfect circle, six miles across. Within that circle the land has been replaced with land of a different nature, made of different sorts of stone. The hills are as different as though in a single step you traveled a hundred miles. In the months since the event there has been some weathering. In spite of that, it is easy to see the perfection of the cut. The evidence we have found is too consistent to be false. They are from the future.

As I write this, I know that you will realize that I am only reporting what I have determined from this up-time history. The news is not good. War with Poland, right now, is destined to fail. Russia does not have the resources needed. As Colonel Leslie has said many times, the army lacks the proper training and discipline.

I must urge that the attempts to modernize the army take precedence. Also, that any attempt against Poland be delayed until that is complete. See the report attached.

Additionally, and this is most important, you are at risk, as is your son, our Most Holy Czar. The death of either of you would leave Russia exposed to more troubles. I include in this package a vial of medicine that may assist you both, in the hope that it may help. The histories speak of your death in the year 1633, but they do not specify the cause. I have spoken to the up-time physicians, who tell me that this medicine is often prescribed to those at risk of heart failures. It has the added benefit of relieving aches and pains.

Also, see the pamphlets translated with the aid of up-timers. They tell much about the avoidance and treatment of disease. I urge you most sincerely to give them full credence. The doctors from up-time are already considered miracle workers by the local Germans...

Vladimir had struggled with that letter. How did you tell a man that the goal of his lifetime was a disaster and that he was scheduled to die soon? Perhaps, though, Patriarch Filaret would be comforted by the rest of the information he was sending.

"When do we go home?" Trotsky asked.

It was a tender subject. Fedor Ivanovich Trotsky was a bureau man from the lower nobility. In essence, he was the expedition's secretary and ranked fourth or fifth in the group—but only second to Boris as a secret agent. So if Vladimir and Boris left for home, Trotsky would wind up in charge. He would run the network competently enough, but with little or no imagination.

"That has become a rather more difficult question," Vladimir said. The mission was to come to the Ring of Fire, find out that it was nothing, then go home. "The Ring of Fire does exist after all, and is a repository of great knowledge."

"Trotsky does have a point, Prince Vladimir," Boris said. "We're here only to confirm the existence of the place, not to immigrate to it."

"I know. But there is so much here that we need in Russia. You know as well as I do that as soon as Patriarch Filaret hears what we have found, he will want a permanent presence here."

"Probably," Boris agreed. "Assuming he believes us."

That's a touchy point, Vladimir thought. It wasn't that the patriarch or the czar lacked faith in their powers of observation. But a town from the future wasn't the easiest thing to believe. "We'll take proof or send it."

"Send it?" Trotsky asked.

Trotsky was a bit of a stickler for authority. A tendency that hadn't been diminished at all by Vladimir's pointing out that he shared a name with a famous revolutionary of the future.

"Yes, send it. I realize that some of us are going to have to go home but..." Vladimir paused, trying to figure out how to put it.

"The histories we have seen have shown Mother Russia lagging behind the West in wealth and prestige," Boris finished for him. "I suspect that the prince is concerned that we will fall even further behind in this timeline."

"Well, at the least I see the Ring of Fire as an opportunity to let Russia avoid the errors of that other history," Vladimir said. "An opportunity that might be lost if we just go home. There will be factions at court that won't want to look ahead and will oppose anything that might upset the social order."

"If some of us are to stay here," Boris said, "we will have to send as conclusive a proof as we can manage."

Chapter 3

Vladimir had been told that the Thuringen Gardens was a good place to relax and have a drink and he was feeling in need of both. The very large beer hall was crowded and noisy. Vladimir found himself a seat against one wall and waved to a waitress, then looked around again while he waited for his beer. At the next table was what appeared to be an up-timer somewhat in his cups. You couldn't always tell. Many of the down-timers had adopted up-timer dress. But the fellow was muttering into his beer in English with the up-timer accent. Vladimir's beer arrived, he paid and drank. It was good beer, substantial.

"I wish all this hadn't happened," the up-timer muttered.

"You wish what hadn't happened?" Vladimir asked.

The up-timer looked at Vladimir a bit blearily, raised his mug and indicated the world around him with a sweeping motion of his hand. Unfortunately, about half the beer spilled. "Damn. Something else to wish hadn't happened."

Vladimir chuckled. "You should be more careful. The beer is good, and should not be wasted. It's a bit, ah, high-priced to throw around the room."

"No shit, Sherlock." The up-timer snorted. "Oops. Sorry. I forget sometimes that I'm not back in the world. I guess I shouldn't say things like that anymore. Somebody might take it the wrong way."

"No" and "shit" were words Vladimir knew, though he could

think of nothing offensive about "No shit." The term "sherlock" was unknown to him. Perhaps it was the offensive party.

Vladimir stood up. "Might I join you at your table?" He walked the two feet that separated them. "I would like to know what 'no shit, sherlock' means. You Americans, you have such odd expressions. Another one I don't understand is 'a screw loose.' How that is different from 'being loose' or 'screwing around'?" Vladimir had spent some hours reading a novel yesterday, trying to gain a better understanding of the changes in English.

"Sure, join me." The up-timer used a foot to move a chair out from under the table. "Have a seat. I'm Bernie Zeppi."

"I am *Kniaz* Vladimir Gorchakov of Muscovy," Vladimir said, taking the vacant seat. Vladimir waved at the waitress and mimed his desire for a pitcher of beer. The waitress nodded.

"Is *Kniaz* your first name?" Bernie Zeppi asked, which told Vladimir that even in his cups the man was observant.

"No. *Kniaz* is a title. It can be translated into English as anything from a prince to a duke or perhaps a count, if the Englishman is being particularly rude." Vladimir shrugged. "I am a relatively low-ranked *kniaz*. So, what did you mean by 'all this'?"

"I mean all of it." Bernie waved at the room, this time with the hand that didn't contain a mug of beer. "The Ring of Fire, it killed my mom, gave me PTSD. I did my part. I was at the Crapper and Jena. But there's too many mechanics for the private cars we have running. And I don't want to sit in a factory, babying an old engine that's been pulled to power it. No way I'm going to tie myself down into the Mechanical Support Division working for the government. So now I'm stuck on the work gangs, trying to get by."

"You are not in your army?" Vladimir asked. "I thought most of the young men were in the army."

"I told you I was at the Crapper and Jena. I'm in the reserves. I go if they call, but not until. I didn't end up covered in glory like Jeff Higgins. Imagine a nerd like Jeff Higgins ending up a hero." Bernie paused and shook his head. "Not me, though. Just the breaks. They haven't been running my way since the Ring of Fire." Another pause. "What's Muscovy? Your turn to answer a question."

It was a question Vladimir had gotten before. "Russia, but most nations of western Europe don't call it that yet."

"So what are you doing in Grantville?"

"Spying." Vladimir grinned.

"Are you supposed to tell people that?" Bernie grinned back. "I wouldn't think an espionage agent would just walk up to someone and say 'Hi, I'm a spy.'"

"Well, it saves time. Officially I'm a representative of the czar, here to determine if the stories about Grantville are true." Vladimir grinned again without a thought. It came easily to him. "Everyone in Europe has spies in Grantville. I'm expecting spies from China to show up any day now."

Bernie laughed. "Yeah, China. Why not? So, what vital secret are you trying to get out of me, Mr. Spy?"

"How many planets are in the solar system?"

"Huh?"

"How many planets are there?"

"Why do you want to know that?" Bernie looked at Vladimir with puzzled face.

Vladimir took a sip of beer. "Do you know?"

"Well, yes. Nine, but so what? Everybody knows that."

"I'm afraid not. What people outside of Grantville know, if they know anything, is that there are six."

"Six?"

"Yes. Mercury, Venus, Earth, Mars, Jupiter and Saturn. And they only know that if they're educated and not too conservative. Otherwise they think that the sun, the Moon, and all the planets go around the Earth on crystal spheres. Now that I have done my work for today, care for another beer?" Vladimir took up the recently delivered pitcher and poured Bernie a refill. "And after that, we can do tomorrow's work, if you like. What are the names of the other three planets?"

"Gee, I don't know, Vladimir." Bernie smirked. "Well, I might know. But a beer isn't going to buy that information. A sandwich might, though."

Vladimir pondered something Zeppi had mentioned earlier. He cleared his throat. "I do not mean to be rude, but is this 'PTSD' a disease I need to worry about? What do you call it? An 'infectious disease,' I believe."

Bernie stared at him for a moment and then barked a little laugh. "No, you can relax. It's not exactly a disease. More like a mental condition. The initials stand for 'post-traumatic stress disorder.' I got it at the battle of the Crapper."

Vladimir considered that information for a moment. He knew enough English to make rough sense out of the expression, but the precise meaning still escaped him.

"You were badly injured?" he asked.

Zeppi drained his beer and set the mug down carefully. "No. It was the other way around. I'm a very good shot and it turns out I don't freeze in combat like a lot of guys do." His face was completely expressionless. "I killed a lot of men that day. At least five, probably more. I get flashbacks about it, still."

The term "flashback" was unfamiliar, but Vladimir thought he understood the essence of the matter.

Interesting. It seemed there were some depths to the man not apparent at first glance.

Bernie wasn't quite sure how it happened but by the end of the evening he had a part-time job. As a spy, no less. He did make it clear that he wouldn't betray the folks in Grantville. That didn't seem to be what interested the Russian spy, though.

Vladimir grinned at Boris' expression or lack of one. "I know that he's not a trained agent or in a particularly valuable position, but that's all to the good."

Boris just looked at him.

"Yes, I want to send him to Russia," Vladimir said. "And not just as proof the up-timers exist. That too, but I've been thinking."

Boris' face got even blanker, if that was possible.

"I can probably get copies of up-time books and pamphlets but translations are another matter. You speak English as well as anyone I know, Boris. How well have you done translating the language the up-timers speak to the English of our time? We want him for his up-time knowledge, Boris, not his abilities as a spy. And he's not as stupid as he seems at first. Just undirected. Remember, these up-timers have their own time of troubles with the Ring of Fire. Bernie's mother died on the day of the Battle of the Crapper for lack of up-time medicines. He's having trouble adjusting to the strange new world he has been thrust into. Also, his life so far has been one of privilege. I know dozens of sons of great houses who are like him. Nothing they really need to do, so they play with their horses and their hawks and ignore the wider world. Bernie has his cars, his computer, and video games."

Boris shook his head. "I don't disapprove, Prince Vladimir. I realize that he has value. Just access to his computer is worth more than we are paying him. I take it you mean to stay here while I take Bernie back to Russia in your place."

"That's an interesting way of putting it," Vladimir said. "But I mean it more as an example of why I have to stay here for a while. We've talked about this a bit, but I've been thinking about it a lot. I think I have come up with a plan that will help Russia and us."

They talked it out, Boris' part and the part that Vladimir expected his sister to play.

Chapter 4

Bernie wasn't drunk but he did have a little buzz going. He'd mostly had something of a buzz going since the Battle of the Crapper and in the process had pretty much alienated everyone in his family. Mostly everyone he knew except Brandy, a waitress at the Club 250. He was a functional alcoholic; he didn't drink enough most of the time to render himself incapable of doing his job, but often he had enough of a buzz to keep him from doing it as well as he might. Most days since meeting Vladimir in the Gardens, he had dropped by and talked with Vladimir or Boris about whatever was on their minds. Or they had dropped by his place to talk and use his computer. Today they were at Bernie's house. At least till his dad threw him out, which was looking like it might come any day now.

Boris was slowly and carefully tapping keys on the keyboard and Vladimir was sipping his beer.

"Bernie," Vladimir said, "we have an offer to make you."

"They've been pretty good offers so far, Vladimir," Bernie said. "What have you got in mind?" Bernie was sort of hoping that Vladimir wanted to hire him full-time so he could quit the road gangs.

"How would you like to live in Russia?"

That pulled Bernie up short. Russia had had a sucky reputation in the twentieth century and it had an even suckier one in the seventeenth. Bernie sat back and gave Vladimir a serious look.

"Honestly, Vladimir? I probably wouldn't. Nothing against your homeland, but from what I understand, life there isn't pleasant. Even less pleasant than it is here, and Germany is in the middle of a war. I'm used to hot and cold running water, flush toilets and the like."

Boris snorted from the keyboard of the computer. "Granted, we don't have hot and cold running water, but we have pretty servant girls in plenty to carry the water. And carrying water isn't all they do. The quality of life in this century—and I would imagine in yours as well—is greatly dependent on your status. Here you are one up-timer among many and while up-timer carries a certain status..." Boris turned from the computer and looked Bernie in the eye. "Your status here is close to the bottom of that of up-timers. In Russia you would be the only up-timer and vital to a project that would be of value to all of Russia. That would naturally entail considerably higher status than you enjoy here. Status in Russia carries more privileges than it does here."

Vladimir shrugged. "Give it some thought, Bernie. But think quickly if you will. Boris must return to Moscow to report soon, and I would like to send you with him."

Bernie did give it some thought, enough that he almost sobered up to think about it. The truth was that there wasn't much here for him except harsh looks from his family and manual labor. Besides, the notion of willing serving girls appealed to him, although it wasn't the big draw that Boris seemed to assume it would be. Even screwed up the way he'd been since the Ring of Fire, Bernie never had much trouble getting laid.

The big attraction was simply that it would be a big change. Bernie wasn't given to what he considered excessive introspection, but he'd have to be a complete dimwit not to understand that if he didn't do something to turn his life around—and dramatically, at that—he'd just keep sliding down into a pit. If he stayed here he'd probably drink himself to death in the next few years.

Still, much as he had come to like Vladimir, it was Boris that he would be going to Russia with and he wasn't at all sure that he trusted the short, bearded, fireplug of a man. So he consulted a lawyer and insisted on a contract of employment. Bernie knew the contract might not be enforceable once he got to Russia, but what the hell. He figured it was better than nothing.

Bernie went to the national library and looked up Russia. That led him to look up Cossacks and Poland. And it occurred to Bernie that Russia was a very dangerous place. In a way, that made it easier for him to decide to go. The risk, in its way, was as appealing as anything else. Risk was usually coupled with opportunity. In Russia, however it turned out, he might actually be able to do something important. Here, he was just pissing his life away.

Chapter 5

It was on a cold blustery November morning in 1631 that Bernie, Boris, and some gear loaded onto the small hovercraft that would take them down the frozen Saale River to the Elbe. The hovercraft would have to make three trips to get their gear and the rest of the party to the Elbe. And each trip would take a day.

Four days later Boris had hired a barge and a small company of guards to take them down the Elbe to Hamburg. Germany was still a war zone, after all. He had also made arrangements with an innkeeper in Barby on the Elbe to forward mail going each way to Grantville and Hamburg. Boris was setting up a secure mail route from Grantville to Moscow and back. From Barby it was two weeks to Hamburg. In Hamburg, Boris renewed his acquaintance with a merchant who had been sending broadsheets from Hamburg to Moscow for years. And informed him that if things worked out he would be shipping a lot more both ways and his recompense would likewise increase. From Hamburg to Lübeck was two and a half freezing, wet days in wagons. And Bernie was seriously wishing he had never agreed to come.

The Baltic coaster that carried them from Lübeck to the Swedish stronghold of Nyenschantz, near what in the original timeline would have become St. Petersburg, was, if anything, less comfortable and more crowded than the wagons. They didn't actually visit Nyenschantz. Boris was in no hurry to bring Bernie's presence to the attention of the Swedes. Instead, they stopped at an inn in the town of Nyen, across the river from the stronghold. Boris sent a courier on ahead while he organized the sleigh trip to Moscow.

Part Two

The year 1632

Chapter 6

January 1632

"Home," Boris sighed, then waved at the red brick walls of the Kremlin that stood sixty feet tall and dominated the mostly wooden city of Moscow.

Bernie Zeppi, after the long trip, didn't care if it was home or not and certainly didn't care about the view. He just wanted in out of the cold. The Russian winter had stopped both Napoleon and Hitler in Bernie's old timeline. In the new one, in the middle of the Little Ice Age, it had almost killed Bernie. He looked out from not-quite-frozen eyeballs under completely-frozen eyebrows, at a snow-covered town. A big town, granted, but it was made of log cabins, not the concrete buildings Bernie remembered from pictures of twentieth-century Russia. What surprised Bernie was that the log-cabin Moscow that was before him looked even dirtier and less inviting than the concrete monstrosities of the Soviet Union looked in the pictures he'd seen. "Where do we go first?"

Boris pointed toward a street. "My townhouse first, then I must make a report and get instructions."

Boris burst into the house roaring something in Russian. Bernie thought it might be "I'm home" or "we're here" or something like that. But Bernie's Russian was still very poor. A short plump

27

woman responded with "*Da* something," in a tone that said she was less than impressed. Boris deflated and gave the woman a kiss on the cheek.

Bernie, not understanding what was going on, looked around. It was a moderate-sized room with a few very small windows. One corner had several of the religious paintings that were called icons, and the other had about the biggest stove he'd ever seen.

Then Bernie was introduced to Mrs. Boris whose name turned out to be Mariya. There was more Russian, including the words "Natalia Gorchakovna," which Bernie knew was the name of Vladimir's sister. So Boris was probably telling Mrs. Boris about the plans. Bernie was to stay with Boris and his family for the next day or so while introductions were to be made.

Mariya spoke a little English with the weird Russian-Shakespeare combination accent that Boris and Vladimir had, but even stronger on the Russian part. Even that little was more than Bernie was expecting. There were, it turned out, English merchants living in Moscow and in other places in Russia. Also English mercenaries hired to modernize the Russian army. At least, that was the impression Bernie got from Mariya's accented comments. Honestly, most of it flowed by him without delivering much in the way of meaning.

They got him seated, then switched to Russian while Bernie sat and thawed a bit.

Boris looked at Mariya, feasting his eyes. "Vasilii said I was to report directly to the patriarch. Otherwise I would have taken the outlander to the Gorchakov townhouse. Vladimir, I wrote you about him, has arranged for his sister to house him rather than putting him up with the other outlanders."

"Is that wise?" Mariya asked as a servant busied himself at the stove. "The bureaus are in an uproar." At Boris' curious look, she explained. "They didn't want to believe that the miracle was real. They especially didn't want to believe that God would leave us on our own in the Time of Troubles, then give the Germanies a miracle in their need. The monasteries especially disliked that part." Then she snorted a laugh. "I wasn't pleased by the implications myself. Even with the letters and books you sent. It seemed, still seems, as though God cares more for Germany than Russia. So there are factions that were arguing that it was a fraud right up until Vasilii arrived to say you were on your way. Some still are."

Boris shook his head. "I didn't want to believe it either, but after the reports we've sent, I would have thought—" At his wife's look, he hesitated. "I guess it is an unbelievable story. But you can't not believe after you've seen the glass-smooth cliffs of the ring wall."

"Is it really that special?" Mariya sounded a bit wistful. Unlike Boris, she had never been out of Russia. "I got your letters but..."

"Yes and no." Boris tilted his hand back and forth. "In some ways it is the most miraculous thing you could imagine and in others quite mundane." He shook his head. "Enough of that for now. I will tell you all about it later. Now I need to know what is going on in the bureaus." So they discussed the different factions that were shifting around the miracle in Germany. The fraud faction, the work of the devil faction, the God's will faction. Which bureau chiefs were leaning which way. How the great families were lining up. The most common reaction was "wait and see," then "how can my family benefit or be harmed," followed closely by "how will it affect my bureau?" All of which was flavored with the question: What's wrong with us that God would leave us to cold harsh winter and give the Ring of Fire to the Germanies?

"From what I hear—" Mariya lifted the pot of water. "—the czar wants to see the outlander as soon as he can but the bureaus want a chance to talk to your Bernie first so they can formulate policy. They have managed to fill the czar's schedule for the next week or so to give them a chance to do so."

"And the patriarch?" Boris asked.

"The czar's father has made no public statements and he's even been quite reticent in private, at least according to rumor. I imagine that's part of the reason you're to report to him."

Chapter 7

Half an hour into the conversation with the patriarch, Boris felt wrung out. Patriarch Filaret apparently remembered every fact he'd read about Grantville, not to mention every bit of the history he'd read. They'd already been through the butterfly effect and every bit of Boris' knowledge of the spies in Grantville. Now, Filaret changed the subject.

"So, this Bernie Zeppi, he has come to work for us?"

"Ah...not quite." Boris twitched in his seat. "In fact, he has come to work for Prince Vladimir. Who has paid—and is paying—his salary, so far. And there is a personal contract." Boris produced the contract for the patriarch's perusal. Filaret took it and read through it rapidly. Several times during the reading he gave Boris sharp looks.

His brow creased. "A rather large salary. Do you feel it will be worth it?"

Boris was surprised at the choice of first question. By custom, outlanders were always hired to work for the czar, not members of the court or the bureaus. "I can't say for certain. The up-time knowledge is worth a thousand times that salary. Patriarch..." He paused. "They could fly up-time. I have seen the movies, heard the stories—they could fly. And I have no doubt they will again, if they survive another five or ten years."

✧   ✧   ✧

Filaret leaned back in his chair. This was the reason he'd called for Boris Petrov to see him. He wanted to hear, first hand. "Yet they don't fly now. None of the machines, the airplanes, was it? None came with them."

Boris nodded. "True. It was a poor village of peasants that was sent back to us. Yet even there they have miracles in every art and philosophy and in things we had not even dreamed of. Undreamed of wealth, Patriarch. The products of mass production, they call it. Everything identical, made by machines. If we can make the machines, we should be able to do the same."

Filaret raised an eyebrow. "Yet you say you're not sure?"

Boris sighed. "You know the problems with hiring outlander experts. If they were really experts they would be getting rich where they were. What we get are the less adept or the ones no one is willing to hire for some reason. We have seen that, time after time."

"Your outlander is a mal-adept?"

"You must remember that there were only around three thousand people brought back in the Ring of Fire. That includes babes still at their mothers' breast and those so... sick that they could not survive without constant intervention from their medical practitioners."

Boris had, Filaret was sure, almost said "so old" but caught himself in time. Filaret hid a smile. He was over eighty and Boris was afraid to offend.

"By their standards," Boris continued, "it was not a particularly educated group. Most adults had high school diplomas... never mind. The point is that anyone who had much in the way of special skills or unusual talent was already employed by their government, or getting rich right there in Grantville, or both.

"Bernie is friendly, willing, and doesn't lie about his abilities. That, above all else, Vladimir insisted on and I agreed. We have had too many master cannon makers who were more familiar with gold than bronze."

Boris paused and Filaret considered. Boris was good at his job and Vladimir was clever. He didn't think that Vladimir was planning anything against the czar, partly because Vladimir was a good lad and a friend of the family, but mostly because he was staying in Grantville. Manipulating court politics from such a distance was almost impossible. Not entirely impossible; Filaret had done it from imprisonment in Poland. But that was a special case and hadn't worked out the way he had wanted. At the same time, Filaret realized that Vladimir was beginning to play politics, albeit at a remove. This project was to be the Gorchakovs' entrance into the ranks of the high families and Filaret thought he could use that. There was a great deal of tension in the *Boyar Duma*, in part because of the Ring of Fire and the general uncertainty of what it might mean, but also because the word from Grantville had weakened the war faction and given hope to the Polish-lovers like his own cousin, Fedor Ivanovich Sheremetev.

By this time Filaret had almost decided to approve the project, but he had a few more questions.

"Then—" Filaret leaned forward with his fingertips steepled. "—if he is so unskilled, what is he doing here? And why did Vladimir hire him into the Gorchakov family's service instead of the czar's? Why agree to pay him so much?" He motioned toward the contract. "This is what we would pay for a colonel of artillery."

"His salary is the least of the expense of this project," Boris admitted. This was one of the most important parts of the plan. "Vladimir had an idea. He will be having copies made of the books in Grantville. They will be sent here. But they are only copies, Patriarch, not translations. Not even Latin translations, much less Russian. He doesn't have the staff, or the cash on hand, to pay to have it done and the time it would take would put us years behind. The books will have to be translated here or our experts must learn up-timer English."

"I still don't understand what we need this outlander for. Not that I object to his presence. The czar has been anxious to meet an outlander from this miracle and I am curious myself. That, however, doesn't justify this salary or this change in our traditional ways." The patriarch waved a hand at the contract again. "Contracts like this . . . well, I suppose I can understand the idea. But it's not the way we have done things and I don't like the precedent it sets."

"I speak the English of England in this century quite well," Boris said. "The American English of the end of the twentieth century is full of words that I don't even have the concepts for. What is an electromagnetic field?" Boris used Russian for field and English for electromagnetic.

At Filaret's look, he answered his own question, sort of. "Had someone asked me that before I went to Grantville, I would have had no idea what they were talking about. Even if I had looked up electromagnetic in a dictionary from Grantville, I would still have thought it a nonsense phrase. The dictionary would tell me that 'electromagnetic' is the adjective form of the word 'electro-magnetism' which is magnetism caused by an electrical current, which is useful to know. But the real trouble comes with 'field,' because the field they are talking about has nothing to do with plowing or reaping nor with grain or grass or battles or the flags and ensigns carried into battle. It's the area where the electromagnetism is, which I didn't find out because though I didn't know the meaning of electromagnetism, I did know the meaning of field.

"When I asked Bernie what an electromagnetic field was. He told me 'it's what makes electric motors work and I'd have to look it up if you want to know more.' I explained that I had looked up electromagnetic and it had not helped much. We discussed it for a while till it came about that Bernie's definition of field contained several more meanings than mine did. Between us we worked out roughly how an electric motor works and how the changing of the electromagnetic field is crucial to its working. I understand it a little, but it feels profoundly unnatural to me, like the incantations of magic might feel."

"Could it be magic?" Filaret asked.

"No, Patriarch." Boris shook his head, trying to put into that gesture all the certainty that he had gained in his time in Grantville. "It feels like magic because it is so different from the way we are used to thinking. There are no demons running their machines and if an electromagnetic field is an unseen force, it carries no motive, no will. It is an effect like water turning a waterwheel. Not magic, just craftsmanship and great knowledge."

"Very well. So this Bernie will tell us what the words from the future mean. What about the contract?"

"Bernie insisted on it, Patriarch. I think he was a bit afraid that once we got him here we'd lock him in a dungeon and use whips and tongs to get him to work."

"Certainly an option worth considering," Filaret said, and Boris knew very well that the patriarch wasn't joking. Not even a little bit.

Boris nodded. "Hence the contract and a share of the money to be paid into an account in Grantville. The contract helps assuage his fears and the fact that we have to send some of the money to Grantville anyway helps even more. We need him enough to make it worthwhile to pamper him a bit before we attempt harsher methods.

"It's hard to explain unless you have seen what they can do and how freely they give out their knowledge. Prince Vladimir is convinced that if we don't have someone like Bernie, if we don't gain this knowledge and do it now while the door is opened—" He paused and took a deep breath. "Russia, without the knowledge— the up-time knowledge—facing a Europe with that knowledge, will not survive more than a few decades."

"Why is Vladimir paying for this?" The patriarch was nodding. Good, Boris thought. He understood why Bernie was needed.

"He wants to set up a think tank." Boris spoke entirely in Russian but the concept didn't translate well.

Boris tried again at Filaret's expression of annoyance. "A gathering of minds, also a research center. A place where concepts and devices from the books and notes he is sending can be tried. Tests can be done to see what will and will not work. A place where the knowledge from the future can be combined with the talents of Russians to make both the things he sends us designs for and new designs of our own."

The patriarch nodded, his mind jumping ahead of Boris' explanation. "Where?"

"The Gorchakov family has a large and comfortable dacha and hunting park a day's ride from Moscow. Close enough to Moscow for convenience, yet far enough away so that it can be kept fairly private. He promises not only its use but money for the materials needed for the experimentation. Some thousands of rubles a year."

"That explains what he wants to do, Boris Ivanovich Petrov. It does not explain why the contract with this Bernard Zeppi is with Vladimir Petrovich Gorchakov, not Mikhail Fedorivich Romanov, Czar of all Russia."

"Vladimir is willing to commit the Gorchakov family to the primary funding of the project."

"And he wants what in exchange?"

"The exclusive rights to produce and sell the products of the dacha." This was common. One family might have exclusive rights to mine iron ore in a certain area, rights they had purchased from the government. Another might have exclusive rights to sell the furs of another area. Filaret was hardly a novice when it came to that type of negotiation.

"No, that won't work," Filaret said. "The Gorchakov family is rich but not that rich."

"He plans to sell the rights to produce individual products," Boris explained. "The research center will make a working model of, say, a reaping machine, and designs for the parts to it, then sell the rights to make the reaping machines to another clan or to a set of villages."

The patriarch nodded and considered. "Exclusive except for the government. I'll not have the government giving the Gorchakov family the rights, then paying for the research as well." That too was standard. The government of Russia maintained first call on everything. If a family gained exclusive control of a mine, what that family got was what came out of the mine beyond the government's share.

"Of course, Patriarch." Boris nodded. As each new device was made both the government and the Gorchakov family would have the right to produce it if they chose. In the case of the reaping machine, the government would be able to either make reaping machines itself or have them made; so would the Gorchakov family. The Gorchakov family might want to sell its rights to make the product but that would not affect the government's rights. "Of course, the research center will need experts from some of the bureaus."

Filaret nodded thoughtfully. "That can be arranged. And the church?"

"Vladimir would prefer not to make an open grant to the church." Boris' answer was delicate. "There have been abuses of such grants in the past. I am very much afraid the bureaus would not like such a blanket grant either." The Russian Orthodox Church was neither monolithic nor free from corruption. Monasteries vied for power and wealth with the great families and each other.

The patriarch grinned rather sardonically and nodded. "The patriarch's office, then." He laughed at Boris' expression. "Not even that?"

Boris steeled himself. "Who will be the next patriarch?"

Filaret nodded, but lost his smile.

"Vladimir did wish me to convey his warmest personal regards to you, Patriarch Filaret. His concern, and frankly mine, is that the next patriarch may not share your concern for the czar or for Holy Rus. Do you remember mention of Patriarch Nikon from the histories we sent?" Boris really wished he could avoid this part of the conversation. He was used to bureaucratic infighting but not at this level.

Filaret grimaced but nodded. "However, I am patriarch now."

"As long as that happy situation remains, the patriarch's office will receive anything the dacha can provide."

Filaret's fingers made a drum roll on the desk as he thought about it. "It is a great risk for young Vladimir. He could ruin his family if it doesn't work." Then he stared at Boris. "What about you, Boris? What do you gain in this? What do you risk?"

"It has been suggested that I would make an excellent candidate for the head of the Grantville section of the embassy bureau." He shrugged. "That is both the reward and the risk. If it doesn't work, well, my position in the bureau would become untenable."

"Yes, it would." Another pause while the patriarch's fingers continued to tap out a strange beat on the desk. "Very well. I will talk to Fedor Ivanovich Sheremetev, then. I'll even do what I can to get the appropriate people assigned to your section and loaned to the Gorchakov dacha."

He gave Boris a hard look, his eyes seeming to glitter for a moment. "You understand what you're risking?"

"I think so, Patriarch."

Chapter 8

Bernie had a private letter from Vladimir to his sister Natasha, whose legal name was Natalia. Vladimir hadn't made a big deal of it, but Bernie had the impression that Vladimir would prefer that Boris didn't know about the private letter. So Bernie waited while Boris sent a message to warn the great lady that Boris was bringing a barbarian to be examined and to put mats down on the floor in case the strange creature should decide to take a dump on it. At least that was Bernie's impression of Boris' attitude. It was hard to tell what the little guy thought.

As promised, Boris delivered Bernie the next day. They were ushered in by an armed retainer who looked a warning at Bernie and left them in a warm, well lit room with a great big stonework heater. In the room was a tall, willow-thin woman with long, black hair and snow-white makeup and red-painted lips. Boris went ahead and kissed her on the cheek as was the custom. She had to lean down to accept the kiss and suddenly they looked to Bernie like nothing so much as Boris and Natasha from the Bullwinkle cartoons.

Boris and Natasha looked like Boris and Natasha. Bernie cracked up. He couldn't help it. He had been nervous all morning after the lecture Mrs. Petrov had given him on how important the Gorchakov family was. And suddenly it was like he was in a Rocky and Bullwinkle cartoon. He cracked up. He almost had himself under control when "Where's Bullwinkle?" slipped out. He lost it again.

Things were getting tense by the time Bernie really got himself under control. "I'm sorry. I'm away from home and nervous about the new job. It was just that you two right then happened to look like Boris and Natasha."

Now the princess was looking confused again. "But we are," she said with a distinctly Slavic accent. "He's Boris and I'm called Natasha."

"I know." Bernie shook his head. "I think that's what really did it. Not like you, Boris and Natasha; like the cartoon Boris and Natasha. Natasha was tall and slinky, ah, beautiful with a very pale face and red lips, Boris was short and stocky. They were spies." Another giggle. "Spies who were constantly trying to blow up Rocky the Flying Squirrel and Bullwinkle J. Moose. I used to watch it on Nickelodeon when I was a kid."

"What is a cartoon?" Princess Natasha was apparently much mollified by the notion that this other Natasha was beautiful. Bernie was less confident of her reaction to slinky, though you never knew.

"It's a simple drawing," Bernie tried to explain.

"Something like an icon but without the religious significance," Boris clarified.

"Except the ones with Boris and Natasha moved."

"Moved how?" Natasha's forehead creased under the makeup. "Did they shake the paper?"

Which led to a discussion of moving pictures in general and how they were made. By the end of this discussion, Natasha was too interested to be offended.

"Now I see how it works." Natasha saw something else too. This was why they needed Bernie Zeppi and why they should turn the dacha into a research center. He had not come here to introduce moving icons on a screen. It had just popped out like a chicken laying an egg. He cackled a bit and there it was. How many other eggs were buried in this stranger from the future and how valuable would they be to the family? Natasha had seen mimes and clowns perform. In spite of his comments, she knew that the movies and cartoons didn't need sound to attract an audience. She was pleased again when, while Boris was talking to her Aunt

Sofia, Bernie managed to pass her a letter "from your brother." Then he had gone on about Rocky and Bullwinkle blundering along and thwarting Boris and Natasha while Bullwinkle at least didn't have a clue what was going on.

Over all, Natasha was quite impressed with Vladimir's up-timer, as were some of the other people Boris introduced him to over the next week.

Chapter 9

"I think we can use him," General Kabanov said. He was in charge of guns and weapons for the *Streltzi,* the musketeers who served Russian cities as guardsmen as well as providing much of the army's infantry. "He does seem to know a great deal about guns and their use."

Bernie had just finished disassembling and reassembling his up-time rifle and then loading it and emptying it into a set of targets. Boris nodded in response to the general's assessment. He saw no need to point out that Bernie's familiarity with the rifle was not particularly unusual among up-timers. Grantville was a town of hunters.

"Why can't we make these repeating rifles?" General Kabanov asked Bernie. But he didn't speak English, much less up-timer English, so questions were funneled through Boris. Which was probably for the best, as it allowed him to edit at need.

"Primers," Bernie said. "You can't make the primers. We went over all this in Grantville."

"In the brass cartridges," Boris translated, "are compounds of a chemical that is difficult and expensive to make in quantity—"

So it went. It was the third interview that day and there were three more to go and still more tomorrow.

"Why did you have to bring us an idiot?" Filip Pavlovich Tupikov was pacing back and forth, scratching furiously at a rather weak beard. "They know how to fly. They can make materials we never dreamed of. And you bring us this? Not a doctor, not a . . . what is the word? Engineer. Not an engineer. Instead you bring us this . . . this . . . barely a craftsman. Why, Boris Ivanovich?"

Boris Ivanovich looked at Filip Pavlovich. The man was a brilliant artisan and a skilled natural philosopher, but had no understanding of how the world worked. Besides, Boris had been getting some version of this from about half the interviewers for the last two weeks. "Ah, how foolish of me." Boris snorted. "I should, no doubt, have asked their president, Mike Stearns, to give up all he had in Grantville and come be a servant in Russia. Or perhaps the master of machining, Ollie Reardon, would have given up his factory with its machines and the electric to run them. Better yet, I could have tried to persuade Melissa Mailey, a qualified teacher in their high school. Of course, she has been heard to say—more than once, I should point out—that they should start by executing nine out of ten of the nobility of Europe. She then suggests that they go up from there. I'm sure she would have been happy to serve the czar."

Filip Pavlovich flinched a bit. Boris felt he'd gotten his point across. "I brought Bernie Zeppi because he was who I could get. He has graduated their high school. He is a qualified auto mechanic with tools. I should know. I had to arrange for their transport. He speaks, reads and writes their up-timer English. English which is not so similar to the English we know as Polish is to Russian. You can get by with practice but the words have changed their meaning and pronunciation as often as not. Believe me, Filip Pavlovich, there are people I could have recruited that you would have liked much less."

Bernie sighed. "When is this sh . . . ah . . . stuff going to be done with? Let me get to work, will you?" Bernie wasn't all that anxious to get to work, just to get out of Moscow and away from the interviews.

"Soon, Bernie, soon," Boris said. "We have the audience today. Princess Natalia will be down soon and we will leave."

"The makeup again?" Bernie chuckled.

Boris glared at Bernie, remembering the silly business about Boris and Natasha. "I trust you will be able to control your sense of humor."

"Wish she'd hurry up." Bernie's complaint brought Boris back to the present. Then Natasha arrived, walked to Boris and said in a deep sultry voice—not her own—but which Bernie claimed was a fairly good imitation of the cartoon Natasha: "Welcome, my little Borisky. This time we will capture that naughty moose, yes?"

Bernie grinned and Boris turned red.

Bernie tried to suppress his grin as Boris and Natasha coached him very carefully for his meeting with Mr. Big. Mr. Big, otherwise known as the Czar of All the Russias. Armed with Vladimir's gifts, as well as his own, Bernie followed their instructions carefully.

Boris whispered names and positions while they stood in the line of people waiting to be presented. "Patriarch Filaret, the czar's father, there to the left of Czar Mikhail. On the right, Fedor Ivanovich Sheremetev, the czar's cousin; he is in charge of the bureau of records. It is an especially powerful post, because he can cause so much trouble for the other bureaus." The list of names went on and on. Bernie quit paying that much attention, except for the fact that they all seemed to be related to the czar. Natasha had left them, and gone off to see the czar's wife. When they got a bit closer, Bernie started looking around a bit. Fortunately, he had good eyesight. The room was huge, at least eighty feet long and broad in proportion.

Mr. Big—no, that really didn't seem to fit—was a pretty ordinary guy when you got a look at him. The czar looked to be in his mid-thirties. He also looked like he didn't want to be here. Sort of bored and sad. He seemed like the kind of guy who got stuffed in his locker in gym class. The patriarch guy, his father, was really old, but looked to be a tough old bird. And all these... *boyars*, they were called. There was some serious money tied up in their clothes. At the same time there was something a bit tawdry about the whole thing. The cleaning staff hadn't done that good a job on the great hall and most of the fancy outfits needed cleaning—but not as much as the people wearing them.

"Dmitri Mamstriukovich Cherakasky." Boris nodded toward another man. "Not a man to cross, that one." Well, Bernie wasn't going to cross anyone if he could help it. This place was to the period movies Bernie had seen as *The Good, the Bad and the Ugly* was to *Roy Rogers*.

Finally, they got up to the front of the line. Boris did all the talking, which was just as well. Bernie hadn't had much luck figuring out the lingo yet. Boris gave the agreed upon signal and Bernie bowed. "Your Majesty."

Mikhail Romanov smiled kindly back at Bernie's attempt to bow. "Welcome to Moscow."

Bernie bowed again and Boris made a gesture, so Bernie presented his gifts. Czar Mikhail looked at the watch curiously.

"It is an up-time 'watch.'" Boris spoke softly. "If you will press that button there, it will light up."

The czar, clearly with some trepidation, pressed the button and managed to say "Very interesting."

They finished the interview, so Bernie and company were ready to leave the next day.

Chapter 10

Bernie sat in the sleigh and moped. He should be interested and excited, but he couldn't manage to feel even an echo of such an emotion. It had just hit him again: the Ring of Fire, the people he'd killed at the Battle of the Crapper and his mother's death. He could quit and go home but it wasn't home. Home didn't exist anymore. Bernie wanted a drink. He knew he shouldn't have one but he wanted one.

He had been drinking a lot less since they started for Russia. Getting out of Grantville had helped, but sometimes it all came back on him. For some unknown reason, today was one of those times. Midwinter this far north had short frigging days. Maybe that had something to do with it. He'd read something about that somewhere.

Natasha looked over at him and grinned. "We will reach the dacha soon, Bernie."

Bernie grunted without much enthusiasm. *God, I wish I had my car. I wish I had some gas. I wish . . .*

"What is wrong, Bernie?"

"Nothing you can help with, nothing anyone can help with really. I guess I'm just homesick."

"You wish you could go back? But we have only begun to become acquainted."

Bernie noted with some amusement that Natasha's vamp routine needed a bit of work. Still it was nice that she was trying to cheer him up. "No, I don't wish to go back. Not back to Germany anyway. I wish I could go home, back to the world I came from. This world isn't home. Even Grantville isn't home. I used to do all right, you know. I had enough money to do what I wanted, for the most part. I dated, I worked my hours. I had a life." *I hadn't killed anyone; I had a mother who was still alive.* "Now, though, well, it's just not the same, not even in Grantville."

Bernie looked at the girl. She seemed nice enough and she hadn't gotten pissed at the Boris and Natasha bit. On the other hand, she was Vladimir's sister and Bernie had finally figured out just how rich and powerful Vladimir was after he had gotten to Moscow. This girl was the daughter of a great house. She was pretty, dark-haired and slim. Slimmer than a lot of the Russian women, with black hair that hung down to her waist. She spoke some English. Funny-sounding English, but English. Mostly, though, she was someone to talk to and Bernie was sick of thinking about his troubles.

"So," he said, "tell me about yourself." Natasha looked taken aback by the question and the old lady, Vladimir's Aunt Sofia, cackled a bit. Bernie didn't have a clue why.

"Ah ..." Natasha stopped. "What do you wish to know?"

"Oh ..." Bernie hesitated a moment. "What do you figure on doing with your life? Do you have any plans to become a doctor or lawyer? What's it like in the summer here? Is there summer here? Do you like parties?" He snorted. "What's your sign? That's probably too many questions, isn't it?"

"Perhaps," Natasha acknowledged. "In any case, I didn't understand what all of them meant. I don't know what my sign is. Unless you mean the family crest."

"Never mind," Bernie scratched his chin. "Why do all the men wear beards?"

"Men wear beards because the church says that it is a mortal sin to shave them. God did not create men beardless, only cats and dogs."

"Not to mention rats and mice," Bernie said. "Goats, though. Goats have beards."

Aunt Sofia was suppressing laughter. Bernie grinned at the old lady. "Of course, goats don't shave either."

"Perhaps so." Natasha sounded like she was trying not to laugh. "But I'm not sure the church would like hearing that ..." She searched for the word. "Ah ... compare?"

"Comparison," Bernie said. "Yeah. I've never met a holy roller yet that liked that sort of comparison. I understand the churches down-time have a lot more power. So maybe I should be more careful about what I say."

"What of your faith, Bernie?"

"Mom was a Methodist, a Protestant I guess you'd call it, and Dad a Catholic, though neither one of them were big church goers. Me, I guess I was an agnostic before the Ring of Fire."

"Agnostic?"

"Someone who doesn't know," Bernie said. "Maybe there's a God or maybe not. If there is a god maybe it cares about people and maybe not. After the Ring of Fire . . . well, something had to do that. Which still leaves me wondering about what it wants, whatever it is."

That statement seemed to set both Natasha and Sofia back on their heels. Which wasn't an unusual reaction. Bernie had had his face shoved in the fact that most people down-time were members of a church whether they wanted to be or not. There was no Madelyn Nutcase O'Hare down-time screaming about atheist rights. And considering what the holy rollers got up to without such people, maybe O'Hare wasn't that much of a nut case after all. "Like I say, someone or something took a six-mile diameter chunk of rock, earth, water, and air, animals, people, machines and books and shifted all of us three hundred sixty-nine years into the past and halfway around the world in a flash of light. I know that there's someone or something that can do that and if it ain't a god, it's close enough for me. On the other hand, whatever it is didn't appear to have much concern for what it was doing to my mom by taking her into the past and leaving the medicines that were keeping her alive in the future. So, yes, I'm convinced there's a god. That God is good and caring, not so much." Bernie ran down and realized he had probably said way too much. *I'm not here to fix their culture or update their religion*, he reminded himself. It was time for a change of subject. "So what do you do?"

"Do?" Natasha asked. "Ah . . . I take care of the family properties while Vladimir is away. Someone must."

As the sleigh carried Bernie, Natasha and Aunt Sofia to the dacha they talked about the roles of women in the future America where Bernie came from and the role of women in Russia. Natasha was clearly shocked at the options open to women in that future. Sofia was more curious and cautious.

Natasha found herself both shocked and intrigued by the up-timer's lack of concern for her rank and station. It wasn't so much that he ignored her rank. Instead, he treated it like some local fantasy that he paid polite lip-service to. In a very real sense, it seemed to Natasha that Bernie did not see himself as outranked by any man. Perhaps not even by God. And that was a truly frightening, and oddly exciting, thought.

Chapter 11

February 1632

Bernie moved in and settled. It took several days to get his stuff and the other gear that Vladimir had sent. They were also putting together a load of goods to go the other way. Boris wanted to make one more trip to Grantville to make sure the path he'd set up was in good working order both for mail and for goods. That had little to do with Bernie, which he was perfectly happy with. He'd already run into one mine field and didn't want another. It turned out Natasha was very interested in women's rights, a subject that Bernie had only a vague knowledge about. In order to hold off her questions a bit he had said, "Look, Natasha, I didn't mean to have you burn your bra in Red Square. It's just the way things were up-time."

Natasha, being Natasha, had come right back with, "What is a bra and why would I want to burn it?"

While Bernie was more than willing to talk about bras and their disposal with servant girls, it wasn't a place to go with the boss. Which, it had turned out, Natasha was, in fact if not in title. Especially when she had a whole retinue of men at arms who gave Bernie hard looks any time he got within twenty feet of her.

Talking to noble ladies about their undergarments was definitely chancy territory. Bernie got his revenge in a way by directing her to a barmaid who could answer her questions. Brandy Bates was a friend of his who worked at Club 250, where Bernie had drunk until the Gardens got its own building. Bernie talked her up a bit because it seemed like a good idea. Brandy had dropped out of high school before getting her diploma but Bernie figured he could get away with claiming she had a G.E.D., even though she'd never gotten that either. Who knew? Maybe the barmaid had something to teach the princess.

Besides, the truth was that Bernie didn't like the way the peasants were treated here and now. Bernie didn't think it had been near this bad in Germany. He had to remind himself quite often that he wasn't here to fix the soul of Russia, just the plumbing. He didn't like it but he kept his mouth shut. So let the princess learn about bras from the barmaid. Maybe she'd learn something else as well.

Natasha was at her desk, at last. There were several letters to write. She, as was her nature, started with the hardest.

> *To the Up-timer Citizen of Grantville, United States of America, Miss Brandy Bates,*
> *I make free to write to you at the suggestion of your fellow up-timer, Bernard Zeppi. I hope that this missive finds you in the best of good health.*

Natasha hated this part. She was a regular correspondent with several women of Russia and even a few men. But writing to someone new was always a challenge, especially someone from a foreign country. Worse, in this case, because the up-timers probably thought of everyone from this century as barbarians. But she really did need an answer to this question.

> *Let me apologize if I have failed to include the titles appropriate to your station. It is not with the intent of insult but from simple ignorance. Goodman Zeppi informs me that you are a woman of great accomplishment and considerable status among the up-timers. Also that you are of good family and possessed of a G.E.D.*
> *I gather that the G.E.D. is a title? But I confess my ignorance in how it is to be applied to a salutation. Mr.*

*Zeppi professes ignorance of your other titles, not being
a student of heraldry.*

*I fear this may be a delicate matter to broach on first
acquaintance, but what is a bra and why should one
burn it in the grand market square?*

Natasha filled in the context of the discussion then added her
signature. *Princess Natalia Petrovna Gorchakovna*

Natasha knew she should be saying more, introducing herself
more clearly, but she was uncertain of what degree of formal-
ity she should use in writing to an unknown up-timer. She set
the letter aside and started working on the next. It would go to
Vladimir, and would discuss the Grantville Section of the embassy
bureau and the agreements reached between the family and the
government.

Chapter 12

"We can't do it," Andrei Korisov said with disgust. "You don't understand what we have to deal with. Less than half the service nobility can read, and just one person in three hundred is of the service nobility. Even with the occasional priest and overeducated *Streltzi*, less than one person in a hundred can read, even in the cities and large towns. In the countryside, probably less than one in a thousand." He paused, allowing the translator to catch up, before adding: "This is not Germany. It's not even Poland."

Bernie listened with a certain amount of irritation. Not only because having a translator was a pain in the rear, but because Korisov was a generally irritating guy. He was very good at his job and more. The man was a master gunsmith who had taught himself to read and calculate ballistics. Through skill and hard work he had moved from the *Streltzi* to the service nobility. Not an easy thing to do in Russia, Bernie had already learned. Still, Korisov's contempt for the average Russian was irritating to Bernie, and he wasn't even Russian.

Meanwhile, Natasha spoke up. "Why isn't it possible, Andrei Korisov?"

"Because they're too complicated. No, it's not simply that. It's a combination of things. I could build a rifle like the American's by hand. It would take me about a month and it wouldn't be as good as his Remington model 7400, but it would work and it would fire a .30-06 round, if we had some to put in it. Then I could build another, and it would take me about a month again. And ten years from now, after Poland had invaded and taken Moscow, I would have made about one hundred and twenty rifles."

Natasha just looked at him and Andrei blushed, then continued. "I'm sorry, Princess. But it's hard to explain. To make rifles like Bernie's, in any number, we need so many tools that we don't have that I can't even imagine them all. Most Russians are still spending all their time growing food."

At this point, Bernie took up the argument. "It's the 'tools to build the tools' problem, Natasha. We had the same problem in Germany, although apparently not as severely. Up-time we could do incredibly complex things, precisely the same way, time after time, very quickly by using a variety of machines, each of which did one simple thing. But to get there, you have to build a lot of machines. I think Russia can get there, and that's what your brother hired me to do, help you get there. But it's not going to be fast. And from what I've been hearing about the political situation, it's not going to be in time to help you at all with Poland."

"Well, can't you build the machines you need to build the rifles quickly?" Natasha asked.

"We don't even know what most of those machines are, much less how to build them," Andrei Korisov said dejectedly.

Natasha nodded and switched to English. "Very well. Bernie, I want you to get together with Andrei, and try to figure out something that we *can* make. Something that will only take a few machines." They had their marching orders, and if Bernie didn't like them much, it was pretty clear that they didn't thrill Andrei either.

Natasha looked around the table, then switched back to Russian. "Now, what's next, gentlemen?"

"I have made a battery," Lazar Smirnov said. "However, coils will take longer and I'm just beginning to study the theory of radio. It will be a while, Princess."

After this, the people at the table began to discuss other projects. The Fresno scrapers were ready to test, but the ground was still frozen, so that project had to wait. They also had a plow, but again, they would have to wait for the spring thaw.

Filip said, "I understand the steam engines. The principles behind them make sense. I'm not sure of their practicality because of the amount of work involved in producing even one."

Filip was the translator, so Bernie interrupted him. "They're worth it. Believe me, engines are worth it. I'm not a big fan of steam, but limiting yourself to muscle power is the wrong way to go."

"It's not that I doubt you, Bernie," Filip said, "but we're back to the tools to build the tools problem. We don't know how much power we'll get and they are going to be built by hand like Andrei's handmade Remington that he is even now building for the czar. Granted, we don't have to make bullets to go in it, but we do have to make boilers and, well, we're a long way from anything useful." He turned to Princess Natasha. "We'll keep working on it, but don't expect much progress soon, Princess."

"The aspirin is not a problem," said the apothecary, Anatoly Fedorov. "But the antibiotics are well beyond us. Certainly we'll try for penicillin, but don't expect much. We don't even know what mold it comes from, much less how to process it to get the effect we want."

Nikita Ivanovich Slavenitsky, who was there by grace of being one of Natasha's most trusted armsmen, spoke up with a smile in his voice, clearly trying to lighten the mood. "Bernie has been teaching us about up-time football, which is played with a ball that is not round, and strategy games. So at least we'll have an amusing winter, Princess."

The princess gave him a quelling look, but Nick wasn't noticeably quelled and Natasha turned back to the table. "What about aircraft?" Natalia asked, but Bernie was shaking his head before she'd even finished the question.

"Not without some pretty powerful engines," he said. "And I don't know anything about aerodynamics. Nor is there anything in the books we brought with us."

The meeting went on for a couple of hours, a disheartening mix of "not yet" and "it can't be done," with only a sprinkle of things they could do.

Disheartening, yes. But not that disheartening. It was early days yet and they all knew it.

Chapter 13

March 1632

Vladimir took one look at Boris and knew he had made a rough, fast trip back. "What's wrong?"

"Nothing. I want to get done here and get back to Moscow as quickly as possible. How is the network progressing?"

"I'm not sure. It seems to me to be working fairly well. The number of spies, artists and philosophers that are living or visiting here seems to grow every day. Trotsky is starting to see spies under his bed."

"I doubt anyone cares what happens in Trotsky's bed, even his wife," Boris said. "Still he knows his business."

"Oh, there are spies enough." Vladimir agreed. "However for the most part they don't seem to care about us." He shook his head, caught between laughter and embarrassment. "What few attempts we've had to penetrate our network have been clumsy. Almost as though they didn't really care what we were doing but were too polite to simply ignore us. The Spanish and the Austrians want to know what the Swedes are doing here and the Swedes want to know what the Hapsburgs are doing here. The French want to know what the Catholics, and, well, everyone is doing here. The Italians want to know what the other Italians and the Spanish are doing here. The closest thing to a real attempt to subvert me has been an offer by a group of merchants and agents to go in together in the copying of the Encyclopedia Americana 1963 and such other books and periodicals as we can agree on. I accepted, of course. They were already doing it and were simply looking for more subscribers to defray expenses."

When Brandy Bates received the letter from Natasha Gorchakova she was on her day off and getting ready to go to a play with her mom at the high school.

Her mom answered the door and the first thing Brandy heard was, "You have a letter for Brandy from who?"

"Who is it, Mom?" Brandy asked as she came into the living room to see a tall, dark-haired man with deep blue eyes and a neatly trimmed black beard.

"I'm *Kniaz* Vladimir Gorchakov," he said. "The letter is from my sister."

Brandy wasn't a true adherent of the philosophy of Club 250, but she had taken in enough of the attitude while working there that she wasn't the least bit awed by the title or the fancy clothes. Well, maybe the least bit. But she responded by being just a bit snooty herself. "And why is your sister writing to me?"

"Apparently Bernie Zeppi recommended you as a correspondent," the guy said.

Bernie had gotten a job in Poland or Russia or someplace like that. The pay was supposed to have been pretty good and Mom was giving her the "you behave" look. Oh, what the hell. She could at least read the letter. "Well, if Bernie suggested it at least it's not out of the blue." Brandy held out her hand and with clear reluctance the guy handed her the letter.

Mom asked him to have a seat as Brandy examined the letter. It was folded over with a wax blob holding it closed and the wax had been imprinted with a crest.

Brandy shrugged, popped the seal and looked at the letter. The handwriting was good but with way too many flourishes. Working through the letter she got to the part about burning bras in the market square and burst into laughter.

Both Mom and the guy were looking at her with curiosity clear on their faces. Brandy handed the letter to her mother and smiled. "For once Bernie did the right thing. This is not a matter for men of any rank."

The guy turned a little pink and her mom, who was struggling though the letter, started laughing too.

All in all, though she wouldn't know it for months, Brandy had managed by accident to make a fairly good first impression on Vladimir.

In the meantime, after they had said goodbye to *Kniaz* Vladimir Gorchakov and seen the play, Brandy was left with the letter. Its very sparseness made it clear that this Natalia Whosis didn't know what or how much she could ask without giving offense. So Brandy put together a female care package. 1995 *Victoria's Secret*, a 1993 *Glamour*, 1997 *Vogue*, a *Better Homes and Gardens* plus cold cream, nail polish, eye shadow, and a pair of the stretchy one-size-fits-all pantyhose, with instructions. Brandy considered sending an actual bra, but she didn't have Natasha's sizes. So instead they sent a tape measure and more instructions.

Chapter 14

Ivan Nikitich Odoevskii didn't look like a book worm. He was tall and as richly dressed as a prince and a member of the *Boyar Duma* ought to be. He rode, he was a skilled falconer, but he did love to read. He read anything. Account books. Treatises. Stories. Anything he could get his hands on. His fierce black beard was twitching and his blue eyes squinted as he thought. "It's complicated, Patriarch. Yes, the up-timers use paper money, but their system is a tortured mix of the government and... well, anarchy."

"Anarchy?"

"They have something called federal reserve banks..." Vladimir had sent several tracts on economics—not very detailed or all that complete—back to Moscow, which had arrived about the time Boris had gotten back to Grantville. Along with them had come a very rough outline of what Vladimir thought might work for a banking system in Russia. That outline would have the great families issue money, having bought the right from the Czar's Bank or the Gorchakov Bank. With some vague limitations based on how much their property was worth. Going from those tracts on up-time economics, Ivan Nikitich explained his understanding of how the future economic system worked.

Patriarch Filaret was a man of no mean intellect, but his eyes were glazing over within a paragraph. He tried to follow the salient points for a while, but finally gave up. "Enough. Can we use it, Ivan Nikitich? Can we use it?"

Ivan Nikitich sighed like the wind gusting from the north. "Yes. But it is dangerous. The tracts made that clear, even if I could only understand one word in three without talking to that idiot Bernie." Ivan Nikitich snorted. "And only one word in two after talking to him. The danger is more than the simple temptation to print ever more and more as it loses its value. That's a danger, true enough. It is made worse by the fact that failing to print enough can hurt the nation even more. That is one thing the excerpts young Vladimir sent taught me. Half of Russia's troubles are caused by not enough cash."

"You needed a tract from the future to tell you Russia is not a wealthy nation?" Filaret snorted in exasperation.

"No!" Ivan Nikitich almost shouted, then visibly got hold of himself. "Patriarch, what I needed the writings from the future to tell me was that Russia *is* a wealthy nation. A wealthy nation with what the up-timers call a 'cash flow problem.' That Russia has everything it needs to have a booming economy, except the economy."

Filaret glared a bit. "Speak sense!"

Ivan Nikitich sighed. "We have grain. We have timber. We have pitch, not to mention furs of all sorts. We have rivers that in summer give us clear roads from China and India to the Baltic Sea. In hard winter, the sleighs are more efficient than wagons are. What we lack is a means of tying all those things together. Much of our trade is just that. A peasant trades a bushel of grain to another peasant for bit of cloth. It happens that way because neither peasant has any money. Did you know that over ninety percent of the up-timers' purchases were made with money? Everything from their homes to a piece of candy for their children. Everyone had money, even the very poor. That—along with their transportation system—made the manufacturing of goods in one place to be sold in another much more practical."

Ivan Nikitich spoke with passion. He even stood and began pacing the room. "The raw materials are here. The trade routes are here, mostly. Even the skills are here. *Every* peasant in Holy Rus spends half the year at some craft because you can't farm ice." Ivan Nikitich shook his head. "The only thing really missing is some practical means of letting the people in one place buy the products from the people in another place. Buy them, Patriarch, not trade for them. Because barter simply won't work for what we need. The things we must have are: money, ways of transferring money from one place to another without bandits robbing the caravan, banks where bureau men and even peasants can save money or get loans. As I said—everything we need for an economic boom except an economy."

"What you're saying is we're rich in goods but not in money?"

Ivan Nikitich nodded. "What we need is money and the writings of the up-timers explain how to do that without silver or gold. The idea, as I understand it, is to have just a little more money available than there is product for it to buy. That encourages the peasants to work harder to get the last bit. It's like hanging a carrot in front of a mule. Too close and he eats it. Too far and he gives up. Russia's carrot is hanging off the mule's ass."

"So, you think Vladimir is right." The Odoevskii didn't get along all that well with the Gorchakov family. If Ivan Nikitich could find a way to say Vladimir's report was wrong, he would.

"No, absolutely not," Ivan Nikitich said by reflex. Then he laughed. "Well, perhaps a little bit. The way the boy proposes to go about it is all wrong. We are not some barbarous western nation. It will need to be the Czar's Bank and all the little banks part of the Czar's Bank. The Gorchakov boy's proposal will just make the Gorchakov family richer than they already are."

Filaret gave the Boyar of the Exchequer a look.

"Very well. The Gorchakov family and many others," Ivan Nikitich conceded. "But the czar should reap a greater benefit if the government owns all the banks, not just the Czar's Bank."

Filaret considered. "What bureau would control the Czar's Bank?" He gave Ivan Nikitich another hard look.

Ivan Nikitich gave him back look for look. "The bureau of the exchequer is the obvious choice," he acknowledged.

In some ways Filaret really preferred Vladimir's plan. As chaotic as it was, it had the advantage of not putting the power of a central bank in the hands of one of the great families. On the other hand, having the Romanov family in charge of the central bank would strengthen them considerably.

The discussion continued for several hours that night and then broadened over the next several days. Eventually, it included every member of the *Boyar Duma* cabinet and many members of the Assembly of the Land. It was pointed out that the institution of this system would probably mean fewer taxes would be needed, at least for now. Which made it quite popular. There was much support among the great houses and monasteries for Vladimir's plan but the *deti boyars*, the service nobility, and the merchants hated it. Both because of the extra power it would give the great houses and monasteries if they could print their own money and because of the difficulty they could see clearly in determining how much this house's ruble would be worth versus that monastery's ruble. That pitted the great houses against the service nobility. Not an uncommon occurrence. But while everyone was fighting over which way to do it, the whether to do it got decided by default.

The czar, at his father's urging, came down on the side of the service nobility. The money would be issued by the Czar's Bank. All banks in Russia would be branches of the Czar's Bank. Which, by the way, would offer nice jobs for lots of the service nobility. Something that didn't make it into the general discussion was the fact that more money would make it easier for serfs to buy out of their bonds to the land. Not that that mattered much. Every year for the last decade and more had had a decree from the czar that the serfs couldn't leave that year, even if they had paid off their debt.

Fedor Ivanovich Sheremetev leaned over to his friend and chief henchman, Colonel Leontii Shuvalov, as the debate went on. "It was good that the note from Vladimir arrived in time to prevent the patriarch from dragging us into war with Poland, but the notion that they are truly from the future disturbs me."

"I'm not entirely comfortable with it myself, my lord, but facts are facts and Bernie is real. The stuff he brought from Germany is real."

"And the knowledge," Sheremetev grumbled. "Slavery and serfdom were both banned in their world. It will give our serfs ideas. There are too many new ideas coming out of Germany these days and they will spread faster with this outlander from the future here. The Gorchakovs are really just puffed-up merchants, even if they did hold their land independently before it was absorbed by Muscovy. Why did Filaret give them the patent on these new inventions?"

He knew why Filaret had done it. It was precisely *because* the Gorchakovs were just puffed-up merchants with little connection to the factions in the great families. He shrugged. "Who knows? Maybe it won't amount to much. Games and rumors are all that have come from that dacha of theirs in the months he's been here."

Chapter 15

Andrei Korisov sawed away at the barrel of the rifled musket. He had taken it out of the musket and was sawing off the breech end. He had, he thought, the beginnings of an idea. He had spent the last three months going over the history of firearms with Bernie, a subject that the up-timer knew rather less about than he thought he did. Andrei was convinced of that. Andrei didn't know what parts were missing, and that was perhaps the most frustrating aspect of it all. But a week ago, they had gotten to talking about movies and Bernie had remembered that the ball and cap pistols of the old west had been muzzle-loaders.

That, of course, wasn't what Bernie had said, but after discussing it with him for two hours, that was what Andrei was convinced the up-timer was describing. Powder, then shot shoved down a short barrel. There were six of the short barrels in a cylinder which was why the pistols were called six-shooters, but the six barrels weren't full length. There was an earlier version that was called a pepper-pot, according to Bernie, in which the barrels were full length but the six shooters had short barrels that rotated into position behind a longer barrel. And that was what had led Andrei to his gun shop in the middle of the night, filled with uncertain inspiration.

How much force did you lose, Andrei wondered as he sawed, out of that gap between the short barrel and the long? It couldn't be so much that the bullet stopped in the barrel. It couldn't even be so much as to rob the bullet of its knock-down power. Not when sent through a short pistol barrel. But how much would you lose when it was fired though a long musket barrel? Would the length of the barrel make any difference? Was that why they only used the technique on pistols?

Having cut the rear five inches of the barrel off, Andrei carefully smoothed away burrs with a fine file, then reinstalled the barrel in the stock. Placing the back of the barrel in a vise, he proceeded to load it with powder and shot. He pressed a lead ball and wadding into the chamber he had created, then reinserted it into the rifle, being careful to make sure that it lined up properly, and then tied it into place. This was simply a test, after all.

On due consideration, Andrei looked at the rifle sitting in the sandbag, then decided that he was too important to risk.

"Ivan, come over here," Andrei shouted. He always shouted, since the peasant workers wouldn't actually do anything if he didn't.

This one, whose name might or might not have been Ivan, came over, looking warily at the rifle.

"I want you to lean down and pull that trigger," Andrei said.

Ivan looked a bit nervous, so Andrei glared at him harder. "Lean down and pull that trigger."

The peasant finally complied. The musket was braced in sandbags for stability and it was at an awkward height. The peasant put his left hand on the sandbag to brace himself, leaned down and put his right hand by the trigger. This put his head just above the gap and his left wrist just beside it.

"Pull the trigger!"

So he did.

"*Yaaaaah!*" Ivan jerked back, grabbed his left wrist and put his right arm over his face, still screaming.

"What's the matter with you?" Andrei shouted. "Get out of here!"

The gun shot didn't attract much attention. But Ivan's continued screaming did.

Filip Pavlovich Tupikov came running from the blacksmith's shop, where the Fresno scraper was being finished. "What happened?" he asked.

"It worked," Andrei said, and then pointed downrange. "See the target?"

There was a little black hole in the paper target, a little below the bull's-eye.

"What was that man screaming about?" The injured man was being helped away by several other workers.

"He put his hand in the wrong place, the idiot," Andrei said with a dismissive wave. He didn't notice Filip's change of expression as he looked at the rifle. The firing chamber, the back of the barrel that he had cut off, had shoved back into the stock and cracked it. Also the same escaping gas that had injured the peasant had cut into the stock of the gun. "Look what happened to the rifle. The stock is damaged. I'll have to work on that. Can't have the stock being damaged by only one firing. Perhaps a shield of some sort."

Andrei ignored Filip as he left, immersed in reworking his rifle design. A few more shots and the gun would come apart, but that was beside the point. His solution had sent the bullet downrange without too much loss of force. Some, yes. There was more drop at twenty yards, but only a little more. Still what about a shorter barrel? Would there be more drop or less?

Andrei started working on how he would mount the firing chamber on a gimbal of some sort so that it could be flipped up for reloading, and flipped back down for firing. And some sort of shield so that the escaping gas from the firing wouldn't damage the stock.

Filip Pavlovich entered the dacha's new "clinic," more out of curiosity than anything else. Andrei Korisov was irritating, but the making of guns was really his responsibility and none of Filip's business. But he was curious, so he intended to ask the injured peasant what had happened.

"Hold him down! And get me some swabs and alcohol!" Vitaly Alexseev said. Vitaly was the Dacha's new barber-surgeon.

From what Filip understood, Vitaly had been a fairly prosperous surgeon in Moscow when Princess Natalia hired him to learn about up-time surgery. Filip watched Vitaly work with a mixture of condescension and interest, which slowly gave way to a sort of grudging respect. Vitaly might not be of the nobility, but he was very good at what he did and had picked up on Bernie's explanations, crude as they were, of sterile technique. He had swabbed down the wound with alcohol, in spite of the increased screaming of the peasant. His thread had been soaked in alcohol, so would not introduce corruption into the wounds. All in all, Vitaly seemed a very competent man.

About halfway through the procedure, the peasant fainted, which made everything much easier. Luckily, whatever had wounded the man had missed his eye, so it was only the fairly shallow cuts along his wrist and forehead that had to be dealt with.

"There," Vitaly said, finally finished with his bandaging. "When he wakes up, I'll speak with Anatoly Federov and we'll decide what type of pain-killers to use. I'm not sure that the aspirin will be enough for these injuries. They're superficial, but they're going to be very painful.

"What did you do to him?" Vitaly asked Filip.

"Me? Nothing. It happened on the firing range. I wasn't even there." Then Filip had a thought and asked a question. "What can you tell me? From the wounds, I mean."

Vitaly paused, clearly thinking about what he had looked at. "It's strange. It was not like a cut. And there was a tattooing of powder residue around the wounds. It was not quite like anything I've ever seen before. A tearing of the skin and the flesh beneath it. As though it were chewed up by a thousand tiny mouths. The good news is, it wasn't deep. He should be fine assuming the alcohol works and he doesn't get infected."

Filip shuddered.

"I wish you people would have a little more care," Vitaly said, "with the people who work for you."

Lazar Smirnov played with wires and batteries in an aromatic room in the Gorchakov dacha. The aromas weren't, perhaps, those that most people might find attractive. But Lazar found them pleasant for what they represented. He had a copper sulfate battery. In fact, he had several and he had copper wire, fine and coated in lacquer, which he had coiled around a wooden dowel and coated in more lacquer, and when he hooked the coil up to the batteries, he got magnetism. An invisible force moving things and under his control. It was magic in every sense that mattered to Lazar. Better, it required no pact with a devil or demon, simply knowledge and understanding.

Lazar was one of the privileged elite of Russia. A member of a cadet branch of a great house, a fifth cousin to the czar, he was important enough to have all the privileges of rank but far enough away from the halls of power not to have to do anything. It made for a fairly pleasant, if somewhat boring, existence. He had been asked by his family head to come to the new research center—usually just called the Dacha—to see what was going on. "You like to read, Cousin. Go have a look around, stay a few months, see what it's all about," he had been told. So he had come and now suspected that he would never leave, given the choice. He liked experiments. He liked learning how things worked and he liked doing magic, even if others called it science.

Lazar looked around his lab and smiled. Here was a piece of iron ore, pounded just enough to turn it into a rod but leave it full of impurities. As Lazar understood the books, it would make a heating element, getting hot as the electricity tried to flow through it and was resisted by the impurities on the metal. Over there was a crystal radio set that he had made carefully to the specifications in the pamphlet from Grantville. It had nothing to listen to, but Lazar had it nonetheless. Next to it, a key to a telegraph. When he pressed it, it let current flow through the electromagnet and the compass moved as he clicked out Morse code. He was a happy man.

Chapter 16

April 1632

"Good morning, Bernie," Anya said with a flirtatious smile as she brought in a pitcher of hot water and a washing bowl. Indoor plumbing was a possibility now that the snow was melting. Still, it would probably be midsummer before it became a reality. So it was chamber pots and maids to empty them. The fact that Anya was willing to do more than empty chamber pots was both a lot of fun and kind of upsetting.

Bernie found the whole class situation in Russia strange and upsetting. More so than he'd thought he would. Bernie had discovered that he *really* didn't like serfdom. Somewhere deep down inside of him was a belief in the basic rights of people and seeing those rights ignored angered him.

The whole issue of serfdom was more complicated than he would have thought, too. He himself was off to the side of the class system somewhere around the upper end of the service nobility and the lower end of the upper nobility. He was a hired foreigner, which would normally put him in or just below the service nobility. But Bernie was special. He had actually and demonstrably experienced a miracle. He was here in this time because God had personally put him here. Of more practical importance, what he could do was absolutely unique in Russia.

Bernie wasn't sure how it had happened. Maybe Boris, maybe one of the letters that Vladimir had sent, in any case the word had been given. Anya had told him about it. The majordomo of the Dacha had picked servant girls for attractiveness and had made clear that keeping Bernie happy was a job requirement. Anya also told him that there was some real competition to get the jobs.

That job requirement bothered Bernie. At the same time, he was a young man with hormones flooding his system. If a pretty girl found opportunity in his bed, that was fine with him. His attitude was hypocritical as hell and he knew it. He was suddenly a bit more understanding of the whole Thomas Jefferson/ Sally Hemmings thing. *There's a profound truth there somewhere,* Bernie thought as he watched the sway of Anya's breasts. *If it's be honest and don't get laid or be a hypocrite and get laid, then a hypocrite most guys will be.*

Bernie had spent the first months at the Dacha getting to know the staff and learning Russian through total immersion. He was getting better at Russian and beginning to know the players there.

There were the philosophers/scientists, mostly the low end of the upper nobility because they were the ones who could afford an education, but with a fair number of the service nobility and more than a few monks and priests. Then there were the craftsmen; they were mostly of the *Streltzi* class. The *Streltzi's* duty to the czar was to guard the cities, so, unlike the service nobility, they weren't granted much in the way of lands but got the right to engage in crafts and trade. Then there were the servants. These were mostly serfs from the Gorchakov estates. About half of them had been at the Dacha before the Ring of Fire. The rest were shipped in to support the additional staff. A few servants had been hired from Moscow and were at the low end of the *Streltzi* class, basically peasants not tied to the land.

At the center of it all was Bernie and the books. Mostly Bernie so far, because Vladimir was still setting up the processes to get the books copied and sent to Russia. While a number of books were sent with Bernie and Boris, there were none that were Russia-focused. They were books and parts of books that had been copied because others wanted them.

"You know what's planned for today?" Bernie asked Anya as he washed his face then headed for the chamber pot.

"It's the scraper," Anya said. "It's a clear day and they want to see how it works."

The Fresno scrapers left Filip Pavlovich Tupikov wondering what they really needed Bernie for. It wasn't that he was unhelpful. "Yes, *da*," Bernie said. "The handles let you control the depth of the cut. Push down for a shallower cut, let them rise just a bit for a deeper cut."

Filip translated.

"How deep can you cut?" Petr Stefanovich asked.

Filip translated the question.

"It depends on the ground," Bernie explained. "If you loosen the earth with a drag board, you can usually cut a couple of inches. You get a feel for it with practice. You start to notice when the scraper is pushing up hard. Then you have to push down and shallow the cut."

Filip translated. Bernie had indeed been of help to the blacksmith and carpenters in making an iron reinforced wooden version of the scraper. That wasn't the reason Filip wondered why they needed Bernie. Filip had seen the design for the scraper, the drag board and a couple of other pieces of road construction equipment. They were all quite clear. Written and drawn to make it easy for a village smith and carpenter.

The horses, small steppe ponies, were hitched and Filip followed along as Bernie demonstrated. A cut about half an inch deep grew quickly to a length of about twenty feet.

"Whoa." Bernie pulled the horses up. He turned to Petr. "You want to give it a try?"

Petr Stefanovich took Bernie's place. At first the scraper slid along the ground. "Lift the handles." Bernie gave directions as Filip translated. Filip stepped between Bernie and Petr Stefanovich to see. Petr Stefanovich lifted the handles about three inches.

"Gently!" Bernie shouted. The next thing Filip Pavlovich Tupikov knew he was being jerked back by his collar. He saw a blur.

He turned on the uppity outlander but Bernie wasn't there. He was checking on Petr Stefanovich, who was holding his arm and looking surprised. The scraper was turned over and the ponies were looking back in confusion.

"Look, man." Bernie's voice was harsh. "This stuff is heavy equipment even if it's run by horses, not a motor. Gentle does it, especially at first, until you get to know it. I don't give a damn how big you are, you're not stronger than two horses working together with leverage on their side." Bernie took a deep breath. "You empty the bucket by lifting the handle, too. As you just demonstrated." Then Bernie turned to Filip Pavlovich, eyes flashing. "That was pretty dammed stupid for a guy who thinks he's smart. The handles on the scraper are like the end of a lever. You just came within an inch of getting your head busted, big time."

Filip Pavlovich looked at the scraper, remembered the blur and decided that perhaps Bernie wasn't totally useless after all. Even if he was rude. Filip went ahead and translated Bernie's speech for Petr Stefanovich.

Bernie wasn't sure whether to be elated or scared to death. He had just repeated, almost word for word, the two lectures he had received the first day he worked with the scraper after he joined the road crew. The combination of his wrenched arms and the fear in the supervisor's eyes had impressed the lecture on him. Petr Stefanovich was a big mother, and proud of it. Bernie should have figured that he would push it, but he hadn't. Worse, Bernie hadn't even considered that Filip Pavlovich, the Russian nerd, would stick his head in the way of the handles. Somehow, it hadn't occurred to him that someone could get killed using the stuff he helped the Russians build.

"Look, guys. This stuff can be dangerous. I guess most of the stuff we brought back in the Ring of Fire can be dangerous, even the medicine." Filip was looking at him funny and Bernie sort of ran out of steam, not really knowing how to say what he wanted to say. He really didn't want to be responsible for getting someone killed.

"I understand, Bernie. You came to help us. It's all right. People get killed using shovels to smooth a road or dig a canal, too. Believe me, this will help."

As soon as the test was finished, Filip informed Natasha and sent a message to the Grantville desk in Moscow. So much he was supposed to do. He also sent one to his cousin who worked in the bureau of roads. That, he did on his own.

The Grantville desk had been pretty much in limbo since Boris had left for Grantville. It was known that Boris would be taking over the Grantville desk when he got back, so not much of anything was being done till they had a boss to blame it on. Put more kindly, they didn't know what to do. Especially, they didn't have a clue what to do with information coming out of the Dacha. It wasn't, after all, coming from Grantville, not directly. So, like several other items, it got tossed on Boris' unused desk to await his return.

Natasha, on the other hand, knew what to do. She sent letters to several potential customers about the new device that could be seen at the Dacha. Among others, the letters went out to the main bureau of roads and several of the local bureaus of roads, the ones for various cities and districts. In part because of Filip's letter to his cousin, Natasha's letters were accepted with less reservation than they might otherwise have been.

Still, things had to go through channels. It was some weeks before they could arrange for a viewing of the scraper and the drag board. In the meantime, both devices had been put to use. The primary purpose of that use was to familiarize the crews with the equipment. But the still small Dacha team also wanted to show off.

Yuri Mikhailovich was in charge of assigning crews to specific roads in the area around Moscow. Yuri pulled up, staring at a ridge in the road—path, rather—he was riding on. About a hundred yards from the Dacha, the road suddenly rose about six inches and became quite smooth. Much smoother than Yuri would have expected of even a good road crew. There were bare sections on either side, where an inch or two of top soil had been scraped away, clearly where the new surface of the road had come from. Slowly, Yuri approached the road. When he reached the road he climbed down and examined the new road. Evaluating.

Yuri climbed back onto his pony and proceeded to the Dacha. Looking for the scraper but not finding it.

One of the kitchen boys came and fetched Natasha when he rode into the yard. She met Filip Pavlovich, with Bernie in tow, on the way to the door. Filip identified his cousin Yuri while he was getting back on his horse.

"Come, come." Filip Pavlovich waved at his cousin. Rather pompously, Natasha thought. Then led the way around back, where the scraper was in use.

Natasha and Bernie let Filip do the explaining. In Bernie's case, it was because his Russian still wasn't good enough. Natasha wanted to see how Filip would present the equipment.

The drag board was just a board with spikes sticking out the bottom. It was used to cut the ground and loosen the soil. In combination with the scraper, two men and four small Russian ponies could do a phenomenal amount of work—more than twenty men with shovels could accomplish.

As they turned the corner and could see behind the main house, Yuri stopped and stared.

"You see?" Filip Pavlovich waved at the project. "You see what can be accomplished?"

The trench was about seventeen feet, just under three scrapers, wide. It was a hundred feet long and about three feet deep, not including the mounds on either side of it. It had ramps on either end which allowed the horses to get in and out of the trench, which the team pulling the scraper was doing now.

"It will take planning for proper use." Filip Pavlovich waved at it again. "With that planning, a team can cut a six foot wide trench at a rate of approximately one mile in four hours in this sort of soil. The trench will be approximately two inches deep. The second pass is actually slightly faster than the first because the ground is smoother. Three teams could do the same but with the trench seventeen feet wide. Or a six-foot-wide trench, six inches deep, could be cut. As the depth of the cut deepens, it gets harder to do, of course. You need a ramp about every hundred feet."

Yuri nodded, still watching the scraper as it dumped a load along the side of the trench. It had climbed the ramp then gone around to the side of the trench to dump the load. He finally pulled his eyes away from the scraper and looked at Filip Pavlovich. "I am impressed with the scraper, Filip Pavlovich. Considering your comments about planning, why didn't you take your own advice and plan the placement of this trench to serve some purpose? You could have made a fish pond if nothing else." There was a grin in Yuri's voice that indicated he was getting back at Filip for his pompous presentation. If so, Natasha couldn't really blame him.

Natasha had found herself twitting Filip on more than one occasion. Filip was what might be thought of as an intellectual snob. On the other hand she knew that Yuri was of higher rank in the bureaus and, according to Filip, had a tendency to lecture.

Filip Pavlovich sighed, and Natasha tried not to laugh as he explained, "It's for the tile field, part of the plumbing system. See the notch halfway down the trench? That will be dug deeper for the septic tank."

"What's a plumbing system?" Yuri Asked.

Filip explained.

"As I said, why didn't you do something useful?"

"We are making something useful," Natasha spoke up. "I have it on good authority that much of the disease we suffer from in spring is caused by the thawing of frozen human waste."

Yuri froze. He'd forgotten that he and his cousin had an observer from a high house, Natasha thought sardonically.

"Bernie, as yet, has little Russian." Natasha waved at him. "But we have pamphlets from Grantville that he has helped us translate. Disease travels from human waste to water to its next victims. Not all diseases, but enough to explain the sickness that comes to Moscow every spring. In general, this process is well-documented, though not in regard to Moscow." Natasha smiled to take a little of the sting out of her words. "Bernie's great concern over the indoor plumbing has, I fear, less to do with protection from disease than it does for comfort."

Filip Pavlovich sighed again, more real this time. "Toilets and showers are his constant obsession. When I first saw the design I thought it would take months. Now it seems we will see it begin to work in a few more days."

"So we are presented with a useful device that is to be used for expensive doodads?" Yuri sneered.

"Not entirely." Filip Pavlovich's admission was a bit grudging. "In spite of Bernie's obsession with what he calls decadent civilization..." He threw a glance at Bernie, who grinned. "The princess is right. Sanitation is an essential part of preventing the spread of disease. It is a complicated field and I have not studied it deeply yet."

Natasha was trying not to grin, both because she was intrigued by the idea of decadent civilization and what you might be able to do in what Bernie called a hot tub, and because she was finding the notion of doing those things with Bernie increasingly interesting, even attractive. Bernie was as different from the men she'd known in Russia as she imagined a bathroom was from an outhouse.

"Princess?"

That was Filip. Natasha had let her attention wander from the business at hand. Again.

"Sorry, Filip. What did you say?"

"We were speaking of sanitation."

Natasha jerked her mind back to the subject of the scrapers. Filip Pavlovich's admission meant that there was another use for scrapers which in turn meant that the scrapers were still more valuable. "Oh. Yes. Sanitation and the involvement of the scraper in removing waste. A very useful application."

Yuri didn't manage to hide his scowl, and looked at his cousin rather than at Natasha. "What else have you got?"

Filip Pavlovich shrugged. "There is a report on something called 'macadam style road construction.' We haven't finished translating it yet. It seems to make for good roads that handle the winter freezing well."

New roads and canals would make trade easier and safer. And with the introduction of a monetary system, there would be better opportunities for trade within Russia.

Natasha smiled as Filip explained. "We used the road out front to practice road work, and then we used this to test its use in digging canals."

"Canals?" Natasha heard the apprehension in Yuri's voice though Filip Pavlovich apparently missed it.

"The scraper works by scraping a thin layer of soil then putting it somewhere else. By going over the same stretch again and again you can go a little deeper with every pass." Filip Pavlovich waved at the trench. "Roads, leach fields, canals, even cellars. Anything where large amounts of earth need to be moved."

The underchief of roads gave his cousin a sharp look, which Filip Pavlovich appeared totally unaware of. The bureaus of canals and river transport were constantly in competition with roads for resources of all sorts. The families that controlled the bureaus disliked each other intensely. *The bidding war has begun*, Natasha thought.

And so it had. Not, of course, without interference from Filaret. While Natasha's family owned the patents on the scraper so, by agreement, did the government. That meant, as Filaret interpreted it, that if the bureau of roads wanted to manufacture their own scrapers, they had a perfect right to. Natasha didn't disagree with that interpretation. Of course, the bureau of roads wasn't really set up to manufacture scrapers. Unfortunately, neither was the Dacha. The Dacha was a research facility, not a manufactory. Worse, they were entering the farming season. For the next six months, the large majority of people in Russia would be working to get grain into the ground, then taking care of the plants and harvesting. The time for making came in winter. What blacksmithing was done in summer was emergency fixes.

"But these *are* emergency fixes," Yuri insisted. "Every one of these frees up ten men for farm work while still allowing the road work to be done. And we are going to need the roads in good order come harvest time."

Natasha completely agreed with Yuri's assessment. "But there is the matter of payment. The blacksmiths and carpenters involved in making the scrapers must be paid. The time taken away from their normal work will also delay the repair of tools used in planting and harvesting. If our family estates are to be used in producing scrapers for the rest of Russia, the family must be compensated for the loss of skilled labor.

"If, on the other hand, you wish to send out plans to the villages and estates all over Russia telling them that they must put aside useful work in order to make a strange new gadget that the bureau of roads wishes them to employ..." Natasha shrugged. "I wish you the best of luck, but don't hold us responsible for the results. Say rather, lack of results, you are likely to achieve."

"Yes, I know, Princess. But how are we supposed to pay for it? We are provided labor for repairing the roads, not money."

So it went. Roads and canals, as well as private organizations, monasteries and land owners all arguing over how to get scrapers without either paying for them or having to pull their already overworked smiths off the necessary jobs they were doing. It wasn't that people were trying to cheat Natasha's family. Not entirely. Mostly it was simply that the equipment was needed and the money to pay for it wasn't there. The *Boyar Duma* and the Assembly of the Land were still arguing over the fine points of the new Czar's Bank and the new money it would issue. The money was not yet issued. And how were people to pay for scrapers without money?

Still, it worked out over that first summer in the same ragged way that such things often work out. Some scrapers were made on the Gorchakov lands by Gorchakov smiths who worked in what was in effect a factory, making the parts and assembling them. These were produced with less time and less effort than the ones where a smith in a village had to work out everything from the instruction sets, and work on the scraper in between his other work. Those who had the cash bought the Gorchakov scrapers, which, aside from everything else, were generally better made because the people making them quickly gained practice.

But not nearly as many scrapers were made as were needed. The scrapers made a difference, but over all that summer the difference was minor. In the spots where there were plenty of scrapers, however, the difference was phenomenal. For instance, the road work that the Gorchakov were required to supply and which generally took several hundred men working for over a month, in 1632 took fifty men working for two weeks. The rest of that labor draft was available for other Gorchakov projects and the Dacha provided them several. All of that took time to happen.

Chapter 17

Spring was in the air and mud was on the ground as Bernie and a small troop of Natasha's guards left the Dacha to travel to the Gorchakov family townhouse in Moscow. It was a pleasant ride on little Russian steppe ponies. The sun was shining and the temperature was in the mid-forties. The breeze was gentle, not the chilling wind of winter. Bernie and the guardsmen laughed and joked about the girls of the Dacha and the visit of the bureau man. Bernie got teased about what invention he ought to introduce and teased the guards back about what inventions they might have to try out.

All in all, it was a wonderful morning right up until they reached the outskirts of Moscow. As they entered the city, they were met with a delegation.

"The slow fever has broken out," said a somewhat chubby fellow in the dress of a member of the service nobility, or perhaps a very wealthy member of the merchant class.

"What's slow fever?" Bernie asked.

That took some explaining and while they were figuring out that it wasn't anything Bernie knew anything about they had drawn a crowd.

The guard captain said, "I know there's probably nothing you can do, Bernie. But at least have a look."

And Bernie couldn't see any way out of it. Moscow in the

seventeenth century didn't have much in the way of hospitals. So it was homes Bernie was taken to; homes of the rich, homes of the poor. There weren't a lot of common factors and for a while Bernie managed to be analytical trying to figure out what was causing the people to get sick. For a while. Then he couldn't any more. These were people…men, women, children. The houses stank and the healers were doing the best they could. There was no way Bernie could think of these guys as doctors what with their talk of balancing humors. But he managed not to call them quacks out loud because it was pretty obvious that they cared about their patients and, again, they were doing the best they could.

But there was this little kid, a boy maybe four or five. He was running a high fever. Even Bernie could tell that much, and his bed was shat in. The healer had just finished bleeding the kid when Bernie got there. He'd be a cute kid, Bernie thought, in other circumstances. It was clear the little boy didn't know what was going on and that he was in pain. It was like one of those ads asking for money for starving kids in Africa or South America back up-time. Except for the smell. The smell of week-old shit and death. Bernie barely managed not to vomit. This little kid who hadn't done anything to deserve it was dying because he didn't have modern medicines, just like Bernie's mom had died because she didn't have medicines.

Bernie stood outside the log house on a Moscow street, breathing in the spring air, knowing that the little boy was almost certainly going to die. God might be a bastard, but he wasn't out after Bernie specifically. The Ring of Fire didn't happen just to turn Bernie's life upside-down. That little boy and all the other people would have gotten sick whether the Ring of Fire happened or not. He'd known that all along, really, but it hadn't felt like it. It had felt like the whole Ring of Fire was just God messing with Bernie Zeppi. Now, suddenly, it didn't feel that way. It was more than a little humbling that Bernie wasn't the center of the universe. The little boy dying in his own waste had had his own life. A life cut short and the kid was going to die in a lot more pain than Bernie's mom had.

What was a whole lot worse than humbling was the thought that maybe if Bernie had known what he was doing he might have been able to save the kid and who knew how many others. Maybe he wouldn't have, but he didn't know enough even to figure out what the disease was. Maybe cholera? He thought he'd read somewhere that cholera had something to do with diarrhea and most everyone who had this had that.

The street was muddy and there was a bit of a taint to the air. Not just from the house where the boy was. Suddenly Bernie remembered a cartoon he'd seen somewhere with this cowboy apologizing to his horse as he hammered a cork into the horse ass. Something about an EPA regulation. That's what he was smelling. Not really a barnyard smell. Not quite. An outhouse smell, that was it. The whole city of Moscow smelled faintly of outhouse. The problem was that Bernie didn't know if it meant anything. He just didn't know.

"Okay, asshole," Bernie muttered to himself. "What do you know? You must know something that will help."

There was one thing that he was pretty sure of. Bleeding didn't actually help any disease he'd ever heard of. Maybe gangrene or something like that, but not an illness. He waved at one of the guards. "Listen, Pavel, I don't know all that much about medicine but this much I do know. In my time we've known for centuries that bleeding people who are sick doesn't help. I'll write Prince Vladimir for confirmation, but I'm not waiting for an answer. The next time I see one of these guys bleeding someone with this, I'm going to bleed them. Cut their throat from ear-to-ear and bleed them right out." Bernie looked Pavel dead in the eye and Pavel went a little pale.

Then Bernie continued. "I know it's not their fault. Doctors were still bleeding people in the Revolutionary War and that's like 1776. But it doesn't work! And it makes the patient weaker, more likely to die. If I have to take down a few of these guys to make it stop, I'm still saving lives."

Well, Bernie was in it now. He'd made his first medical pronouncement and it was a doozie. He knew that he wasn't going to be able to leave it at that.

In all the doctor shows back up-time, the doctors wore masks when they were doing surgery and he knew that when there was fear of an epidemic in places like Japan sometimes people wore masks. He knew that that was because some diseases were transmitted by air, by people sneezing on each other or even breathing on each other. Was this disease like that? Bernie didn't know. He knew that in hospitals and restaurants they were fussy about washing your hands. And he remembered something about childbed fever being carried by doctors who didn't wash their hands. Besides, all the hospital shows always had doctors and nurses washing their hands and wearing rubber gloves before and after they treated anyone. If the masks didn't help, washing hands might. Or the other way around. Maybe if he could get people to do both it might help keep this sickness from spreading.

Bernie started improvising. He sent one of the guards back to the Dacha to get anything they had on diagnosing disease. And while they were there, to pick up Anatoly Fedorov, the apothecary and Vitaly Alexseev, the barber-surgeon, who were staying at the Dacha.

It turned out that there was almost nothing in the Dacha about diagnosing or treating disease. However, Anatoly and Vitaly had known Bernie for months by now and had talked to him before about up-time medical and sanitary practices. So while they weren't entirely convinced of the importance of such things, they had at least been exposed to the germ theory of disease. They'd even seen a couple of pictures of cells. Not photographs, but drawings copied from up-time books.

It was in their interest that the up-time techniques worked. It would give them an advantage over their competitors. This, it seemed, would make a decent test case. So they supported Bernie's recommendations. For the next weeks Bernie, the guards, and the medical community, such as it was in seventeenth-century Moscow, fought a holding action against an enemy everyone except Bernie knew too well. Bernie worked as hard as anyone and in the process got up close and personal with the grinding poverty and squalor of seventeenth-century Russia.

Were they successful? Who could say? The annual spring epidemic of typhoid fever was less severe in 1632 than it had been in 1631. Fewer people caught it and fewer of those who caught it died.

The reason for fewer deaths could have been the washing of the hands. It could have been the masks. And it could have been the boiled water with a touch of salt and sugar that Bernie called Gatorade that they gave to the sick to try to stave off dehydration. It could be those things made a difference. It could also be the placebo effect of Bernie's masks and his being an up-timer touched by God. Or it might have just been a mild year.

The little boy died barely a day into the fight. But, though he would never know it, he left a legacy for Russia. By the time Bernie returned to the Dacha he knew that his getting it right made a difference. That difference was the difference between life and death. Not just for little kids who might catch a disease but for thousands of other kids and adults. Kids who would go hungry without better plows, or better crops. Craftsmen who couldn't get their goods to market without better roads. What had been a job for Bernie Zeppi had become a calling.

Chapter 18

May 1632

Bernie missed the progress meeting where Andrei Korisov announced the AK1. He was still in Moscow. Andrei didn't let Bernie's absence slow him down in the least. He didn't believe that Bernie either needed, or deserved, much of the credit. "There is some loss of force from the gap between the firing chamber and the barrel, but surprisingly little. And a shield to protect the stock from outgassing must be installed. There is some danger from outgassing, but, again, the shield, plus moderate care, should avoid any serious problems."

Natasha didn't scream at the man. Four of the servants in the Dacha had been debilitated by the squirts of gas from the gap between firing chamber and the barrel, and one poor lad had been killed when the firing chamber had broken though the stock and hit him in the head. What she really wanted to do was have Andrei Korisov shot with his own gun, but she couldn't. He was a *deti boyar*, and one of Fedor Ivanovich Sheremetev's at that. It was early days yet, but Sheremetev was starting to get interested in the Dacha and what it was producing.

She wanted Andrei Korisov out of the Dacha, but she couldn't do it by punishing him for the people his experiments had hurt. Suddenly, she knew what to do. Vladimir had friends in the army and so did Boris. Fedor Ivanovich Sheremetev was arguing that the arming of Russia shouldn't be left in the Dacha, and he probably already had the full particulars about Andrei Korisov's cut-up gun. In a few weeks, she would make a trip to Moscow, visit some of Vladimir's friends in the army and, perhaps, Boris. Meanwhile, she held her face steady while Andrei Korisov gloated over his new toy.

Then she went on to the next person.

"I've produced electrical sparks, miniature lightnings," Lazar Smirnov said. "But I can't tell yet if they are producing the electromagnetic waves the papers talk about. I've made a crystal radio set, but I have no way of telling if it works. Certainly, one of them doesn't, because the sparks aren't making the crystal set make noise, which, if I'm reading all this right, it should."

"What about the heating units?" Natasha asked.

"I think they're too big for the batteries, Princess," Lazar said. "I'll know more when Bernie gets back and translates these pamphlets for me."

The princess looked over at Filip, knowing what he was going to say.

"We had a boiler blow up," Filip said. "We had used a copper pot and had a coppersmith weld the lid on. We had a steam pipe going from it to a bellows, the idea being to use the steam to expand the bellows. Using pressure to get work rather than work to get pressure, as it were. But we did something wrong. I'm not entirely sure what, but I think we had a valve in backwards.

"We put the fire under it, we waited for the bellows to lift but it didn't. We added more wood, and then the pot split. We had injuries, Princess. The coppersmith's apprentice was standing too close when it split. But we had no warning. Nothing at all to indicate what was going to happen. There must be a way to tell that sort of thing, but I don't know. I won't even know what to look for until Bernie gets back. I've written to your brother, asking for more information. Maybe internal combustion is safer." Filip shrugged. "We just don't know enough."

"I know and I am sorry, Filip," Natasha said. "I went by and saw the boy. He is doing well." She took a deep breath and continued, "Some good news to end the meeting. The plows and scrapers we sent to Murom are in use and our road preparation and plowing are well ahead of schedule. We'll meet again when Bernie gets back. But know, my friends, that the Dacha is producing good results in the wider world."

Chapter 19

June 1632

Boris got back to Russia while the fight against the typhoid fever outbreak was still going on but after Bernie had gone back to the Dacha. The Grantville Section was, so far, not doing all that well. Boris was having organizational problems. Pavel Borisovich, his eldest son, shook his head at him. "They won't authorize his transfer, Father."

"Why not?" Boris felt he was asking the question with considerable restraint.

His son shrugged. "The official reason or the real reason?"

"The official one; I know the real one." The real reason was resentment. The patriarch had gotten Boris the Grantville Section and a reasonable budget. That only fueled the resentment. There were other people who were in line for the promotion; people with better family connections. That would normally mean that if a new section was established, those people might reasonably expect to be selected to head it up. Assistant section chiefs—in and out of the embassy bureau—were angry that Boris had been jumped a rank.

"Priorities." Pavel squinted and hunched over as though he expected a strong wind.

"I was given to understand that we had a rather high priority?" Boris tried to keep his voice calm. Perhaps too calm.

"I'm just passing on what I was told." Pavel waved the report, then began to read. "'Because of the requirements of the grain shipments to Sweden, Yuri Petrovich Gorbochov is desperately needed to expedite the harvest in the Gdansk region.'"

"They picked one that has a higher priority than we do." Boris had to give that section chief credit. It was cleverly done anyway. There might even be some truth to it.

"Father, I'm not sure you do know the real reason. At least not all of them. I was talking to Petr Somovich. He said that a lot of people are starting to be afraid that this is a job that leads nowhere. Bernie is popular enough, though some of the healers are pretty upset with him. Not that much has come out of the Dacha yet. The scrapers, if they turn out to be useful, and a few other things. We have some books that mostly don't make sense, not even to people who do speak English. Who cares that someone named Audubon painted birds? Russia has real issues to deal with."

"I know, Son." Boris had to concede that some of the objections to working with the Dacha crew seemed to be valid. Among the other things that Boris had brought back was an up-time copy of the first book of the *Encyclopedia International*, 1963 edition, that had been in someone's garage. They had refused the outright sale of the books but had rented them to Vladimir and his friends for an outrageous sum. "But you never know what might combine with something else to solve a problem. We saw it again and again in Grantville. There would be an article on something that they needed but it would be missing some vital piece of information. Then that needed piece of information would show up in the biography about the man who discovered it. Something like where he was when he found the first deposit of some rare earth."

"So you decided to send a copy of everything. I know, Father. I even agree." Pavel's face was serious, his dark eyes intent. "That doesn't change the fact that spending the next ten years of their lives translating minutia about people who will never even be born seems a pointless, career-ending job to most people."

Boris sighed. "I had hoped it would be more popular. It is a secure position, doing important work, if not the most exciting. A safe place in the bureaus."

"That's the problem, Father." Pavel shrugged. "It's not secure unless the Grantville Section becomes secure."

Boris was left with an office and a budget and not nearly enough

people who read and wrote English and Russian. The budget...
for the moment he had plenty of money. Well, lands. The government of Russia ran on a formalized barter system because
there was not nearly enough money to support the economy they
had. That would be changing soon. The Assembly of the Land
and the *Boyar Duma* were almost agreed on the form the Czar's
Bank would take.

The delay in the formation of the Czar's Bank wasn't caused
just by the haggling over who got what. There was plenty of that,
to be sure, but the politicians were also waiting for more excerpts
from up-time economics books. They all wanted the money to
work, even the fair number of boyars and other officials who
didn't believe that paper money would ever be worth anything.

Two days after Boris got back he had a visit from Princess
Natalia. She came to his home, had tea with his wife, and talked
to him about getting Andrei Korisov out of her Dacha.

"I don't care that much that he is no doubt spying for Fedor
Ivanovich Sheremetev or one of that clan. Anyway, they have other
spies, I don't doubt. It's what he's doing with the servants of the
Dacha. They are terrified to go near his little shop for fear of
being drafted to pull a trigger on the latest of his experiments."

"Is he getting results?"

Natasha sighed. "Yes, I think so, and so does Bernie. Not that
Bernie is any more pleased about his methods than I am. Bernie
and Filip worked up a string and pulley system for pulling the
trigger and a paper cage to measure the outgassing.

"Andrei Korisov thanked them for the paper cage because it gives
a more accurate read on the direction of force than a screaming,
running peasant does. He just grunted about the string and pulley system for bench-firing the rifle. Apparently, saving peasants
from maiming or death is not an issue of concern. Bernie, just
back from Moscow and the slow plague, wanted to kill him and
I wanted to let him. Even Filip was upset, and you know how
conservative he is."

Which Boris actually didn't, but he nodded anyway. It was
what you did when a princess told you that you knew something
you hadn't known. "So, Princess, clearly you have something in
mind?" he asked when she had run down a little.

"Yes. I want to give him to the army or to the Grantville desk.

Anywhere. I don't really care. I just want him out of the Dacha. Bernie will still consult on weapons development and maybe the army can find him some criminals to pull his triggers for him. As long as they aren't my people, I don't really care."

This was a very natural thing for a member of the nobility to say, though Boris knew most up-timers wouldn't think so. There was a certain coldness that came with the territory. Let the monster go kill other people if it was inconvenient to stop him, just so long as they weren't her people.

"If you try to give him to me, the bureaus will scream," Boris said with some regret. There were contracts to be had, not just with the main army but with the *Streltzi* of all the towns and cities in Russia. "I would suggest you give him to the *Streltzi* bureau, and through them to the army. They will be thrilled."

Which was what they ended up doing. The Gun Shop, as it came to be known, was placed at another small town about thirty miles south of Moscow and about twenty miles away from the Dacha. If there was need, they could get in touch with the Gun Shop or it could get in touch with them. And in the meantime, Andrei Korisov was out of Natasha's hair and no danger to her servants.

Chapter 20

July 1632

"Order Kameroff to take his battalion to the west." Bernie grinned as the barely bearded Russian wearing two stars on his collar moved his finger along the map, over a set of hills then northwest along a river. "He is to take dispatch riders and notify us at the first sign of the enemy."

This was not the war games Bernie had played as a kid. There was no fog of war in *Afrika Corps*, or the other war games Bernie played. There, everyone could see what the other side was doing. Not in this game, which had been designed by army officers instead of geeks.

"Yes, sir," said the veteran with the graying beard halfway down his chest and a single bar on his collar. There was probably a bit of amusement in his voice. But if the "general" felt any offense at that amusement, he kept it to himself.

The "lieutenant" left to deliver the orders. The "general's" sigh was barely audible. This was his first time in the war room and he was clearly trying hard to keep up a good front.

It was Bernie's first time in the war room, too. Bernie had told some of the guardsmen at the Dacha about war games and football last winter. He'd drawn plays on a slate, and a small hex grid map on another. The guards had been less interested in the

87

football plays than in the grid map. Perhaps because the grid map war game was a game that involved dice. And in Russia, in winter, playing dice was something to do. Anyway, Bernie had spent many evenings with the guards and the serving maids building a simple war game for the guards to play and insisting that the maids should be allowed to play if they wanted to.

The guards gave in pretty easily. The girls were pretty, after all. The game was based on some battle that Ivan the Terrible had fought. The guards told Bernie the situation, how many troops of what kind Ivan had, how many the enemy had, the terrain, the supply situation, stuff like that, sometimes consulting with Father Kiril, a priest and historian, to get the details right. As they gave Bernie details, he would fold them into the game. The supply situation became supply units that had to travel back and forth to the front. Terrain was added to the map and restricted movements, till they had something approaching a working game.

Then Bernie had gotten busy with other stuff and forgotten about it. The guards, a couple of the maids and Father Kiril hadn't. They had taken the game and continued to refine it, added other maps and other battles. The guards had told their friends in the Russian military about it and word had gotten to the generals, who in turn became interested in it as a teaching tool for young officers and some not so young. It had become quite the rage in the Kremlin.

General Mikhail Borisovich Shein, the hero of the defense of Smolensk who had avoided being the goat of the Smolensk War only by the intercession of up-timer records, said the games by themselves were the next best thing to useless, perhaps even worse than useless. Still, when combined with the experience of senior officers, they would allow the learning of war with much less loss of blood. So he had let them be played and even incorporated them, with modifications, of course, into the training of his officers.

General Shein wanted the fog of war in the games. So the official games were played in three rooms—the commander of one force in one room, the commander of the other force in another, and finally the judges in a third. This way the players could see only their troops and not all of them. Only the judges in the third room could see it all.

Bernie thought that sounded neat, but obviously entailed a great deal of work. It *was* a lot of work, but almost nothing compared to the actual moving of troops and staging mock battles. He looked back at the kids doing their planning on the game board.

"General" Ivan Milosevic was clearly a very nervous kid, as well he should be. Bernie had been briefed over beers last night. The lad had been cleaning up at the standard games, with his partner in crime, Boris Timofeivich, acting as the bank and the person the bets were made with.

The members of the service nobility didn't choose to believe that a lowly baker's son would be able to beat them at a game so clearly based on the arts of war. Yet the boys had been cleaning up, and because Timofeivich was not just service nobility but a member of a cadet branch of one of the great houses, they were finding it difficult to welsh when they lost. Clearly, the lads must be cheating somehow, else the arrogant little baker's boy would have been losing. Either that or the games were not an accurate reflection of real war. Well, they probably weren't, Bernie figured, but that wasn't why the members of the service nobility were getting their clocks cleaned by the kid. The kid was good.

The "general" looked over at the "captain," Timofeivich, then back at the map. It was a carefully drawn map of western Russia, Lithuania and eastern Poland, that had elevation lines in some places and little humps drawn for hills and trees drawn for forests in others.

One of the things that Vladimir had sent—before he'd sent Bernie, in fact—was a map-making kit. The Russians had been putting it to good use. It and quite a few copies of it. The kit wasn't that much. A pair of sighting devices that could be placed at a known distance from one another. A compass and plumb bob for each device so that the direction each was pointed could be determined precisely. And something for them both to look at, a stick stuck in the ground some distance off. The rest was recording and calculation. Dictatorships do have their advantages. It wasn't hard for the czar and *Boyar Duma* to order the maps made in this new way and to have survey teams trained. The new maps were a combination of the surveys and the maps they already had. Even though several hundred people had been put to work on the project, the results were as yet spotty. Very good right around Moscow where the teams were trained and along the rivers where the surveys were concentrated, not so good in forests where it took more work.

Hence the contour lines here and little trees over there. The map was actually fairly pretty. Which was beside the point. Ivan pointed at a hill, just a little bump drawn on the map. "If it's high enough," he said, "we'll build a temporary fort here..."

While Ivan talked, Bernie looked at the map and nodded. He hadn't seen it till Ivan had pointed it out, but it was clear enough now. If they were going to be attacked, that would be one of the ways that the attack might come. If the map was accurate, the other ways would be easier to reach and see from up there. The kids really were good at the games. But Bernie had no idea how well that would translate into being good at war.

The "lieutenant," Gorgii Ameroff, came back into the room and nodded to Bernie. Gorgii was an old veteran and had seen war firsthand. He also had his doubts about how well the skills of the gaming room would translate into the field. As best as Bernie could tell, Gorgii was a staff officer looking after the training of young officers under the command of a higher officer.

Bernie wasn't sure, but from Gorgii's expression the kids were doing pretty well and Gorgii didn't quite know how to take that. Totally aside from his youth, the fact that Ivan was from a modest family, more merchant class than nobility, annoyed Gorgii. Bernie knew Gorgii was still trying to work out how he felt about that. It just didn't seem right that this baker's son would have such talent or potential. The changes brought on by the Ring of Fire were disturbing.

The question wasn't just how well the games would translate into real battle, but also how much practice at war could be gained. Stories told around campfires of battles fought a generation ago didn't necessarily translate all that well to the real world. But they were a real part of teaching the young men the art of war. With the games, a young student might command in a month the same number of battles he would fight in a dozen years of service. Experience, even the sort of pseudo-experience provided by the games, might make the difference between seeing or missing a danger or an opportunity on which a battle might be won or lost.

Bernie waved to Gorgii and quietly left the room. He needed to get back to the Dacha.

Chapter 21

Bernie was going nuts. After all his talk about the joys of decadent civilization, he had failed to provide the decadent civilization. It had taken a while to get the parts to the new bathroom made. Now they were made and installed, but there were still a multitude of problems. And the brain cases wanted to know why. Heck, the brain cases wanted to know why *everything*. Bernie had tried to explain and run headlong into a massive wall of ignorance and arrogance. Mostly, but not entirely, his own.

"What is a gravity feed?" Filip Pavlovich asked. "How can one make water grave and serious? Water does not flow because it is serious. Water flows because water wants to return to its proper level, just as Aristotle said two thousand years ago. So to make this 'seriousness feed' the book speaks of, you would have to make the water serious. How do you do that?" Bernie was pretty sure that Filip Pavlovich was having a bit of fun at his expense, but there was a core of truth in the complaint. He'd run into the philosophers' faith in Aristotle before. It was akin to their faith in God.

"It didn't say water falls because it is serious." Bernie tried clenching his teeth and counting to ten. "It said that the force of gravity causes it to fall. It didn't say anything about water being serious, for crying out loud. The force of gravity is a force of nature. Oh, hell...never mind. Let me think a minute."

Bernie stormed away from the workshop. He wasn't completely sure about it, but from the timing and some of the symptoms he'd seen in Moscow, the "slow fever," whatever its proper name was, seemed likely to be transmitted by bad water. If that was true, then indoor plumbing, septic systems, and getting human waste away from things like drinking water or washing water, might mean the difference between hundreds of people dying of "slow fever" every spring and maybe none dying.

He had never thought himself arrogant. He just figured that among people who thought there were only six planets, he'd do all right. He'd tell them how to make stuff and they would. The problem was, Bernie didn't really know how to make stuff. He had quite a bit of the knowledge needed, but he had no idea how to put it together into a form that would produce a product.

That should have been all right. There were a number of very bright, very creative, people at the Dacha. They had been arriving a few at a time. However, as yet there was very little crossover between what Bernie knew and what they knew. Their map of the world and his were so different that communicating, even with a good translator, was difficult.

Right at the moment, the problem was with the toilets. The manuals talked about a gravity feed. To the local experts, gravity meant "dignity or sobriety of bearing." In fact, though Bernie didn't know it, the gravity feed was something they already understood quite well. However, the terms were different. They would have called it a "natural flow feed" or something similar. That would have referred to Aristotle's assertion that there were natural and unnatural types of motion. Water flowing downhill was natural motion. There was no force that made things fall. Things fell because things had a natural desire to go where they belonged. Steam went into the air and rocks onto the ground because that's where they belonged. Water, as was the case here, just naturally wanted to travel to the lowest point. Granted, Galileo had chipped around the edges of Aristotle, but just around the edges. Besides, few people here had read Galileo.

Bernie didn't know it, but an extension of this Aristotelian world view had led to many of the concepts that the up-timers thought of as superstition. After all, if water just naturally wanted to flow downhill, didn't it make sense that a wheel would just naturally want to turn, that a candle would just naturally want to burn? That any device that was made well enough would want to perform its natural function and, given the opportunity, would do so on its own? And if water had a natural desire to flow downhill, what about people? Was it not self-evident that people were innately good or innately evil? Innately superior or innately inferior, good blood, bad blood?

It was a subtle but profound difference in the way people thought about the world. The early modern period, the period the Ring of Fire had thrust the West Virginia mining town into, was when that notion of a world where things did what they did because it was their nature to do so was being replaced—slowly, one chip at a time—with the notion that things happened because of external forces like gravity and drag. But it hadn't happened yet. It would have been Newton who really shifted the world view and he hadn't been born yet. Now, because of the Ring of Fire, he wouldn't be born at all in this universe. Here it would be Grantville that the change spun on, and the change would come much faster. Worse, Russia, in general, was lagging about two hundred years behind the rest of Europe.

Bernie didn't know any of that; he didn't even know that Aristotle had gotten it wrong. He knew Newton had some laws—three, he thought. He sort of thought that Einstein had gotten it right and corrected the bits that Newton had gotten wrong with his theory of relativity. That was how the A-bomb worked. More importantly, Bernie didn't know that the problems sprang from a difference in world view. Half the time he thought the people at the Dacha were playing with him. Half the time he thought they were idiots, and half the time he thought he must be the idiot. There were too many halves of Russia and not nearly enough working toilets. At the moment there weren't *any* working toilets.

Bernie entered the kitchen of the dacha and sat at the table. "Marpa Pavlovna, may I have a beer, please?" When the cook nodded, Bernie leaned back and tried to figure out how to explain gravity.

The cook handed him a beer. His "thanks" was a bit absent-minded. She also put a plate of ham and cheese sandwiches in front of him. He'd had a little trouble explaining that no, he didn't want to stop work in the middle of the day and have a big meal, then take a nap. It was weird. Everybody in Russia took a siesta in the middle of the day. Bernie had thought that only happened in, like, Mexico. Well, not totally weird. Moscow in summer was as hot as Mexico, or at least he thought it was. Bernie didn't have a thermometer. Bernie knew good and well that they could make a thermometer here but he needed an up-time thermometer to get temperature to make the marks on the thermometer made here. Not that he really needed a thermometer right now. What he needed was a plumber and the nearest one of those was in Grantville.

Bernie rubbed his temples with his fingers, trying to ease the headache he invariably got when he tried to explain a complex concept to Filip Pavlovich. In a few moments a pair of cool-feeling hands began rubbing his temples for him. Bernie leaned back against the chair and let one of the maids, Fayina Lukyanovna, take over. One of the things Boris had not lied about was the availability of willing women. Unfortunately, though, the woman who was increasingly working her way into his fantasies was unavailable. Bernie couldn't quite imagine Natasha rubbing his temples for him. Well, he could imagine it, all too easily, but it wasn't going to happen.

"What is now, Bernie?" Fayina's voice was low, gentle. "'Sewer system' again?"

Gravity was the least of his problems with the sewer system. Bernie had arrived at the Dacha with complete designs for a toilet and complete designs for a septic system. But it wasn't working right. The toilet had backed up, the sink had backed up, the bathtub had backed up. Each and every one of them was producing the most awful stinks it had ever been his misfortune to smell. He couldn't use the indoor bathroom anymore. The room had been closed off and some pretty horrible sounds came from it. Bernie was pretty sure that the problem was in the septic system or in the pipes. He had finally remembered the U-shaped pipes just below the sinks. He had had those installed and that had seemed to fix it for a little while. But then things got worse.

"I don't know how to fix it." Bernie groaned. "God, your hands feel good. The bathroom is going to drive me crazy until I figure it out."

"Princess Natalia Petrovna wishes to speak to you." Fayina stopped rubbing his temples. She was dark-haired and short, well-padded. He noticed that she was wearing one of those crown-looking head-dresses with her hair loose. Customs were different here. Confusing.

Single women wore a smaller headdress than married women and left their hair loose. Married women kept their hair covered all the time. "New books have arrived from Grantville."

"I have good news for you, at any rate," Natasha said. "Here. You have letters. I have letters, as well. And more books. Perhaps the answer will be in the new books."

Bernie took his stack of letters, wondering who had written him. Dad wasn't much of a letter writer and his sisters were busy. The handwriting on the top one was vaguely familiar. And the envelopes, some of them, were from up-time. Bernie opened the first one carefully and read:

> *Dear Bernie,*
> *Thanks for recommending me to the Princess Natasha. What's she look like, by the way?*
> *I just wanted to let you know that I sent her a* Victoria's Secret *plus some other stuff. So the consequences to Russian culture are on you. Anything else you want me to send them? I don't think the library has a copy of the* Communist Manifesto, *but I'll see if I can find Mao's Little Red Book* if you like.

Bernie's reading stuttered to a stop as a sudden vision of Natasha in a black teddy swam before his eyes. With some effort, he brought himself back to the letter.

> *Also, your whole family is fine but still a bit pissed about your crawling into a bottle and running off to Russia after your mom died. Bernie, I know it was hard on you and your family does too, but, well, the world's not a nice place sometimes. Deal with it.*

Bernie snorted. It was good advice, he knew, but he figured that Brandy Bates ought to be taking it, not just giving it.

> *I don't know if you were sober enough to notice but Grantville was turning into a boom town even before you left and you're not the only guy that got hired away. Folks are getting rich right and left. I don't know how,*

but they are. I'm still working at Club 250 which sucks, but what can you do. A lot of the folks that got rich since the Ring of Fire have bought estates in the country with servants and the whole bit. But for every one that moves out, two or three down-timers move in. Then there are the tourists! Grantville is more crowded than ever. There's talk of people moving factories to Halle because the Saale's closer to navigable that far down river. Others are talking about going all the way to the Elbe. But people are nervous about getting too far from Grantville.

Anyway, things are happening here even if it does seem it's all skipping past me and Mom. Write me, and tell me what else I can do to save Russia from male shovanism.

Good Luck.

Brandy.

"Thank God." It was a relief to read something that wasn't an encyclopedia, Bernie thought, utterly failing to notice that Brandy had misspelled chauvinism. "Someone who speaks my kind of English. Natasha, when can I send a letter back to Grantville?"

Natasha looked up from her own letters. "The courier will leave tomorrow. You can send a letter with him." Bernie knew Natasha didn't approve of his tendency to sit in the kitchen. She was also the reason he was growing a beard, even though it itched. He still wasn't going to wear some silly robe out in public, though, no matter how much she nagged at him.

"Good. I'll get right on it and have Gregorii make a drawing as well." Gregorii Mikhailovich was the artist whose job it was to take Bernie's descriptions and very rough sketches and turn them into usable drawings. "Brandy can probably find out what I've done wrong. It's a darn good thing your brother stayed in Grantville. When I've finished the letter, I'll take a look through the books and stuff he sent. Maybe I can figure out how to explain gravity."

"Seriousness?" Natasha's voice was curious. "Don't they know what seriousness is?"

Bernie groaned. Then headed back to face the brain cases.

"Bernie Janovich, what is the center of gravity?" Petr Nickovich had been waiting impatiently while Bernie was out of the room. His English was not good and the discussion of gravity was more confusing than helpful. He knew there was something there because the notes he had received on flight mentioned gravity regularly. Center of gravity, specifically. He sat and thought, giving no sign how much it hurt him not to understand about gravity and how to fly. Finally, Bernie returned with the letters and Petr asked his question before the sewer system could distract them again.

"Hey, I actually know that one." Bernie grinned at Petr. "Cars need a low center of gravity for stability."

Petr just looked at him. As usual, Bernie hadn't explained anything.

Bernie lost his grin. "Okay. Try it this way. Bend over." Bernie bent over. "As your head moves forward, your rear end moves backward, otherwise you fall on your face. That's to keep your center of gravity over your feet." Bernie stood up again. "Try to balance something on one finger. It's the same thing. To keep it balanced, you have to keep your finger under the center of gravity."

"You mean that center of gravity just means the point of balance?" Petr couldn't help his look of shock. "The place where you would place the fulcrum?"

The outlander shrugged. "Pretty much."

Petr considered, then asked. "Then why does how high the center of gravity is matter?"

"There is other stuff besides gravity. Centrifugal force and stuff."

"Explain that, if you would." Petr tried not to grit his teeth. He knew he was close to something but wasn't sure what. He listened to Bernie's rambling explanation. It was there he knew, if he could just grasp it. The secret to everything. It came in bits and drabs . . . gravity was a force like centrifugal force. Then another piece when Bernie squared his stance and had someone push from the side. The person pushing on him to try to over-balance him was a force. The key came when he asked why they used rockets to get to the moon. "Why not wings?"

"No air in space."

"Why not?"

"Gravity," an obviously frustrated Bernie insisted.

Petr froze. He could see it in his mind's eye. "How much does air weigh?"

"I don't know." Bernie shrugged. "It's pretty light; we can look it up. Uh . . . maybe not, but we can write Vladimir about it."

The outlander didn't realize. How *much* air weighed didn't really matter. What mattered was *that* air weighed. That it had weight. It was pulled down to the ground by a force; water was, too, but more so. They wouldn't have to look the weight of air up, Petr could think of several ways to work it out. Looking it up might be easier if it was in one of the books. The important point was that air had weight. That was how the balloons worked. That was how it *all* worked.

Vesuvius erupted. Russian words spewed forth. Bernie didn't understand. Didn't want to understand after he caught the Russian words for "idiot" and "uncultured" repeated several times. At least this time everyone was an uncultured idiot, not just Bernie. Which was a relief. Everyone, Petr included, everyone from Adam to Aristotle…especially Aristotle. Everyone in the entire history of the world, both histories. Only two exceptions could be made: God and Sir Isaac Newton. God for creating such a complex world from such beautiful simplicity and Sir Isaac Newton for understanding it.

"Don't you understand, you uncultured buffoons? We can fly!"

"What in blazes are you talking about?" Filip Pavlovich was not one to accept being called an idiot by anyone. "Of course we can fly, once we know how. If the outlanders from the future could do it, we can learn to do it." He froze then. "You know how?"

"It's all forces, don't you see…damn Aristotle to the worst region of hell. Innate desire. Natural tendency. Bah…it's forces. Water is heavy, air is light, the force of gravity works better on heavy than light, that's what makes it heavy."

Bernie almost laughed at the man's odd combination of enthusiasm and exasperation. "Think you can explain a gravity-feed system to these guys, Petr?" he asked, half-jokingly.

"*Da*," followed by about three sentences in Russian said too fast for Bernie to understand. Which led in turn to several voices from around the room saying, "Oh, we understood that part! We thought he was talking about something else." Bernie just shook his head and left the geeks to their talk. Somehow, he couldn't stop grinning. These guys got such a charge out of this stuff. Now maybe they could get the plumbing to work.

That night, instead of studying, Bernie wrote a letter to Brandy Bates.

Hello, Brandy

If you really want to change Russia send me instructions for fixing the plumbing. Creating the plumbing, rather. They have a disease here that they call slow fever. It lasts a month or more with the fever getting worse and the people getting weaker. I watched a little boy and a lot of other people die of it this spring. We've sent its pathology to Prince Vladimir in hopes that he can find out what it is and how it's cured from the up-timer docs. But diarrhea is one of its main symptoms and I figure it's getting into the water supply and spreading that way.

I got to tell you, Brandy, these folks don't wash much. Steam baths, sure. Washing your hands before you prepare food? Not so much. Washing dishes is pretty slapdash, too. I already had that fight with the kitchen staff here at the Dacha and won it, with the support of Princess Natasha. Working after school at the Burger Barn has paid off.

Anyway, if we want to stop the slow fever and probably a lot of other deaths, we need hot running water, hand soap, and toilets. I tried putting a septic system in here at the Dacha and it isn't working. I haven't been able to figure out what's wrong but . . .

Bernie spent the next three pages describing in great boring detail what he had had installed and the symptoms of its failure.

Brandy, I'd write this on my knees if I thought it would help. Please find someone there in town who can tell us how to make this work. You'll be saving lives if you do.
Bernie Zeppi

Chapter 22

Freshly ensconced in his new kingdom, Andrei Korisov didn't hear about the new understanding of gravity in the Dacha. He wouldn't have cared that much anyway, because it didn't change ballistics, just the reason they worked. If he had cared at all, it would have been to be concerned about the allocation of resources away from his guns to flight. That, however, was no longer a problem. He had his own resources now. Well, he was in charge of them. Which was the same thing. He went back to working on the Andrei Korisov rifle.

The mechanics of holding the chamber in place while allowing it to rotate up and out for reloading weren't very complex, but they were an added complication. The gimbal was constantly breaking under the stress of firing, then having to be redesigned and strengthened again. Andrei was sure he was missing something. He went out to the range, where one of the apprentice gunsmiths was testing the latest version. Andrei had decided to go with a smaller bore and a shorter barrel, mostly for ease of construction. He would use much tighter rifling and count on the greater spin to keep the smaller bullet accurate. But that wasn't what these tests were about.

These tests were to determine how much wear was caused by the outgassing. They would fire one hundred shots, then measure the wear on the protective plate Andrei had installed. It was still basically a Russian muzzle-loader with the back five inches of the barrel sawed off, but some things had been added. A heavy iron gimbal had been added to let the firing chamber be rotated up for loading and back down into alignment, and Andrei's protective plate, a relatively thin piece of curved iron, had been inserted into the stock where the firing chamber muzzle almost touched the open back of the barrel.

Oleg had the new rifle clamped to the bench and was using the string and pulley system to test fire the rifle. Andrei watched as the boy pulled the string and the rifle fired. Then Oleg made a mark in a slate. Fourteen shots since the start of the test. It was going a little faster than Andrei had thought it would.

Oleg went over to the rifle and pulled out the spent chamber and put in another one. He poured a little powder into the pan, cocked the lock, and went back behind the bench and pulled the string. The rifle fired again. The chamber slammed against the back plate and the stock cracked. The stocks weren't handling the strain.

"Where did you get that chamber?" Andrei shouted.

"Which one?" Oleg asked, then continued quickly, seeing it was his boss, "One is from this rifle, sir, and the other one is from the last one. It's quicker to load the two chambers together, then just switch them out. I didn't know I wasn't supposed to."

"How do you get one chamber out to put in the next?" Andrei asked.

"After the gimbal broke. Ah . . . they do that a lot," Oleg said, clearly anxious not to be blamed for breaking the gimbal. "It was just easier to put the chamber in by hand than fix the gimbal every time."

But Andrei wasn't concerned with that. He had just found the key to making the rate of fire for the Andrei Korisov rifle much higher, at least for a short while. A chamber was a lot shorter than a barrel and a lot easier to make. He could make several chambers for each rifled musket. The soldier could carry them loaded and have several fairly quick shots before having to reload the chambers.

It was weeks later that he realized that the chamber didn't have to be the same shape as the barrel. At least in its outer dimensions. And he still hadn't realized how necessary it was to have the chamber holder attached to something.

Chapter 23

Grantville
August 1632

"Well, the problem is that we can't foreclose on it." Dori Ann Grooms hesitated and Vladimir saw the blush rise. "I'm sorry. That really wasn't the best way to put it, Herr Gorchakov. What I mean was that your collateral is simply too far away for the Bank of Grantville to accept it as surety for a loan. It's not like it was in the old, ah, new, back up-time. And even then there would have been issues with using property in a different country."

Vladimir nodded. He'd thought that might be the answer, but it had been worth a try. He needed more money, cash on hand. Most of his family's wealth was tied up in land. Much of the rest was tied up in the Dacha research center. "Do you have any suggestions, then?"

Dori Ann shook her head. "Edgar said you might have better luck with the Abrabanel Bank. Seems like they've got agents everywhere."

The young man ushered Vladimir into Uriel Abrabanel's office in the Bank of Badenburg, closed the door and left. Uriel was behind the desk, while Don Francisco Nasi sat in a corner and grinned.

"Ah..." Vladimir was clearly unprepared to discover that Don Francisco would be sitting in on his conference with the president and primary owner of the first down-time bank to become a member of the New U.S. Federal Reserve System.

Don Francisco waved reassurance. "I'm not here to interfere in your business with Cousin Uriel, Prince Vladimir." He smiled at the look on Vladimir's face.

"You do understand that I will not..."

"Betray your people? Please. Do I look like John George of Saxony?" Francisco waved away the whole idea. "All that is going on here is that when I learned of your appointment with Uriel, I decided to take the opportunity for a semi-private meeting. But I am more than willing to wait my turn. Please go on with your banking."

Then for a while Francisco mostly watched as Vladimir and Uriel discussed banking matters. He did put in a comment here and there. "Vladimir's Dacha has already produced half a dozen products that are being licensed to various groups in Russia. Are you sure, Cousin, that speculative venture is the right description?" That got Francisco a dirty look from his elder cousin. And a curious one from Vladimir.

Then, some time later, Francisco said, "Paper rubles with the printing in the hands of the *Boyar Duma*? No disrespect intended, Vladimir, but the czar's cabinet isn't exactly known for its restraint."

"A lot of that was simply not being aware of the consequences. Printing gobs of money would not benefit the great houses," Vladimir said.

"If they realize that and if they care," Uriel said. "Printing gobs of money, as you put it, may not be good for the economy but in the short run it can be very good for the printers. Even if they show restraint, determining the amount of money needed to run the economy without causing hyper-inflation is no easy task. Not even with computers. I can't avoid the conclusion that accepting payment in the czar's paper would be a speculative investment. I really have to insist on New U.S. dollars."

So it went for about two hours. Francisco mostly watched the exchange, and kept Uriel from skinning the Russian prince too badly. Vladimir wasn't as good at this as he apparently thought he was. But, finally, agreement was reached and Vladimir was provided with a letter of credit.

At which point, by prior arrangement, Uriel excused himself and it was Francisco's turn.

"The reason I invited myself to your meeting was that I wanted to talk to you about where you think the alliance between Sweden and Russia is headed. Also what role you see the New U.S. playing in those relations."

At first Vladimir demurred, pointing out that primarily his mission had to do with information that was mostly free for the asking, from the National Library and the Research Center.

Nasi grinned. "That is true enough, but incomplete. Yes, your shop is getting most of its information from legal sources, but you are also involved in what the up-timers call 'industrial espionage.' For instance, the sewing machine that went to Moscow with Bernie Zeppi was accompanied by rather copious notes on how it was made and what machines would be needed to make more. And your tour of the power plant was unusually focused on their new steam engines."

Vladimir smiled. "The twins were more than happy to explain how it was done. It isn't like I broke into their factory in the middle of the night and stole the designs. And as for the tour of the power plant, that was all perfectly legal."

"And Fedor Ivanovich Trotsky? Is he also staying within the bounds of law?" Nasi laughed at Vladimir's expression.

"Never mind. Trotsky is competent but unimaginative. We aren't that worried about him. However, I'm not here to threaten or browbeat you. I have an offer to make. I can provide you with information that Trotsky would find difficult to gather and all I want in return is the same consideration. Please consider my offer. There are things I won't tell you, but I won't lie to you unless absolutely necessary. All I ask from you is the same courtesy."

"I think I understand," Vladimir said. "However, I'm just a part-time spy. Little more than an apprentice. You'll have to be more explicit."

"Because of its situation, Grantville has a large group of spies working here. When you combine that with the ease of transferring information provided by the phones and computers, you get a situation ripe for counterespionage. The fact is that spies tend to know a lot about what their employers have in mind, both because you tell something every time you ask a question and because if a spy lacked curiosity he'd probably have gone into another line of work. Put it all together and you have a whole other reason to come to Grantville to spy. Information is our stock in trade. We trade it amongst ourselves. So a spy for Monsieur Gaston and one of Cardinal Richelieu's *intendants*, while not fond of each other, might trade information about the actions of Spain and Sweden. And each benefits by being able to inform their employer both bits of information."

Vladimir nodded sagely and Don Francisco grinned at him.

"All of which puts you in a most enviable position," Don Francisco said.

"Ah, how?" was all Vladimir could come up with.

"Because with only a few exceptions, nobody cares what Russia knows about anything," Don Francisco said bluntly. "Poland, certainly. England, if it has to do with trade. Sweden, if it's to do with the grain Russia sells to the king of Sweden every year at very low prices. Other than that? No. If you should learn Spain's military dispositions for the next two years the king of Spain would lose not a wink of sleep over it. Cardinal Richelieu's upset would be strictly a matter of principle and what the cardinal doesn't know won't hurt him. Ferdinand II, under other circumstances perhaps. But between the Lion of the North and the Turk to the south?" Nasi shook his head. "Russia barely makes a blip on the radar."

None of which was very complimentary but all of which Vladimir had to acknowledge was true. He nodded reluctantly. "And this situation is enviable how?"

"Because as a spy who must report back to the embassy bureau you have every reason to be asking the sorts of questions that will make you look good to Moscow and there is very little reason for people to be unwilling to answer them. I, on the other hand, am all too well known as an associate of Mike Stearns." Nasi gave a histrionic sigh. "No one wants to talk to me."

Vladimir barked a laugh. "So you want me to gather information and give it to you instead of my government."

"Oh, not at all. In addition to, not instead of," Nasi said. Which was precisely what Vladimir thought he was going to say.

"And for providing you with a carbon copy of the information, you will provide me what?"

"Why, carbon copies of the information I gather about places like Poland and England. And occasionally I'll be able to direct you to people who won't talk to me, but will talk to you."

"I see a problem," Vladimir said. "No one is going to be all that surprised that you happened to be visiting your cousin while I came seeing about a loan...once. But if we keep meeting like this, what will it do to my reputation as a titled nonentity? People might stop talking to me. That would be a disaster for me and inconvenient for you."

"That's what makes Grantville such a nice place with its phones and computers."

"Even I know the phone system has been penetrated," Vladimir said. "If you start calling me a lot or I start calling you a lot, someone will notice."

"That's where the computers come into play. You know that the local nodes of the internet came through. There is in Grantville a local area network that covers the town and several outlying areas. You can post encrypted information to various sites and no one will the wiser about who is posting what. There's also an encryption program that is called *Pretty Good Privacy* that came though the Ring of Fire. Apparently it was free for anyone up-time. I understand you bought a computer?"

"Yes." That was one reason that Vladimir had needed the loan. He knew that they were only going to get more expensive for the foreseeable future.

Nasi passed him one of the compact disks. It was unlabeled in its jewel case. "On that disk is a copy of the program *Pretty Good Privacy* including the source code and one of my public keys."

"What's a public key?"

"The thing that makes this such a good system is that it has two keys. One key encodes and the other decodes. What you encode with the public key can only be read with the private key. What is encoded by the private key can only be read with the matching public key. I would suggest that after you've had the program checked you make yourself some keys and post a key to one of the message boards listed on the CD. Encode it using the public key I included on the CD and only I will be able to read it, so you know that any message using that key is from me."

They talked about processes and procedures, which mostly came down to neither seeking each other out nor avoiding each other. They would use the local area internet in Grantville to transfer data. For the foreseeable future if anyone wanted to transfer information without anyone else knowing they were doing it,

Grantville was the place to be. In effect, each became a part of the other's spy network. For Nasi it was one more tiny link in an increasingly extensive network. For Vladimir, even with the filtering that he was sure Francisco Nasi would do, it represented a doubling of his capabilities or more. It was not a bargain he could afford to pass up.

When Vladimir got home he found mail had arrived from Moscow and the Dacha. There were several letters, requests for specific information for him, packages of goods for trade, mostly furs and pearls. There were also a set of letters and packages, to be delivered to Brandy Bates, some from his sister and some from Bernie. Vladimir thought for a moment about delivering them himself. He was a bit curious about what they might contain. But the truth was he simply didn't have time. He was snowed under trying to find answers to the questions sent to him. He sent his man Gregorii.

Chapter 24

Brandy Bates woke up the morning after her mom had read her the riot act about getting her G.E.D. rather less sure of herself than she had been the night before. Yes, it would be a lot of work and what would it actually get her? It wasn't like she was going to go to the library and find a way that the down-timers could make microwave ovens or washing machines. She was sitting at the kitchen table half-trying to work up her nerve to go see Mrs. Whitney about getting her G.E.D. and half-trying to come up with an excuse for her mom as to why she hadn't. Brandy's procrastinating was interrupted by the doorbell.

"Yes, can I help you?" Brandy asked the rather dangerous-looking bearded man at her door. He was carrying several packages.

"Have . . ." He paused looking for the next word. Then apparently gave it up as a bad job. "Stuff. Have stuff for Brandy Bates." The accent was almost unintelligible and it wasn't German. Something eastern-European.

"What sort of stuff and from who?"

He pointed at the packages. "From Berna Zeppa, from Kazrina Natalia, from Czarina."

Oddly enough it was the word "Czarina" that clarified things. The stuff was from Bernie and Natasha. And apparently something from the czarina.

She let in the man, who muttered his name. Gregorii something, she thought he said. He stacked the stuff on the coffee table in the living room and went on his way. Then Brandy started sorting through the stuff. The packages were from Natasha and the czarina of all the Russias. Apparently she, Brandy Bates of Grantville, was now pen pals with one of the crowned heads of Europe. Maybe if she'd graduated high school she could show them all up at the ten-year reunion. Then she stopped and thought. No, probably not. Her classmates, the ones who were caught in the Ring of Fire . . . Well, a lot of them would probably know crowned heads of Europe by the time the ten-year reunion came around. It would be "which crowned heads do you know?" and Russia would be near the bottom of the list.

Brandy laughed out loud. "Gee, Brandy. Only pen pals with the czarina of all the Russias? You can't win for losing, can you, girl? They do keep moving the goal posts, don't they just!"

She read Natasha's letter first. It was full of questions and observations that girls talk to girls about. It had requests for items that she might be able to send: plastic just about anything, aspirin, marijuana, medicines in general, pictures printed or photographed. It acknowledged that acquiring that sort of thing might be difficult and professed to understand if she was too busy to worry about them. A nice way of saying "we understand if you can't afford such things." Which, to be honest, Brandy mostly couldn't.

The letter directed her to a couple of the packages. One contained forty matched pearls. Another contained, according to the letter, enough treated pelts of Russian mink to make a mink coat for winter. These were not payment but a simple thank you for the magazines and makeup.

The letter also introduced the czarina and her letter. The czarina's letter was similar but different. There was a feel of condescension about it. Perhaps because she was the czarina or perhaps because she was a married woman. But mostly, it seemed to Brandy that the czarina was a bit nervous and a bit stilted. Both letters were written in seventeenth-century English with all its irregularities in spelling and differences in word usage. The czarina's was probably written by a scribe, which might well be part of the slightly more distant feel that the czarina's letter had. The czarina was a bit more upfront about payment and made it clear that she was interested in those things that were of interest to women and tended to make men uncomfortable. Her package also had pearls, as well as Chinese silk fabric.

Finally, around noon, Brandy got around to Bernie's letter and almost wrote nasty letters to both Natasha and the czarina. There had been a plague outbreak in Moscow and all they wrote about were doodads and trinkets! She actually wrote the letter to Natasha and started the one to the czarina. It was in that one that she stopped and thought. She wrote, "What if it had been your kids?" And that was what had stopped Brandy from irrevocably putting her foot in her mouth. The czarina and her children had been in Moscow when the outbreak had happened this spring. She went back to Bernie's letter, yes. It happened every year. Every year the czarina, the czar, and the czar's children lived in the path of the disease, whatever it was. They didn't write her about it because it was a part of life that you lived with, not something you could do anything about.

But Bernie wanted to do something about it. Football jerk Bernie, quiet drunk Bernie after the Ring of Fire. "Off to Moscow for the vodka and the hot and cold running servant girls" Bernie. What had happened to Bernie? Had something made the friendly but perpetually spoiled boy grow up? His letter sure read like it had.

Maybe it was time for Brandy to grow up, too. There were indeed people who were worse off than she was. In a way, the czarina of all the Russias was worse off than Brandy Bates. At least if Brandy got sick she could go to a doctor who wouldn't bleed her to balance the humors.

She would send Natasha and the czarina everything she could. She'd get the czarina's little girls plastic baby dolls if she had to sell the pearls and the mink to pay for them. She would send Natasha naughty underwear and strappy high-heels to help make her feel pretty. She would do those things, but first she was going to find out about the plumbing. And if she could, she was going to find out about the disease, too.

As it turned out, requests for help had already gone out to the doctors from Bernie and Natasha by way of Vladimir. The disease, the doctors were almost sure, was typhoid, spread by human waste in the water supply and curable with antibiotics. Of which there were not nearly enough to go around. The techniques to make the one they could produce down-time had been sent to the Dacha but it would be a while before the Russians could develop the tools to follow the recipe. How long a while was anyone's guess.

Washing hands before preparing food, using antibacterial soap and only using water that had been boiled to wash foods were all essential to stopping the disease, or at least decreasing its spread. All this information had already been sent to the Dacha, though it might not have gotten there yet. Yes, plumbing was essential, too. If the waste didn't get into the water supply and the cooks washed their hands, the disease couldn't get to the victims. Absent antibiotics, the treatment was to fight the fever, replace electrolytes lost through diarrhea, and otherwise fight the symptoms while the patient fought the disease. That treatment would decrease the percentage of deaths, but it would still be the very young and the very old who were hit hardest.

Vic Dobbs was helpful; he went over Bernie's letter and made recommendations, focusing on the vent stacks. Which Bernie had apparently not known about. With the help of her mom, Brandy put together the second care package, selling the pearls, mink and silk as needed to gather the goods. Which included some children's vitamins, dolls for the royal daughters and a cap pistol for the heir to the throne, along with various odds and ends to make ladies feel pretty and information on the rights of man and the rights of woman, too.

Brandy's mom took the care package to Prince Vladimir for further shipping because by then Brandy was hard at work on her G.E.D. while working as a researcher in the New U.S. National Library.

Chapter 25

Moscow
September 1632

The older he got, the less he slept. Filaret paced around his room, thinking. God had made his presence known. In that other history, Russian forces would even now be moving toward Smolensk and that whoreson, Sigismund III, would be dead this last half a year. That the war Filaret urged on Russia would have ended in disaster wasn't something that the patriarch doubted, much as he wanted to. God had spoken though the histories of that other time.

The question of whether God existed was clearly answered. That was perhaps not the sort of question that the patriarch of the Russian Orthodox Church ought to be asking, but Filaret's approach to religion had always been more pragmatic than pious; more a means of control than a way to heaven. Well, it had seemed more pragmatic. Maybe the pious fools had been the pragmatic ones, after all. God apparently did exist. Oh, Filaret supposed that an atheist could argue himself into believing that the Ring of Fire had just happened, or was some previously unknown natural phenomenon, but that would take more self-delusion than Filaret could manage at this late date.

All this, of course, raised the question: *what does God want?* Filaret had lots of priests who could tell him that, based on the

Bible. Unfortunately, not one of them had predicted the Ring of Fire and the scriptures that they had found after the fact predicting it were so vague and contradictory that they might well mean anything.

It was apparent that God wanted the best for Germany rather more than he wanted it for Russia and that posed a problem. The God who had let Russia and Filaret himself suffer through the Time of Troubles without lifting a finger to help, then moved heaven and earth in time as well as space to aid Germany? That wasn't a god that Filaret could follow. In fact, if old Nick had shown up in Filaret's room that night he would have gotten the patriarch's soul cheap, on the basis that even the Devil has to be better than such a god. With effort, Filaret turned his thoughts away from that well-worn path and onto the equally familiar path of politics.

They were on a dangerous path. No . . . they had been on a dangerous path before the Ring of Fire. Now it was worse. The knowledge that he had been wrong about attacking Poland had weakened him, and the information about the revolution of 1917 was being used as proof that the Romanov dynasty would lead Russia to disaster. Never mind that it wasn't scheduled for almost three centuries. Now wasn't the time to go experimenting with new ways of governing Russia, and he didn't think Mikhail realized just how dangerous this situation was. Mikhail was a good boy, but too gentle for the real world. Still, something he'd said kept coming back to Filaret. *Knowledge, freely given.* Filaret had started the only print shop in Russia. Like most things, it was a royal monopoly. He had also been instrumental in starting schools in monasteries. Again, control resided in Filaret, this time as the patriarch. Giving things away didn't come naturally to him, especially something as valuable as knowledge. Freely giving knowledge had its drawbacks, didn't it?

But the more he thought about it, the better it sounded. *Freely given. Charity. A gift to the poor. Alms of knowledge?* What an interesting idea. The agreement with the Gorchakov family was that the government could do what it wanted with the knowledge from the Dacha. It wouldn't do to give everything away. But some of it . . . Things that would help a lot of people and would cost a lot to administer. *A gift from the czar, granted freely to every citizen, peasant and serf in Russia. The right to make the turning plow.*

One of the new plows produced by the Dacha. And, of course, the Gorchakov family could still sell the right to make the plow to anyone who would buy what had already been given them for free. It would serve as a reminder to the Gorchakov family who was czar. At the same time, it would remind everyone that even knowledge was the czar's, to give and withhold at his will.

Chapter 26

"Why not an airplane, Pete?" Bernie asked.

"We're not sure of the math, Bernie," Petr Nickovich said, and then grinned when Father Kiril held up his cross as though fending off an evil. Father Kiril, Bernie had long since learned, was quite good at history, language and medicine. But math, especially algebra, gave him the heebie-jeebies.

"Don't worry, Padre, airplanes work. I've even flown in one," Bernie insisted.

"I don't doubt you," Petr Nickovich said, "but according to Newton's second law the wings should be much larger than this Bernoulli seems to think and..."

"You trust Newton like he was holy writ," Bernie finished for him. "Bernoulli, not so much. I get it."

"And if we are calculating all this properly," Fedor continued, ignoring Bernie's interjection, "we can probably build a half-dirigible easier than we can build an airplane. The problem is with the engines. A dirigible gets its lift from its lightness, not its motors, so it needs a lot less motor to move a given weight."

The discussion went on and Father Kiril was forced to bring out his cross several more times. Also the D books of two encyclopedias from Grantville were brought forth. Drawings were made and calculations calculated.

Anya brought sandwiches and Magda apple cider, only slightly hard. Gregorii Mikhailovich drew pictures. Bernie did calculations on a solar-powered calculator from Grantville, while Fedor checked him by doing the same calculations in his head and writing them down. By evening they had a plan. There would be a series of tests with hot air, then hydrogen. Each of increasing size.

Boris stared. A flying ship. Not a little airplane that they talked about in Grantville, but something the nerds—Boris liked that word—at the Dacha were calling a half-dirigible. There were drawings, still rough sketches, and rough estimates of carrying capacity, all of which seemed to agree that bigger was better, to the extent that they could build bigger. Everyone in the section would have seen it by now. The rumors would be flying faster than the half-dirigible could travel. And he had to come up with a recommendation. How was he supposed to know if it would work? Meanwhile, he had dozens of requests for things he knew they could make. And suddenly hundreds of requests for transfers to his section. "Pavel, get in here."

Pavel came quickly enough. Boris smiled. Pavel looked nervous, as well he should. "You will be missing dinner at home again." Boris handed him the report. "Go out to the Dacha and find out about this."

"But, Papa—" Pavel started to complain.

Boris cut him off. "I know all about the party at the Samelov house. They want you to get their little Ivan a job in the section, but he doesn't speak English and the only thing I've heard he's good at is getting drunk. Make your apologies, but get out to the Dacha."

Boris put the rest of the reports in his Grantville-style briefcase and headed for home, wondering how Princess Natasha's meeting with Czarina Evdokia was going.

"So, now that you've had a chance to get to know him, what is this Bernie like?" Czarina Evdokia took a sip of strong Russian tea.

"Different from when he arrived," Natasha said. "When he first arrived he was very sad and he didn't, I think, care very much for anything or anyone. He was useful enough, helpful and willing, and the things he knows are so many and varied that he has no idea how much he does know. Yet it's not as though he knows more than we do. He doesn't."

Natasha paused because this was something that she wasn't sure she really grasped. "A carpenter knows wood and he knows his village. A blacksmith again knows iron and his village. I know my family's lands, but the individual villages...not so well as the blacksmith or the carpenter each knows his own village. And I know more of the rest of the world than the carpenter or the blacksmith. Bernie might as well be from a village of magi in a nation of magi in a world of scholars. He knows auto mechanics as a carpenter knows wood, but he also knows his much wider, wealthier village. In his village there are aircraft and fruits delivered from around the world. There are cartoons, computers, television and a thousand other things we have never heard of. None of which he really understands, but all of which he knows enough about to make understanding possible with effort.

"Last winter, when he first arrived, he was willing enough to give the knowledge but the effort was to be all ours. He simply didn't care if we succeeded or not. Still, even then he was worth the money my family pays him, because between him and the books my brother sends, we could work out what was meant most of the time. But then came spring in Moscow and the slow fever."

"Yes, I know," the czarina said. "It's still the talk of Moscow. You should be aware that there are factions in the church that want to burn Bernard Zeppi as a witch. Mostly in response to those who want to saint him. Saints are much more convenient when they are safely dead."

"The words 'saint' and 'Bernie' don't really belong in the same sentence," Natasha said, smiling. "But something happened in Moscow that changed him, or changed his attitude anyway. For a little while after Moscow, he was fierce in his focus on study. But that's not the sort of pace that can be maintained. Now he's mostly gone back to being Bernie, but there is a core of fire there that wasn't there before. He's pushing everyone in the Dacha to learn something. Servants, craftsmen, scholars, even our guards, and it's catching.

"Honestly, it started before Moscow just from having all the scholars and craftsmen together but with Bernie's fire it's changed. There is an awareness that what we are doing is important. It helps that a cook from the Dacha who has learned techniques from the future has better opportunity. But that's not all of it, not even most of it. We are saving and improving lives and the people at the Dacha know it. There is a feeling around the place that this is the most important thing any of us have ever done or ever will. You can smell it in the wood chips and lacquer, see it in the new things being built and modeled, hear it in the conversations. You breathe it in with the air and all you want to do is get on with it." Natasha ground to a halt, embarrassed by her outburst.

The czarina kindly changed the subject. "I find the possibilities of the future amazing," she said. "Do you believe they sent someone to walk on the Moon?"

Natasha considered. "Yes. I do believe it."

"Why?"

"Partly because Vladimir confirms it in his letters, but mostly because Bernie talks about it the way we would speak of Ivan the Terrible or the Mongol rule. Not a fantastic tale, just something that happened in the past."

"Can you imagine? And women went, too. Russian women."

"Valentina Tereshkova. Vladimir wrote about her and Yuri Alekseyevich Gagarin. Bernie didn't remember her name but didn't dispute that the first man and the first woman in space were Russian." Natasha paused and looked at the czarina. There was a look in Evdokia's eyes. A dreamy, hungry look. To Natasha the fact that the first man and woman in space were Russian was an interesting piece of information and made her feel good about being Russian. For the czarina, it seemed more somehow.

"I have always dreamed of flying," Evdokia's voice had a soft faraway tone. "Since I was a little girl. Floating up to the clouds and looking down to see the whole world spread before me." She visibly pulled herself back from dreams of flight, but a bit of the smile lingered. "Child's dreams, but it warms me somehow that it was done, and by Russians first."

"Who knows?" Natasha offered. "What those people from the future could do, we can learn to do. Petr Nickovich says we can fly. He thinks he understands gravity and has built model hot air balloons that work. You may fly yet."

Evdokia laughed a bit sadly. "Even if we learn to fly, it will not be allowed. It is a pleasant thought, though. Now tell me of the progress of the Dacha."

Natasha grinned as she began her report. "As I said, Petr Nickovich thinks he understands gravity. Fedor is not convinced..." Not of the feel of the Dacha this time, of the particulars. Then there were the letters from Grantville. Natasha almost always had a new one to share and now the czarina had her own.

"Thank God," Bernie said when Natasha handed him the latest batch of letters. "There wasn't anything about plumbing in those books. I hope I've got an answer to that problem." Natasha had made a rare foray into the kitchen, searching for him. He was having his usual sandwich lunch.

Dear Bernie,

Vic Dobbs says you left out the vent stack for your plumbing and that's most likely the problem. I typed out the sections he suggested in some of his plumbing books. Without the vent stack you get a buildup of pressure or a vacuum in the septic system and it forces the dirty, yuck, water back up or clogs up the system. He made a drawing to show you what you did wrong. I've included that along with the notes I typed. He also said you'd probably never seen one, since they're usually inside the walls, so don't feel bad about it. This ought to fix the problem. Just in case, you might want to have that Vladimir guy contract to have some books on plumbing that Vic recommends copied or scanned and reprinted. A list is included.

I saw your father in town yesterday. He said to tell you hello and wants to know can he sell your car? It's in the way, he said. But, Bernie, a car engine is worth a small fortune these days. He also said you should write him and your sisters. They want to hear from you, too.

Old Grantville is rocking along just fine right now. We've got, I swear, thousands and thousands of people around here now. It's so different from before.

I hope you're doing well and I hope the plumbing helps. The docs think your slow fever is typhoid, and that you're right. It's shit getting into the water supply that causes it. I bet it's a lot different than working on cars was. But then, who'd have ever dreamed I'd wind up working in a research center, of all things? For both of us I think it's more important work than we would have had up-time.

*Well, gotta go. I need to have this done before I get
to work so Mom can drop it off at your Russian spy's
place to be sent on. Tell Natasha I said hi!*
                                        Best,
                                        Brandy

"You have wood in your hair." Natasha grinned. Bernie needed
some management and she found she liked that. She peered at
his hair. "Quite a bit of wood. What have you been doing out
there in that shop of yours?"

Much to Natasha's surprise, Bernie went outside to shake off the
wood shavings. "Sorry about that," he said when he came back to
finish his lunch. "I didn't realize. I brushed myself off, but didn't
know I had it in my hair. We were working on the pattern lathe.
Finally got the setup for that connecting piece Ivan the Tolerable
wanted." Bernie had gotten into the habit of giving various people
at the Dacha nicknames. "Now I need to talk to the guys about
this vent stack thing. Maybe we can get the bathroom back in
operation." Bernie gulped down the last of his sandwich and beer
and rose from the table again. "Excuse me. I really want to get
the plumbing working. We can't persuade anyone else to install
it till we get it working and winter is coming on pretty quick. I
really don't want another spring typhoid outbreak.

"Oh, Brandy said to tell you hi. And I'm going to be up late
studying, again."

Natasha barely repressed the snort. Studying, he said. Studying
that little blonde, more likely.

She shouldn't mind it, Natasha knew. It was common with
men. But this was Bernie, and for some reason it bothered her.

"Could you light a couple more candles?" Bernie smiled at Anya.
"I can't tell you how much I miss good lighting, I really can't."

Bernie liked Anya. She was smart, willing and practical. Bernie
was perfectly aware that she was using him. He was using her, too,
but it was friendly and fun. Anya went off to get more candles.

Bernie sat down with the book, a hand-typed and drawn copy of
freshman algebra. Algebra had been one of his "did well" courses.
One of the ones that he had found fun. But it had been a few
years and the nerds were desperate to get through algebra so that
they could get on with calculus. Not one of Bernie's good courses.

"Bernie, could you teach me math?" Anya asked. Her English was still far from good but it was getting better every day.

"Sure. Algebra?"

"No. Math of accounts."

"Accounting?" Bernie stopped and considered. Actually it made quite a lot of sense. Russia was trying desperately to move from a primarily barter economy to a moneyed economy. That would require bookkeeping and accounting. A growth industry, they would have said up-time. "Yes, that makes a lot of sense. I'm not sure I have all the stuff we'll need. In fact, I'm darn sure that I don't. But we can make a start. I don't know all that much about double-entry bookkeeping, but I'm pretty sure it involves something like this."

Bernie pulled over a sheet of paper and drew a grid. "The item bought or sold. The amount it's bought for here or sold for here that way you have a record as it comes in and goes out so..."

They got a start on it, then Bernie got back to refreshing his memory about algebra.

All the things he didn't know meant Bernie had to study. It was a lot more intense than school had been and he had come to think of it as much more important. Importance didn't make it easier or more fun. But, as with anything, practice did. All the stuff that he had been sure that he would never need once he graduated high school, he needed now. He had to interpret words he'd never heard and in contexts he'd never dreamed of. What the hell was calcareous grassland? Calcareous turned out to be to do with chalk or calcium; at least that's what the dictionary said. But calcareous grassland? How could chalk grow grass? He had to go to the dictionary all the time to find the weird stuff that the Russian nerds wanted.

Then there was Bernoulli's Law. Petr Nickovich had found a description of how wings worked in one of the books. The explanation described a wing's dependence on Bernoulli's Law. Then they had compared that with Newton's three laws and the effects hadn't matched up. The nerds had come to the conclusion that it couldn't work that way. Newtonian physics, Bernie was assured, would require a small plane to be traveling at over three hundred miles an hour to fly. They believed Bernie that powered flight was possible. They even believed him and the books about the size of the wings and the speed of the aircraft.

They knew and understood that they were missing something, but they didn't know what. Bernie didn't know what either. He built paper airplanes and wooden airplanes that flew, based on the rubber-band-powered airplanes he had played with as a kid, but he couldn't explain how they worked.

What Bernie didn't know, and for that matter most people in the Ring of Fire didn't know, was that Bernoulli's equations were a way of describing the actions of large groups of air molecules that were in turn following Newton's laws of motion. And when they had tried to integrate the two different ways of describing the same event they had, in effect, added everything up twice. The mathematicians and natural philosophers who surrounded Bernie now might have understood the complex explanation. They were still somewhat trapped by Aristotle's assumptions but they were some really bright guys. It didn't matter. Bernie didn't have the science to explain it. He had seen the drawings of air flow over a wing and assumed that they were accurate. They weren't. This didn't mean the shape of the wing was wrong. They weren't really inaccurate, either. Just simplified. Using the drawing out of those books for the cross-section of the wing would produce a wing that would fly quite well. Assuming, of course, that you added the ailerons and the rest of the plane.

Every day Bernie had people asking him questions that he didn't have the answers to. They weren't meaningless questions that didn't really matter, like how many planets there are in the solar system. Well, most of them weren't. The astrologers were nuts to know the locations of Neptune, Uranus and Pluto. Mostly, though, the questions were about how things worked and how to treat injuries and diseases. And that's what kept him up late studying.

Chapter 27

Andrei had it. He was sure now that after months of experimentation, he had the right chamber shape. The outside of the chamber was shaped like a long barn with a peaked roof. The inside, of course, was a round hole of the same size as the barrel. After the chamber was loaded, it was simply inserted into the rifle, roof down and muzzle forward, which put the touch hole on the right side, aligned with the pan. He had tested it on the firing bench, fired dozens of rounds through it with no real problems. He reported to Fedor Ivanovich Sheremetev that they were ready to go into production. Granted, Fedor Ivanovich Sheremetev wasn't the official person he was supposed to report to, but he was Andrei's patron, so he was who Andrei told first.

Sheremetev told him to make two dozen of the rifles and to have them sent to the Sheremetev estates. Andrei did so. It was a disaster.

In the field the chambers had a bad habit of slipping out of the guns. Even worse, sometimes they didn't slip out of the rifle, not all the way. Instead they got shifted just a little so that the touch hole was still aligned enough to fire the charge, but the muzzle of the chamber wasn't properly aligned. At which point the gun had a tendency to blow up. Any bit of dirt that got into the chamber lock misaligned the chamber and caused it to misfire or sometimes escape from the chamber lock when fired. One of

the Sheremetev *deti boyars* had died when an escaping chamber
had hit him in the head.

Boyar Fedor Ivanovich Sheremetev was not amused. Worse, Fedor
Ivanovich Sheremetev was embarrassed, because the first guns
shouldn't officially have gone to him but to the army. Sheremetev
excused the slip by saying that he was having the sample tested to
help out his *deti boyar* and wasn't it a good thing that he had. For
if he hadn't, the army might have got stuck with rifles that weren't
ready yet. The explanation was accepted but not believed and Fedor
Ivanovich Sheremetev resented Andrei. But even more he resented
the Dacha and Natasha for the fact that he had to ask them for help.

Filip, Bernie and the team came out to look at the AK2 and
discussed how they might be fixed. There were a lot of problems
with it. The upside down barn shape of the chamber was supposed
to provide a guide to position the chamber. And it sort of worked,
but a bit of dirt in the chamber lock or a burr on the chamber took
the chamber out of position and there was still the gap between
the chamber and the barrel. Unlike a six-shooter, the way a rifle
was shot put that gap altogether too close to the face of the person
firing the weapon for comfort. So the barn was modified. Just the
back of the chamber was shaped like a barn. Just enough to allow
the chamber to be positioned in the dark. The rest of the chamber
was basically cylindrical. That went a long way to fixing the dirt
and imperfections problem, but made the alignment problem worse.

One of the team members, who had been in charge of the
actual installation of the plumbing at the Dacha, remembered that
they had used pipe sections inserted into the expanded end of
the next pipe section. He suggested that the back inch or so of
the barrel be resized so that the chamber could be shoved into it.

As stated, the idea wasn't workable, but it suggested possibilities. Rather than inserting the whole front end of the chamber,
a round lip, not very big, that could be shoved forward might
work. It would have the problem that it couldn't simply be slot-
ted in like the chamber of the AK2, but maybe a lever that
opened up the slot that the chamber fit into then closed it back
might be the answer. But Andrei didn't like that way of doing
it. It introduced moving parts and, worse, introduced them right
where a great deal of force would be exerted. It was clearly not
yet ready for the army

Chapter 28

October 1632

The Ring of Fire had happened a year and a half ago and Bernie had been in Russia the better part of a year when he was given the first official pronouncement on the Ring of Fire. It was far from the first pronouncement. Monasteries had pronounced first that it hadn't happened at all and later that it was the work of the Devil because if God had done it He would have put it in Russia, not the Germanies, for not even God could care much for those barbaric people. Certainly not more than he cared for Holy Russia.

Through it all, the office of the patriarch had made no pronouncement, taking a wait-and-see attitude. From what Natasha had told him, that had been a very near thing. But here it was. In Russian, of course. Bernie could struggle through Russian writing by now, but not well. Natasha read it to him.

> *Patriarch Filaret's Advisory*
> *on the Ring of Fire*

> *It is clear through multiple sources that God, in his infinite wisdom, has chosen to take a hand in the conflict among the German States. He provides through this*

example clear evidence of both His infinite power and His will, that the Roman Church and the Protestants, whether Lutheran, Calvinist, or other peculiar sects, are wrong. God has endeavored to make clear to them that which of their errors is most wrong is not a matter worth fighting over.

That is clearly God's message to them. But what is God's message to us? It is obvious that we are not in need of the sort of correction the German States required, else surely God would have placed the Ring of Fire here, in Holy Rus. While His admonishment, gentle as it is, is for the Germans, the gifts which He sent with it are clearly for all the world. Willingly or not, the knowledge the up-timers bring is spreading to all the world. To their credit, the up-timers themselves seem willing enough to share most of the knowledge that God gifted their ancestors and our descendants with. This is an especially gracious gift to Holy Rus. For, while we have been strong in our adherence to scripture and the true faith, circumstances have left us behind the more western nations in some of the more mundane and earthly matters. We have been blocked by Poland from sharing in the technical advances made in the west.

The czar, in his wisdom, has long had a policy of trying to correct that problem so that we, the true heirs of Christianity and the Roman empire, could maintain the faith in relative safety, while at the same time limiting the corrupting influences from the west. God has smiled on Czar Mikhail's endeavor by providing new skills developed over time; many of them developed right here in Holy Rus. Yet like greedy children we complain "Why an American village? Why not a Russian village?" We know, after all, that in the twentieth-century Holy Rus was one of the two great powers. After studying the history, it is obvious that God chose an American village to protect Holy Rus, especially the church. The Russia of that time had fallen into corruption. For most of the twentieth century the Russian Orthodox Church, in fact all Christianity, had actually been banned. It was to protect us from this corruption that God chose an American village.

He placed it in Germany to remind us that He sees the whole world and cares about even those who have fallen away from the true church. More than that, He placed it in Germany to remind us not to be too proud to listen and learn from others and to protect us from too much of their direct influence, so that we might learn from them without becoming them. To protect our great Russian culture and still allow us the benefits of the good things they brought with them.

"That," Bernie said with a grin, "is the work of a top-flight spin doctor."

"What's a spin doctor?" Natasha asked.

"Someone whose job it is to spin the facts so that the best possible face is put on them."

Natasha looked at him.

"God didn't put the Ring of Fire in Germany because he likes Germany better but because none of the faiths the Germans are fighting over are the right one," Bernie said, shaking his head in admiration. "I never would have thought of that."

"Do you think God cares more for Germany than for Russia?" Natasha asked quietly. Natasha had never struck Bernie as all that religious but the notion that God didn't think you were worth worrying about had to hurt.

"No," Bernie said with more conviction than he really felt. "What I think is that if the Ring of Fire had showed up anywhere where there was just one established religion, that religion would have landed on it with both feet. If the Ring of Fire had landed Grantville, say, here in the Time of Troubles, then we would have been hit by Russian troops with Russian Orthodox priests urging them on before they knew anything except that something strange and scary had happened. And by the time anyone really figured out what had happened, it would have been really hard for them to backtrack. The Russian Orthodox Church would have been stuck with a policy of kill the daemons."

Natasha slowly nodded, thinking it through. Russian civilization had come apart in the Time of Troubles, but the church wasn't seriously challenged. If something like the Ring of Fire had happened, people would have looked to the church for answers and there was a very real chance that the church would have seen the town with Catholics, Protestants, and even atheists—but no one from the Orthodox Church—as a threat.

"Yep. Would have scared the hell out of just about anyone. The difference between here and there is just that there, there was nothing strong enough to hit us before they got to know us at least a little. And they had Lutherans, Calvinists, Catholics, some killing each other, some running each other out of town, and a few sort of getting along. We were easier for them to get used to."

"So not virtue or vice, but circumstance?"

"That's the way I figure it, but I ain't God. Not even a priest. But, as to that bit about 'gift to all the world'? Come see the balloon tomorrow."

Natasha watched the balloon as it lifted into the air. Petr Nickovich was doing "a preliminary experiment into the lifting power of hot air." In other words, he was playing. It was his third balloon so far, each larger than the last. This one was as tall as a man and as wide as it was tall. And it trailed a series of lead weights. Lifting first one, then the next into the air below it. It lifted five of them, then stopped rising, proving that hot air is lighter than cold air. Which any five-year-old in any peasant village in Russia could have told him. Natasha knew there was more to it than that. The weights told Petr how much lift he was getting from that volume of heated air. There was also a thermometer in the balloon that told him how hot the air was. A thermometer by the wall told him how hot the outside air was so he would have the difference.

Petr Nickovich was holding his experiment in a corner behind the main building of the Dacha where it would be out of the wind. Which also meant out of the sun. It might have been prettier if his balloon was in the sunlight. It would certainly have been warmer.

What had really brought her out into the cold to see it was the idea that, some day, a much bigger thing like this might let people fly. Petr Nickovich wasn't looking at the balloon; he was writing out calculations. Then he looked over at Filip Pavlovich. "I was right. The heated air lifts a little more than a quarter of an ounce per cubic foot."

Filip Pavlovich just nodded.

"I must have the hydrogen you promised me," Petr Nickovich insisted.

"Yes. Fine. We'll talk about it, but inside." Filip Pavlovich was visibly cold even in his heavy clothing. "Where it's warm."

Natasha smiled, though she didn't let it show. Petr Nickovich was not one to take being laughed at well and keeping the peace was part of Natasha's job.

As they blew out the candles that were heating the air for the balloon, Natasha thought about what was going on at the Dacha. It wasn't just Bernie, the person that this was all about. There was Lazar Smirnov, a member of a cadet branch of a great house, who was sitting in one of the buildings, winding wires in a coil. Slowly, carefully, making what he said would be a generator of electric. He carefully painted the wire with lacquer and laid one circuit around the coil, then waited for it to dry before he did the next. He was a volunteer, here because he wanted to be. Sure, he and Bernie had talked about insulation and electromagnetic fields but he was the one doing the work. And Lazar could have hired a small army to do any work he wanted done. But he wanted to understand electric power, so was doing the work himself.

It was a strange attitude in Lazar and it had come from Bernie. "You want to learn how a machine works, build it yourself. Set someone else to doing it and they'll learn it instead of you." Bernie had said that more than once and clearly it was having an effect. Servants here were treated better, talked to, not at. You might need the expertise they had gained on your next project. Natasha was not sure where it would all lead.

Part Three

The year 1633

Chapter 29

January 1633

It worked. Andrei Korisov had tested it, even firing it several times himself. The results were good. Not perfect by any means, but the third major version of the Andrei Korisov Rifle was a workable weapon, even a good one. It seemed to Andrei that it had taken both more and less time than it had. More because of all the frustrations of the last two years and less because it was a genuine revolution in the design of fire arms.

He sent a message to Fedor Ivanovich Sheremetev telling him so. Sheremetev sent back, "Send some to the Dacha. Let's see what they say," by which Andrei was allowed to know that he was not forgiven yet for the failures of the AK2.

Bernie knelt on the blanket laid out at the Dacha firing range and fired the new gun from the gun shop. It was the third day of testing and it had passed the bench tests pretty well. The lip had helped a lot with the outgassing. It no longer cut you if you had your hand in the wrong place, it just hurt like the blazes.

Bernie wanted to make sure that the outgassing had been licked enough so that it wasn't a danger to the user. He was also making a point. Andrei wouldn't get it, but by now Filip would. So would Natasha. Leaders lead. They don't assign some poor peasant to take the risks.

Bernie opened the chamber lock by the lever-action and pulled the spent chamber. The lever-action allowed the back of the chamber lock to be pushed forward, forcing the lip of the chamber into the barrel. It also allowed for the quick removal and replacement of the firing chamber. Bernie knew that Andrei hated the added complexity of the lever-action. But by now the fact that Andrei didn't like it made Bernie at least open to the idea. Andrei was probably right that simpler was better both for production and for ease of maintenance. But the lever-action of the chamber lock was simple. Four moving parts, all of them interconnected. Levers moved the back block of the chamber lock back when opened and forward when closed. The back block of the chamber lock was shaped like an upside down barn with a peaked roof, and fit into the back block in only one position. That meant that to line up the chamber only the back and front of the chamber had to be precisely finished, precisely fitted.

He was about to stick another in when he had a thought. He half cocked the lock, flipped up the frizzen, tapped the touch hole on the chamber over the pan. Sure enough, a few grains of powder fell into the pan. Bernie closed the frizzen, inserted the chamber, closed the lever action cocked and fired again.

He looked over at Nick. "How am I doing? Hitting anything?"

"You're hitting a bit low, Bernie," Nick told him.

"It's the black powder drop," Bernie complained. "After a life time of shooting smokeless, I can't get used to it. What about adjustable sights, Andrei? I know we talked about them."

"They are an added expense and no one will know how to use them."

"Cheap asshole," Bernie muttered under his breath. But in a way he knew that Andrei was right. Russia wasn't like Germany, where you published a cheat sheet and suddenly everyone knew how it worked. Likely as not, in a Russian village, there was no one who read or wrote. And if someone did happen to be literate, having something read to you once was not the same thing as having the cheat sheet there to look at. It made it a lot harder to disseminate information in Russia than it was in Germany. And, as best as Bernie could tell, that was just how the powers that be liked it. Bernie reminded himself again that it wasn't his job to reform Russian politics, then went back to leading by example.

"Okay, Nick. I've tried it now. Ten rounds as fast as I can. Time me."

It took him two minutes to send eight rounds downrange. Call it four rounds a minute as long as he had loaded chambers and used his trick of tapping the chamber to prime the pan. Theoretically, you could do that with a muzzle-loader, though, in the real world, two or three rounds a minute was more likely. And Bernie was firing a new weapon. Given some practice, he could probably get faster. A pro with this thing might get to five or six rounds, though Bernie doubted that even the Russian Davy Crockett would manage more than that. Well, maybe if he had the chambers lined up and handy and didn't worry about where the chambers went after he fired them.

The AK3 could be reloaded kneeling or prone, and that went for reloading the chambers too. They were only five inches long, after all. With loaded chambers, five to eight rounds a minute. With unloaded chambers, two or three, about even with a muzzle-loader. And as of late January of 1633 there were a grand total three of them in existence.

Bernie stood up. "All right, Andrei. You have a working prototype. We can add a couple minor tweaks, but overall it looks like as good as we are going to get with the tech base we've got. How can we help you guys get it into production?"

It was educational, Natasha thought, *to see the effect Andrei Korisov has.* He was undoubtedly brilliant and often right, but so self-centered and irritating about it that you wanted to argue the other side just to be against him. Andrei's negative example had helped to open Filip's eyes to the virtues of treating peasants and servants with respect. Not as much as Bernie's positive example perhaps, but it had its effect. Natasha knew she was affected the same way Filip was by both. Andrei would point out that Russian peasants couldn't do this or that. Natasha would immediately want to find one who could—and she usually could. Individually. But how did you get enough of them taught?

And that was the issue Andrei Korisov brought up in regard to getting the AK3 into full-scale production. There were armories in Russia. Some of them were quite good, so far as quality was concerned. But even Andrei's Gun Shop was incredibly slow by German standards, much less up-time standards. And it wasn't just guns. It was everything. Oh, Russians knew how to do things—but that was half the problem. Russians knew how to make a gun. You made it the way your grandfather did. They knew how to make a plow and how to use that plow to plow a field...which was precisely the way their grandfather did it, and at the same phase of the moon.

Not that there weren't creative people and original thinkers in Russia. It was just that they all seemed to live at the Dacha. Well, perhaps a few at the Gun Shop.

The specific issue now was getting the gunsmiths in Russia to make the new guns, much less use the new techniques. There was nothing about the chamber-loading flintlock rifle that they couldn't make, but Andrei was insisting that they were too stupid to learn. And Filip was insisting that if Andrei could learn, a donkey could learn. Bernie was insisting that there was no reason for the gunsmiths of Russia to object to the AK3 and plenty of reason for them to embrace it.

But Bernie didn't understand. Andrei was unpopular and well-known enough that the mere fact that he had invented the rifle—and named it after himself—was plenty of reason for most Russian smiths to hate it, sight unseen. Add to that the general illiteracy, and what Bernie called "the not invented here syndrome," and they were facing an uphill battle.

Meanwhile Natasha was getting a headache.

"What was it like to live in the future?" Anya asked.

"Easier, freer, but less important." Bernie shrugged. "I never thought much about the future when I was living in it. What I did didn't matter much to anyone, not even me. I was in no hurry to grow up. There was no real need. I had a pretty good job. Enough money for most of what I wanted. Never found the right girl, but had a lot of fun looking." Bernie grinned at Anya. He wasn't her right guy and she wasn't his right girl, but they had fun anyway.

"Right after the Ring of Fire, and especially right after the Battle of the Crapper, I was just caught up in what I had lost. I couldn't get over the way my mother died and I kept seeing those guys falling down like tenpins at the Crapper. It didn't help that like a damn fool I made the mistake of going out there after the battle and looking at the corpses. There was one kid—I'm sure I was the one who shot him, because he was wearing this odd-looking hat—"

He broke off for a moment, then shook his head. "So I didn't give much thought to what it meant for anyone else." Bernie looked into Anya's pale blue eyes made darker by the candlelight. She was trying, but she didn't get it. He hadn't expected her to. It made little enough sense from the inside; it had to seem totally nuts from the outside.

"Like everyone else, I was in shock at first. But I just couldn't come out of it. People started doing things, things that mattered. President Stearns, Jeff Higgins...everyone was making it work and I couldn't get past the Crapper and Mom's death. I was sitting around doing what I was told. The same old Bernie. No direction, no drive.

"I couldn't think of anything useful to do. Truthfully, I wasn't even trying. Then Vladimir offered me this job. I had no idea if I could do it, but I couldn't take much more of Grantville. It wasn't home anymore, but it was too much like home.

"I think the trip out here was the first time I had been sober for three days running since the Crapper. Now, I'm too busy to worry about it that much." Bernie grinned again. "Too much to do. The Nerd Patrol is always hitting me with new questions and I spend so much time reading and helping out that there isn't that much time to mope anymore. That's the secret to a happy life, kid. Have something to do. It's even better if it's something that matters. But have something, whether it matters to anyone else or not."

Lazar Smirnov worried out the words in the pamphlets. Flipping back and forth between them, trying to divine meaning from two directions. Along with the copies of English books and parts of books that Vladimir sent them were the occasional German translations. Lazar had a bit of German, almost twice as much German, in fact, as he had English. He didn't have all that much of either. He spoke Russian, read Latin and Greek, but that was about it. His reading of Russian was problematic and his writing was quite idiosyncratic. So trying to read the pamphlets on electronics and radio was an uphill task at the best of times.

But he had been doing it for over a year now and he was gaining, he hoped, an understanding of how it all worked. He had a spark gap transmitter and it now seemed to work. That is, the crystal set clicked when it should if it was close enough. What was the difference between a Leiden jar and a capacitor? He was beginning to think there wasn't one. He went back to the little pamphlet on the capacitor and noticed the word mica, looked up mica and noticed that the best was muscovite mica.

At which point Lazar wrote to Vladimir about the potential for profit if they could determine what muscovite mica was.

Having written his letter and had his man put it in the pouch to be sent to Grantville, Lazar went back to trying to improve the tuning of his tuned-circuit spark gap transmitter. That evening he went on to trying to figure out how to make an alternator so that he could produce inductance and an inductance furnace for the melting of metal.

Chapter 30

February 1633

Natasha alighted from the sleigh at her family's dacha outside of
Moscow, along with her aunt, Sofia Petrovna. Both were wearing full
regalia. And they were attending this function almost against their
will. Over a year ago the Dacha had been converted into a research
and development shop. For a while there had been very little notice
taken of what was going on at the Gorchakov dacha, but for months
now there had been increasing pressure to provide demonstrations of
what rumor said the Gorchakov family was keeping secret. Natasha
had resisted for several reasons. But resistance had proved futile.
Well, not entirely futile. She had gained time and, though the Dacha
leaked like a sieve, there was a difference between hearing about
something and seeing it. Meanwhile, through some mystical combination of personalities and mutual support, the Dacha produced
magic. Magic which had allowed the family to gain support and
favors from several of the most important bureaus and great families.

The Dacha was still not profitable in terms of money and it would
be some time before it would even start to pay back the money
invested in it, at least to the family. But politically it was a gold
mine. Natasha, with Aunt Sofia's guidance, had been selectively
generous. Rewarding friends for friendship and strengthening the
more liberal factions at court.

Aunt Sofia served as her chaperone, necessary in Muscovy's culture. While her brother, Vladimir Petrovich, was away in Grantville, someone had to assume responsibility for the lands. That responsibility fell on Natasha. Young for it she might be, but she and Vladimir were the last of their branch of the family. It was a wealthy branch. Thankfully, she and Vladimir had been raised by a free-thinking father who had been rather enamored of the west. She had been educated alongside Vladimir. Fashionable or not, someone had to take care of things.

Aunt Sofia turned to Natasha. "Well, girl, what do you suppose Bernie has done this time? I thought the stinks and noises from his bathroom were quite enough. And the hundred ways he has discovered not to make a light bulb was rather less than impressive."

Natasha looked at her diminutive aunt and raised an eyebrow.

"Fine, he and the electric nerds have made working light bulbs now." Aunt Sofia admitted. "And their light is much better for reading than candlelight. But it took them long enough, considering the information Vladimir sent."

"It's not Bernie we need to worry about. It's the nerds," Natasha corrected.

What she was worried about wasn't Bernie. It was Russian culture. In the Dacha they had developed their own little world of cooperation. But in the bureaus, among the service nobility and great families, there was a culture of back-stabbing and credit-stealing that had been all that Natasha had known, as unnoticed as the sea to a fish. Until the Dacha—and now she was very afraid that with the presence of the guests the nerds would revert to bureaucrats.

But it was unavoidable. After spending too long informing their superiors and themselves that the Dacha was an unimportant flash in the pan, that the items that were pouring out of it were all there were or were ever going to be, and besides, they were all really coming from Grantville anyway—the bureaus, the monasteries and the great families had suddenly noticed that the Dacha was changing the political equation. Now the members of the *Boyar Duma* and the high and the mighty in general wanted to see what was going on and how much things were going to change. There was also a faction that was anxious to shut the place down and set the clock back.

✧　　　✧　　　✧

The czar and czarina, Patriarch Filaret, several members of the *Boyar Duma* and some of their wives, and three of the highest-ranking prelates representing three of the most powerful monasteries in Russia, arrived over the next few hours and had to be provided quarters in the Dacha for their stay. The normal inhabitants of those rooms had been moved into outbuildings, and some of them even into a large, heavy, double-walled tent. Natasha greeted each guest as they arrived.

Natasha listened to the lecture on soil chemistry with half an ear. It wasn't that it was unimportant. In the long run, it might turn out to be drastically important. But Natasha had already read the reports on fertilizer and had other things on her mind.

It had taken a while for the other great families and the bureaus to realize what the deal her brother had struck meant, but eventually they had gotten it. By now there was considerable pressure to provide them with up-timers or, better yet, to shift Bernie to their service. The roads bureau wanted Bernie to spend all his time on road-making equipment. The farming bureau wanted him making farming machinery. He was also wanted to make medicines, concrete, steel, plastics, and who knew what else.

There had been time for some of the effects to be felt since Bernie had arrived in Russia. Some road crews had the equipment he introduced and had been building and repairing roads much faster. A new quick-loading rifle was in limited production. Bernie insisted on calling it the AK3. And Natasha, after some explanation, liked the joke a lot better than she liked Andrei Korisov. Andrei Korisov was head of the team that had developed the new rifle, after all, and the up-time AK47 had been simple and massively produced, just like the AK3 was supposed to be.

Both the Swedish and Polish sections of the embassy bureau wanted Bernie transferred to them, and the Grantville Section shut down. The Swedish Section claimed jurisdiction because Bernie had become a subject, sort of, of the king of Sweden since he had left Grantville. The Polish Section claimed jurisdiction because Bernie was teaching what he knew about firearms. In fact, both claims were to get Bernie into the control of the great families most connected with those bureaus.

The knives were out, all over Moscow. Some of them were

political and some made of steel. The political ones were by far
the more dangerous.

"By introducing nitrates into the soil . . ."

For a moment Natasha was distracted from her thoughts.
Nitrates and the nitric acid that could be produced from them
played an important role in the production of smokeless gun
powder and that process was looking to produce nitroglycerin
and then TNT in the next couple of years. No, the lecturer was
talking about using clover and beans to enrich the soil on the
Gorchakov family estates last summer. It had only been test plots
but the tests had been quite successful.

Vladimir had made his deal with the patriarch and the family had gained the Bernie franchise. It had been an expensive
investment, both in goods shipped to Germany and in wealth
spent here. The return on investment was small so far. But the
favors flowed like rivers. And favors were the currency of political power in Russia. If the mining bureau wanted a road to a
new mine, it would not have to come just to the roads bureau,
not now. Now it would have to come to the Grantville Section
and the Gorchakov clan. Boris Petrov had collected more favors
since being made head of the Grantville Section than in all the
rest of his career. And Boris' gains in influence hadn't even really
compared to the Gorchakov clan's gains.

And that was dangerous. While they had been a minor, mostly
unconnected family with few important ties, they could be safely
ignored and mostly were. But over the last year and a half, they
had become noticeable, the unavoidable consequence of success
in Russia. The Sheremetev clan was showing particular interest in
wresting any potential profits from the Gorchakov clan, though
they seemed happy enough for the expense to remain with the
Gorchakovs.

With Bernie placed in their Dacha, it was unavoidable that
the Gorchakov family backed and influenced the Grantville Section. So far, no one had had enough influence to change that.
Which also meant that the Gorchakov family was passing out
favors. Natasha was picking up more and more owed favors from
the high nobility. The Gorchakov family wasn't being stingy in
a monetary sense, but there was a degree of political selectivity
in their choices.

But this was Moscow. Alliances could change at a moment's

notice. Now the patriarch was nervous, Natasha knew. There were rumors that the Gorchakov clan would try for the throne, which was insane but power carries its own implications.

A more realistic concern was that they would gain influence with the czar. Which in fact was true indirectly through Czarina Evdokia. Natasha, and now Brandy, had considerable influence with Czarina Evdokia and the czarina had considerable influence with the czar. Czar Mikhail was loved, but not that well respected. Not considered . . . particularly strong. Of course, his hands were tied. The Assembly of the Land, the *Zemsky Sobor*, had seen to that when he was elected. Those limitations might well explain why he was so popular. When the government got blamed for something it was usually his advisors, not the czar, who got the blame. It was known that Mikhail had cried when told he had been elected czar. As well, it was known that he had refused the crown. He had continued to refuse until told that if he didn't accept, the blood of the next Time of Troubles would be on his hands.

Natasha knew the czarina, Evdokia. Before Bernie, that acquaintance would have given her family protection, but not much influence. Now that acquaintance was a way for up-time ideas to reach the czar without going through his father, who was also the patriarch of the Orthodox Church. And the ideas had gotten to Mikhail. Some of them, anyway.

Fedor Ivanovich Sheremetev, Chief of the Bureau of Records, had read the reports. That was one of the reasons that he had pushed for this general demonstration of the products of the Dacha. One of the reasons—the other being his increasing concern about the influence of the Grantville Section and the Gorchakov family. He had been forced, almost against his will, to realize the importance that the Ring of Fire was going to have on the rest of the world, including Russia.

He watched Petr Nickovich pace about in a dither, getting in the way of the workmen handling the ropes, and found himself tempted to do the same thing. He knew what was about to happen; he'd read about it in the reports. Then, as the ropes were let out, the thing began to rise. Two poles, about five feet apart with ropes going from them to a basket below and balloons above. He had thought that he knew what was going to happen, but he hadn't realized what it would feel like. Twenty feet into the air, then twenty-five, thirty, supported by nothing but air. Its only connection to the earth the ropes that held it down. And in the basket that hung below the dirigible testbed, Nikita Slavenitsky smiled and waved to the crowd of dignitaries.

Sheremetev waved back; it was absolutely the least he could do. What he wanted to do was jump up and down and shout. A Russian was flying in the air, held aloft by the knowledge and craftsmanship of his fellow Russians. He had read that the up-timers had already flown. But knowing about it from a report was one thing, seeing it was something altogether different. The up-timers with their machines doing it was one thing. Russians making a flying device out of wood, rope and cow guts—that was something altogether different. Even in his excitement about the flight, he realized that it meant that one of his goals in forcing this demonstration had backfired. If anything it would increase the influence wielded by the Grantville Section. He looked over at the czar's pet up-timer, in time to see Bernie looking bored. Then the outlander snorted a laugh.

Bernie could understand why Petr Nickovich was so nervous. Today the czar, the czarina and some members of the cabinet had come to see his baby fly. Bernie looked over at the big shots. They were gawking. Totally gone. You'd think the aliens were landing or something. Then he thought about it. Granted, it wasn't that much of a dirigible. It had no power and there wasn't much you could do with it, not yet. But, Nikita was the first Russian to fly in this timeline.

Wow! This was history. For here and now, this was like the first rocket ship to the moon or something. Bernie found himself giggling a bit. Nikita Ivanovich Slavenitsky was a nice guy and usually had a joke to tell or a dirty story. But he wasn't the sort of guy you would think of as Yuri Gagarin or Neil Armstrong. But Nick was going down in history anyway.

One of the big shots was looking a bit offended. "You find this funny?"

Bernie had forgotten the guy's name. He was the head of one of the bureaus, Bernie knew that much. "It's not that, sir. I just never thought that a guy I had a beer with every now and then would make history."

"History?" The guy paused. Looked up and nodded. "The first Russian to fly."

"Yes, sir," Bernie said. "Nikita Ivanovich Slavenitsky and Petr Nickovich have done Russia proud today. Real proud."

The big shot looked at Bernie a bit sharply for a moment, then he smiled. "You will excuse me, Bernie Janovich. I must speak to the czar."

Fedor Ivanovich Sheremetev headed back to the czar in a rather bemused state of mind. He wasn't sure what to make of the up-timer. Bernie Janovich hadn't tried to take credit for the flight, even though Sheremetev knew that his explanations had been a large part of making it possible. Nor had he been demeaning of the Russian efforts. Sheremetev didn't know what to make of the man, and that bothered him. Over all, he rather liked Bernie Janovich. And that was unfortunate because sooner or later the Gorchakov clan had to go. There was too much power in the Dacha, even with the Gun Shop separated out. He glanced up at the flying carriage. Much too much power. Control of such devices and the knowledge that allowed them to be built must be tightly held and controlled, lest it destroy the social order. Control of such knowledge was important; important in more ways than one. Nikita Ivanovich Slavenitsky, a *deti boyar* of the Gorchakov clan, would go down in history as the first Russian to fly. More status to the Gorchakov clan. Too many things like that could change the rank of a clan. Things like that flowed out of the Dacha, and the Gorchakov clan was gaining too much status to be allowed to survive.

Fedor Ivanovich was effusive in his praise of the device and the Dacha in general and concerned about leaving such an important project in the hands of such a minor house. He argued intensely that even the flying device wasn't enough to justify any renewal of the conflict with Poland. And he argued that, with the changing state of things, Poland was less of a threat and the Swede was more of one. "The CPE is potentially the most powerful nation in Europe and we are likely to be thankful for Poland as a buffer state in a few years." That position didn't please Patriarch Filaret, but much of the *Boyar Duma* was more worried about the Swede and the CPE than they were about Poland.

The first radios were now working, though less well than they had hoped, and there was one in the Moscow Kremlin and the test one at the Dacha. Fedor Ivanovich Sheremetev wanted one for the Gun Shop and he wanted one for his estates. Actually, it would take more than one radio to reach his estates. They had limited range. More power for the Gorchakov clan, even if that idiot cousin of Pavel's had done most of the work developing it.

"We can fly," Evdokia, Czarina of All Russia, insisted. Mikhail looked at his wife and sighed. He knew he was going to lose the argument. They were in the best room in the Gorchakov dacha, and it had been an interesting day.

"I know how you feel," he tried, though in truth he didn't. He knew his Doshinka had dreams of flight but he never had. Mikhail's dreams tended to be dark things, best forgotten. "But we have real problems that we must deal with."

Evdokia, thankfully, didn't ignore the problems, though Mikhail was fairly sure she wanted to. "I know, Mikhail. But I think that Petr Nickovich made some excellent points about the usefulness of such a flying ship. More importantly, though, is the useful thing he didn't mention."

"What useful thing is that?"

"Pride. Pride in being Russian. Pride in being a part of something great. Who is, ah, was . . . will be that up-time general that Mikhail Borisovich Shein is always quoting about eggs?"

Mikhail shook his head, not able to remember the name. He thought the general was French but that was all he remembered.

"Well, that's not the only quote. The general Nappy-something also said that the moral is to the physical as three to one." She grinned. "I think to the fiscal, it's even more. Let us fill the hearts of the people of Russia with pride in who they are. Not with fear of the bureaucrats."

Mikhail looked at his wife for a long time, just taking in the bubbling excitement. She fairly glowed with it. Could Petr Nickovich's assemblage of balloons really produce such a reaction? And if it produced that sort of reaction in the Russian heart, what effect would it have on the Polish heart and the Cossack heart? "Very well. I will support the project. I can make no promises, mind."

Somehow, as pleasant as his wife's resulting smile was, it made Mikhail a bit nervous.

✧   ✧   ✧

Bernie had spent most of the last three days explaining that it was really Vanya, Misha, Filip, Gregorii, Lazar and even Andrei at the Gun Shop who had actually worked out all the improvements. He had just helped a bit. It was becoming increasingly clear not everyone at the Dacha agreed with that assessment, though. Some of the folks who worked here had even said so, though that was less common.

Bernie had been in Russia long enough to know how dog-eat-dog the bureaus were, so he was surprised and impressed that any of them were willing to share credit. But some of them were. Not Andrei, of course. But some were, and not just with Bernie, but with each other. Which was even more impressive.

All of which didn't make orbital mechanics one whit more interesting. When Gregorii Mikhailovich started explaining orbital mechanics and Newton's laws of motion, Bernie's brain started to fry. He just didn't want to hear it again, not right now.

He was having a beer in the kitchen when the door opened unexpectedly. At first Bernie was afraid that one of the brain cases had come looking for him again. But, no...the boss.

"Howdy, Boss." Bernie snaked out an arm and grabbed a chair. "Have a seat."

"Thank you," Natasha said taking the offered chair. "Petr Nickovich is going to be impossible."

"Why?" Bernie asked.

"Because the czar—and as of this morning, a majority of the *Boyar Duma*—wish a dirigible or half-dirigible built. They are going to build a facility at Bor on the Volga to build the main ship and others to follow it, but we will be building a test device here. Things are going quite well."

Maybe, Bernie thought, *but it's still a pain in the butt.* "Glad to hear it," he said.

Natasha lifted an eyebrow at him and he shrugged.

"I am. It's still a pain, but I am glad it's going well. The politics are something I'd just as soon avoid, but I realize that it's necessary."

"It is necessary, Bernie, and I'm not sure how much we're going to be able to avoid them." She then told him a bit more about the structure of the Russian government. How the bureaus were traditionally nonpolitical—at least how they had remained nonpolitical in the Time of Troubles, working for whichever claimant was holding the throne at the time. How Mikhail Fedorovich Romanov had been a dark horse candidate who didn't want the throne.

Bernie snorted. Then at Natasha's look, he elaborated. "Isn't that the standard line? After working for years to get the throne, the new king or dictator or whatever says 'I didn't want it, it was just my duty.'"

"Perhaps that is how it happens in most cases, but my family has known the czar since before he was the czar. And my father was with the delegation that went to him. Mikhail was a teenager, old enough to know that being declared czar was a short step away from being declared dead. His mother and father each had more than their share of ambition, but they passed none on to Mikhail. He was precisely what the *Boyar Duma* and the Assembly of the Land wanted, a figurehead to move the battle for control of Russia back out of sight. Even so, the *Boyar Duma* and Assembly tied his hands with a set of restrictions."

Bernie held up his hands in surrender. "I wasn't there," he said, "and I don't doubt you. It's just that the king that doesn't want the throne is a stock item in fairytales, but pretty darn rare in a world of elected officials, where if you don't want the office you don't have to run."

"In any case, the czar is generally quite impressed with your accomplishments and so are the patriarch and Prince Cherkasski."

Bernie knew that Cherkasski was the czar's cousin and was the boss of three of the bureaus that ran Russia.

"With their support," Natasha continued, "Sheremetev won't be able to do anything."

"What bugs this Sheremetev about the Dacha?" Bernie asked.

"Primarily that he doesn't own it," Natasha said. "The Sheremetev family are famous for their corruption, but also very good at politics. They know all about bribery and blackmail, having accepted more bribes than any other great family in Russia. But we'll be all right here, as long as Patriarch Filaret can keep a leash on Sheremetev. The brain cases will be fine."

Mikhail and his father were already consulting with the "brain cases." Mikhail wanted a way out of the trap the up-time history had put him in. Since the history of that other future had leaked, people with power were not happy. He and his father, as czar and patriarch, had been carefully dancing in the mine field of Russian politics, focusing on the danger of a return to the Time of Troubles to keep the various factions in check. Even so, power was shifting between the factions. The one led by Fedor Ivanovich Sheremetev, for instance. Their cousin or not, Sheremetev felt that the information from the up-timers and the actions of Peter the Great really destroyed the Romanov credentials as arch-conservatives.

"Interesting, perhaps." Sheremetev set his glass on the table. They had been discussing the history of the United States of America and its Constitution. "Interesting, but not that impressive. It was their day in the sun, that's all. The Mongols had theirs and this United States had theirs. They were only two hundred years old. Barely a youth, as nations go."

Mikhail looked across the table at him. There were only three men at dinner tonight. Filaret, Mikhail and Fedor Ivanovich Sheremetev. Mikhail wanted Sheremetev's support. "I am more concerned with something else," he said "The general agreement— and I read this over and over again—was that Russia continued to lag behind much of the rest of the world. We can change that, and I believe we should. Right now, we should start. Because right now, everyone is four hundred years behind Grantville. We have Bernie here and Vladimir in Grantville. We can modernize."

Sheremetev nodded, but Mikhail didn't think he was listening. Not properly at any rate. "The army, most assuredly. Right away. That I agree with. But this other? This constitution? Why? A firm hand on the reins. That is all that is needed, Mikhail. A firm hand on the reins of Rus."

Mikhail shook his head. No, Sheremetev wasn't listening.

Fedor Ivanovich Sheremetev left the dinner and considered the evening most of the way home. He understood what Mikhail and Filaret were contemplating. *Let every peasant vote. Introduce a constitutional monarchy, then gradually give away the power, not only of the monarchy, but of the great families as well.*

He would not, he could not, let that happen. They said it was to prevent the revolution that had come in three hundred years hence in that other history, which they thought would probably happen even sooner in this one if they didn't act to forestall the causes for it. But to Sheremetev, such reasoning bordered on sheer insanity. Who could predict what might happen in three centuries? In any event, if preventing a revolution was the issue, surely a policy of more severe and consistent maintenance of order would work far more reliably than introducing chaos.

But Sheremetev suspected that the real reason for their schemes, at least for the czar himself, was that Mikhail was afraid of power. When they had offered him the crown he had cried like a babe.

Sheremetev had a lot more sympathy for Joseph Stalin than he had for Nicholas Romanov. And more for Nicholas than for Mikhail. It was God's whimsy to sometimes put a peasant in the blood line of kings, or a let a king be born in a peasant's hovel.

Stalin was a king born of base blood. And Mikhail was a peasant borne of some of the noblest blood in Russia. But that whimsy of God's didn't invalidate the concept of royalty, any more than the occasional sport in a fine bloodline of hounds or horses invalidated breeding.

Filaret would have made a better czar, except for his fanatical hatred of Poland. Couldn't they see that the Swede was the danger now?

Chapter 31

Grantville
March 1633

Vladimir was running late. He had just about given up on doing his own research. There wasn't time. There wasn't really even enough time to provide supervision of the researchers. Not with the sources Francisco Nasi pointed out to him. Yet here he was, because someone in Russia had found something about mica capacitors and wanted to know more because apparently Russia had the best mica in the world. At least, so he was told. He was looking around trying to decide where to start, when he heard a voice.

"Well, hello, Prince Vladimir. What brings you here?"

Vladimir looked around and saw a vaguely familiar young woman. He couldn't quite place her though she was clearly an up-timer.

While he was trying to figure out what to say to the young woman, she spoke again. "I thought you master-spy types had minions to do this sort of thing."

Her knowing that he was a spy wasn't much help, but it did offer something to say. "I think you must be thinking of Boris, who has gone back to Russia. I'm just a journeyman spy. Besides it's amazingly hard to find minions for this sort of work. Do you know some of them actually insist on having their eyes open when reading the books?"

"How horrible for you," the young woman said. "Why, someone might actually find out what they were learning about for you. Now I understand why you hired Bernie for your Dacha. He can read the entire encyclopedia without learning anything."

Bernie? Yes. This was Natasha's correspondent that Bernie had recommended to her, the one that wrote to her about bras and things. Brandy...yes, that was it. This was Brandy Bates. "Regretfully, Miss Bates, you do Bernie an injustice. From all reports he has proven to be both hard-working and capable."

"So Natasha keeps saying in her letters. But I've known Bernie all my life and it's a bit hard to believe that he's taking anything seriously for more than a couple of months." Brandy shrugged "Maybe he's grown up."

Actually Brandy's assessment of Bernie would have fit Vladimir's perfectly, when he'd sent Bernie off to Moscow. He'd thought they'd have had to use much more stick to keep him at his work. "Apparently things changed this spring in Moscow."

"Yes, Bernie wrote me about that. I hope you can get plumbing in before it happens again next year."

Vladimir felt his head shaking before she had finished her sentence. "It's most unlikely. Frozen ground is almost as hard to dig as stone. I do understand that there will be some rather draconian punishments for emptying chamber pots in the street and they are going to have barrels and workmen to move those barrels out of town."

"Barrels?"

"To empty the chamber pots into."

"It might work as a stopgap measure. Is that what you're doing here, looking for new kinds of barrels or ways of carting them off?"

"No, the *Streltzi* of Moscow, who have apparently taken Bernie to their bosom after last spring, are taking care of that. I am in search of information on mica, muscovite, or Muscovy-glass. It's sometimes used as glass in Moscow windows and someone at the Dacha seems to have discovered that it is an unusually good insulator. It's a potentially high profit export for Russia."

"So, why don't you have your minions doing it, Prince Vladimir? Surely a prince has minions?"

"It's that same problem again. The minions insist on reading with their eyes open. Plus the fact that my main researcher just got hired away by a French marquis who may be working for Cardinal Richelieu or the king of France's little brother Gaston. But what are you doing here? Surely no one could hire away your minions. Besides, you're an up-timer. Probably you already know all of this." Vladimir waved at the thousands of books casually.

"No minions, I'm afraid. I'm a researcher. Have card catalog, will cross-reference."

"Ah!" *Perhaps I can get back to work.* Vladimir felt himself grinning. "A minion for hire. I pay standard rates."

"Yes, but you see I read with my eyes opened," Brandy said, grinning back.

"Well, in this case it doesn't matter. Poor spy that I am, I've already let you discover that I'm seeking information on mica. Are you sure you're not a spy?"

Brandy giggled. Then quickly regained her composure and asked what he wanted to know about mica. He told her and they discussed hourly wages, the cost of copying and other fees involved. They reached an agreement and Vladimir was free to get back to his organizational duties.

Brandy went to work on the mica research, but her tummy was jumping a bit. Well, maybe not her tummy. But something inside her was jumping a bit about something.

The last thing she'd ever expected was to feel this way about a down-timer. Down-timers were . . . well, down-timers. They didn't quite get civilization.

Over the next few days, she saw Vladimir quite a bit. And that jumping feeling became rather more intense.

Prince Vladimir had his own sensations. And the more he saw Brandy Bates, the more interesting those feelings got.

It was hard to know what to do about them. Up-timer women were . . . different. Not suitable for a casual dalliance. And, by Russian standards, not suitable for anything else. Still, he couldn't help wanting to see her.

He kept finding jobs for her. And then, when he'd worked up the courage, he suggested they have lunch. And lunch led to dinner. And without really realizing it, he had become involved.

✧   ✧   ✧

"Vladimir." Brandy waved the letter. "What precisely is a clan?"

"Excuse me?"

"Your sister is talking about clans. I'm not sure what she means." She handed him the letter and waited impatiently as he read it.

"Clan seems a fairly good word." He pursed his lips like he wasn't quite sure. "I think I would say family connections, but I am not sure. From what I understand, your government frowns on what you call nepotism, right?"

Brandy nodded, wondering where this was going.

"Russia is different. Nepotism is an institution of government."

Brandy giggled, thinking he must be exaggerating to make his point. But Vladimir was looking serious, even concerned. "You don't mean *literally*?"

Vladimir nodded. "Yes. If a person whose extended family is of lower rank is placed over a person whose family is more highly ranked . . ." Vladimir hesitated.

Brandy had seen it before, both in Vladimir and other down-timers. She had even done it herself, trying to explain things like the Goth style of dress. It wasn't just that the concept was missing; it was that there were half a dozen interrelated concepts that were all a bit different from the down-time concepts.

"A person's rank in Russia is determined by three things," Vladimir finally continued. "His personal rank in the bureaucracy, his family's rank and his inherited rank. However, they are all at least somewhat mixed together. My family is small but descended from independent princes. Because it is small and doesn't have a lot of connections to other great families, it's fairly weak. In my case, that is somewhat counterbalanced by the fact that I am the prince. But a cousin of mine, if I had one, would be of significantly lower rank than a cousin of Ivan Borisovich Cherkasski, because the Cherkasski family has connections by marriage to many other great families. Also, because the Cherkasski family has served in the government of Russia for many generations and counts several boyars among its ancestors.

"So, say my cousin and Ivan Borisovich's cousin both get jobs in the bureaus. My cousin, through talent or luck, advances more quickly. So my cousin is placed as section chief over a section in which Ivan Borisovich's cousin serves."

"Makes sense."

But Vladimir was shaking his head. "Because the Cherkasski clan is higher ranked than the Gorchakov clan, it would be against the law for my cousin to be placed in authority over Ivan Borisovich's. He could have higher personal rank, but still could not be put above Ivan Borisovich's cousin in the same chain of command."

"Like, say, he's a prince?" Brandy tilted her head to the side.

"No." Prince Vladimir got a bit red in the face. "I was talking about his rank in the bureaus or the army. Say a colonel in command of a battalion . . . a captain with the higher family rank could not be placed in command of one of the companies of that battalion because that would put him under the orders of the colonel. If the colonel was also a prince, it would be all right because his personal rank would trump the family rank, sort of. It gets a bit complicated. It's the rank of the family as much as that of the individual. The family's situation must be considered first. Before individual wants. Which is one of the things that has made it so hard for our people to accept your innovations. It's common knowledge that you're a 'peasant village' from the future."

"We're not, you know," Brandy said. "I know that's the way we have been portrayed and even how we tend to present ourselves. A village from a nation that didn't have nobility. In a way, it's true, but it would be just as true to say we were a nation of nothing but nobility. What we really don't have, Vladimir, is the distinction."

"And that, Brandy, is even harder for my people to accept," Vladimir said, though in his heart he had accepted it. Accepted it because he had to. The proof was here before his eyes and before his heart. In the person of Brandy Bates who was as noble as anyone he had ever met and as common as the barmaid she had been before the Ring of Fire. All classes, all in one beautiful young woman.

Chapter 32

The Kremlin
April 1633

"Death and taxes," Bernie muttered as he fell into the chair. "I'd really prefer a visit from the tax man." It was April 15 and Bernie was in the Kremlin. Not because he was really needed but because he was the up-timer and the Muscovites believed that his presence was a shield against the slow fever. Typhoid, that was, in up-timer English. So he went through the hospices where the people who had gotten typhoid fever this spring were being treated with down-time made Gatorade. At least this year they had real instructions on how to make the stuff, not just what Bernie could suck out of his thumb. And they were making their own aspirin for the fever even if they couldn't make chloramphenicol yet.

"It really does help, Bernie," said Father Kiril. "You up-timers even tested it and gave it a name. Not that they were telling any down-time doctor anything they didn't already know. Or any priest, either, when you come down to it. The placebo effect, they called in your future, and you, Bernie, are a very effective placebo."

"Yes, everything's great," Bernie said sourly. "Natasha, Anya, Filip the whole staff of the Dacha, the mayor of Moscow, the rich and powerful, and the poor and huddled all agree. It's likely that this spring's outbreak of the slow plague will kill fewer than a hundred people. Which is great, if you don't happen to be one of those hundred people. Sorry, Padre. It's just that I know that we could cure this if we had the right antibiotic and we knew how to make them up-time. We even had the knowledge in the Ring of Fire, but we haven't been able to make it. And 'sorry, kid, maybe next year . . . oh yeah, you'll be dead next year' just doesn't make me feel any better."

"All we can do is the best we can do," Father Kiril said. "The Ring of Fire didn't change that. I suspect that nothing ever will."

Guba Ivashka Kalachnikov was very interested in the knowledge from the future. He hadn't been last year, much to his regret. He had found the up-timer uncultured and rude to people who had practiced the healing craft for decades. It wasn't that Guba had any profound objection to washing his hands. True, it wasn't a lot of fun in icy water and heating water was expensive. Boiling it, as the up-timer wanted, was even more so. But he had seen the results. He had seen patients that he would have said would die, live. If the Gatorade had that effect, what about the hand-washing? Since spring of last year Guba had been trying to learn more of the up-timer knowledge so that he might determine how much of what the up-timer said was knowledge and how much ignorance.

"Quicksilver, mercury," he whispered, "is a poison?" He wasn't that concerned about the lead that the ladies used in their makeup. There were other things that would work as well for that. He was busily trying to integrate the things that were coming from the Ring of Fire with his experience. He had a lot of the latter; he had been a healer for over forty years.

He listened to the rest of the list. It was something called a cheat sheet and was being read to him by a clerk from the Grantville Section of the embassy bureau. The clerk was a lad of fifteen and, even though he was Guba's social superior, worked for him doing reading and writing. He paid the boy and thanked him for the service. Guba had never bothered to learn reading and writing. At least not what most people would think of as reading and writing. He used a set of symbols that was partly inherited from his teacher and partly made up by himself to keep track of what drug, prepared in what way, was in each container.

He worked with potions to relieve pain and balance the humors. He had mixed potions for Czar Ivan when he was an apprentice.

Potions that included mercury. The knowledge that his potions might have been what drove Ivan mad didn't sit well. "Mercury causes delusions?" he repeated. "I made drugs that drove Ivan Grozny mad? Drugs without which he would not have killed his son and the Time of Troubles would not have happened?"

No! he thought. *It's lies. It must be.* And yet . . . He could think of no reason for them to lie. At least none that made sense given the circumstances.

The shop was in Moscow and upscale. Guba knew about drugs and acupuncture and a number of other treatments. He had a large number of very wealthy customers, and he wasn't sure what to do. In more than one way. First, the potion for relieving the pain of swollen joints worked. He knew that; he had seen it. Mercury potions were also the only effective treatment for syphilis that he knew of. The dementia, if it was caused by the drug and not the pain, was a side effect that took multiple doses over a period of time to manifest.

Nor did he have a replacement for the drug. Not one that was nearly as effective. He understood from some of the things the boy from the Grantville Section had said that Grantville did have drugs that were effective. The little blue pills of happiness that were supposed to relieve pain and restore manhood. Another called Mary Jane. It didn't matter; he didn't have them and had no practical way to get them or make them. Now he had to change or he would lose all his clients.

Chapter 33

May 1633

Vladimir had just opened the packet from Moscow when Gregorii knocked on the door. He looked at Gregorii, then looked
at the clock and stifled a curse. Time had gotten away from him
again. Brandy Bates and her mother, Donna, had agreed to come
to dinner tonight. It would be a quiet dinner, just the three of
them. "All right, Gregorii, show them in."

One of the letters in the packet caught his eye. Surely it must
be important. As all of them were—to their originators, at any
rate. Vladimir was beginning to dread the packets, in truth.
There was yet another over-large stack of letters in this packet.
Vladimir knew they would contain more requests, demands, and
commands, depending on who the writer was. And probably half
of the questions would have already been answered.

The turnaround time for communications was over two months.
The message packets came every week or so. Often he got requests
for clarification of some point, did the research and sent an answer.
Then a week or two later he got another message saying "never
mind, we figured it out." They had obviously solved the problem
before he ever got the request. Sometimes their solutions matched
the answer he had sent and sometimes not.

Sometimes their solutions were better than the answer he had sent. That meant opportunities Vladimir could take advantage of here in Grantville. There were, as of his last report, something like a hundred of the brightest minds in Russia living in his dacha a few miles outside of Moscow. This wasn't anywhere near the number of bright minds that were in Grantville by now, but still constituted a fairly robust R&D facility, to use an American term. Sometimes they came up with solutions that the up-timers wouldn't because the up-timers "knew" it didn't work that way.

Vladimir averaged sending one message packet a week back to Moscow. Usually it would include the most recently copied up-timer books and what answers he had been able to get for the lists of questions that came in every packet.

Gregorii announced Brandy and Donna moments after he broke open the impressive looking letter. As they were shown in, he read the first paragraph. "Will you look at this!" Vladimir stood and stomped around the room. "Just look at it!" The letter had the imperial seals as well as those of the Russian Orthodox church. It was from Filaret, the patriarch of the church. Who also happened to be the father of the czar.

"Well, I could." Brandy shrugged. "But it wouldn't do much good since I can't read your language. Not enough, at least. Suppose you just tell me what it says."

Vladimir stopped his pacing and looked startled for a moment. "Ah . . . yes. I forget. You've learned so much about me and my country that I feel you must know the language better by now. Silly of me, I suppose. Come, ladies, come. Sit down, please. Will you have a glass of wine?"

Brandy smiled. "I do the same thing. It always surprises me when you need a word translated these days. Anyway, what does that very impressive looking letter say? It must be important, considering all the seals and ribbons. And yes, please. After this day, I could use a glass. I could use several, for that matter."

"Tell me, Donna Ivanovna, was the government in your America as impossible to please as mine is?" Vladimir's face was still a bit flushed with irritation. "The patriarch, of all people, sends me a request to have the entire library sent to Moscow. Impossible, totally impossible. Have they no idea of the size of such a project? Have they any idea of the expense?

"Oh, and you will love this part." Vladimir waved the paper again. "At the same time, I am to prevent the sale of up-timer books to other nations. Especially Poland and nations ruled by the Habsburgs. And I am to prevent the books from falling into the hands of the Roman church. The group that's reprinting the Americana has three priests and an agent of a Polish magnate in it! Let me read you this. It is impossible."

"To Kniaz Vladimir Petrovich Gorchakov

It is most necessary that the knowledge of the up-timers be limited to those of the true faith or at the very least provided to those of us of the orthodox church first. This must happen before it becomes available to those influenced by Rome. You must acquire the library, especially the National Library, mentioned in your dispatches and send it to the Church as soon as possible.

You are to be congratulated on sending so many books so rapidly. As you know, I am an expert on books and the time it takes to make copies. It is clear that you are somehow acquiring originals of the books you have sent because so many could not have been copied so quickly.

The spiritual tracts and philosophical knowledge gained by the up-timers must especially be sent to the church first. This is so that they may be reviewed before they are released. We wish to avoid partial understanding and crisis of faith among the followers of the true faith.

Further, it is essential that advances in techniques, new techniques and the knowledge of science be limited to nations that share in our beliefs. Some Protestant nations, particularly Sweden, may be allowed this knowledge but it must be kept from Poland and the Habsburgs. Especially, knowledge of medicines and healing must be controlled, lest the unscrupulous Roman clergy use it to bolster faith in their misinterpretation of God's word.

"Can you believe it?" Vladimir asked.

Mrs. Bates very nearly snorted wine up her nose.

Brandy was looking both concerned and confused. "He knows better, doesn't he?"

Vladimir was still stalking around the room and waving his arms in the air, but Brandy's question brought him up short. The answer was; of course, the patriarch knew that the demands were beyond impossible, well into the range of ridiculous. So what would make him write such a set of demands? It almost had to be that someone else was reading them or that they were being put on the record to demonstrate that the patriarch had instructed Vladimir thus and if Vladimir had failed to act on his instructions then it wasn't the patriarch's fault.

But now wasn't the time to go into all that. Vladimir slumped into a chair and poured his own glass of wine. "Every week I send a report. And every week I get more and more impossible requests. And I have no doubt that there are at least half a dozen more in this packet alone." A piece of paper fell out of it.

"Well, if it isn't going to violate national security or something, why don't you pull them out and read them to us?" Brandy suggested. "That way you can blow off steam before you try to answer them."

Vladimir dug into the packet of letters and grinned mischievously. "Oh, you're going to enjoy this, Brandy. Here. You have a letter from Bernie." He handed her the letter.

After she took it, he picked up another missive. He was glad to see it had fewer ribbons and seals.

"Oh, no." Brandy stared at the letter like it might be a snake. "Two months ago it was 'send me an egg beater.' Last month it was 'send me a generator.' And we've done it, every time. What do you suppose Bernie wants now? I'm almost afraid to read it." Brandy glared at the letter, suspicion all over her face.

Mrs. Bates stifled another snort at the look she wore. "Come on, Brandy! At least it will be in English. Read it to us."

"Okay, Mom." Brandy gingerly opened the letter. "I'll read it. But hang on to your hat. There's just no telling, there really isn't."

   "Hey, girl."

"You know," Brandy muttered, "he could use my name, just to freaking be polite." She continued,

> *"Well, if Dad really wants the old car out of the way how about we do this? I'm sending you an authorization to take money out of my savings account. Will you give Dad some money for me? Tell him it's a storage fee, or something. Anything to keep him from getting rid of the*

car. Then, if you could have Vladimir get someone to pull the engine out of it for me, I'd really appreciate it. I'm enclosing a bill of sale from me to you, just in case.

The body doesn't really matter that much, but I want the engine and the transmission. Actually, I'd like to have all of it, but there's probably no way to ship it, not in one piece. Ask Vladimir, will you? I'd take it all if I could get it.

I've asked Natasha to ask Boris (I love that... Boris and Natasha, the Russian spies) to authorize paying for the transport back here. If worse comes to worst, we'll tear the whole thing apart and try to build our own version. God, I miss the car, I really do.

Thanks, Bernie

"Oh, Lord." Mrs. Bates giggled. "Bernie wants his car. In Russia. In the year 1633. That makes a lot of sense."

Brandy, Vladimir and Mrs. Bates laughed. "I can't imagine what he'll do with it." Brandy shook her head. "What do you think, Vladimir? Should you send Bernie his car?"

Vladimir slumped farther into his chair but smiled. "I told you there would be more impossible demands, didn't I? As to whether or not we should send the car, yes, we should. And also anything else that might help. I sent them information on the steam engines you built for your power plant months ago. They can't build them. Natasha tried to have them built in Murom and they failed completely. But Russia needs some kind of motive force even more than Germany does."

Brandy grinned. "The difficult we do immediately. The impossible takes a little longer. As it happens, there's a new booklet out on making steam pumps. We can send them that. It might help. So what's that other thing you got in that letter?"

Vladimir waved a piece of paper. "Money. Money like yours, in fact." He passed it to Brandy, who looked at it and passed it on to her mother.

"Colorful," Mrs. Bates said.

It was. About four by eight inches, printed in red, yellow and blue. "Who's this?"

"Czar Mikhail." Vladimir pointed at the images. "A cross, a proper cross, on the other end."

Mrs. Bates flipped the paper over. "And that would be the palace, I suppose? Or a government building of some sort?"

"The Kremlin." Vladimir took the bill back.

"And what does the writing say?" Mrs. Bates looked at him curiously.

"This bill is legal tender for all debts, by order of the czar, with the support of the *Boyar Duma* and the *Zemsky Sobor*. One ruble."

"Bernie or you, Vladimir? I mean, this isn't the sort of thing that Bernie would come up with." Brandy had known Bernie Zeppi for years. This wasn't his sort of thing.

"Me, mostly. I started sending information about your banking system before Bernie left. On the other hand, I'll wager any amount you name that members of the *Zemsky Sobor,* that's the Assembly of the Land, consulted with Bernie before they signed off on it."

Chapter 34

Vladimir believed in going to the best source he could find. He discussed the matter of book copying with the staff of the research center, then sent the patriarch information on the book-copying system they had instituted. Parts of it, like scanning pages into computers, could not be replicated in Russia. Other parts could, like the waxed silk sheets for the new duplicating machines.

Having, he hoped, explained to the patriarch, or whoever the patriarch thought was reading their mail, that he could not just buy the National Library and ship it off to the Kremlin, he set to work on the next impossible demand. He made an appointment with Wilkie Andersen, the Tech Center teacher of auto mechanics. The man had the strangest desk he had ever seen. It was red and appeared to be the front end of a truck. Wilkie noticed him staring and pressed a button. The blaring noise rocked Vladimir back on his feet.

Wilkie grinned. "That always got the students' attention. Yes, it is the front end of a S10 pickup truck. And I've hooked the horn up to the electricity. I don't honk it that much, but I still enjoy seeing people jump. Now, what can I do for you, Mister ... ah ... Gorchakov?"

"I came because I have a question. Is it possible to 'pull the engine' of a 'car' and have it transported to another place?"

Wilkie nodded. "Sure You can pull any engine. But some of

them won't do you much good. What kind of engine is it? And what do you want to use it for?"

"I'm told it is a 1972 Dodge Charger." Vladimir waved the bill of sale Bernie had sent. "I don't really know what that means, but that's the car. Bernie Zeppi wants me to pull the engine and transmission and send it to him in Russia. I'm here to find out if that is possible."

"Not a bad choice." Wilkie leaned back in his chair and motioned Vladimir to another. "It's a good bit less complicated than some. No computers in it, at any rate. And I remember that car. Bernie bought it for a couple of hundred dollars back when he took my classes. We restored it together, out in the shop. Me, Bernie, all the class. Leon McCarthy, from the body shop classes, even got involved and fixed a couple of dents. But why pull the engine? Why don't you just put it in neutral and pull it with horses? Bernie's car has a stick shift so you don't have to worry about protecting an automatic transmission over a long tow. That car's got a rear wheel drive, though, so make sure you disconnect and remove the drive shaft or you'll wreck the transmission. How far does it have to travel and what are the roads like?"

Most of the response was meaningless to Vladimir, beyond the apparent assurance that the vehicle could be towed intact as long as certain precautions were taken. He could figure those out later. For the moment, he concentrated on the last question, which he did understand.

"It has to go to Moscow and will make a good part of the trip by way of the Baltic Sea." Vladimir shrugged. "The roads are fairly bad. Horrible, by up-timer standards. On the other hand, we can use more than two horses if we have to."

"Russia used to have oil wells up-time." Wilkie leaned forward. "Are you folks planning on getting into the oil business or do you figure on buying gas from the Wietze oil fields? I gotta tell you, they aren't getting much high octane yet."

"I have no idea," Vladimir admitted. "For all I know they want to use the engine as a planter for up-timer roses. I am also told to send those."

"Well..." Wilkie shrugged away the possibility of Russian oil fields. "If you can get it onto and off of the boat, it really might be easier just to tow the darn thing. Sure, it weighs more than a wagon. But it's also got shocks and ball bearings on the wheels.

Most of the time it'll be easier to pull than a wagon, even with the engine in it."

Brandy was in the research center when Vladimir found her. "What's up?" she asked.

"Your Mr. Wilkie says that Russia in the up-time had oil fields. If they were there in the up-time, they will be there now. I wish to locate them. And I shall have to arrange for some people to come here for training at the oil field. In fact, I should probably have a number of people come here."

Brandy sat down at the table across from Vladimir and nodded. "Probably not a bad idea. Who will you have come?"

"We already have a fair sized staff at the *Residentz*." Vladimir had bought a half-acre lot in Castle Hills, the upscale housing development that had grown up just north of the Ring of Fire. Then he'd put a fair-sized mansion—or smallish hotel—on the lot. "But this is too much for just a few people to absorb. I'm going to write Natasha and have her pick the best of the people from our lands. As well, I'm sure she knows some students who would be interested." Vladimir looked Brandy in the eyes and said in a serious tone, "Russian politics are not pretty, Brandy. Not pretty at all. It hasn't been that long since Czar Ivan the Terrible and the Time of Troubles. It will take a lot of work, but I believe most strongly that Russia must take advantage of the knowledge in Grantville. That is why, although it will be atrociously expensive, I will send Bernie his car. I will send books. Eventually, I hope to send teachers."

"You're not trying to be Peter the Great, are you?" Brandy asked. "I just don't see you going around cutting off beards and all that silly stuff."

"Not silly, my dear. Not silly at all." Vladimir made a vague gesture and frowned. "It was a symbol. And symbols can be very powerful. The beards might have been the wrong symbol at the wrong time, perhaps. But something had to be done. Or rather, would have had to be done, had it not been for the Ring of Fire."

Vladimir sighed. "The history of my country isn't a happy one, not according to the very few books here in Grantville. These books, they barely mention the time of troubles after the death of Ivan the Terrible, the three false Dmitris that left Russia bleeding and broken. Poland invaded and took Patriarch Filaret prisoner. The Poles held him prisoner for years, Brandy. That was after he was forced to take a vow of chastity by Boris Godunov. The purpose of the vow was to disqualify him from the throne."

Vladimir stared into the distance. "It hardened him, Brandy. Which may well be to the good. I don't know whether it was being forced to take holy orders or the imprisonment. Whatever it was that caused it, he was different when he came back. There is a cold-blooded practicality that wasn't there before. He manipulates everyone. The czar most of all. Mikhail Fedorovich is not in control. His father is."

"Do you know him?" Brandy settled in for a long talk. "The czar, I mean." She couldn't help but be interested. Vladimir attracted her in a way that few people did. She wanted to understand him and his country.

"Yes. My family is very wealthy, on the whole. And the treasury was bare when Mikhail came to the throne. My sister and I are the last of our particular branch, which concentrated the wealth even more. So we were invited to court quite a bit. Not as much as some, but fairly often. Our father traveled for the embassy bureau for many years; it gave us a different outlook. Natasha and I were educated more than most." Vladimir's face grew more animated. "Natasha does know the czarina quite well, and I have sent her letters and books. Perhaps the czarina, with Natasha's help, can become more of an influence."

"I've gotten to know the czarina fairly well through the letters we've traded," Brandy said. "I don't think that she's in a position to do much. You said once that the czar supports Gustavus Adolphus, didn't you? Or is that his father's doing?"

"Some of both, I think." Vladimir leaned forward. "Money. Always a problem, the money. The Poles cleaned out the Russian treasury. The Time of Troubles left roving bands of thieves that traveled through Russia, some of them even now, after nearly twenty years of Mikhail's rule. Mikhail is loved by the people but he is not very strong. He is governed by the boyars and the great houses. I respect your system of government, Brandy. I really do. But how much of it can be adapted to Russia . . . that is hard to say. I don't know how much we can do. We have Natasha. We have your Bernie, even. I will work for change, with all my heart."

"I'll help." Brandy stood up. "As much as I can."

Chapter 35

June 1633

"Well, let's see." Bernie said, pointing. "The acquisition is recorded here and here because it's a . . ." He continued doing his best to give Anya an idea of what the accounting book said about how to prevent or catch different ways of cooking the books. By now Anya was better at accounting than Bernie was or wanted to be. But the expertise was in English and while Anya was learning accounting, English and the way of thinking that went with modern English was still mostly foreign to her. By now Bernie had gotten really good at translating between modern English and seventeenth-century English. And not bad at taking the next step and translating from modern English to seventeenth-century Russian. So he explained about the esoterics of accounting, and neither he nor Anya noticed Filip Pavlovich standing in the background listening. Not till Filip cleared his throat.

"What?" Bernie looked up. "Oh, hi, Phil. What are you doing up at this—" Bernie looked at his watch. "—ungodly hour?"

"The bathroom woke me," Filip said sardonically. "Chamber pots are quieter and they can be emptied in safe ways."

"Can be," Anya said, "but rarely are." Which, though Bernie didn't notice it, brought Filip up short.

"That's an interesting observation, Anya," Filip said. "And not the sort of thing a maid would say."

Bernie felt himself stiffen and Filip waved a gentling hand. "I wasn't criticizing. I know I often sound like I am even when I'm not." Filip grinned at them. "Which is rare enough."

Bernie's lips twitched.

"It was simply an observation. What drew me up short when Anya spoke up wasn't that she was getting above herself, but that I didn't mind that she was getting above herself. If that makes any sense?" He looked between them. "Bernie, before you arrived in Moscow I would have been offended. Deeply offended. Offended enough to have her dismissed or seriously punished. I would hazard a guess that before you arrived, Anya would never have thought to say such a thing in my presence." Filip looked to Anya for confirmation and got it from a clearly anxious woman.

"There is nothing to worry about, Anya, at least not here," Filip said. "What it did was bring into focus something that has been bothering me for some time now. Petr was explaining to me yet again how everything was an interaction of forces."

"For the hundredth time," Bernie said.

"Oh, much more often than that," Anya said.

"And I couldn't get him to shut up about it. 'Fine, yes, water flows downhill because of gravity. I understand already' I told him. 'No you don't,' he told me. 'It's not just water and it's not just gravity, it's everything. Magnetism, electricity, alchemy... it's all forces acting on things.' Well, naturally, I didn't pay all that much attention to it, but still there was something about it that bothered me. Something I couldn't quite figure out or get out of my head. Not till just now." Filip paused, lost in thought again.

"Well, go on!" Bernie said.

Filip looked over at Anya and there was something in his expression like he was, well, almost scared. Certainly cautious. Then he visibly squared his shoulders, and went on. "If a rock doesn't keep going on and on forever because of external forces, if rocks aren't lazy by their nature as Aristotle said, what about serfs?"

"What *about* serfs?" Bernie asked.

Still looking at Anya, Filip said. "Are serfs tied to the land because it's their nature to be so or because some external force like social drag or social gravity is holding them down?"

"Because they are held in serfdom, of course." Bernie was more than a little confused. There were laws in Russia that prevented a serf from leaving the land he was bound to. Filip knew that.

Hell, Filip was the one who had told Bernie. Bernie looked at Anya and she was looking at Filip like she was seeing a ghost.

"Okay, guys," Bernie said slowly. "I'm clearly missing something here. Serfs are serfs because they are forced to be. There are laws that tie them to the land. Slaves are slaves, again because they are forced to be. Once again, there are laws that allow them to be held against their will, bought, sold, and generally abused." Bernie hesitated, then went on. "I know I'm a stranger in a strange land here. I know I was not hired to change your society or your laws. But the laws that make people be treated like property are wrong. They are self-evidently wrong. But they are there and I can't change them and if I try it will destroy all the good I'm trying to do here. I figured that out before I left Grantville and I was drunk as a skunk then. That's why I've never made an issue of it. I knew it was wrong, and, to be honest, I figured you had to know it was wrong too. But you weren't about to give it up, so what was there to say?

"So, now you're both sitting there shocked as hell about something as simple and obvious as water flowing dow..."

Filip was looking at Bernie like *yes, go on, shove your foot the rest of the way into your mouth.*

"But there are laws," Bernie said "Clearly an external force. Right?"

"Yes, Bernie, laws," Filip said. "But laws to do what? To force the serfs and slaves into a state of servitude or to keep those whose nature is servitude from misbehaving and causing trouble?"

"I have, you know," Anya said, "always believed deep in my heart that I should not be a servant...but I never really thought that forced servitude was wrong. I just felt that it should be forced on someone else, not me."

Bernie looked at Anya and Filip and they were looking at each other like they were both watching a horror movie and couldn't look away. Servant and master, not directly, not to each other, but the odds were pretty good, Bernie knew, that Anya was actually a runaway serf or possibly a slave. She'd been working as kitchen help, and whatever else she could find, when the job at the Dacha had come up and she'd gotten it because she was pretty.

Bernie was still confused. He knew something important had happened, but he didn't know what. Another truth, as important, or perhaps more important, than the change from Aristotle to Newton had occurred in this candle-lit room, and somewhere

deep down inside Bernie sensed that this was a lot more dangerous than Newton's three laws. He wondered how long it would
be before the pebbles dropped in this room started an avalanche.

As it happened it wasn't long at all, though avalanches do take
time. The next pebble was dropped by Filip. "Did you know," he
said to Natasha, "that Anya is learning accounting?"

"What? Bernie's tart?" Natasha asked. "What on earth for? It's
not like she gets paid by the...encounter." Natasha wasn't pleased
with Bernie's extracurricular activities but men were men, especially in Russia. Then Natasha noticed that Filip had stiffened.

"Never mind, Princess, It wasn't important," Filip said.

"I think perhaps it is," Natasha said. "Clearly it's important to
you. Why don't you tell me why?"

Filip did, stumbling a bit but clearly showing he was impressed
by Anya. He explained about his finding Bernie and Anya studying
accounting and the ensuing discussion. Filip impressed by Anya?
Filip, who couldn't see past the edge of the book he was reading and didn't care about breast size, just brain size? Anya had
a brain? Well, yes, apparently she did. That was a pretty astute
observation about chamber pots and the safe emptying of same.

After Filip ran down she thanked him for his help, asked a
few questions and let him get back to work. Then she thought
about it a bit and had Anya fetched.

"You called for me, Princess?" Anya entered the princess' office
with more than simple trepidation. She was scared to death. She
remembered the conversation of the night before and she was very
much afraid that in spite of Filip's assurances that it was all right
here at the Dacha, it wasn't. At least it wasn't when a great lady
was looking for a reason to discipline a maid who was having a
bit of fun with a guy the great lady was interested in. Women
in power were dangerous to girls like her.

"I understand you're having Bernie teach you accounting?"
Princess Natasha said.

Anya thought this was a set up to punish her for getting above
herself. "Yes, Princess. Of course, if you feel it's interfering with
my duties..."

"Not at all." The princess actually smiled a bit. Much to Anya's
surprise.

"Ma'am?"

"I said, not at all," the princess repeated. "I'm a bit, um, startled by it, but why would you want to learn accounting . . . considering your other assets?"

The princess was blushing a little bit as she said that. There was an edge. Natasha didn't like what Anya was doing with Bernie. Or no. Anya realized Natasha didn't like that *she* was doing it with Bernie. The princess really was jealous of the serving girl, though she probably didn't realize it.

They talked about Anya's observation about chamber pots. Which led to questions about what else Anya had observed. They talked books. Bernie had taught Anya to read and she had picked it up well. Anya had gotten the job in part because she had a bit of English from a previous employer who had been all hands. "Why did he teach you to read?"

"Because I asked."

"Why did you ask? I don't mean, why did you want to know how to read, I mean why did you think Bernie would teach you?" The princess' blush was even brighter now. "When men are, ah, with girls like you, that's not what they're interested in."

"Not all men are the same, Princess, not even about that. The English merchant who was all hands never would have taught me to read." Anya shrugged. "Bernie likes smart women. That's why he likes you. Besides, he's a nice man and wanted someone to talk to in his up-timer English and teaching me to read helped with that."

They ended up talking girl talk for quite a while that afternoon and the beginnings of a friendship were put in place. After that, Anya became Natasha's personal maid and confidant.

Lazar Smirnov barely noticed that Anya's status had changed. Lazar had his own companionship and wasn't any more interested in politics than he could avoid. The gradual change in attitude of Filip Pavlovich Tupikov that had been crystallized by conversation over accounting books a few nights back had passed him by completely.

Lazar had his own problems. Granted, none of them were all that severe taken on their own but they couldn't really be taken on their own. Lazar was trying to build an entire infrastructure. Storage batteries required lead plates and sulfuric acid. Enough batteries to power a spark gap transmitter of good range required lots of lead plates and lots of sulfuric acid. Not that much of a problem. Lead, after all, was not gold, and improved processes for the production of sulfuric acid had been forwarded to him by Vladimir and his friend Lady Brandy Bates, G.E.D. So there was a factory on the Muskova River that producing the stuff by the gallon. Which was good, because he needed gallons for each spark gap transmitter.

He had serfs on his estates making clay battery jars to hold the acid and the lead plates. Or at least they were till a few weeks ago. Now they were planting, sowing the seeds of the fall harvest. But once that was done, many of them would go back to making the parts he needed to create an electronics industry.

Like copper wire to make the generators to charge the batteries, to use to make the permanent magnets to make more generators. And it wasn't just radios Russia needed, whatever the *Boyar Duma* said. What Russia needed was the whole infrastructure. Even if they had only needed radios, the number of parts in a radio network was significant. The transmitter tuning coil, the transmitter spark capacitor, the transmitter spark coil, the transmitter spark generating buzzer, a telegraph key, a switch to switch between the receiver and the transmitter for the antenna, an earphone, a receiver tuning coil, a receiver capacitor—which was not the same thing as a transmitter capacitor—a grounding rod, wire going to the grounding rod. None of these things were really hard to do, not by themselves. It was just that there were so many.

There were four radios in Russia. Two that Lazar had made and two that had been imported. Of the two that he had made, one was here at the Dacha and one was in the Kremlin. But Lazar was also building, a bit at a time, the infrastructure to build more radios, faster. They would have one for the Gun Shop by month after next, and by then—if all went well—they would be turning out about one spark gap transmitter a month. It would be a while before the government got the network it desired.

In a vague way Lazar Smirnov knew that he was making central control in Russia much easier, but he didn't give it much thought. That the increasing awareness of the rights of people in other parts of time and space were making the ties to the land insufferable to some and others were increasingly threatened by the notion of freedom? That, he didn't notice at all.

Chapter 36

July 1633

A Dissertation on the Value of Freedom and Security

"Those who give up their freedom for a little temporary security deserve neither freedom nor security and ultimately will lose both." So goes an up-time quote. This humble writer doesn't know whether that is true or not, but it is demonstrably true that the nation it comes from—founded on principles of freedom—grew to be one of the richest and most powerful in the world.

That nation had no greater resources than the Russia of its time. But it had a great deal more wealth. Why is that, I wonder? The question troubles my sleep at night.

The Time of Troubles is a weak name for what Russia went though at the beginning of this century. It has perhaps made us a bit timid, afraid of freedom. It's so much easier when everyone knows their place and no one is allowed to argue or try something new. So much safer it seems. But I wonder, safe for how long?

Bandits are mostly gone from our roads and villages now. Surely that is a good thing. It seems worth a bit of freedom. What use, after all, is freedom to a man

175

murdered by bandits? Is it worth, perhaps, the right of a serf to leave the lands of his lord? Some of those serfs might become bandits and make our roads unsafe yet again. Yet, why was this America, with its freedom, so rich? Where did its great wealth come from?

Much of it came from people leaving their work and striking out on their own. From people who left their homes and tried to do something that they had never done before. A man named Bell tried to find a way to make the deaf hear. Instead he found a way to send his voice and thousands of other voices thousands of miles along a wire. Another man, named Edison, hated transcribing the messages he received to send on. So he made a machine that did the job. This type of event happened again and again and made the land that the up-timers came from the richest in their world. Was it the freedom that did it? I think it may have been. For the same rule that prevents a serf from becoming a bandit also prevents him from becoming an inventor, or a merchant.

As I think of these things I can't help but wonder if we are beggaring our children to buy a bit of security for ourselves. The history of Holy Mother Russia that was written in that other time saw the fading away of the Zemsky Sobor. It is barely even mentioned in their records. How did we allow that to happen? Are we, perhaps, afraid of the responsibilities of voting for representatives we trust? How will Mother Russia compete with nations that have spent a bit of their security to buy a little freedom for themselves and their posterity?

                                        The Flying Squirrel

Natasha set the pamphlet aside. What Russia was, she decided, depended a lot on how you looked at it. She had looked at it one way all her life, now she was looking again. "Aunt Sofia, what do you think of American democracy?"

The woman chuckled. She was tiny, four foot ten and weighed all of eighty pounds. Yet, when needed, she could put on such an expression of fierceness that boyars and bureau chiefs blanched. Fortunately, at the moment she didn't have her game face on. Her eyes twinkled. "Bernie again or one of the pamphlets? I don't know enough about it to have much of an opinion. From what I've heard, I cannot imagine it working, but obviously in some way it did. It must be different from what the Poles have that leaves their government so paralyzed."

"Well, according to Bernie, women vote as well as men, peasants as well as princes."

"I approve of the first and disapprove of the second. Peasants lack the knowledge of the wider world to understand the issues of a great nation. They lack the intellect for matters of state. Instead, they have low cunning." The eyes laughed. "Of course, I am a woman of the nobility. Were I a man—and a peasant—I might have a different opinion."

Natasha looked up at her smiling aunt with some irritation, then back down at the piles of papers on her worktable. She had two inboxes and two outboxes. One set was for what the Dacha was doing and what the nerd patrol wanted to do and her approval or disapproval of the same. The other had income and expenses for the Dacha and, for that matter, the rest of the Gorchakov estates. The pamphlet on the cost of freedom and security was an issue she didn't have time for.

"I have another letter from Brandy." Natasha changed the subject, setting down the pamphlet and picking up the letter.

"And what does she have to say?"

"Quite a lot. They are making electric crock-pots in Grantville now and she is sending me some." Natasha scanned down the letter. "Well, well. It seems that Brandy is now working part-time for my brother. I wonder if I should warn her of his defects of personality or pray that she can cure them?"

Sofia gave her a suppressing look. "Warn her off. The political consequences could be difficult."

"I was joking." Natasha gave back the standard look of young women who are hearing silly advice from old women who don't understand. "Brandy is doing research in the National Library of theirs. Finding answers to the questions we send them."

"Perhaps." Aunt Sofia didn't sound convinced.

Natasha went back to her letter. "She repeats that we should stay away from lead-based makeup. And sends some cheat sheets on making white makeup without lead oxide. In Grantville, and to an extent in the rest of the New U.S., women can pursue any career that men can. A woman can be an artist, an engineer, a person of business. She mentions a group of young girls who have gotten rich investing in many and varied enterprises since the Ring of Fire and she, as a researcher in the library, makes quite a good living for herself. She goes on to say how rewarding the work is in ways other than financial. She, her work, is making the world a better place." Natasha's voice, in spite of her intent, had risen in tone and volume as she said that last.

Aunt Sofia lifted her arms and patted the air. "Calm, child, calm. Stop and think a moment. Women do the same in Russia. Not all calls to holy orders are calls to God. Quite a few are calls away from the restriction of the outside world."

"But they don't—"

Aunt Sofia was holding up her hand. "I understood what you meant," Sofia said. "My point was that there was already an acceptable way to avoid the responsibilities of family. And how do these women live? They get jobs, just as your friend Brandy."

Natasha nodded cautiously.

"And, Natasha, what do you do in the Dacha?"

Natasha stopped dead. What she did in the Dacha was run it. She used Vladimir's authority as head of the family, but she ran the Dacha. Her authority there was pretty much unquestioned. "I wasn't just thinking of me. Though I would like to see Grantville. Perhaps even live there for a time. I was thinking of all the other women of Russia."

"Of course you were." Aunt Sofia sounded doubtful. Then she laughed at Natasha's expression. "But all the women of Russia can't move to Grantville! What would the men do? Nor can we make Russia into a copy of Grantville, not without losing Russia and ourselves in the process. Quietly, calmly. Think each step through. Plan. You are a *knyazhna*, not a peasant. Consider the church, also. Think about what the church will have to say. If that doesn't calm you down, consider how most of the women of Russia will react."

Sofia held up her hand. "Consider," she insisted again. "If a woman can be a soldier, then a woman can be made to be a soldier. Yes? Would you have women of the boyar class working in the fields like peasant women? Would Madame Cherkasski agree to have her status based on her position in the bureaucracy? She can't read, you know. And she heartily disapproves of those who can. It wasn't the men of Russia who poisoned Mikhail's first choice for a bride. Think about that. For now, at least, leave politics aside and concentrate on the Dacha."

That was, Natasha knew, very good advice, though the pamphlet suggested that not everyone followed it. Natasha wondered again who the writer was. She remembered for a moment the joke about Boris and Natasha and the hunt for the moose and the flying squirrel.

Russia had flying squirrels. They were hunted for their fur and were elusive and hard to catch.

Sofia shook her head as she left Natasha to her work. The degree to which her brother had sheltered his children from the realities of Russian politics sometimes appalled her. The degree to which Natasha's mother had shielded her from the reality of sexual relations appalled her even more. The girl knew nothing about the emotions involved. So little, in fact, that she failed to recognize her obvious—to Sofia—interest in Bernie. This wasn't the first time Sofia had tried to get her niece to notice how she was reacting.

Natasha was always aware of Bernie. She was aware of him even when he wasn't in the room. She listened to every casual comment and even though she clearly knew better, she gave those comments and beliefs considerably more weight than they deserved.

Why, Natasha didn't even realize that she was envious of the various servant girls who saw to Bernie's needs!

Not that Sofia wasn't concerned by Vladimir's interest in the Bates girl, but at least he had been encouraged to get a certain amount of practice, as were all men of his class in Russia. Natasha was most certainly a virgin and, because of her mother's attitudes, Natasha had had very little even theoretical knowledge until she started corresponding with Brandy Bates. She was totally unprepared for the feelings Sofia could tell she was having for Bernie, which effectively prevented Sofia from being able to offer advice on how to deal with them.

The only good news here was that Bernie was also unaware of Natasha's interest. Sofia hoped he continued to be unaware. The political consequences of Vladimir getting involved with an up-time woman would be bad. The political consequences of Natasha getting involved with an up-timer would be worse. Partly because Natasha was a woman, and partly because Bernie was right here in Russia.

Perhaps Sofia should encourage Natasha to visit the estates in Murom. Take that new steam barge downriver. That should keep her distracted. Sofia could only hope that the distraction wasn't fatal, considering that the first boiler they made had blown up.

"It must have come from the Dacha!" Sheremetev roared at the patriarch. For most people roaring at Patriarch Filaret was a serious, sometimes fatal, mistake. Fedor Ivanovich Sheremetev wasn't most people. He was a cousin of the czar and one of the most powerful nobles in Russia.

"Do not shout at me, Cousin," Filaret snarled back. "It may have come from the Dacha or it may have come from the bureaus—not even necessarily the Grantville Section. The same sort of thing is coming from Germany and Sweden. The up-timers' founding fathers are often quoted."

"Wherever it comes from, the writer, this Flying Squirrel, needs its pelt removed and publicly. We can't allow this sort of rhetoric and you know it. After what that fool Zeppi did in Moscow last spring, anything attributed to an up-time source is given extra credence almost as though it were holy writ."

"I know, and that is the very reason we must tread carefully. Aside from offending the Gorchakovs, who have shown themselves both loyal and of considerable financial worth to the czar, a raid or attack on the Dacha would engender quite a bit of ill-feeling among the people. Further, I don't want to give it that much credence."

Sheremetev wasn't satisfied but Filaret wouldn't budge. The American had become a danger to Russia, Sheremetev thought as he left the meeting. It was time to consider removing that danger. Besides, without the Zeppi fellow, the Sheremetev clan would have a better chance of getting control of the up-timer knowledge away from the Gorchakov clan.

Chapter 37

On the Oka River, between Moscow and Murom
August 1633

"Hey, Stinky. What do you have there?"

Pavel Mikhailovich didn't much like being called Stinky, since he didn't stink any worse than his brother did. "I got a pamphlet, Shorty. There was this kid handing them out in Moscow."

"What'd you want a pamphlet for that you can't read?" Ivan Mikhailovich demanded. He didn't much like being called Shorty, since his brother was only one inch taller than he was.

"Well, I figured you'd read it to me. Oh, that's right! You can't read either." Pavel Mikhailovich made a rude gesture at his brother, then continued. "The kid stuck it in my hand. I wasn't going to stop in the middle of a Moscow street and explain to him that I couldn't read. So I stuck it in my pocket and forgot about it."

Pockets, not entirely by chance, had become the mark of a well-dressed man—to the extent that someone had suggested a law forbidding them to peasants and *Streltzi*. The notion hadn't gotten very far, but just the fact that it had been broached was enough to make pockets a fad.

"Fine, then. How's the engine doing?" In theory, Ivan, being three years older, was the captain and Pavel was the engineer. In fact, they switched off and both turned their hands to whatever needed doing on the Gorchakov Steam Barge One. It was the only steam barge in Russia and it was brand new. The barge was thirty feet long and twelve feet wide. The front twenty feet had boxes and barrels like any barge on the Moskva river might. But the back ten feet were different. They contained a Frankenstein monster of an engine that James Watt wouldn't have recognized in his worst nightmare. The engine started with a big iron pot, the boiler, which was connected to a big wooden tub by a copper pipe. More copper pipes led to two wooden cylinders, each about six feet long, held together by what a wine merchant would call an excess of barrel hoops.

Though you couldn't see it from the outside, the inside of each cylinder had a piston a bit over a foot across. From the piston, a piston rod extended out of the cylinder and attached to a connecting rod, which attached to a flywheel, which was connected by way of a belt drive and an assortment of other wheels and belts to a rod on the end of which was a propeller. The power was controlled by a valve that restricted the flow of steam to the cylinders, and the direction of rotation by a lever that added a reversing gear.

"Well enough," Pavel said. "It's leaking a bit more than I like out of cylinder two. When we get to Murom, we should pull the cylinder head and check the greasing. But it should get us there."

Ivan nodded. They had to do that every so often to one of the cylinders or the other. The inside of the cylinders were coated with lard, the steam melted the lard, and the piston shoved it to the ends of the cylinders.

Then he turned and went forward again.

Struck with an idea how he might twit his younger brother, when Ivan got to the middle of the barge he asked loudly, "Say, can anyone read? My brother can't and he got given a pamphlet in Moscow." The front half of the barge was stacked with boxes and barrels of goods from Moscow and the Gorchakov Dacha, on which sat half-a-dozen passengers, all of it, and them probably, headed for the Gorchakov family estate at Murom.

There was a general shaking of heads. The passengers were mostly *Streltzi* on this run, which varied a lot. But there were generally better odds of finding a literate person on the barge than most places. The barge made a local, then an express, run in both directions. This was the express run from Moscow to Murom, a bit under four hundred miles by river. They would next hit land in four days or so. For safety's sake, they threw out an anchor and stayed in the middle of the river at night.

One woman asked, "What have you got?"

"Just a pamphlet some kid gave my brother in Moscow," Ivan answered.

"Sorry I can't help."

"Doesn't matter. We're sure to find someone in Murom who can read it to us. Why are you going to Murom?"

"I've got a cousin there. Maybe I can get work, what with all the new business Princess Natalia is promoting."

The other passengers had similar stories. Looking for work, looking for opportunity. Bright people, hopeful people, but not literate people. So they wouldn't find out what the Flying Squirrel had to say till they got to Murom.

Meanwhile, they cooked their meals over the boiler fire and had a generally good four-day vacation, talking about the goings on in the wider world.

"What's the Dacha like?" the woman who had a cousin, second cousin actually, in Murom, asked the first night.

"Confusing." Pavel laughed. "I don't have any idea what they are talking about most of the time."

"So how did you get the job?" asked a big man who was going to Murom in hopes of work as a blacksmith or maybe a foundry man. Not belligerently, just with the assurance that comes with being the biggest man around most of the time.

"Because we are very good boatmen," Ivan said, with a touch of belligerence in his tone. This was their barge, after all.

The big man waved off any offense. "I didn't mean that. I don't doubt your skill, but I heard that those folks at the Dacha are dead set on reading and writing and figuring. I heard even the servants are learning to read at that Dacha place."

"That's true enough," Pavel agreed after swallowing his mouthful. "But the princess said they'd never find enough river men to handle steam barges if they insisted that they all be able to read."

"So they plan to make more of these?"

"They're already making them at Murom," Ivan confirmed. "We got the first one because we're the best boatmen out of Murom and even the princess had heard about us."

"We're part of a test," Pavel explained. "Us and the steam engine. We were shown how to operate the steam engine and sent out with it to see how it worked. Every time we go by the Dacha they ask us about what has gone wrong and how we fixed it. At first it was really bad, but we got to know the engine pretty quick and we have fewer breakdowns every trip."

Not no breakdowns as it turned out. That trip, on the second day, they had a pipe come loose from the number two cylinder and they had to repair it as best they could with rags and pig fat and continue on. It was during the pig fat repairs that Pavel explained that what they had was a low-pressure steam engine. "See," he explained amiably, "the piston is so big so that the pressure on any little bit of it can be less and you still get the same total power."

Chapter 38

Grantville
September 1633

"So what else is on the list of impossible demands this week?" Brandy asked.

"Bernie, or rather 'one of the brain cases,' wants a computer. The patriarch wants proof of the dangers of lead poisoning and an alternative makeup, because certain women in Moscow are having fits. Also, tons of antibiotics. Apparently they are having trouble with the instructions already sent."

"That's not surprising. Cloramphenicol is doable, but not easy." Brandy said.

Vladimir nodded. "I have one here from the Polish Section demanding a generator 'if such things really exist.' We sent one to Bernie a while back; that must be where they heard about it."

"According to Natasha, they have a group at the Dacha who are hand-making generators and batteries. Why doesn't the Polish Section get one from them?"

"Ah, that explains it." Vladimir grinned. "The Polish Section wants a generator all right, but they don't want to go through the Grantville Section or the Dacha to get it. Russian politics. I'll direct them to the Dacha. Here's one . . . they want the precise location of all gold mines in Russia. I already told them that the best we've found is general areas. So, make unreasonable demands of me, Brandy. I'm getting used to it."

"Hmmm." Brandy considered. "Hmmm. No one has ever suggested that to me before, I don't think. I'll hold the unreasonable demand for now and use it when it's really inconvenient. For now, how about a reasonable demand? Let's take off early? I want you to tell me about Moscow."

Vladimir shrugged. "Why not? The demands will still be here tomorrow."

It was three nights after the car had left for Russia that Vladimir made up his mind. He would ask for permission to marry the girl from the future. He pulled out a pen and began the two letters. One to Natasha informing her that he would be seeking Brandy's hand and asking for her help in persuading the czar. One to the czar asking his permission to marry a foreigner. He would wait to ask Brandy until he had permission because he didn't know what he would do if the permission was not forthcoming.

Having written those letters, Vladimir began to write this week's report to the embassy bureau, attention Grantville Section. First he wrote about Hans Richter and the political implications that were already bouncing around central Germany. That was an event that would change the politics of Europe. He included some of the newspaper coverage and turned to the next item.

> *The steam engines are on order. The younger Herr Schmidt may prove even more suited to the new future that sits before us all than his father. I include fairly extensive notes on the tour of his plant. Herr Adolph Schmidt charged two thousand American dollars for that tour. He said he understands that he can't prevent others from profiting from his work, but he can at least get them to pay for the privilege if he doesn't charge too much. It would have cost more to steal the information, so I guess in this case he didn't charge too much. I think we got our money's worth, anyway.*
>
> *In spite of your efforts in Murom, I don't think the infrastructure is in place to support a steam engine factory in Russia like the one in Magdeburg. Herr Schmidt's factory doesn't exist on its own, but is a part of an industrial*

community. Herr Schmidt gets parts from three different foundries and is looking for more. The machines he uses to finish those parts were produced by other suppliers, mostly from near Grantville. But he is looking into having a tube bender made in Magdeburg. I mention this to emphasize again that what we need more than a steam engine shop or a gun shop—or any other shop—is that community of industry. A place where the parts for machines may be bought and new machines built, not out of raw iron ore but out of parts that are already on a shelf in another shop.

We do need steam engines, yes. Besides the tour and the order for two twelve- and four twenty-horsepower steam engines and the accompanying boilers and condensers, I have included the booklet that Schmidt Steam sells with instructions on how to make the less efficient, but easier to produce, low-pressure steam engines, which it seems every other blacksmith or carpenter in Germany is building. When combined with my notes on the tour it should give our craftsmen a better steam engine.

Rudlinus Nussbaum, who took me through the factory, explained it this way. There are two extreme forms of steam engine. The ones like they make in the factory are high-pressure steam engines that use what he calls super-heated steam to produce pressures of hundreds of pounds per square inch. That's still lower than the pressures and heat in an internal combustion engine, but it's very hot and very high pressure. Rudy, as he asked that I call him, said that a piston escaping from a high-pressure steam engine would go right through me and the door behind me. He then assured me that I was perfectly safe. Grinning like an idiot the whole time.

In any case, high-pressure steam engines require good quality steel and fairly tight tolerances. We have craftsmen that could handle the tolerances, but it would take a long time to build each cylinder.

However, there are also the low-pressure steam engines I sent you the booklet about. In general, a low-pressure steam engine uses steam that is not that much above boiling and works at pressures as low as a few pounds per square inch. Rudy said, "To get useful work out of *that weak a head of steam, they use large cylinders and large pistons. A piston head with a diameter of one foot has a surface of 113 square inches. At a steam pressure of ten pounds per square inch, that comes to a stroke force of 1130 pounds or half a ton. Say half of that is lost to friction and other factors... that's still 565 pounds of work. Just over a horsepower, assuming a foot-long cylinder and a cycle time of a couple of seconds. Actually, with a one-foot diameter, four-foot cylinder and a decent flywheel, at ten psi you should get about two and half horse power once it gets going."*

I take Rudy at his word and I believe you should as well. What this means to us is that a wooden cylinder three feet long and a foot across—essentially a barrel with the proper attachments—can provide the work of three or even four steppe ponies. According to the booklet and the experiments they did at the Smith Steam engine factory: "The low-pressure steam engine can be made mostly of wood and leather with iron reinforcements." That is not true, as I understand it, of the boiler and the pipes. For one thing the highest pressure is always in the boiler not the engine, since the engine is releasing that pressure to get work. The best boiler is steel tubing. But making steel tubing would be prohibitively expensive. We will probably be forced to use a steel pot or even an iron pot and copper tubing to take the steam from the pot to the engine.

Chapter 39

October 1633

"What's taking so long with the car?" Bernie asked. "We asked for it six months ago."

Anya hid a grimace. Bernie was increasingly upset about the delay in sending the car.

"According to his last letter, Vladimir says that he's trying to find an up-timer to come with it," Natasha said. "There are also other requests he has to deal with. To use the up-timerism, he wrote he has more on his plate than just your car. The politics of the CPE are increasingly fractious. The embassy bureau is concerned that the League of Ostend will defeat the CPE and relieve the pressure that is the only thing keeping Poland from invading us. So, more of his time and energy is being used acquiring political information, and he can't take the time to find shipping for your car, Bernie."

"I know that, but we need that engine as an example. The steam engine project is hitting snags all over the place. And I'm pretty sure it's the tolerances."

"Tolerances?"

"How tightly the piston sits in the cylinder," Bernie explained, which wasn't a particularly good explanation, as far as Anya was concerned.

✧   ✧   ✧

"Oh, man." Bernie sounded worried. "Why him?"

Natasha looked up from her latest letter from Brandy Bates and watched Bernie for a moment. His beard had grown in rather nicely, she thought. His clothing, though, was a disaster, and worse, he was influencing the staff at the Dacha and even people in Moscow.

"Why who?"

"Cass Lowry." Bernie waved the letter at her. "He used to be a friend of mine when we played football together. I thought he was so cool—and he is clever. He was always coming up with stunts to pull. The thing is..." Bernie paused and looked at Natasha, then went on. "He always had...I guess you'd call it a sense of entitlement. His stunts usually had a nasty edge to them, getting back at someone who had dissed him. Ah...shown a lack of respect for him. He was going to go to college on a football scholarship. Studying was a waste of time.

"I was the same way, I guess. Everything that happened to us was someone else's fault. I was right with him all through high school. Then, after his football scholarship fell through, Cass blamed me for keeping him from studying." Bernie looked over at Natasha and gave a shrug. "There may have been some truth to it but other guys on the team did study and went on to college. Somewhere in there, I got over myself and started to grow up. But from the letter, it doesn't sound like Cass ever did. Now he's blaming everything on the down-timers and Mike Stearns." Bernie waved the letter. "That's what this letter comes down to. I hope no one ever reads this, Natasha. Because it's pretty rude."

Natasha knew that quite well. It took some effort to control her expression. Cass Lowry's comments about "krauts," "russkies" and "I guess you're living in the armpit of the universe" had not gone unnoticed. Not in the least. "Brandy says it is because he was the only person who knew cars well enough who was willing to make the trip. Vladimir wanted, very much, to have someone who knew cars travel with your 'Precious.'"

"My what?"

Natasha looked at Brandy's letter again. "Brandy says 'tell Bernie that Cass is traveling with Precious because Cass is the only guy we could find who wasn't doing something else.'"

Bernie's face was a study. Part outrage, part pout. "The car is not named Precious. Are you sure she didn't say 'your precious car' or something?"

Natasha shook her head. "No. It even has the capital P. I assumed it was the name for it. At any rate, your Cass will be arriving in a month or so. We should probably arrange for you to meet him. He, according to Brandy, wants to visit us for a while. And you never know, he might help."

Bernie slumped into a chair. "I doubt it. Don't get me wrong. Cass is smart, smarter than me, I always thought. It's just . . . I don't know . . . he has a knack for screwing things up. You're probably not going to care for him one little bit. Neither will Boris or Filip." Bernie shook his head in disgust. "Why did Brandy have to send him?"

Brandy had not sent him, Vladimir had. He had been fully aware of Cass' drawbacks and had stressed the need to put up with them while he was milked for information, especially on weapons and tactics used by the up-timers. "Mr. Lowry," Vladimir had written, "is not a person we would want in our home. But he does have knowledge that could be useful to Russia. Try to keep anyone from killing him for the insults he will surely give." Natasha had wondered if Bernie's view would agree with Vladimir's. While there were subtle differences, for the most part it did.

Chapter 40

On the road to the Swedish Border
November 1633

Bernie shivered. Theatrically, Natasha thought. She exchanged an amused glance with Anya. Anya rolled her eyes and Natasha had to struggle not to giggle.

Oblivious to the byplay, Bernie went on, "Well, at least it's not a horse. It may be colder than a witch's . . . ah, never mind. It may be really cold, but at least we aren't riding horses."

"Indeed, we aren't." Natasha smiled. "And you must admit that it's a very nice sleigh, Bernie, very nice."

And it was, in fact, a very nice sleigh. It had special springs for the skis. Outside it was bitterly cold and the snow was still pretty deep, but the streamlined sleigh had double-walled construction and a lacquer polish job that acted as sealant, as well as making the whole thing shiny. It was relatively warm inside, even if it did look a bit peculiar. The sleigh needed high road clearance because even the improved roads weren't exactly highways in the up-timer sense of the word. They were reasonably well-graded dirt roads with a bit of crushed rock spread over them. Plus, at the moment, a layer of snow.

Only a relatively small part of the design for the coach was from up-timer information. More of it came from a Russian coach maker who had joined the team after the czar had seen some up-time car magazines. Czar Mikhail had liked the idea of cars and smooth rides. He'd decided that if he couldn't have an engine, he at least wanted a streamlined design and shock absorbers.

The coach maker, Ivan Egorovich Shirshov, had taken note of that desire. The czar had seen to that. Ivan Egorovich had arrived at the Dacha with a medium-sized chip on his shoulder over the whole mess. Then he talked to Bernie and found that Bernie agreed with him. But it was no more up to Bernie than it was to him. They had gone over Bernie's car magazines, then over sleigh designs and coach designs, trying to figure out what they could do. Ivan Egorovich now had a permanent dent in his forehead from pounding it against the wall in frustration. And Czar Mikhail had a new coach. So did Bernie.

Bernie grabbed the edge of the seat. "Hang on. We're about to hit another rutted bit. And I still can't figure out why you wanted to come on this trip, ladies. You're probably going to get frostbite on your noses."

"The 'advance team,' as you call it, has made arrangements, Bernie. We will be comfortable. And I like traveling. Vladimir and I did quite a bit of it, you know, back when our father was alive."

Aunt Sofia grinned widely. "The weather, it is not so bad."

Bernie shuddered. If it hadn't been for the long johns, he'd have had frozen b...ah...parts by now.

The trip to the Swedish border had several purposes. One was to investigate the road work. Road work had been continuing apace since a few months or so after Bernie's arrival. Since he had worked on the road gangs around Grantville and had a mechanical turn of mind, he had a good knowledge of the horse-drawn grader and other horse-drawn road improvement equipment. The equipment he had helped design for Russia had been used extensively for more than a year now and was showing real effect. The czar's highways mostly went south and east, roughly toward China. One, however, went north and west toward the coast of the Baltic Sea.

That was the highway they were traveling. It was a fairly slow trip. They stopped occasionally to examine the road work. Most important to Bernie, though, was that the trip's second purpose was to pick up his car. It had been shipped from Grantville by way of the Baltic Sea to the Swedish-owned coast.

Russia had lost this particular bit of land to Sweden a couple of decades before. Thankfully, relations between the two nations had greatly improved in the ensuing years. This was mostly because both Sweden and Russia disliked Poland more than they disliked each other. But, also, Czar Mikhail Fedorovich Romanov was honestly impressed with the charismatic Swedish monarch.

Natasha had decided to join the party and she brought Sofia and Anya, so there were more women than Bernie thought there'd be. The amount of advance planning needed to travel just a couple of days was mind boggling to Bernie. And this trip would take at least a month, new coach or not.

"I can't believe it." Bernie knew his voice was harsh and his nose bright red from chapping. He was also angry. "I can't believe it took five freaking weeks to get here and the ship still hasn't made it." Which wasn't what he'd started to say but was more politic. He stomped around the room for a bit, working off some excess energy and tying not to say what he wanted to say.

"Now, Bernie." Vladislav Vasl'yevich Vinnikov, Natasha's captain of guards, tried to soothe him. "It was a long way, a hard trip at this time of year. I would imagine that it was even worse on the sea. Your friend will be here. You must just be patient."

"Why can't we just go to the coast to meet him?" Bernie asked, in spite of his better judgment. The truth was Bernie was pretty sure he knew why. He wasn't going to be allowed to leave Russia. Not for the foreseeable future, anyway. They had their up-timer and weren't going to chance losing him. That had become obvious once they got to the Russian/Swedish border and stopped. He threw his hands in the air.

Bernie knew Vladislav Vasl'yevich wasn't about to answer his question directly. It wouldn't be the correct thing to do.

"The villages in the area, Bernie. We should look at the villages. The soil is a bit different, perhaps. You could take notes; it would help with the development of the plows and reapers, I'm sure."

Bernie brightened a bit, not much. "Well, it's something to do anyway. Sure, we'll go take a look."

Natasha, who had been quiet for a few moments, added, "As well, Pavel Andreyevich would like you to design your plumbing for his home. He is most interested in it. And you are invited to utilize his sauna, if you wish."

Bernie grinned. The word Natasha had used was *banya*. The Russian multi-leveled sauna was certainly a way to get warm. Overly warm, if the truth were known. Bernie hadn't quite been able to make it to the third level back at the Dacha, not yet. Nor had he quite had the guts to roll around in the snow afterwards, although he had progressed to dumping buckets of not-quite-cold water on himself. The process also involved a massage with leafy twigs that was called *venek*, that had been sort of a revelation. Bernie didn't know of the reports up-time that *venek* worked better than Viagra, but if he had he would have agreed with them.

"Sounds like a plan." Bernie sniffed. Cold always made his nose run. "After four hundred miles in this kind of freaking cold, a sauna sounds really good." *And as pissed and, tell the truth, Bernie,* he thought, *scared as you are. Now is not the time to make an issue of it.*

Natasha smiled as Bernie left the room. "That might have been more difficult."

Vladislav Vasl'yevich shook his head. "He knows. He just doesn't want the confrontation any more than we do. I wonder what delayed the ship."

They had planned not to reach the border till after the car was already there, but didn't want it waiting too long. Natasha had spent a worried week thinking up things to keep Bernie occupied. As yet, Russia had been able to recruit a total of one up-timer. That up-timer was Bernie Zeppi. Cass Lowry was a temporary hire.

Czar Mikhail and Patriarch Filaret were quite insistent that Bernie not leave Russian territory. At the same time, Mikhail Romanov expressed a personal desire that Bernie not be made to feel abused or trapped. Natasha was stuck with the job of keeping Bernie from leaving Russia while keeping him from realizing that he couldn't. A task which, if Vladislav was correct, she had already failed at.

It was important that Bernie remain willing to stay in Russia. Bernie was in regular correspondence with Brandy Bates and his own family in Grantville. A sudden end to those letters would be reported to the government of the USE, most likely. Russia, decidedly, didn't want to annoy the USE at the moment.

Chapter 41

"What the hell took so long, Cass?" Bernie asked.

Cass Lowry glared at him from beneath the hood of his camouflage-fabric parka. "Everything you can think of, dude. Everything. Hail. Freezing rain. A goddamn storm at sea. So don't gripe at me. I got the damn thing here, didn't I? Not to mention the drums. And let me tell you, those were a ring-tailed son of a bitch, they really were. And expensive! You'd never believe what Gorchakov had to pay for those fifty-five gallon drums, not to mention what's in them."

Bernie decided yelling at Cass wouldn't help, so he grinned. "You're right. I'm happier than you know to have fifty-five gallons of gas, I promise you. And motor oil. That's a bonus I didn't expect."

Cass smirked. "I told Brandy. I told her and that Vladimir the same thing. 'It's not going to do any good if you just send the car,' I said. 'You've got to send some gas and oil.' It cost Vladimir a bundle, Bernie. But he did it. And there's a whole pile of boxes in the wagons, too. Everything anybody could think of to send you is in a box or wrapped up in the trunk of the car. Brandy hit every garage sale and junk sale she could to find stuff to send you. And books—you'll never believe the books. Piles of them."

"Great. We need every one we can find. Come on. Let's go get the introductions over with. Things are kind of formal around here, Cass. You need to watch your step. Just follow my lead and things will probably be okay."

"Natalia Petrovna Gorchakov, may I introduce Cass Lowry. Cass, this is Vladimir's sister, Natalia Petrovna. And this is her aunt, Madame Sofia Gorchakov. And this is Anya, our accountant."

Bernie thought he'd done a credible job on the introduction until Cass opened his big mouth.

"If you're Vladimir's sister, why isn't your name Natasha? That's what Brandy said, Natasha."

Bernie sort of kicked Cass in the ankle and made a face at him. "I'll explain later," he murmured. "Just say hello—and be polite, will you?"

Cass glared a bit, but nodded. "Ma'am, I'm pleased to meet you. I did bring a load of letters for you. They're from your brother and Brandy. And there are some presents, too. They're in one of the boxes."

Natasha nodded graciously. "My thanks. We appreciate your trouble and invite you to share our hospitality at the Dacha for a while. Vladimir Petrovich was pleased that you accepted his commission."

"Yeah, well, I stung him pretty good on the fee." Cass snickered.

Bernie knew there was going to be trouble sooner or latter. Cass was acting like he was still up-time and still a football star. "Natalia Petrovna, we will take our leave of you for the moment," Bernie said. "My friend and I need to have a talk. If you will excuse us?"

Natasha inclined her head. "Certainly, Bernie. Perhaps we shall see you and Cass at dinner?" Bernie suppressed a groan. Cass, Natasha, dinner...what was wrong with that combination? Bernie didn't want to think about it.

Dinner was tense, to say the least. The Russians were showing restraint and Cass needed to be in restraints. He was behaving like a boor, to the point where Bernie was seriously considering knocking him out. Unfortunately, most of the Russians present understood quite a bit of English. Natasha had an aptitude for language and was getting fairly close to fluency.

To make things still worse, it turned out that Cass had an apti-tude for language also. Bernie hadn't expected that at all. He was certain that if she'd been present, their former Spanish language teacher in high school, Guadelupe DiCastro, would have been struck dumb with astonishment. Bernie had gotten a B-minus in her class but Cass had almost flunked it completely.

Cass wasn't actually stupid, though, although he could sure put on a good imitation. When he decided to learn something and applied himself, he could usually manage it pretty well. So, on the long trip here he'd apparently learned some Russian. Not enough to really get by, but enough to be able to insult people in two languages instead of just one.

It was worse for Anya, Bernie was pretty sure, because this was her first time at the nobility's table. Her friendship with Natasha was still fairly new, after all.

"Yeah," Cass was saying, "winding up back here before the world got civilized was sort of hard. It was a boon to the here-and-now, but God was playing a nasty trick on us up-timers. Wars all over the damn place, the food sucks, and there's all this religious bullshit, too. Every time you turn around someone is in your face about religion. When the Ring of Fire made it clear that none of your religions had a clue what God had in mind."

Father Kiril was having dinner with them. Kiril was a nice guy. Luckily, he spoke almost no English at all so he couldn't follow what Cass was saying,

Natasha could, however. Her face was cold as she regarded Cass. "Indeed. And you did? Have a clue, I mean. Didn't you say that back up-time you could have avoided all the difficulty by simply moving? Could you not?"

"No. The big guy didn't tell us either, but then if he had you would have gotten a ghost town."

Cass managed to leer and look superior at the same time, and Bernie was more and more sure he was going to have to hit him. The problem was that what Cass was saying was close enough to what a lot of up-timers, and more than a few down-timers, believed to hurt. Certainly if Bernie's family had known the Ring of Fire was coming, they would have gotten his mom out of the Ring. Bernie would probably have opted to stay in the twentieth century, given the choice. He hadn't joined the Peace Corps, had he? It was also true that the presence of the up-timers had turned out to be of considerable benefit to the down-timers, at least the large majority of those affected, one way or the other. Looked at one way it looked like God had drafted the up-timers to rescue the seventeenth century from itself. That the up-timers were God's chosen representatives; whether they wanted to be chosen or not.

Then Cass laughed raucously and snorted beer up his nose.

When all the spewing and coughing was finally over, Bernie looked at Cass. He was pretty drunk. "I think I've had enough, Cass. I'm going to crash. You ready?"

Cass was a little bleary from the vodka he had consumed, but wasn't ready for sleep, apparently. "No, dude. I don't think so. You go on. I'll just keep this lady company." He was eyeballing Anya in a way that Bernie didn't like at all.

Natasha's already cold face froze. Anya looked scared. Bernie could see it happening.

"I, myself," Natasha said, "am quite tired. You gentlemen feel free to enjoy...whatever it is that you enjoy. Until the morning, then. Come along, Anya, Aunt Sofia." Natasha rose and swept from the room, casting a telling glance over her shoulder. Aunt Sofia's glance was even more telling.

Bernie got the message. Cass had to learn to behave properly.

"That one will get himself killed," Vladislav Vasl'yevich murmured. "Soon, I expect."

"Not by us, though, and preferably not in Russia. Let some other nation do the world the service." Natasha agreed with his assessment. Cass Lowry was a barbarian. "I know he's already said things that would be reason for a duel. Certainly most would already have been punished for those remarks. But the czar will want to meet him, just as he met Bernie, and Russia needs what he knows. Vladislav Vasl'yevich, we need to avoid any incident. You'll have to restrain yourself and your men."

"At least Bernie did not intentionally insult. This one, though..." Vladislav shook his head. "He is a different type of man. He thinks himself a boyar's son, protected by his father's position. He seems to think that everyone in Russia is a peasant."

Cass was a bit drunk. Not much, just enough to take the edge off. He was wondering what the fuck was Bernie's problem. After all, Bernie got the fancy job here in Russia, with all the servants and lots of money. What did Bernie have to complain about? Had the idiot gone native? Could have happened, he figured. Bernie had been all alone with a bunch of down-time barbs for over a frigging year. "What is your problem, man? They're just down-timers. They need us, we don't need them. Ain't you figured that out yet? Hell, even up-time kids are getting rich."

"So what are you doing here, Cass? Since you're so rich, I mean?"

Cass flushed. "Cheap shot, man. The breaks haven't been going my way. It's Stearns' fault. Treating the down-timers like they're real Americans and selling us out to the Swedes like he done."

"Cass, we're not in high school anymore." Bernie stared at him intently. "Some breaks are coming your way, sure enough. Broken arms, broken legs and a busted head. One of the ladies you were hitting on is a frigging *knyazhna*, Cass. That's Russian for princess. Don't think for a minute that her guards won't cut off your dick and feed it and the rest of you to the pigs."

"What the hell is your problem, Bernie boy? Afraid of the competition?" Cass pulled his new Peacemaker and pointed it casually in Bernie's direction. He liked the gun and how it made him feel strong and dangerous. It was modeled loosely on the Colt Peacemaker but made in a down-time gun shop. "Anyone wants to cut me, they had better bring a whole lot more firepower than these candy-asses have."

Bernie froze.

At first Cass thought he had made his point, but Bernie wasn't really looking scared. Mostly he was looking pissed off.

It occurred to Cass that pointing a loaded gun at Bernie might be pushing it a bit. He really hadn't meant to piss Bernie off, not till he got the lay of the land, anyway. Especially, he hadn't meant to let Bernie-boy know that he was competition.

"Hey man, it's no big deal," he said, putting away the gun. "If you got dibs on her, I'll back off."

Cass knew he was smarter than Bernie. He hadn't done well in school, but that was because school just bored him. Besides, he was a football star. He didn't need to bust his hump in English class. He knew he could pick up what Bernie was doing pretty quick. He could probably push Bernie out, if he wanted to. But he wasn't going to put up with much crap from the dumb-ass down-timers. Not him. Not ever.

Chapter 42

Cass winced at the bright sunshine when he walked out the door three mornings later. "Oh, man, that hurts."

"Think you might want to be a little more careful with the booze?" Bernie's smirk was irritating. "Sun shining off snow can really dazzle you, but the biggest part of your problem is your hangover. Three days and three hangovers. No wonder it hurts."

"Maybe," Cass muttered. Drinking was about the only thing he was enjoying. Well, that and the girls. Every place they stayed had servant girls. Even staying away from Bernie's boss—and wasn't it a laugh that a girl was the boss in Russia—wasn't hard, not when you had all those other girls around.

Bernie put on his heavy coat. "You ready? Let's get a move on. This trip is taking forever. I wish the car was running, I really do. Steering and braking with no power while being towed behind a team of horses is a real pain."

"What did you expect? The thing sat on blocks for years, man." Cass snorted. "Let's go. Get to this Dacha place and see if you can get it running."

Hours in the carriage with only a couple of troops who didn't speak English was a real bore. But Cass didn't want to ride on one of the carts out in the open and especially didn't want to be on horseback. Too cold for that, by half. It was the usual order today. Out ahead of everyone, a double column of ten guards on

horseback spread out. Then came the rolling stock. First came the
fancy-ass sleigh that the women were in. Cass hated to admit it,
but it was actually kind of neat. Boxy, but still sort of streamlined
and buffed to a high gloss. Then Bernie was freezing his ass off
in that old junker of his. Cass was behind Bernie's car in his
carriage. Then all the carts with all the stuff the Gorchakov dude
had sent. At the end of the line there were six more guards. Plus
guards in some of the rolling stock.

Bernie patted the dash. "Oh, yeah. Once I get it running it will
be able to do thirty miles an hour at least. Even on these roads
and pulling a bunch of stuff."

Vladislav Vasl'yevich was riding beside Bernie's car just then.
Partly because he was actually interested in how it worked and
could see lots of military applications for these motorized vehicles.
Mostly, though, over the course of a day's travel, he would spend
time all along the column. He checked everything, several times a
day, to make sure everything was working and looked for trouble
before it happened.

Vladislav had seen and reported on hundreds of military
applications in the time that Bernie had been at the Dacha. He
hadn't exactly been ignored. The czar now had a .30-06. It was
handmade with gold engraving, but there was a very limited
supply of bullets. There were people making new guns, flintlocks,
but only in small numbers, as experiments. There were the war
games in the Kremlin. But in Vladislav's opinion the military had
been slow to consider the potential usefulness of the up-timers'
innovations in weapons and tactics.

"I wouldn't mind seeing that . . ." Vladislav stopped at the shout
from the front of the column and shots ringing out. "Bandits! To
the *knyazhna*!" He looked around to assess the situation.

The road here curved from southeast to east. The bandits had
either been spotted by the guards out in front or had sortied too
early. Probably spotted—that shout had been Petr Kadian's. It was
a large party, it must be. This many trained solders wouldn't be
easy to overcome. From the noise, there were probably around
thirty or forty bandits. Most were hitting the front of the column,
and the outriders on the north side, which was the inside of the
curve. That meant that Vladislav's men were more spread out
than the bandits were and the bandits could react a little faster.

Vladislav noted in passing that Bernie was trying to get his .30-06 out of the back seat of the car. That could help, depending on how Bernie held up in combat.

Surprisingly, the other outlander, Cass, was out of his carriage and running toward Bernie's car. "Get down!" Vladislav shouted. "Get down before you get shot!"

What was the man doing? Vladislav wondered. He was playing with the back of Bernie's car. The back of the car opened like a great mouth, hiding Cass from Vladislav's view.

There hadn't been bandits in this area for years. It was too well patrolled. Not out of fear of bandits, but to provide warning of an attack by Poland. Vladislav waved to the embassy bureau troops who were bringing up the rear. "To the *knyazhna*! Don't worry about the carts, protect Natalia Petrovna and Bernie!" They could probably replace the stuff in the carts if they had to, but they had to protect the princess and Bernie. Vladislav shot one of the bandits and dropped the pistol. He drew the second. He always carried one in each boot and two in his belt.

"*Yeeeehaaaw!*"

Vladislav looked around, startled by the scream. Cass had reappeared from the back of Bernie's car and was carrying a long gun of some sort. He was running at the woods on the north side of the road, screaming like a banshee. *Clickety boom*, came the noise. And again. *Clicktey boom. Clicktey boom.* Two bandits were down, one with most of his head blown away. Vladislav watched as Cass cut to the right. *Clickety boom.* Cut left. *Clickety boom.* Cass ran in some sort of wild pattern that the attackers couldn't follow. Neither could Vladislav.

Crack. A different noise sounded. One of the bandits fell from a horse. Since most of the bandits had been on foot, Vladislav figured he was probably their leader. They should have been paying attention to Bernie instead of Cass, who stood behind his car taking well-aimed shots at the attackers. He was propped up on the front of it, rather. Vladislav could see his head and shoulders. The bandits would be lucky to see his head, or the .30-06 that was killing them. It would take a special miracle to actually hit a target that small.

Bernie had frozen for a moment, when the attack began, immobilized by another flashback to the battle of the Crapper. But as he usually did, he managed to shake it off quickly. Store it away, rather; he never did really shake off those memories.

A familiar detachment came over him. He reached over the back seat, got his rifle, opened the glove compartment and took out a box of ammo. Then he got out of the car and took position using the hood as a firing stand.

Immediately, he spotted a man on horseback and shot him out of the saddle. Then he looked for Cass. The idiot had managed to take out at least two attackers because they'd been completely caught off guard by his broken field charge and weren't accustomed to the rate of fire of an up-time pump-action shotgun. But they were fighting men and they were all around him. Bernie could see a bandit already taking aim at Cass from the side.

Bernie took him down. One shot. All he needed. He wasn't in the league of someone like Julie Sims when it came to sheer marksmanship but he was very steady in a fight. At this close range and with a modern rifle, that was plenty good enough.

Lowry gunned down another bandit at point blank range. But for the first time one of his opponents fired back before he fell. He missed because Lowry's rush unsettled him, but they wouldn't all miss.

There was another bandit just beyond Cass, aiming at him. Bernie took him down. A bandit next to him. He went down too.

Another flashback paralyzed Bernie for an instant. Furiously, he drove it under. But he'd been out of it long enough for Cass to shoot down another bandit—and three bandits to fire at him.

Blind luck—Cass lost his footing and fell. The bullets passed harmlessly over him. He hadn't done that intentionally, though. In fact, it was obvious he hadn't even seen the three men to his left.

Bernie shot one of them. The other two immediately ducked for cover. Bernie fired two more shots to keep them down, giving Lowry a chance to get away. Then he started reloading the rifle.

Vladislav looked around again. The situation wasn't as bad as it had at first appeared. The attackers had been spotted before most of the column was in the trap. Bernie had apparently gotten their leader, who'd been trying to shift his troops. And Cass, the madman, had spread panic in their ranks—which was made all the worse by Bernie's deadly covering fire.

Meanwhile, Vladislav's men were pushing against their northwestern flank and pinning most of them away from the body of the column. Vladislav wanted to charge the bandits; to use the loss of their leader and the panic. A charge now, even with the few men he had, would break them and send them running. If these were all there were. But, what if there was another group? His job was to protect the *knyazhna* and Bernie, not to leave them unprotected while he went on a boar hunt.

The American madman was now out of position. Hopefully, he was out of ammunition as well and would choose to stay down. Cass was well into the trees. Vladislav knew he was going to lose men he couldn't afford if he rescued the maniac. Yet keeping the up-timers alive was vital. While he was considering his options, there was another new sound.

Bernie was firing again, having apparently reloaded. It was a heavy covering fire, not aimed at anyone in particular—the bandits in that area were all cowering from him now—but just intended to protect Lowry.

That should do, Vladimir thought. And now he could see that the bandits were falling back.

"Hold!" Vladislav shouted. "Don't chase them. Hold your positions." Vladislav hated to do it, but their job was to protect, not chase. "Back!" he shouted. "Back!"

Lying under some bushes, Cass let the adrenaline leak away from his system. He'd been an avid hunter since he was ten and a halfback all though high school. Since the Ring of Fire, he had hunted wild boar a lot. Moving fast, moving through woods, and shooting were all things he did quite well. Being shot at in return was a lot less fun.

He reloaded the shotgun, as much for something to do with his hands as anything else. His hands were shaking a bit.

Bernie's marksmanship had been too good. The man whom Vladimir thought was the commander of the bandits couldn't be questioned because he was dead. Bernie's shot had gone into his chest just above the chest bone, shredding the aorta and cutting the spine—as deadly a shot as could be made. He must have been killed almost instantly.

The attackers who had been captured were run-of-the-mill

bandits, collected for this. They knew very little. Just that they had been hired and paid unusually well to attack this particular group. They were to kill everyone, take as much as they could carry and burn the rest. His equipage and clothing suggested that the commander might be Polish, but anyone could have hired him. The troops were spending quite a bit of time talking about Cass' "broken-field running," as Bernie called it. It made up some for the things he had been saying since he arrived. If he could learn manners, he could be an asset.

"Vas'ka Kadnitsa will probably recover." Bernie washed his hands. "But I wish we had a real doctor." He didn't specify what he meant by a real doctor. Another example of Bernie learning manners. By now, even the doctors at the Dacha acknowledged that they needed to go study with the up-timer doctors in Grantville. Bernie knew it, Natasha knew it, Vladislav knew it. There was no reason to harp on it.

"I have sent a man to the nearest village to report and bring more troops," Vladislav reported. "About all we know is that it wasn't a random attack. It could have been the Poles trying to deny us access to up-timer knowledge. That will be what most people will assume. On the other hand, it could well have been a faction in the court, perhaps someone who opposes the income tax or the constitution."

Vladislav paused a moment, then his curiosity overcame him. "Bernie, what was that long gun Cass used?"

"A pump-action shotgun." Bernie grinned, albeit mirthlessly. As though he knew that more information would be requested, he continued. "It's a smooth bore weapon that can fire a solid shot or a bunch of smaller pellets every time it's fired. Cass was apparently using buckshot. It spreads, so you don't need to be all that accurate and is heavy enough to take a man down at close range."

A scout rode up. He and Vladislav conferred for a moment. "We will camp a mile or so up the road. There is a good spot that can be made quite defensible. I don't want to do any more traveling than we have to, not before we are reinforced."

Bernie and Natasha nodded. He was the captain and knew what he was doing.

Chapter 43

Dinner had been served outside and Natasha, Anya and Sofia had gone to their tent. Cass Lowry remained at the table, drinking vodka. The American had been drinking all afternoon. Vladislav kept a close eye on him. Lowry was a dangerous man—savage in a fight, and reckless and careless even when sober. He was also apparently a drunkard, judging from the relentless way he'd been working on the vodka.

It was a volatile combination. The camp was defensible, which left the *nyekulturny* outlander as Vladislav's major worry. Lowry hadn't let loose of the shotgun all day and had been passing out insults ever since the battle. After-combat jitters, perhaps. Trying to convince everyone, especially himself, that he wasn't afraid. Vladislav had seen the reaction before. Then Cass had gotten quiet. Vladislav expected trouble. Soon.

The madman stood up and began to walk toward Natasha's tent. What were his exact intentions? He was probably too drunk to know himself, beyond a raw desire to enter a tent that held two very attractive young women.

Bernie stepped in front of him and said something. Vladislav didn't quite understand the words he spoke, since his English was still poor. But it was obvious he was trying to deflect his fellow American.

Lowry shoved Bernie away and said something Vladislav also

didn't understand. It was obviously rude; viciously so, Vladislav thought.

More so than Bernie had expected. That was also obvious. Bernie had the disadvantage of being a sane and civilized man dealing with someone beyond those boundaries. The uncultured outlander's shove had pushed him back and his foot slipped on some rocks.

Vladislav stepped in. The shotgun had to go. He grabbed it from Cass and tossed it to one of his men, keeping the barrel pointed to the sky. Fighting man or not, valuable outlander or not, this one needed a lesson in manners. He hit Cass in the gut. Hard. Then in the face.

Vladislav had been restraining both himself and his men with some difficulty. He had orders to treat the new American carefully. He actually did respect the courage of the man in combat, though no more than he respected Bernie's cool-headed shooting or his own men's courage and discipline. But now that Lowry was posing a clear threat to the *knyazhna*, he had crossed the lines.

Lowry had gone down at the second blow but he was getting back up. He went for the pistol holstered at his side and Vladislav kicked him in the head. The American boor went down again.

"I've been protecting *Knyazhna* Natasha since she was a child, little man." The outlander might not have been little physically, but he had a little soul. "I can live with your uncultured ways if I have to..."

Vladislav pulled Cass up from the ground, took the pistol out of the holster and set it on the table. Behind him, he heard Bernie talking to the guards. "Hey, guys, I can wait my turn, but at least let me watch."

His Russian had gotten quite good, idiomatic and almost fluent. Vladislav chuckled. Some of the guards must have thought Bernie was coming to the outlander's defense.

Still holding Cass by his collar, Vladislav said, "I can put up with your arrogance but you won't lay a hand on her. Not if you want to keep that hand." Vladislav hit him again.

Cass flew into the table and made quite a racket going down this time. Then Natasha appeared.

"What are you doing, Vladislav?" The noise had brought her from the tent. She was shouting. "And why are your men holding Bernie? Neither of these men is to be harmed. You know that. Let them go."

Vladislav let go of the outlander, who promptly fell on the ground, holding his guts, trying not to heave. The other guards let Bernie pass.

Bernie took a few steps and bowed graciously to Vladislav. "I didn't really mind waiting, Vladislav Vasl'yevich, but you might have left a bit more for me. Don't worry about it, Natasha. Every man here has wanted to give Cass a lesson in manners from the moment he arrived. He's earned this, in more ways than you know."

Bernie picked Cass up and leaned him against the handy cart, propping him carefully. Cass' knees buckled and he went down again. "I do think you could have left me some, Vladislav. Considering it was me he pushed."

"I apologize, Bernie Janovich." Vladislav bowed precisely. "But there was very little to it. I thought there would be more. Perhaps tomorrow." Cass groaned.

Natasha sniffed loudly and retreated to her tent. "Men!" She stopped at the entrance. "It has been a busy time and I do not read well in a sleigh. I have not had time to read any but the most essential messages from Grantville. We finally have an evening not filled with politics and you children decide to throw a brawl. Keep the noise down. I don't wish to be disturbed again tonight."

Fifteen minutes later Bernie and Vladislav had arranged the semiconscious Cass on one of the carts. They were about to walk back to the fire when Natasha came storming out of the tent again. There was a letter in her hand.

"You fool!" she shouted at Cass. "Why didn't you tell me that my brother wishes to marry Brandy Bates?" Then she hit him.

"Darn it!" Bernie complained, laughing. "I never get a turn."

Of that charge, at least, Cass was innocent. He hadn't known. He had left Grantville before Vladimir had sent the letter and it had caught up en route.

Chapter 44

December 1633

"Vladimir sent a whole packet of letters with your car, Bernie, and even more of them with Cass," Natasha said. "There's more about the steam engines." She handed Filip the booklet, since he spoke better German than Bernie.

Filip started reading the booklet and less than a page in began to ask Bernie to define some of the terms. They went over the directions and the calculations in the booklet and called in a few more of their experts, and started working up a modified design for the steam barge engines. These new ones would have slightly tighter tolerances, more wood, less leather and be more powerful for their size. They would still, in essence, be low-pressure steam engines, but with this new information they felt they could push the envelope a little bit.

"What are we going to do about Cass?" Natasha asked Bernie two days after that meeting. "He managed, just barely, to be polite to the czar. Other than that, he has offended everyone who has met him."

Bernie grinned. "Give him to the military. Specifically to the *Streltzi* bureau." The Russia military was a weird mix of feudal duty and bureaucratic confusion. The bureaucratic nobility included the officers in time of war. They were the officer corps and the cavalry. The *Streltzi* were the infantry in time of war and the city guards in time of peace. One of the things that the *Streltzi* had picked up from Bernie was fingerprinting. By now most of the criminals in Moscow had had their fingerprints taken or paid considerable bribes to avoid it. The *Streltzi* hadn't picked up on the notion of civil rights, though Bernie had offered it up. In the last few years, mercenary companies hired from the west had been added to the mix. The mercenaries who had a different way of fighting weren't mixing in too well. "We get more requests from them than anyone else. Besides, it might do Cass some good to be surrounded by cops for a while."

Natasha was nodding. Bernie had been urgently called to various military bureaus over the last few months. Especially the *Streltzi* bureaus. The *Streltzi* preferred to fight behind walls, city walls. When they could not fight defensively behind the walls of a city they wanted to fight behind walking walls. The "stand and take it" philosophy of the western mercenary infantry was not in their traditions. They had no objection to dishing it out and did not lack courage, but standing in the open and taking it just seemed stupid. "Do you think it will work?"

Bernie sighed "Maybe, but I doubt it. But worst case, it gets him out of our hair and gets the military bureaus off my back."

"So the Gun Shop will have their own up-timer." Natasha laughed out loud. "Who knows? Maybe General Shein can handle him."

"I don't care if he wants to fuck the czarina," Mikhail Borisovich Shein said. "We have our own up-timer now, and he's one who can fight."

His aide took it in stride. General Shein was a volatile man by nature. The calculation hidden by the volatility was harder to see; most people never did. "What should we do with him, sir?"

"We do what Princess Natalia suggested. Assign him to the Gun Shop with Korisov." The general snorted. "And keep him away from anyone important. Question him extensively, but not harshly. If that doesn't work, we can use stronger measures. From what I understand, the main reason we got him is that he managed to miss out on, or fail at, the opportunities in Grantville. No one will miss him much."

The aide made a note and went on to the next item on the

agenda. "The *Streltzi* are arguing with the outlander solders about their walking walls again." The aide was a bureaucratic noble and therefore an officer in the Russian army. He didn't think all that well of the foreign mercenary companies or the *Streltzi*—who, when not called to active service, made up the merchant class in Russia.

The general gave him a cold look. Mikhail Borisovich Shein had commanded a force made up mostly of *Streltzi* at Smolensk during the last war with Poland. They had held out for twenty months against a force ten times their size. Whatever the traditional animosity between the two classes, General Shein didn't share it. At the same time, he was fully conversant with the Russian army's need to modernize. Slowly, he began to smile. "But what is 'modernize' in a world where we have people from the future? Find me two men, Georgi Ivanov. One outlander officer and a *Streltzi*. Send them to the Gun Shop. Put them in a room with the up-timer and let them argue about it. Even Korisov might have some thoughts on the matter."

Part Four

The year 1634

Chapter 45

January 1634

After some initial sparring, Cass and Andrei got along quite well. Each was convinced that he was the only person that mattered and each held the other in none-too-veiled contempt, but they were useful to each other and knew it. Andrei made sure Cass had access to a plentiful supply of young girls, vodka, hunting, and other sport. In return, Cass provided Andrei with a good, and in a way more up-to-date, up-timer knowledge base.

Cass really was bright and his Russian was improving rapidly. He had lived in Grantville for a year and more after the Ring of Fire. A lot of tricks and workarounds had been developed in that time, so Cass was quite a bit more familiar with the how-to of building a modern tech base than most up-timers had been before the Ring of Fire. For instance:

"What you need is a drop forge, Andy," Cass said a few weeks after he had arrived at the Gun Shop. "Instead of building AK3's by hand."

"A drop forge?" Andrei was none too fond of being addressed as "Andy," but it wasn't worth it to fight through his current hangover.

"Yep. Take a big-ass weight. Lift it up about ten feet, then drop it. Force is mass times velocity, and by the time it hits, it has some velocity to multiply the big-ass weight."

"And how do you lift the big weight?"

"It doesn't matter. Look, a couple of peasants turning a crank will get the job done. Sure, a steam cylinder would do it faster and more efficiently, but you want to wait for those prigs at the Dacha to get around to providing you a steam ram?"

That was a point. Andrei was increasingly upset by the way the Dacha was being corrupted by western notions. So he nodded and they worked on the design of the drop forge. A very hot piece of iron would be placed in the bottom form. Then the weighted top form would be dropped. After which four slaves would crank the weighted top form back up and the part would be removed.

It would take four big, strong, men almost ten minutes to crank the "hammer" up to the top of its arch. During which time, another dollop of iron would be heated white hot. Wham! Another part.

Not a completed part. The chambers had to be finished using a boring machine, also human-powered, this time two men on a stationary bicycle. The chamber locks, which on the AK3 were a lever-action made of several parts, would have the parts stamped out by drop forges, then be finished and assembled. The chambers were all of a standardized size. But Russian gunsmithing, up to this time, hadn't focused at all on heavily standardized calibers. There just weren't that many rifles in Russia that had precisely the same caliber of barrel. So the new guns almost had to come out of the Gun Shop, which, when it came down to it, suited both Andrei and Cass just fine.

All this took time and it wasn't the only thing they were working on. The czar, the patriarch, and Sheremetev wanted cannon. Good cannon. Breech-loading cannon. Cass told them they couldn't do it, that they didn't have the quality of steel needed for up-time cannon.

Andrei, a fairly bright guy in his own right, wanted to know why.

"Strength and flexibility," Cass told him. "Modern metals are produced using precise mixes of elements: just enough carbon, just enough tungsten, just enough chromium, for a weight of steel heated to just the right heat for just the right amount of time."

After some consideration, Andrei asked, "What has to be strong and what has to be flexible?"

The question brought Cass Lowry up short. The whole damn thing had to be strong and had to have some flexibility which was why you didn't make cast iron cannons. But he got the point. They had muzzle-loading cannons down-time. They apparently made them strong enough and flexible enough so that they didn't blow up all that often. What aspect of an up-time cannon had to have fancy modern steel? "I'd say it's probably the breech mechanism," he said after a pause. "Modern cannon use an interrupted-screw breech lock."

"And how does that work?"

Cass described the way the screw had parts of the threading cut out of it so that it could be slid into the breech, which also had parts of its threading cut out and ended with, "You see, the threads of the breech and of the breechblock have to be really strong and take a tremendous amount of force."

"Yes, I see," Andrei said. "But you wouldn't need an interruption if you didn't have lots of threads. That is right, yes?"

"Well, sure."

"So why can't you add more threads to the interrupted screw to compensate for the weaker metals that we have now?"

Cass didn't know and hated admitting it.

"We will experiment. We will make interrupted-screw breech locks and see how well they withstand the force of firing."

"Fine, as long as you know I won't be standing anywhere near them when we do the test firing."

Andrei shrugged. "That's what slaves are for."

Chapter 46

February 1634

Filip and Gregorii looked over the new steam barge design before they sealed the packet.

The more standardized design the Dacha had developed after looking over Vladimir's notes was two ten-inch-wide cylinders side-by-side, with the stroke of the first setting the second and vice versa, to produce a reciprocating engine. They didn't bother with a condenser on the ones for the steamboats and steam barges, as there was generally water available in a river. So they released the steam to the same chimney that carried the smoke fire. They used a pot boiler and ceramic tiles for the fire bed. The engines built that way—and especially the boilers—were so inefficient that they were an insult to steam power. However, they would fit on a thirty-foot-long, ten-foot-wide river barge and they would push the thing through the water.

"I think it's ready," Filip said. "We'll send it on to Murom in the next pouch."

In the Dacha, Sofia's eyes sparkled like cold black diamonds. "Nevertheless, it cannot be you that goes. You are needed here. Bernie needs you. Boris and Mariya need you. You may not abandon that trust."

218

Natasha stopped her pacing. She'd been trying too hard to justify being the person who went to Grantville to determine whether or not Brandy Bates was acceptable to the czar as her brother's wife. She knew it. "But I so want to see it, Aunt Sofia," she whined. "So very much." She threw herself onto a bench. "Vladimir is there. I miss him. And I want to see it."

"Even so." Sofia's eyes softened. "I know, dear." She patted Natasha's hand. "I know." She grinned. "So do I want to go." Then she straightened her shoulders. "But we must carry on here. Czar Mikhail has said that he will consider this marriage, but there must be a senior female of the family to examine Brandy. And I know just who to send." She cackled in laughter. "Oh, my. It will do them so much good."

As it turned out, Aunt Sofia was not entirely in control of who was sent to Grantville. The other great houses wanted their say as well. A friend of Sofia, true enough, would be one of the three dragons sent; the next would come from the Sheremetev clan and an aunt of the czarina would be the other.

All of which would come as a surprise to Vladimir back in Grantville.

"I didn't really believe it. Not until I saw that." Vladimir watched the *Las Vegas Belle* until it was out of sight. Even after the months since the first flight, he still wasn't entirely sure he believed it. And slowly he began to smile. "I believe that turnabout is fair play, Brandy. Perhaps I should write Bernie that I insist that he build me an airplane. And a factory for cars. And an oil refinery."

"Soda pop." Brandy looked in the direction where the plane had disappeared. "Real, old-fashioned Coca-Cola. I miss those. New movies, instead of rewatching all the old ones. Xerox machines for quick copies. Um, we can probably think up a bunch of other stuff to demand. They won't be very realistic, I imagine, but it might be kind of fun to make a demand instead of trying to satisfy them. Besides, they might just do it."

They walked slowly to Brandy's house thinking up ever more outrageous things to demand of Bernie and the "brain cases" in Russia and laughing at their demands. No one could be sad on a day like today.

They turned up the walk to Brandy's house and she hesitated a bit. Vladimir knew that it was because her mother had died there.

He'd been surprised, three days after Donna died, by the atten-
dance at her funeral. It seemed like a large number of people
showed up. Most unusual was the cluster of young girls around
Brandy. One of them was one of the most beautiful girls he had
ever seen. Her hair was a deep auburn and her skin was clear
with just a few freckles.

Brandy had, in compliance with Donna's wishes, arranged a
simple graveside service. It was very brief. Afterward, people visited
with one another and everyone spoke to Brandy and her father
Vernon for a moment or two. Brandy introduced Vladimir to the
cluster of young girls. They were . . . quite exceptional, he thought.

Much to Vladimir's surprise, Vernon was one of the first to
leave. "He's just not good at emotions." Brandy had noticed Vladimir watching Vernon. "He never has been. He's closed up, like in
a shell or something. It drove Mom crazy. That, I think, is why
they got divorced. Mom was too emotional for him, I guess."

Vladimir looked down at her. "I promise you. I promise you
that I will never be so, so . . ."

"Calm and dispassionate?" Her tears started flowing again.
"Good. I don't think I'd like it any better than Mom did."

The sound of the doorbell jerked Brandy to alertness. She
smoothed down her dress and checked her reflection in the mir-
ror before opening the door. *Here goes,* she thought.

Vladimir stood on the porch, smiling at her. Her breath caught
a bit. They'd been dating a long time, but this was the first time
they'd been alone together. Really alone. No servants. No Mom.
Brandy still felt Donna's loss keenly. But a person had to move
on. This dinner was an effort to do that.

"Come in, please." Brandy smiled as Vladimir brought his left
hand from behind his back with a flourish. His eyes twinkled a bit.
"A guest should not arrive empty-handed. So, I brought you this."

This was not flowers or candy, or even a bottle of wine. Vladi-
mir had brought a bag of coffee beans. Brandy grinned. "Good.
We'll have some later." She stood aside and waved Vladimir inside.
"Dinner will be ready in just a moment. I hope you like it."

Vladimir looked around the room. "You have changed a few
things, Branya. Not much, just a little. The home seems somehow
more your own, now."

"Just a little." Brandy felt sad for a moment. "I loved my mother, but I never cared for that 'country' look she liked so much. So I sort of streamlined the room a bit." A dinging sound came from the kitchen. "One thing about a house this size, you can hear the timer. Come on in. The table is ready and it sounds like dinner is, too."

Brandy ushered Vladimir into the small dining area where she had used Donna's best china and crystal to set the table. "Have a seat. I'll be right back."

Brandy came back with a large platter of something. Noodles, Vladimir thought. He was fond of noodles. But what was covering them? It smelled wonderful, whatever it was.

Brandy set the platter on the table. "I've got no idea if this is really a Russian dish. But Cora said it was, so I tried it. I hope it's good. I'm not really much of a cook. Mom tried, but I wasn't very interested, to tell the truth."

The smell had Vladimir salivating. "I don't care if it's Russian, Branya. It smells wonderful. Just wonderful."

Brandy smiled widely and served Vladimir a portion of the dish, whatever it was. She poured wine for them both and indicated the salad and bread on the table. "Thank heaven for greenhouses. We always had lettuce back then. I'd miss it if we didn't have it here, even if it isn't the iceberg I'm used to." Apparently noticing Vladimir's hesitation, she urged, "Go ahead. Dig in."

Vladimir did. The scent was marvelous and the taste even more so. It only needed one thing. "Is there, perhaps, some *smetana*?"

Brandy gave him a look and he grinned guiltily. Brandy had commented before about his liking for *smetana*. He put it in nearly everything he ate, including stew. "It has quite a bit in it already." She passed him the dish full of sour cream. "But I knew you'd want more. Is it all right? Does it taste good?"

Vladimir nodded, busying himself with the dish. "Marvelous." He added sour cream to his plate. "Marvelous. I'm afraid I'm ruined for Russian cooking, at least the cooking back in my Russia. Ruined. I may never wish to go back, just for the flavor of the food alone. What is this called?"

"Beef Stroganoff."

Vladimir ate until Brandy was pretty sure he was about to explode

"Marvelous," he said. Several times. Well, it was, but that was only part of the reason he kept saying it. Vladimir was terrified.

✧   ✧   ✧

After dinner, over coffee in the living room, Brandy began to feel a little awkward. What did you say now? How did you handle this kind of privacy when you didn't have any intention of needing, well, this kind of privacy? Not yet, at any rate.

Vladimir solved the problem by beginning to speak. "Natasha tells me that the situation in Russia is quite tense. Czar Mikhail has vaguely suggested a constitution to replace the agreement he made on assuming the throne. Such a document would be binding not only on him, but on all future czars. Most importantly though, it would also be binding on the *Boyar Duma* and bureaus and replace the *Zemsky Sobor* with an elected legislature or perhaps turn the Assembly of the Land into such a congress."

"Yes. Natasha mentioned it. I understand that the income tax and the business tax are meeting quite a bit of resistance."

"That's a diplomatic way of putting it." Vladimir laughed. "I worked it out. It would cost my family several million of your dollars every year. While my family is quite well off, we're not the richest nobles in Russia, not by any means. If that tax is done just a little bit wrong, it could ruin half the nobles in Russia. I sent my sister a description of your system of tax deductions for things like capital investment along with Cass and Bernie's 'Precious.' Frankly, I don't think it will happen unless Czar Mikhail can come up with something to sweeten the pot."

"So, what can he give them?"

"For right now, I'm not sure." Vladimir leaned back on the couch. "But in a few years, relief from having to have serfs might do it."

"Don't count on it, Vladimir." Brandy shook her head. "The serfs could end up as factory workers and have even less freedom than they have now. 'I owe my soul to the company store.' If it could happen in America, where we—at least in theory—all had the same rights, think how much easier it could happen in Russia where serfs are already restricted in when they can quit."

Vladimir sighed. "I know. Adam Smith and all your economists tell us that free labor is more productive than slaves or serfs. That slavery and serfdom is bad for the economy of the nation. But what they usually neglect to mention is that it's still very profitable for the people who own the slaves." He looked down at his coffee cup.

"Brandy, I've lived here for a long time and have accepted

many of your principles, but that doesn't mean my countrymen have. I agree that serfdom must be eliminated but I don't see any way to do it."

When Brandy got up to light the gas lights against the darkening of the room, Vladimir moved just a tad closer to her end of the sofa. Whenever she leaned forward to pour more coffee, or stood to busy herself with something, he moved just a little bit closer. Eventually, Vladimir was right where he wanted to be. Close, nearly touching.

Brandy looked a little nervous when she discovered just how close he was. Deciding not to give her, or himself, a chance to bolt, Vladimir took one of her hands in his own. "Branya, I have something I want to speak of, something that is not about Bernie or even about Russia."

Brandy's breath caught just a bit before she nodded at him. "You can speak to me about anything, Vladimir. What is it?"

He had been quite confident of her response when he had written the letters asking permission from Czar Mikhail and informing Natasha of his intent. Somehow, that confidence had disappeared when he had been informed that Mikhail had agreed to the marriage—at least conditionally. The condition being that she make a valid conversion. And Natasha had informed him that several ladies from Russia would be coming to Grantville to look Brandy over. At that point he had seen the looming disaster of the dragons arriving to inspect her before he even asked for her hand.

But Vladimir was still hesitating and Brandy was looking at him expectantly. "I am not one of your up-time men, Branya. And I may not have the correct words. But I have grown very...fond of you. Very fond. And I, I..." Vladimir paused a moment. "I wish you to be my wife, Branya. I wish it very much."

Brandy's eyes glittered in the candlelight. "Wife? You want to get *married*?"

"I do," Vladimir said. He watched her face closely. What would she answer?

"Yes."

Half an hour later, after some very pleasant kissing and some not so pleasant explanation. Brandy wasn't quite so sure.

"We don't do that," Vladimir said, sounding a bit desperate. "Abandon thy family, abjure thy name." He shook his head. "It sounds glorious, but Romeo and Juliet ended up dead. Were I to marry without the czar's consent, our family's property could be seized and my sister could end her life in a convent. Forced to take holy orders. Not because Mikhail would want to do it, but because the cabinet would insist."

Brandy knew that was all too likely an outcome. But Vladimir was continuing. "If I asked the czar first and you said no, I would look foolish. But if I asked you first and the czar said no, I didn't know what I would do. I didn't wish to make a promise to you until I was sure I could keep it."

"All right!" Judy the Younger Wendell was grinning from ear to ear. "So, when's the wedding, Brandy? What are you going to wear?"

"I don't know to the first question." Brandy took a sip of root beer. "And I don't know to the second one, for that matter."

Brandy's friends looked confused. As a group they were often called the Barbie Consortium because they were teenagers who had gotten rich selling their old dolls—which, in one of the Ring of Fire's most quirky ramifications, turned out to be highly prized objects for Europe's wealthy classes. They were quite bright, generally speaking, but as could be expected from girls most of whom were no older than sixteen, their experience with life in general was limited.

Marriage was simple and straightforward, in their world view. Fall in love; get married; the bride wears a really nifty outfit and the bridesmaids wear outfits that are almost as nifty, there's a big cake which is usually cut by the groom and in the seventeenth century they thought he got to use a really nifty sword for the purpose.

"It's more complicated than I knew," Brandy sighed. "It turns out that Vladimir is sort of a prince or something like that. He can't just get married, not to a foreigner, not to anybody, really. He has to get permission."

Vicky Emerson looked outraged. "What, from his father? He's a grown man! Why does he have to ask for permission?"

Brandy shook her head. "His parents are dead. Both of them. He's got a sister, Natasha. No, it's not his parents, it's the czar.

He had to get permission from the czar. He apparently asked him before he asked me. And the czar has already sent a bunch of dragon ladies from Russia to check me out," Brandy added, with some resentment. Vladimir had explained that they had to do it that way but it still ticked her off. "And then there's the religion thing, too."

"Religion thing?" Hayley Fortney paused in the act of sipping tea. "There's a religion thing, too?"

Brandy nodded again, and sort of sighed. "Yeah. It's all going to take a while, it looks like. I'd just as soon go down to City Hall and have a civil ceremony, get all the hoopla over with. But Vladimir's church will not recognize a civil ceremony, he says. It's against canonical law. And, it turns out that if he gets married in any church except a Russian Orthodox church, he could be charged with treason. So we figure we better wait."

"That's kind of hard, isn't it?" Judy looked around at the girls. "Your Vladimir is a nice-looking guy. A nice guy in general, for that matter. I bet you hate waiting."

"Well, one thing about it." Brandy shrugged. "At least we ought to be really sure about it when it does happen. Vladimir says he probably ought to have a priest come here, anyway. Natasha is sending a bunch of people from his lands and they're all going to go to school here. And to the oil field. So they need a priest. They wouldn't be comfortable going to St. Mary's. We're probably looking at another three months to wait. If we're lucky."

"That's just about enough time," Judy muttered.

"Enough time?"

"Yeah," Judy grinned. "Just about enough time to plan a really big, really nice wedding, no matter what else is going on here. Or in Russia, for that matter."

Chapter 47

March 1634

Cass Lowry grinned as he idly played with an AK3 chamber, thinking about his profits. He was indeed still working at the Gun Shop, and it was proving very profitable. From his reassignment to the Gun Shop back in January, he had been helping Andrei, not just in gun production, but in gun allocation. Because in Russia everyone was on the take and everyone could be bribed. He casually slid the chamber back into his bandolier. It was nice, that bandolier. Tooled leather with gold leaf, and it really set off his midnight blue jacket.

Well, almost everyone. There were half-a-dozen steam-ram drop forges in Murom, the seat of the Gorchakov family, and one at the Dacha. But Cass and Andrei couldn't get any of those. There were too few for any to get "lost." A steam-ram was a single-cylinder steam engine, but it had to be a high-pressure steam engine because of the amount of force it had to deliver to lift the incredibly heavy weight of the drop hammer. Made of metal and with the need to withstand hundreds of pounds per square inch, they were very hard for the smiths of Russia to make, so there still weren't many available.

Slaves and serfs, however, were not a problem. The Sheremetev family and their *deti boyars* had lands all over the place and they were looking for things to put their serfs to work on over the winter. And they weren't the only ones. In winter you could get the labor of serfs for little more than their maintenance. So the Gun Shop had gone with the serf-powered-crank drop forge rather than the steam-powered one. It took ten minutes to slowly crank the hammer up to drop height, but that was still three chambers or chamber locks an hour. Besides, the time it took to crank the hammer up gave the die time to cool between drops, and given the quality of the metal, a hot die wasn't a good idea.

The crank version, though simpler than the steam-ram would have been, still took a couple of weeks to build. Russia had lots of rivers but the Gun Shop had no waterfalls handy. There were, though, lots of peasants and more than a few out-and-out slaves. So a two-man crank to lift the hammer, which had a die of pretty good high-carbon steel, was more than possible. The hammer dropped on an anvil, which had its own matching die, and *wham*, one semi-finished part. The flash, the excess material, had to be removed and the part had to be finished, but that could be done by hand.

There had already been a couple of puddle steel foundries when Cass had gotten here. And the Gun Shop had a high enough priority to get some of the steel and have it shaped into the dies they needed.

It was when they were working on getting the steel that Cass remembered the advantages of a high failure rate. Andrei had been complaining about the crappy progress of the drop forge for making the chambers. Too many of the chambers were not fully formed. Cass remembered something about a supply of black-market computer chips, some spy story or cop story, where the chips turned out to be being made in the factory that made the legal ones, but were marked down as defective, then sold. So they worked out a deal where the parts that were "not good enough" were sold as scrap to an iron monger. They ended up having to cut in the iron monger for a small piece of the action and a cousin of Sheremetev for a bigger one, but it worked. And Cass had had a down-time made Colt six-shooter with him when he'd arrived. So they started making those on the side, and they were selling faster than he could make them. Not that they could make them all that fast here in Russia. These people were even more primitive than the Germans.

The door slammed open, jerking Cass out of his daydreaming. "What is it?"

"We got a message from Moscow," Andrei said. "A rider brought it."

"Why didn't they use the radio?" Cass asked. He and Andrei

generally preferred to only deal with the spies they knew about. They weren't fond of visits from Moscow.

"It's broken. Again," Andrei said. The radio network was new, incomplete, and full of problems. It was plagued with equipment failures because each and every radio was hand-built, as were the alternators that powered them. Andrei handed Cass the message.

Cass looked at it blankly. Cass couldn't read Russian, as Andrei well knew. It was just one more of Andrei's little digs. Just like the double bandolier Andrei was wearing. More tooling than Cass had, and way the hell more gold leaf. Cass had introduced the bandoliers less than a month after arriving at the Gun Shop and over the past couple of months they'd become all the rage. The advertisement of personal power and wealth that a bandolier full of chambers represented was irresistible to a certain class of Russian noble.

"General Kabanov wants to know when we will be delivering the shipment of AK3's to the Moscow *Streltzi*. He's getting impatient. If we don't get them there soon, he's liable to call for an investigation."

"Ivan Petrovich Sheremetev will never let that happen," Cass said. "He's in this up to his eyeballs. We had to pay him enough. Tell Kabanov a month, just like we agreed. Look, Andrei, we've talked this out before. Everybody knows that we're skimming. Only you, me and Ivan Petrovich know how much. This is brand new stuff. There's no way for anybody outside to tell how many failures we have for every working gun. A fifty percent failure rate isn't unreasonable. And a forty percent failure rate, with us skimming ten percent, that's pretty good. Most of your guys aren't going to realize how well the drop forges are working now. So we sell one gun for every gun we deliver and we make a fortune. We deliver two chambers with every gun and sell five, and we make another fortune. We keep it up a few years, then we retire to rich estates, just like we planned."

Andrei was rubbing his hands together but it was clear to Cass that Andrei's sense of entitlement was winning out over his caution.

"So we write General Kabanov a nice letter, telling him that we've had serious quality control problems, but we will, through long hours and hard work, soon have the full complement of two hundred rifles for the Moscow *Streltzi*."

"And what do we tell him about the cannon?"

Cass winced. The cannon were a whole other issue. Cass

wasn't the most sensitive guy around and he had killed people in the heat of a fight and worked the servants hard in the Gun Shop, but the casual way Andrei sacrificed serfs and slaves to the development of new weapons had horrified him. Well, bothered him, anyway. The problem with the cannon was figuring out how many teeth an iron breechblock needed—or even a moderately high carbon steel one.

When Cass had arrived, Andrei was working up an interrupted screw ten threads deep. Vladimir had provided the basic designs. When a double-charge, the standard testing charge, was tried in the gun, it had blown the breech out as though it hadn't had any threads. The breechblock had sailed like a cannon ball, bounced off the ground, shifting fifteen degrees to the right, torn through a wall twenty meters behind the gun, and killed four people. Kill was really too mild a word. It had pureed four people. Or at least the parts of them that had been in the way. The only good thing you could say about it was it had mostly been quick.

Andrei wanted to try a fifteen-thread interrupted-screw design next and that was what they had done. Andrei also wanted a Welin breechblock, but he couldn't have one. The Welin was a complex breechblock with levels of threading so that more of the breech could be threaded. But while Russian craftsmen were good they were *slow! slow! slow!* in terms of making something as big and complex as a Welin block. Between the Russian craftsmen and the Dacha, they could make standard bolt-cutting and nut-cutting tools in the sizes needed, so the Gun Shop could cut the threads in the breech and the breechblock. But the sort of complex shaping necessary for the Welin would have to be done by hand. And it would take months for a single breech to be hand cut. They made do with an interrupted-screw. Cut the threads into the block and the breech, then grind down the threads so that the block could be slid into the breech and screwed a quarter turn to lock it in place. That meant they needed a longer block and more threads to hold the same amount of force and the metal they were using wasn't as consistent in its strength as twentieth-century metals which—again—meant a longer, heavier block.

Cass' first contribution had been the notion of starting with a quarter-charge and gradually increasing the charge till they got to the standard double-charge or the breech blew so they would be able to tell how much they needed. "After all," Cass had argued, "with a breech loader we can open the breech and use a ramrod to clear the barrel if we need to."

That had saved time by letting them know just how much of a charge was needed to blast out a fifteen-thread deep breechblock. It turned out that to be safe they needed a thirty-thread block and that made for a very heavy breechblock. It needed supporting gear and bearings to hold it up and make it movable. And it was what would be called in another universe a "three-motion" block. Rotate, pull out, swing aside—four actions in point of fact—because a blast shield had to be swung into place. Some of the charge leaked out the less-than-perfect seal between the breechblock and the bore of the gun. Enough to be deadly dangerous to the gun crew without the shield.

All of this made the process of loading the rifled piece cumbersome. Not, however, as cumbersome as loading a muzzle-loader. They were small-bore guns for the weight of shot they fired and because they were rifled, they had a smoother, straighter trajectory. But they were slow to make and expensive. The Gun Shop had two of the eighty-caliber light cannon ready and parts for four more, but it took weeks to finish and fit the breechblock and threading for each gun. They might have four ready by the end of May, but three was more likely.

Cass shook his head. "Tell him we'll try, but we don't expect to have four by the end of May or five by the end of June. We'll send him the guns as fast as we get them made and we'll go ahead and send the two we have to now so he can train crews on them." Cass paused. "The volley guns are doing well. And we should have half-a-dozen of them by the end of May." Fortunately the volley guns used the standard chamber and barrel of the AK3. It just used twenty-four of them in three rows of eight. All they needed was the plate that held the chambers in place and the mounting carriage. It would divert some of their on-the-side AK3 rifle production, but this way they could claim that the volley guns were the cause of the delay.

Chapter 48

April 1634

"The police want to talk to you," Gregorii said in his heavy Russian accent.

"Oh, Lord," Brandy muttered. "What's gone wrong now?" She picked up the phone receiver and said, "This is Brandy Bates. How can I help you?"

"Is that you, Brandy? I was trying for your Russian," Angela Baker, the police dispatcher said.

"He's off doing spy stuff, I bet, Angela. What's up?"

"Well . . . we've got a caravan of Russians downtown. Lots of them. Are they yours?"

Brandy's heart sank into her stomach. "Probably. We were expecting them around now. More or less."

Angela laughed. "I'll send them out to you."

"Gee, thanks."

The dragon ladies didn't arrive alone. Over a hundred Russians came with them: a priest, his family, students of medicine, engineering, architecture, aeronautics, oil wildcatting and a host of other interests. But the dragon ladies ruled the caravan, three ladies of great houses. All three of them were mothers or grandmothers of boyars. One was a friend of Vladimir's Aunt Sofia, Madam Lukashenko.

She was, Vladimir insisted, Brandy's friend at court. Brandy's enemy at court was Madam Sheremetev, as the old bat made clear with a sniff the day they arrived. The neutral, Madam Streshnyova, was a friend of the czarina's mother, which Brandy figured was at least marginally a good thing. By now Bernie had been in Moscow for over two years. A Russian had flown not that long after Jesse Wood did. Admittedly, in a lighter-than-air balloon rather than an airplane, but flying was flying. There were plows and Fresno scrapers being made in some place called Murom. And an essential element to it all was Vladimir Gorchakov. Increasingly Brandy Bates was another essential element, doing for Vladimir here in Grantville what Bernie was doing in Russia.

As she did right now, arranging for housing for the flood of new arrivals. A number were allowed to rest from their trip, then sent on to the Wietze oil fields. Some were set up in one of the new subdivisions that had sprung up outside of the Ring of Fire and some were installed in the *Residentz*. But while Brandy could place most of them, the dragon ladies were unwilling to go where they were told.

"What about suites at the Higgins Hotel?" Brandy asked, feeling a bit desperate. Madam Sheremetev and her kabuki makeup was about the scariest woman she'd ever met.

"Oh, not for me," Madam Lukashenko said. "I told Sofia that I'd stay with you. Natasha said that you have a fine house, the one your mother left you."

Great, Brandy thought. *A built-in chaperone, what a thrill.* She forced a smile. "That will be splendid, Madam Lukashenko. I do have three bedrooms, if another of you would like to stay with me."

Madam Sheremetev sniffed. Again. That sniff was beginning to make Brandy jump, because it always boded ill. "The, ah, Higgins, you said? A suite there, I think."

Brandy couldn't resist. "I'll call and see if they have one available. They might not have room."

"Of course, they will make room for me."

"I'd be very careful of expressing that view at the Higgins," Brandy said, enjoying the moment. "You wouldn't be the first great lady to be told that there's no room for you there, even if the hotel was empty. Delia Higgins does what she wants."

That sniff again. A big sniff this time.

"And you, Madam Streshnyova? Where would you like to stay? The *Residentz* is pretty full."

Madam Streshnyova was Brandy's favorite so far. It didn't seem to matter to her that her niece was the czarina. And Brandy could tell that Madam Streshnyova was sick to death of Madam Sheremetev.

"Oh, anywhere is fine for me," Madam Streshnyova said. "I don't need the Higgins. Perhaps there's another hotel? Or a room at the *Residentz*, if that's possible."

Brandy decided to make it possible, one way or another.

Since Brandy had gone and fallen in love with the dashing Russian prince, she buckled in and the Barbies helped. Well, the Barbies helped some, as they had time. They were still going to school, they had their business interests, but they did manage to pop up and save the day more than once.

The wedding had a tentative date sometime in the summer of this year. Meanwhile, the dragon ladies were going over Brandy's pedigree and tut-tutting all the while because they couldn't find any nobility at all in Brandy's recorded ancestry. They were discovering for themselves what any number of western European down-timers had already learned—that Americans just didn't fit neatly into established lines, pedigrees and social estates. Technically, all up-timers were commoners. In the real world . . .

It wasn't that simple. Any number of down-time prominent families had already tacitly decided that for all social purposes up to and including marriage Americans could be considered equivalent to the aristocracy. "Honorary noblemen," as it were. But the Russian delegation was made of sterner stuff and not yet ready to call it quits.

By May, Brandy was ready to pull a Saint George on all three of the dragon ladies. But letters were still flowing back and forth between her and her Russian pen pals. The czarina was enthusiastic about the dirigible they were building in Bor on the Volga, though it was expected to take over a year to complete. Natasha was enthusiastic about the new industries that were starting up in Russia, especially in Moscow and Natasha's family seat, a town called Murom on the Oka River. The Oka, Brandy learned, was the river route from Moscow to the Volga and Nizhny Novgorodi. The Volga was developing into the Russian industrial corridor.

And, in some ways, it was doing it faster than it was happening in Germany. Russia had farther to go and fewer people to take it there, but it was an autocratic state. If the government decided there would be a dirigible, there darn well will be a dirigible. If Princess Natasha decided that they would build steam engines in Murom, they will darn well build steam engines in Murom.

An open society whose economy was based mostly on free enterprise might be great for innovation and dynamic in the long run. But over the fall of 1633 Brandy had been forced to the realization that when it came to putting innovations into production... well, the expression "shoot the engineer and put it into production" took on a whole new urgency when the authority really could shoot the engineer. It wasn't nice and it didn't fit with her image of either Natasha or the czarina, but it did get results. It got results even when neither Natasha or the czarina had any intention of shooting anyone. Just the fact that they could brought results.

Brandy paid attention to these things in part because it was increasingly her job as Vladimir's primary up-timer consultant, but also because it gave her something to distract her from worrying about what the dragon ladies from the Russian steppes were sending home and whether they would be able to scuttle the wedding.

"That... that... raving bitch!"

"What's the matter now, my darling?" Vladimir asked. "Which of our dragon ladies has made you angry?"

"Madam Sheremetev."

"Because..."

"She said that if she sends a bad report about me, the czar would change his mind about letting you marry me. And you told me he said yes already. So which is it, dammit?"

"Yes, the czar gave his consent," Vladimir said, suddenly even more worried. "But a bad report—if it is bad enough—*might* cause him to reconsider. That is, I agree, what Madam Sheremetev strongly implies at every opportunity."

"Does the old bat actually have that kind of power over us?"

"Probably not. But she does want you to believe that."

"What can we do?"

"It's the way they are, the Sheremetevs. Obviously, she wants something else. Some kind of procedure, some kind of machine, something her family can make money and power off of."

"Well, do we bribe her? Or just blow her off? We better decide something quick. She said, not quite in so many words, that she's going to send her report pretty soon."

Vladimir knew this was pretty standard procedure for the Sheremetev family and confirmed that she was likely to write such a letter. He wasn't all that worried about it actually convincing the czar to cancel the wedding. After all, Brandy was friends with the czarina, which equated to having a pretty good friend at court. "If there is something you can think of to give her, go ahead."

After some consideration, Brandy decided to try giving the old bat photography, or at least to point her in that direction. Brandy had a talk with Father Gavril, the Orthodox priest sent to Grantville, and they determined that photographs didn't count as prohibited drawings any more than icons did, but for a different reason. Photographs were in effect drawn by God—His light painting the image rather than the corrupt hand of man. Brandy put together a packet and gave it to Madam Sheremetev who sent it off to Moscow and was almost nice to Brandy for a week or so before she started asking for something else.

By the time the ice would start forming on the Oka River in the fall of 1634, the Sheremetev family would be making photographs on their estates and arguing that they didn't owe any duties on them because they had gotten them directly from Grantville not from the Dacha.

By that same time, of course, Natasha already had a steam engine factory, a celluloid/cellophane/rayon factory, a wood pulp-based paper mill, a shop making capacitors and half a dozen other projects up and running. Each managed by a member of the *Streltzi* class who was becoming effectively a *deti boyar* of the Gorchakov family.

Brandy would never be more glad to see the back of anyone as she would be to see the backs of the dragon ladies when they headed back to Russia.

Brandy was plenty busy with her correspondence and her work with Vladimir.

As the wedding approached, Brandy got a letter from Natasha describing the Sheremetev's machinations with the photography.

Having established that because the Sheremetev clan got the photographic process directly from Grantville instead of from us, Natasha wrote, *they are now claiming that they got everything from the Fresno scrapers to steam engines directly from Grantville and not from the Dacha.*

Cass Lowry is still working in the gun shop, Natasha's letter continued, *and has made friends among Sheremetev's supporters. I find myself wishing that he was either a little less useful or a lot less obnoxious. He seems to think that he was literally adopted into the clan, not just that he's become one of their supporters. The idiot. The Sheremetevs are just using him. Apparently, Cass was given a harem and quite a bit of money and lands. For which Sheremetev gets his own Bernie, though not one who seems to work as well as the real Bernie does with us down-timers.*

Chapter 49

May 1634

"Princess?" Anya said. "What are these?" Anya held up some sheets of paper and Natasha looked at them.

"Oh. Those." Natasha sat down next to Anya and said quietly, "You know the dies we made for the Gun Shop?"

Anya nodded.

"I had an extra set made and sent it to Murom. I'm having AK3's made for my armsmen."

"How many?"

"Not a lot. A couple of hundred. You know that we'd be last in line, with Andrei Korisov and Cass Lowry doing the distribution."

"Have you seen the latest?" Pavel Egorovich Shirshov asked, handing a pamphlet to Ivan Mikhailovich Vinnikov.

The guard captain looked at the pamphlet and began to read silently.

"Out loud if you don't mind," Pavel Egorovich said testily. Though a skilled craftsman, he didn't read.

Ivan Mikhailovich cast him an apologetic look and began to read out loud. "If we are to have a constitution it must ensure the rights of all Russian citizens..." He continued reading. It was an argument that without a section limiting government, the constitution would be just another way to tie the people down. The writer actually seemed to wonder if a constitution was a good idea at all. Then he went on to—purportedly—quote a conversation between members of the boyar class. A cousin and a younger son of one of the great families. They were reported to have said that the great families thought that a constitution would be a great thing if they got to write it. The conversation was supposed to have been overheard in a brothel.

"Any idea who wrote this?" Ivan asked, a bit nervously. This was the sort of thing that could get people in serious trouble.

Pavel shook his head. "A boy in Moscow was selling them on the street. Couldn't have been more than ten or so." That was happening more and more frequently. Scandals mixed with political opinion.

"I talked to one of them a bit a few days ago." Pavel commuted back and forth between the Army's dacha and the Kremlin every few days. "He sells his papers to make a bit of money. He buys them from a man he thinks is a bureau man, but it could be a merchant. There is apparently more than one man, and they don't all meet in the same place."

"It says here that this Patriarch Nikon caused it." Colonel Pavel Kovezin stared at the broadsheet with distaste clearly showing on his face.

Machek Speshnev, who had brought this news to the colonel, nodded. A lieutenant in this regiment of *Streltzi*, Machek was a pious man. This information had struck a chord with him, as well as with many other members of the Palace Guard Regiments.

"I'm surprised this information became public, but it has. The question is, is there anything we can do about it?" Machek's family would most definitely wind up as oppressed "Old Believers," he was sure. "I don't think I'd care to be sent up north, chasing, beating and killing priests."

The very idea was repugnant.

A lot of information that was coming from the up-timer histories was repugnant. Inconceivable, a lot of it.

Colonel Kovezin stopped staring at the broadsheet. "How many people have seen this?"

"A lot of them," Machek admitted. "The things have been being passed around all over the city. Along with the ones about killing rats, boiling water, not drinking so much . . ."

"This city is being buried in paper," Colonel Kovezin said. Then he grinned. "We live in interesting times. Never mind this. I'm sure the patriarch is well aware of it and will make a pronouncement. Try to keep the men calm. Today is a big day for us and I want everyone's attention kept on his duty."

Machek grinned back. "Today is the day?"

"Yes. Today we receive our new rifles. Never mind the flurry of paper coming out of the Dacha. It's not our problem."

Chapter 50

Moscow
June 1634

Third Lieutenant Boris Timofeyevich Lebedev was savoring the victory. Right up to the time he was called into the commandant's office. He had beaten Third Lieutenant Ivan Maslov in the Polish invasion scenario two weeks ago and won a nice purse in the bargain. The betting had been five to one against him. Lebedev, known as Tim to his friends, had been playing the Polish and he had won by ignoring Smolensk. After all, Poland already held Smolensk. They had held it since the Time of Troubles. And Poland, just like Russia, only had to worry about Smolensk if they didn't have it.

Now he was trying to figure out what he had done wrong, that would get him summoned by the commandant. Tim put his shoulders back and entered the commandant's office not looking left or right, stood at attention and saluted as smartly as he was able. The commandant returned the salute with a casual half wave. Then he asked him the last question he ever expected to hear. "So, Third Lieutenant Lebedev, how did you manage to defeat the entire Russian Army and take Moscow, in just ten weeks?"

"Sir?"

"Come now, Lebedev. It's all over the Kremlin. I understand the odds were five to one in favor of that baker's son, Ivan Maslov?"

"Sir? Are you talking about the Polish invasion scenario?" Tim was out of his depth. It wasn't one of the official war games.

"Yes, of course, Lebedev." The commandant pointed to a map on the left wall. The map showed part of Russia and part of Poland. "Show me how you did it."

Tim walked over to the map pointed where he placed his troops and how he moved them using the River Volga as the supply line. "Russia is not Moscow; Russia is the Volga. In the Time of Troubles, Poland took Moscow but they couldn't keep it. But the Volga controls transport..."

Just as Tim was getting into his description of what he'd done, he heard another voice.

"Would it interest you to know, Lieutenant Lebedev, that Polish troops took Rzhev three days ago? From the somewhat vague first reports we have, there are around ten thousand troops there now, a mixture of the magnate's personal troops, mercenaries and Cossacks."

"What?" Tim faced the new voice and recognized General Mikhail Borisovich Shein. Then, in a state of shock, he blurted out the first thing that come to mind. "But that's the wrong place, sir."

"I'm relieved to hear it," General Shein said wryly.

Tim stood mute.

"Speak up, Lieutenant," the commandant said. "Why do you think Rzhev is the wrong place?"

"It's too far upriver, sir. The Volga is navigable at Rzhev but only barely. Tver would be a better choice, even if it is farther. You'd want to take Rzhev, too. Later. After the first strike. But if you take Rzhev first, you warn Tver and give them time to fort up and block any river traffic from going past."

General Shein looked at the commandant. "He'll do."

After that, things moved quickly. Third Lieutenant Boris "Tim" Lebedev found himself suddenly assigned as aide de camp to General Artemi Vasilievich Izmailov.

"Third Lieutenant Boris Lebedev reporting as ordered."

"Who are you?"

"Sir, I'm to be your cadet aide de camp."

"I asked for Maslov! The baker's boy." General Izmailov was clearly not pleased.

"Ivan?"

"You know him?"

"Yes, sir. We're friends at the military academy." That was the semiofficial name of the still semiofficial officer training school that was growing in the Kremlin.

General Izmailov paused and give Tim's uniform a careful once over. "Let me guess. Your father is a boyar or duma man?"

Suddenly Tim understood. "A great uncle, sir." The pride that Tim's voice usually had in that announcement was notably missing. The general had asked for the best student in the cadet corps, Ivan Maslov. Instead he had gotten . . . well, not the highest in family rank. There were a lot of high family kids among the cadets. It was quite the fashion these days. No, what the general had received was a cadet of acceptable social rank and lesser skill. Even if Tim had beaten Ivan once.

General Izmailov was not usually placed in independent command. For the same reason—he didn't have enough social or family rank. In fact, he was officially second in command of the army they were raising right now, placed temporarily in command of the advance column.

General Izmailov shrugged and got down to business. "I'll be leading a reconnaissance in force and—if necessary—a delaying action while the reserves are called up. The reconnaissance force is made up in part from *Streltzi* Prince Cherkasski has loaned us from the Moscow Garrison." Prince Ivan Borisovich Cherkasski was the chief of the *Strel'etsky prikaz*, Musketeer Bureau. "They're under Colonel Usinov. We have small detachments from the Gun Shop and from the Dacha. And two regiments of cavalry under the command of Colonel Khilkov." General Izmailov gave Tim a look. "Usinov has more experience but Khilkov's family is of higher rank. We have peasant levies for labor battalions. About four thousand of them. We have four brand-new cannons from the Gun Shop and some of the *Streltzi* we're getting have been equipped with the new AK3's. From the Dacha we're getting *Testbed*, the flying machine. I am told it is to be used only for reconnaissance. And we're getting thirty of the scrapers. There won't be time to use them much on the march, but they should help a lot with fortifications when we find our spot."

Tim nodded his understanding. "What about the radio network, sir?"

"Apparently there is no link going toward Rzhev. There is one going toward Smolensk, which would have given us warning if they'd come that way. Which may have something to do with why they're coming from Rzhev. Unfortunately, most of the radio network has been put in places where it would be convenient for members of the great houses, not where it would help the army."

The assumption was that they would meet the advancing Polish forces somewhere between Rzhev and Moscow. Meanwhile Tim was assigned fourteen different jobs, some of them in direct conflict with the others. Or at least that's how it seemed. He was to coordinate with the labor battalions, the *Streltzi*, the Dacha contingent as well as the Gun Shop contingent, and make sure that all the various units were in the right marching order. Except that the people in charge hadn't actually decided the marching order yet. So he was given one order and then fifteen minutes later given a different order by someone else.

By noon Tim was considering the value of getting rid of the beards, as he'd read Peter the Great had done. But in his own mind, "the beards" were the idiots who kept harping on their noble rank, regardless of their true ability at war. *At this rate we'll meet the Poles thirty miles out of Moscow.*

On the first day Nikita—"call me Nick"—Ivanovich's dirigible contingent ended up at the back of the line of march, which meant that by the time they reached the campsite it was already getting dark. Tim watched as *Testbed* lifted into the night sky and disappeared. All Tim could see was the rope from the wagon, climbing into a bit of deeper blackness which hid the stars.

"Of course, it could be that there simply wasn't that much to see," Nick reported a half hour later. Tim could see that General Izmailov was less than pleased. But Nick didn't seem to be worried about it. Which Tim thought was very brave or very stupid. Then he looked over at *Testbed*, which the crew was still tying down for the night. He remembered that Nikita Ivanovich had been the first person to climb into it and had flown it without ropes to keep the wind from carrying it away. Tim still wasn't sure whether that was brave or stupid, but the "very" gained a whole new level of magnitude.

"Tim! *Testbed* will be placed near the front in tomorrow's order of march," General Izmailov gritted. Tim knew that the general had seen the demonstration at the Dacha and had been planning to use the dirigible. But how were they supposed to know that it didn't work at night? Granted, it was pretty obvious when you thought about it. Dark is no time to observe things.

"I don't believe this," Tim muttered. "We'll never get there at this rate." The march had put them about twelve miles west of Moscow. Worse, they were *trying* to move fast and doing it over good roads. The scrapers had improved the roads around Moscow quite a bit.

His friend and fellow student at the cadet corps, Pavel, nodded in agreement. "Bad enough the delays because of the confusion. But Colonel Khilkov and the fit he threw when we were setting out and he discovered that we were ahead of him in the line of march was just plain stupid."

Tim figured the flare up was at least half Usinov's fault with all the gloating he was doing. But he didn't say so. Pavel was Colonel Usinov's cadet aide de camp, and thought quite highly of him. "Just wait till he hears that General Izmailov is going to put *Testbed* near the front of the line tomorrow." Tim threw his arms up and pretended to be having a fit. "Never let it be said that mere military necessity should trump social position in the Russian army. 'My cousin is of higher rank than your uncle, so of course my company must be ahead of yours in the order of march.'" Tim spat on the ground. "Idiots. We're all idiots. If we go on like this we'll be defending Moscow from another Polish invasion and we'll be doing it right here. You can bet that the Poles aren't sitting on their asses in Rzhev arguing about who should be first in the line of march."

Chapter 51

Tim could have bet that, but he would have lost. Because sitting on his ass arguing was precisely what Janusz Radziwill, the commander of the Polish forces, was doing. Not about the order of march, but what they should do now. Janusz, in his early twenties, was already the court chamberlain of Lithuania. That was a high post in the Polish-Lithuanian Commonwealth, which he had gotten because of the influence of his cousin Albrycht Stanislaw Radziwill, Grand Chancellor of Lithuania. Janusz was sitting with his two main subordinates discussing the absence of the arms depot that they had been expecting. It was a rerun of several discussions they had since they had gotten to Rzhev and discovered that the Russian invasion Janusz' spy had informed him of was not nearly so near as they had expected.

"Ivan Repinov has confirmed everything," Janusz insisted again.

Mikhail Millerov, commander of his Cossacks, snorted. "You can't depend on anything that rat-faced little bureau man says. I've questioned many men and his sort is the hardest to get the truth out of. Not because he's a strong man, but because he's weak. He'll tell you anything you want to hear and change his story five times in as many minutes."

"Yet what he said makes sense and fits with what the agent reported," said Eliasz Stravinsky, the commander of the western mercenaries. "Ivan Petrovich Sheremetev is as crooked as a dog's hind leg."

"Yes!" Janusz exclaimed. "That by itself explains the situation to anyone familiar with Russia. Ivan Petrovich commits graft as other people breathe, continuously and with very little thought. And as the nephew of Prince Fedor Ivanovich Sheremetev, the third power behind Cherkasski and the patriarch."

"Fourth, if you count the czar," Mikhail Millerov corrected.

"I don't," Janusz insisted. "Mikhail Romanov is his father's puppet and everyone knows it. In any case, Ivan Petrovich has ample opportunity for that corruption. He got the contract for the depot and pocketed the money."

Millerov nodded a little doubtfully, and Janusz continued. "My agent in the Muscovite treasury bureau spent considerable time putting together the pieces. Prince Fedor Ivanovich Sheremetev was clearly in charge of making the arrangements. And naturally shifted contracts to where they would do his family the most good. Corrupt, every last one of them." It didn't occur to Janusz to wonder what someone on the outside might think of the Polish nobility.

"Possibly . . . or possibly your man misinterpreted a scam of the Sheremetev family and the only place the depots were ever intended to be was in the pockets of the Sheremetevs." Millerov shrugged. "At this point we'll likely never know for sure and it doesn't matter anyway, because we are sitting here in Muscovite territory. They aren't going to apologize. They're going to deny and the depot isn't here. They'll demand reparations. Granted, the Truce of Deulino expired in July of 1633. His Majesty has refused to give up his claim on the Russian throne and Russia hasn't given up its claim to Czernihów or Smolensk. So legally Poland is at war with Russia, but up to now it's been a pretty phony war. Little fighting and even less talking. The war is going to get a lot more real now, one way or the other. So it would be best to win it. Yes?"

Eliasz Stravinsky nodded. "If we go back now, we'll look like idiots. Not very good for the career, that."

Janusz Radziwill nodded almost against his will. He was still convinced that the reports had been accurate. The Muscovites were planning to take Smolensk and much of Lithuania, just like they had tried in that other history. But probably—as had happened before—corruption in their ranks had interfered. Still, the Cossack was right. It didn't really matter now.

Chapter 52

"Men coming in," the scout said as he rode up to the general.

"That'll be the mercenaries from Rzhev," General Izmailov said, then looked at Tim. "Take word the column is to halt. Officer's Call at the front."

"Halt the column. Officer's Call, sir, at the leading unit," Tim told the commander of each unit as he rode down the line.

It was the third day of marching toward Rzhev. And this halt would probably cost them two miles. When he got back to the front, Tim saw that General Izmailov was speaking to the sergeant leading the mercenaries who had sent the riders to inform Moscow of the invasion.

"So tell me, Sergeant," General Izmailov was asking, "why did you abandon your post?"

"What post, General? We were ordered to Rzhev to guard a supply depot. When we got there, there was no supply depot. No quarters and no pay. My people were living in tents outside Rzhev. You can't guard what isn't there, sir, and we were never assigned to guard Rzhev." The sergeant pulled a set of orders out of his pack and handed them to General Izmailov.

General Izmailov looked over the orders and snorted. Then he handed them to Tim and went on to the next question. "Did you keep in contact with the invading force?"

The burly sergeant shook his head. "No. We didn't see any more of them and I don't have the men to spare."

"Are the invaders coming this way? Heading to Tver? Did they even continue on past Rzhev, or did they stop there?"

"I don't know, sir," Sergeant Hampstead admitted.

Tim read over the orders and information in the packet, and stopped. *Ivan Petrovich Sheremetev.* Well, that explained why the foreign mercenaries had been sent off to guard a nonexistent supply depot. It was almost funny. The lesser Sheremetev's greed had, for once, worked to Russia's benefit. If the mercenaries hadn't been in Rzhev, the Poles might have bypassed the place altogether and headed straight for Tver. With no warning to the Kremlin until they had already taken Tver.

General Izmailov turned to a discussion with the dirigible's pilot. After discussing the dirigible and its capabilities for a few minutes, the pilot, "Nick" Ivanovich, said, "General, if we loose the tether, we can see more. I can usually get twenty miles an hour when I use the engines, assuming the engines work. And if the wind isn't bad when I get up there."

"When they work?" Izmailov looked dubious. "*When* they work?"

"They do . . . mostly," Nick said. "The engines aren't really the problem. Sometimes there is considerable leakage in the steam lines. If the steam isn't leaking too bad, I can stay up for ten hours or so. If everything goes right, I can get from here to Rzhev and back before dark."

Izmailov thought for a few moments. "All right. We'll try it. But at the least problem abort the mission and get back here." He turned back to the mercenary. "Sergeant, your officers were delayed in Moscow but we expect them to be joining us in a day or so. You and your men are to fall in at the end of the column as we pass."

Everything didn't go right for Nick Ivanovich. The problem was the winds. They were southerly and fairly strong at five thousand feet. Weaker, but still southerly, at five hundred. *Testbed* didn't have a compressor; it couldn't lift the weight. So it couldn't pump hydrogen out of the bladders and then get it back. Once the hydrogen was gone, it was gone. It did have a couple of hydrogen tanks so it could go up and down a little bit.

Nick ended up using more fuel than expected to keep on course. There was some steam leakage but it wasn't too bad. All of which meant that he *might* have made it to Rzhev and back.

Or, if he went all the way to Rzhev, he might run out of fuel or water before he could get back.

"I was forced to abort, General." Nick shook his head. "Wind was awful and kept blowing me off course. But I did get a bit better than halfway and didn't see the first sign of the Poles. No advancing troops, not in this direction."

Izmailov turned to the mercenary sergeant. "Did your scouts see the entire army? This so-called ten-thousand-man army?"

"No," Hampstead admitted. "My scouts saw the leading elements. About three thousand men. And that's still more than my five hundred could face with any hope of victory."

"How do you know it was the leading elements? Not the whole force?"

"The formation was spread out like a screening element. Why put a screening element out when there's nothing to screen?"

The answer to that seemed obvious to Tim—to hide the fact that that was all you had. To bluff. Still, the sergeant's point about the size of his force was well taken. Why bluff against a force of only five hundred men? Tim could think of two reasons. If the attacking force didn't know how big the force in Rzhev was, they might try a bluff to get a force of a thousand or fifteen hundred to retreat and avoid a battle against an entrenched opponent. Two-to-one odds aren't that great when the enemy is behind walls.

Or it could be that the bluff—if it was a bluff—was intended not for the sergeant but for... well, them. The relieving force. Tim looked over at the wagons holding *Testbed* and smiled.

General Izmailov was shaking his head. "There are a lot of reasons why you might arrange your troops in a pattern that will, at first sight, look like a screen..."

Though General Izmailov didn't know it, the commander of the Polish invaders had not, in fact, formed his force into a screen. He had split his force into three columns of a thousand men to facilitate gleaning. The scout had spotted the center column and swung wide around it which had taken him right into the second column. He had assumed that the two columns were the ends of a large screening element but hadn't checked.

✧   ✧   ✧

There were four wagons in the dirigible contingent. One carried the dirigible while on the march—or served as a moving anchor for it, rather. The dirigible floated about fifteen feet above the wagon and was cranked down to ground level and tied down with spikes driven into the ground at night or in bad weather. That wagon also carried the pump that was used to compress hydrogen gas for the canisters. Another wagon carried equipment and materials for the production of hydrogen gas. A third carried equipment for field repairs and the fourth carried the repair crew. After the aborted trip, they spent two days worth of breaks on the march doing maintenance before they felt safe with the thing untethered again. General Izmailov was not pleased.

"I'm sorry, General," Nick Ivanovich said. "But there is a reason we call the dirigible '*Testbed.*' It's an experimental design to test concepts in aviation." The term "aviation" was English but Izmailov was familiar with it by now. "To the best of our knowledge, nothing quite like it has ever existed in this or any other history. The engines are handmade by Russian craftsman, as are the lift bladders, the wings."

Nick hid a grin. The designer would hate him calling the control surfaces "wings." They weren't designed to provide lift, but control. In fact, they provided a bit of both. The "wings" acted as elevators at the tail of the dirigible. More were located between the gondola and the motors. They didn't provide much lift, but by pointing the dirigible's nose up or down, he could gain or lose a little altitude without having to dump ballast or gas. Or use the emergency tanks to refill the lift bladders.

"They were well made, but by people who had no way to do more than guess about the stresses they would face. It's steam powered and if they had steam powered dirigibles up-time, we haven't heard about it. That's why they built it—to see."

"So why don't we have an improved version or one of the airplanes that the up-timers have?" Izmailov sounded impatient and gruff.

"Engines, sir. Ours are both heavy and weak They wouldn't get a heavier-than-air craft off the ground. There is one engine in Russia that might lift an airplane off the ground. That engine is in the car Bernie Zeppi brought to Russia." This wasn't entirely true, as Nick well knew. The engines they had built for the dirigible would get an airplane off the ground just fine. It was the added weight of the water, the boiler and the steam recovery that had so far made down-time-built steam-powered heavier-than-air craft impossible. Without the recovery system, a steam powered aircraft would work fine for a few minutes before the water was all used up. Water weighed a lot.

"So I will have the intelligence you can gather from your *Testbed* only when and if everything goes right? If nothing breaks on your toy and the weather is just right?" The general glared, then visibly shook himself. "All right, Captain. That's all."

The cavalry were equally unimpressed with the intelligence gathered by Nick. And more than a few of the cavalry were resentful. Scouting was a part of their function and, as far as they were concerned, the infantry was looking to take away the other part. They rode out almost gaily for the two days the dirigible was being repaired.

But, just like the dirigible, they found no traces of the enemy.

Chapter 53

July 1634

Sixty miles as the crow flies from Moscow, Nick was ready to try again. Mostly because they were launching from closer to Rzhev, but also because it was, luckily, a still, calm day. Nick made it to within five miles of Rzhev. At five thousand feet, he feathered the engines so he would have a stable platform, pulled out his telescope and started counting outhouses and camp fires.

"Three thousand men, General, more or less. They haven't burned the town, but it's not big enough to hold them all. They have built a camp next to it. No walls, not much in the way of defensive fortifications."

"Did they see you?"

Nick shrugged. "I can't say for sure. *Testbed* is big and quite visible, but I was five miles away and a mile in the air. It depends on where they were looking. No one took a shot at me and they didn't seem disturbed when I looked at the town."

"Three thousand? Is that all?" Colonel Ivan Khilkov said. "General, we've got almost that many cavalry. Send us ahead; we'll ride them into the ground." The colonel was not a fan of the new innovations in warfare provided either by Western Europe or the up-timers.

General Izmailov hesitated and Nick knew why. Ivan Khilkov was young, but from a very old family. A very well-connected family, since one of his relatives was Patriarch Filaret's chamberlain. The general could deny him once or twice, but if he did it too many times, Izmailov would find himself relieved of command and his career ended. Nick prudently kept his mouth shut.

Four days later, General Izmailov could no longer say no. Colonel Khilkov had sent mounted scouts directly to Rzhev.

"They are fortifying the town, albeit slowly. By the time the full column reaches Rzhev, the town will be fully fortified," Khilkov said. Then he sniffed. "Send us, General. We can get there quicker than this"—Khilkov waved an arm at the wagons—"torturous mess. The cavalry can get there in two days. By the time you can get all this there, we'll have taken the town."

"The *Streltzi* may not move as fast as cavalry, but they are equipped with the new rifles." Then Colonel Petrov stopped and grimaced. Although the *Streltzi* were supposed to be the first to get the new rifles, Colonel Khilkov was wearing a fine leather bandolier with twenty loaded chambers across his chest. And it wasn't just for show. Colonel Petrov knew that Colonel Khilkov had his own AK3, as did quite a number of his men. In fact, the AK3's that had been sold on the black market were one reason it had taken so long before they were finally issued to the Moscow *Streltzi*.

Colonel Khilkov casually patted his bandolier. "I'm familiar with the AK3, and quite impressed by them. But it is the shock of cavalry that wins battles. Not footmen plinking from behind a wooden wall."

There was no way to avoid it, Izmailov knew. Against his better judgment—and with a tiny bit of worry for his future—he agreed. He might very well be ruined either way. If Khilkov won, he'd look bad. If Khilkov lost, his angry relatives would blame Izmailov.

"Khilkov and his forces are about ten miles from Rzhev, sir," Nick Ivanovich reported.

"Very well," Izmailov said. "Do whatever it is you need to do with your ... Testbed. If he's that close, you should see the battle tomorrow." The general paused. "Take Lieutenant Lebedev with you." When Nikita started to object, General Izmailov held up his hand. "There's no choice in this. He is from a good family. If things go well tomorrow, it won't matter—but if they don't, you and I will need his report."

By this time, the main column was only about forty miles from Rzhev by air. Which, unfortunately, meant quite a few more miles on foot. Fortunately, it was short-hop range for *Testbed*. Nick spent the rest of the day doing maintenance and preparing for the overloaded trip to Rzhev. The general consensus was that tomorrow he would have a ringside seat for a glorious feat of victory by Russian cavalry. General Izmailov clearly wasn't so sure, and Nick shared his doubt. There were probably a few others who were less than sanguine about the outcome. Sergeant Hampstead was one of them; his commanding officer, Captain Boyce, who had joined them on the march was another.

"I'm going with you."

Nick Ivanovich looked over at the young lieutenant. "So General Izmailov told me. That's why I'm pulling two of the four hydrogen tanks. We'll also be taking less ballast water and less fuel." Nick wasn't happy with the situation but he rather liked Tim, one of the more innovative young officers in the Russian army. And young was the word. Tim might be seventeen, but he looked closer to fourteen. "Bernie Zeppi said once that the glamour of flying would get to almost anybody. But it's *dangerous* up there. A dirigible is a balancing act. Look there..." He pointed. "Those are the lift bladders. They pull the dirigible up but not by a constant amount. There are several factors involved. At night, for instance, the hydrogen gets cooler and loses some buoyancy. Flying one of these things is more like horsemanship than you'd think."

"A matter of feel and instinct, rather than science, you're saying."

"Right. If you gauge it wrong, you're likely to crash. Fortunately, you'll probably have more time to react than you would falling off a horse. On the other hand, *Testbed* here has as much surface area as a three-masted schooner has sails." *Well, not really,* Nick admitted silently, *but it doesn't have a hull in the water holding it in place either.* "So a sudden change in the wind and we can be a hundred yards away from where we want to be before I can even start to compensate. If we are facing into the wind, or close to it, the engines are enough to move us through the air.

But if the wind is from the sides, the wind wins. If it rains on this thing, the weight of the water means even with all the ballast overboard and the bladders at capacity, we don't have enough lift. We had to drop the radiator more than once in tests at the Dacha and the aerodrome where they are working on the big one. We haven't had to drop the engines or the boiler yet but it's rigged to be able to."

Nick went on to explain about the various controls. The fifty-pound weight that didn't seem like that much till you realized that it could be moved from the tip to the tail of the dirigible to adjust its balance and angle of attack. That not only the wings, but the engines at their ends rotated as much as thirty degrees, to provide last minute thrust up or down for takeoff and landing. Especially landing. The steam engines could reverse thrust with the turning of a lever, so *Testbed* didn't need variable pitch propellers. It was all a bit intimidating.

Chapter 54

Rshev, on the Volga River

"It is a beautiful sight," Tim said. "Banners flying..." He paused a moment, then sighed. "A beautiful sight, noble and glorious. But at the Kremlin in the war games they treated pike units as fortified. Not easy to overrun. Colonel Khilkov didn't think much of the war games." In a way, this was like one of those war games, an eagle's eye view. Tim had played a lot of them, and suddenly, as he watched, he could see the little model units on the field below. He remembered one of the games—an unofficial game—when one of his fellow students had had a bit too much to drink and ordered cavalry to attack undispersed pike units. You were supposed to hit them with cannon first, to break up their formation. And he remembered those cavalry pieces being removed from the board. Ivan had stood, held up one arm, wobbled a bit, lifted the arm again and proclaimed "But, I died bravely!" They had all laughed. Suddenly it didn't seem funny at all.

"Colonel Khilkov thinks the Poles will break when faced with a cavalry charge... and General Izmailov didn't seem to agree."

"You're sounding a bit, ah, concerned there, Tim." Nick peered though his telescope toward the Polish forces.

Tim nodded. "Colonel Khilkov is... a bit difficult."

The Polish forces didn't flee. Three thousand Russian cavalry faced a wall of about two thousand Polish infantry, armed with pikes and muskets, as well as the Polish cavalry. The infantry stood in ranks and waited. Then they lowered their pikes and the Russian cavalry charge ran headlong into a porcupine made of men. Then the Poles fired. It was unlikely that the volley killed many men, but it was enough to shatter the Russian formation.

Then it was the Polish cavalry's turn. They were outnumbered but they were fighting a scattered unit. Colonel Khilkov tried to rally his men and almost managed it. But the Polish infantry had slowly—as infantry must—advanced while the Polish cavalry had been cutting its way through the Russians. Once their own cavalry was mostly clear, the Polish infantry opened fire again.

"It's all over, mostly," Nick said. There was, it seemed to Tim, a coldness in Nick's voice he had not noticed before. "We'd better head back to General Izmailov and tell him."

Tim nodded, tears blurring his sight. He kept seeing little cavalry units being picked up off a playing board while he looked at the clumps of bodies on the field. It was too far to distinguish individuals but he knew some of the cavalrymen whose bodies made up those clumps. "The general's not going to be happy."

The little boyars with their fine horses had left the field, those that still could. Routed by soldiers who worked for pay, not glory.

By the time they got back to the column, it was crossing the Volga at Staritsa and Tim had himself well under control. He made his report and the general discussed the way the battle had gone. Whoever had commanded the Poles had kept his Cossacks in reserve. Which was a bit of a surprise; since probably the greatest Russian weakness was in tactical mobility. Of course, a Russian army that was mostly cavalry was unusual, too.

"I am concerned about the loss of the cavalry," General Izmailov echoed Tim's thoughts. "The cavalry units were most of what tactical mobility we had. We can't afford to be caught away from the Volga. We'll need it for supply. It's a hundred miles along the Volga from Tver to Rzhev. I am going to take the main force straight to Rzhev. But I am sending Captain Boyce and his people along the river to grab up every boat they can find."

Tim said, "But the supplies are coming up by steam barge, aren't they?"

"They're supposed to be," General Izmailov said. "But the latest steam barge is overdue. The steam barges don't work that consistently yet. So I want regular boats to fill in the gaps. I also want to deny them to the Poles. So, you're going with Captain Boyce and his troops, Tim. I don't really think they'll run again, but better safe than sorry."

"Yes, sir. What do I do if they do run?"

"They won't. That's why you're going. I'm sending a squad of *Streltzi* with you, but they are just to keep you safe. Captain Boyce knows that if his company fails in its mission, you'll take the *Streltzi* and come tell me about it. Then he and his people won't get paid."

"Yes, sir," Tim said. "I'm sure the steam barge will arrive soon."

Chapter 55

On the Volga River

"God cursed piece of crap!" Shorty shouted as the pressure valve started screaming again.

Ivan couldn't really blame his brother. Besides, it wasn't really blasphemy, more a statement of fact. The new barge that they had received had a real pressure-relief valve. The pressure-relief valve blew a whistle when it let off excess steam. The whistle wasn't removable. Whenever the steam got a little strong, the thing started screaming at them like some sort of demented banshee and didn't stop till the steam pressure had dropped to what the builders in Murom thought was a good pressure. Which, they had told Ivan Mikhailovich, was about thirty pounds per square inch.

When they had gotten to Murom they had been informed that they weren't going back to Moscow. They were instead taking supplies to "our gallant troops," which meant they were going up the Volga almost all the way. Except, of course, the Volga wasn't their river. Never mind. It didn't matter. They had the most experience with steam barges. So they were given this brand new and improved steam barge with a donut boiler. Which wasn't quite a tube boiler, but better than a pot boiler since the chimney for the fire box went through the boiler. It had better, more finely worked, cylinders and pistons and worked at higher pressure, so used less fuel and went faster. It had two propellers, one on either side. What a glory of Russian engineering!

Crap!

There had been four explosions of steam barges since Ivan and Pavel Mikhailovich had taken out the first one. Four out of the thirteen barges that had been launched. Each and every explosion had been blamed on the barge's engineer over-pressuring the boiler. Maybe that was the cause. The engineers weren't here to argue the point. The experts at the Dacha and Murom hadn't actually said that a dumb peasant couldn't be trusted to manage the steam pressure, but the brand new release valve didn't have any sort of adjustment that the engineer on the barge could make.

They were going up an unfamiliar river in a brand new barge. So far this trip they had lost two seals on the right piston and run aground once.

"What is it this time, Shorty?" Ivan shouted. He had to shout. The god-cursed pressure valve was still screaming. The passengers had retreated to the front of the barge.

"What?" Shorty shouted back holding his hands over his ears. "I think the release valve is getting looser. If we had the sort of head of steam we should need for it to go off like that, we'd be going twice as fast." Shorty banged the boiler with his wrench and it finally stopped screaming.

Ivan looked at the shore and at the water. This wasn't their river, but it looked to him like Shorty might be right. He looked for something to toss over the side to get a clearer notion of the speed of the current. Mostly they were carrying food. Barrels of beans and rye, flour, beets and even some freeze-dried fruit.

Up front, there were four barrels of gunpowder, a box of one hundred chambers for the new AK3 rifles and another crate full of the rifles. There was also some lamp oil, but nothing that Ivan saw was trash that would float and tell him how fast the river was running. He watched the ripples off the bow and they didn't seem to be going that fast. "I think you're right, Shorty."

The passengers were still at the front of the barge. Four boys, ensigns, and *deti boyars* off to win glory, who had decided that going to battle by steam barge would be a lark.

The ensigns had changed their minds about that when they first experienced the pressure valve screech. By now they had decided that it was unsuitable for them to arrive at Rzhev on a boat since they were cavalry. However, there were no horses for them to buy. By now Dmitri Borisovich was discussing the advisability of arriving in Rzhev on cows.

"Cows are useful animals and holy in India or someplace like that. Surely it wouldn't diminish our dignity too much to arrive on milk cows," said Dmitri Borisovich in a voice that was an artful mix of wistful and jesting. He was the youngest and the friendliest of them. The others had started out superior and by now were making threats of dire consequences if Ivan and Pavel didn't magically get them to Rzhev.

"What is the problem with this scow?" Mikhail Ivanovich, the eldest of the four, asked.

Ivan gritted his teeth. They were boyar's sons, and in at least one case that was probably literally so. Mikhail Ivanovich was probably the son of Ivan Corkiski, born on the wrong side of the blanket. So telling him to shut up and mind his own affairs while Ivan and Pavel saw to the boat wasn't advisable.

It only made it worse that they were mostly justified complaints.

"It's not their fault, Mikhail," said Dmitri Borisovich. "They didn't build the thing."

"No, the Gorchakov clan built it. Holding the rights to every-thing to themselves, the Corkiski clan could have..." Mikhail stopped at the glare one of the others was giving him.

Alexsey Sergeyivich was a Gorchakov *deti boyar*, which was why the four had been in Murom when word of the invasion had arrived. He had promised his friends that he'd be able to get them the new AK3 rifles. Which he had, indeed, accomplished.

Dmitri interrupted the stand-off with the comment, "The barges are made by men. Men who are imperfect. Why should we expect that the barges would be perfect?" Then, looking toward the shore, he said, wistfully, "Still, there is that cow..."

After some more mutual glaring, the four passengers moved to the front of the barge, which was continuing its trip upriver. Albeit more slowly, it seemed.

"Ivan, see this?" Pavel said, pointing at a spring-loaded screw in the assemblage that led from the boiler to the pressure valve. "I think it's gotten looser."

"Well, tighten it, Shorty!"

"I'm not sure I should, Stinky. What if it breaks something?"

"Don't call me Stinky. You may be right, it might break something. Or it might fix something. Look, here. See? There's a lever that's pushed on by that screw. I think it controls the pressure valve, but I'm just not sure."

"So I tighten it, right?"

"Yes, but if we do we risk blowing up the boiler."

"I'm going to watch it for now, to see if it loosens any more."

They added more wood to the firebox and a few minutes later the pressure valve popped again and it started to scream.

Mikhail Ivanovich had had enough. This was ridiculous. He stood quickly and marched back to the back of the barge. "Give me that," he shouted, grabbing the wrench. He swung at the screaming whistle, and hit it. It dented, but kept screaming. He swung again and the whistle went flying off into the river.

The bargeman looked stunned. "B-b-b—"

Mikhail cut him off. "There, that's fixed." He handed the peasant the wrench and marched back to the front of the barge.

What neither Mikhail nor Pavel knew, was that as the whistle bent before it broke, it had blocked the pressure valve from opening properly. Some steam still escaped, so it looked like the pressure valve was still working as it should.

After thinking about it for a minute, and examining the damage, the best Pavel could tell was that the damage wasn't too severe, aside from the removing of the whistle. Pavel shrugged. At least they wouldn't be hearing that damned whistle anymore.

He threw some more wood on the fire.

Things were going much better now. They were making much better time. The steam pressure valve was constantly open, but doing its job. So it seemed.

Pavel checked the screw and it was looser, he was almost sure. He was considering tightening it, when it happened. The pressure in the boiler had been building gradually for several hours and the iron was not as strong or as well welded as it should have been. The seam broke and ripped loose, happening faster than the eye could possibly follow.

Pavel was cut in half by the jet of steam before he knew anything had happened. And the shattering boiler sent burning wood from the firebox and shrapnel from the boiler flying everywhere. The rest of the water in the boiler flashed into steam in an instant.

Ivan, Stinky, took a piece of shrapnel in the belly and went down screaming. Mikhail Ivanovich, who had been bragging that it was he who was responsible for their increased speed, was only slightly wounded by a piece of boiler that struck him in the arm, but was shocked and confused by the noise. More importantly, the same piece of boiler that struck Mikhail's arm bounced into a barrel of lamp oil, ripping it open and spilling the contents across the deck.

For fateful moments, as the lamp oil spread across the deck toward bits of burning wood, the survivors were held immobile in shock. Then, as the oil reached a burning shard, fire covered the front third of the barge. And that brought Dmitri and Alexsey out of their shock. Alexsey grabbed Mikhail Ivanovich from the deck and Dmitri went to try to rescue Ivan, who was still screaming.

Neither of the rescuers was in time, for the flames breached one of the gunpowder barrels. And the newest, fastest, most technologically advanced riverboat in Russia ceased to exist.

Chapter 56

July 17, 1634

"Oh!" Judy the Younger Wendell heaved a great sigh. "She's beautiful."

The bride *was* beautiful. Brandy Bates wore a flowing, white, angora/wool gown with a Chinese silk veil. The veil was attached to a wreath of white roses mixed with baby's breath and myrtle leaves. The leaves were said to bring good luck to the marriage. Brandy carried a bouquet of more white roses, baby's breath, ivy and pale pink carnations.

"She's probably melting in that wool," Vicky Emerson muttered. "God knows, I am."

The Barbie Consortium were bridesmaids at the wedding of the season. Wedding of the year, could be. And in spite of Vicky's every effort, the skirts were long and the dresses modest. Not her favorite look.

"Shh!" Millicent hissed. "She's almost here."

The wedding was being held in the formal garden of the *Residentz*, the home and offices of Vladimir Gorchakov's Russian delegation. Father Kotov had pushed for the wedding to be held at St. Vasili's Russian Orthodox Church, but there were just too many people who needed to be invited. And most of them had shown up.

✧   ✧   ✧

"Brandy is just gorgeous." Tate Garrett, Vladimir's chef, wiped her eyes.

"Prince also," said Father Kotov's wife Kseniya. Her English was so heavily accented it was barely comprehensible, but given that the woman had only been in Grantville for three months Tate was impressed she spoke any English at all. She herself had only learned a handful of Russian terms and was still incapable of following any sentence spoken in the language.

Kseniya was right about the prince, too. Vladimir had suffered the indignity of Grantville's eclectic fashion mix—with Russian tradition thrown in—but somehow, magically, it had all come together in a cohesive whole. He wore a Russian style fur hat and cape and trousers that were so tight they might almost have been hosiery. The ceremony was nice, too...if a bit long and convoluted with the greater part of it in a language hardly anyone understood. The reception was more interesting.

The wedding cake Tate had worked on decorating for two days stood tall and gleaming in the center of a table, flanked by molded Russian Creams on each side. Every kitchen maid at the *Residentz* had learned to make mints whether she wanted to or not, because there were literally thousands of them. Tate blessed Vladimir several times for choosing an afternoon reception. She might have had a nervous breakdown if she'd had to do a formal dinner for all these dignitaries. Instead, they'd set up an informal buffet. People were circulating freely, murmuring to one another about various things.

Tate began to relax. It was going well.

"No, it's not that simple," Kseniya Kotova said. "The czar can't make laws, not without the consent of the Assembly of the Land or at least the *Boyar Duma*. It's not just that it would be unadvisable; he literally doesn't have the authority to change the law on his own."

Reverend Green waited for the translator to finish. Once he was done, Green frowned and spoke in English. "So if he wanted to end serfdom, for instance, the *Duma* would stop him?"

Most of the Russian delegation in Grantville was well-versed in English because England was Russia's biggest trading partner in the early seventeenth century. But not all of them were—and, in any event, the English they knew was quite different from the version spoken by up-timers. So, they'd brought a number of translators with them.

Kseniya's husband had been chosen as their priest partly because he was fluent in English. With his help, she'd grown fairly adept in the language, so she thought she'd understood what Green had said. But since the third person present in room, Colonel Leontii Shuvalov, was one of the Russians who spoke almost no English, she waited until the translator was finished just to be sure.

She then glanced over at Shuvalov. Kseniya was by now fully aware of the up-timers' attitude toward serfdom, but this was not the place to discuss it. While she was still trying to figure out how to guide the conversation to a safer topic, the colonel spoke up. "It probably wouldn't be the *Boyar Duma*, what you would call the royal council, that stopped him, but the Assembly of the Land. The ah, middle class I believe you call it. The great families have never been the ones pushing to limit the rights of departure."

Again, they waited for the translator. Once he was done, the American priest—no, she thought he was called a pastor—looked surprised.

"I would have thought they would want it most."

Kseniya understood that quite well. She waited for the translator to interpret for the colonel and then said: "Yes, I know you would. You up-timers tend to simplify things." Kseniya was a bit annoyed at Reverend Green. "It isn't a conflict between the evil lords and their suffering serfs. The great families can afford to... what is it you call it up-time...go head-hunting? Though, in the case of serfs, it's more back-hunting."

Reverend Green snorted.

"I'm not sure that Boyar Sheremetev would agree with you," Colonel Shuvalov said.

"Of course not." Kseniya regretted saying it as soon as it came out but the truth was she despised Fedor Ivanovich Sheremetev though she had never met him. From all reports he was ill-tempered and not very good at dealing with the bureaus. Still, the news that the Smolensk war would have been a disaster had brought him back into politics. So she explained a bit more. "Russia lacks labor, and the weather conditions that make it the next thing to impossible to work the land for half the year don't help. If the serfs were released from the land, the only people in

Russia who could afford to hire the labor needed to run a farm would be the great families and the big monasteries."

"Don't forget the new innovations," Colonel Shuvalov pointed out. "While there is truth in what you're saying, there is less of that truth now than there was before the Ring of Fire."

Kseniya hesitated. What she wanted to say was unsafe, more for her family than for her. But spending time in Grantville had made it harder to keep her mouth shut. "It takes time to put those innovations into production, Colonel. Can you afford to lower your—" A quick glance at Reverend Green. "—tenants' rent?"

Colonel Shuvalov grinned at her. It was a surprisingly friendly grin. "Actually, yes. Though I will admit that it's only because Boyar Sheremetev has been quite generous with my family." Then the colonel turned back to Reverend Green and addressed him through the translator. "Kseniya's father-in-law and I aren't really in the same position, not quite. We are both Russian officers. He a captain, I a colonel, but the larger difference is that aside from the lands granted me by the czar, Boyar Sheremetev provides additional support. So my financial position is a bit better than his and less likely to be swamped by changing economic tides."

"Speaking of the army, how are the negotiations with the Polish-Lithuanian Commonwealth going?" Kseniya asked.

"Negotiations?" Reverend Green asked, after he got the translation. "What are you negotiating with the PLC?"

Now Colonel Shuvalov did look shocked. "Surely you knew! Poland and Russia are at war! We have been since the Truce of Deulino expired over a year ago. The negotiations are an attempt to prevent the shooting war from resuming." Then he looked back at Kseniya. "Not well, when I left Russia. King Wladyslaw is insisting that he is the rightful czar." He snorted. "And I believe the rightful king of Sweden, as well. Boyar Sheremetev is convinced that he, like we, has read the history of the other time Smolensk war. So he knows, probably, that it is unlikely that he can actually gain the throne. But considering the degree to which he trounced us in that other time, he seems to expect to receive the war indemnity without actually having to fight the war."

"How likely is he to trounce you this time if it comes to a shooting war?" Reverend Green wanted to know.

"I wish I knew," the colonel said. "The patriarch was sure that we would win before Prince Gorchakov sent his letter, and we might have been in a shooting war before now if Sigismund III had died this time around when he did in that other history. But he lasted six months more. Boyar Sheremetev was less convinced of our chances in a shooting war and remains so. At the same time, we have learned a lot from the Dacha and the Gun Shop. Even from those silly board games they are playing in the Moscow Kremlin now. Still, it will be better for all if we can reach a negotiated settlement."

Which was, Kseniya knew, the stance of the Sheremetevs and their supporters. None of them had any way of knowing it, but just then a young lieutenant named Timofeivich was reporting to his general in a place called Rzhev.

Chapter 57

August 1634

To supplement their rations, the *Streltzi* with their new AK3's went hunting between villages. Russia was sparsely populated compared to the rest of Europe and there was quite a bit of game. Captain Boyce and his sergeant were impressed with the guns. When they asked Tim about it, he called on one of the *Streltzi* to do a show-and-tell.

Daniil Kinski set the butt of the AK3 on the ground and the tip of its barrel came not quite to his shoulder and Daniil Kinski was a short man. If any of them had been familiar with the up-time weaponry, they would have thought of the AK3 as the illegitimate child of a Kentucky long-rifle and a Winchester 73. Like the long-rifle, the AK3 was a flintlock, and like the Winchester it had a lever action. But the AK3 had a removable firing chamber. Daniil lifted the AK3 and showed them how the chamber was removed. He opened the lever action chamber lock and pulled out the chamber.

"The chamber, as you can see, is a steel case, two and a half inches long including the quarter inch lip that inserts into the bore of the barrel. Behind the lip, the front of the chamber is flat and supposed to fit flush to the bottom of the barrel. It doesn't always fit as flush as we'd like, so we made some leather gaskets." He pulled the gasket off the chamber and showed them. "We still have the flash from the pan and the touch hole, but that's no worse than any flintlock."

269

Daniil stuck the gasket back on the chamber, then opened the frizzen and tapped the touch hole of the chamber on the pan to prime it. He closed the frizzen, inserted the chamber in the rifle, then he pulled the lever up flush with the stock which pushed the back block forward, forcing the lip of the chamber into the barrel. Finally, he cocked, aimed, and fired.

Crack!

Then he opened the chamber lock, pulled the chamber out, stuck it in his pouch, primed the pan with a loaded chamber, inserted the loaded chamber with a gasket already on it into the AK3, closed the lock, aimed, and fired again.

Crack!

Relative to muzzle-loading a musket it was very fast. Plus, since both shots had been aimed, they had both hit the tree that was his target...some eighty yards away from where they were standing.

Daniil pulled the second chamber from the AK3, then leaned the rifle against a tree while he showed them how to reload the chambers. Daniil filled the chamber with a measured amount of black powder then pulled out a lead cylinder. "It doesn't use a round ball, it uses a Krackoff ball." Which, an up-time observer would note, had a certain resemblance to a Minié ball, in that it was a cylinder with one flat end and the other rounded. But it fit snugly into the chamber.

"Push down till the Krackoff ball is flush with or a little below the lip of the chamber," Daniil said. The chamber had an oddly-shaped back end and Daniil showed them how it fit into the back block of the chamber lock. It was designed to fit into the AK3 only in such a way that the touch hole lined up with the flint lock on the side of the rifle. "It can be inserted into the rifle with your eyes closed and the touch hole will still line up," Daniil told them. It was an impressive demonstration.

A week later, while Tim and his crew were still collecting boats on the Volga, the Russian force surrounded Rzhev. In a way, General Izmailov was surprised. His force seriously outnumbered the forces in Rzhev and he had half-expected the commander of the Polish mercenary force to realize that and withdraw.

Janusz Radziwill had considered doing just exactly that. His officers had suggested it. However, Janusz was a young man who had already thrown the dice. If he retired from the game now, things could get really difficult at home. Besides, the ease with which they had dispatched the cavalry suggested that they could hold and break the Russians against their recently built ramparts. So he allowed General Izmailov to reach the town, hoping to bait him into to another rash attack.

General Izmailov didn't take the bait. Instead, he surrounded the Polish encampment and started fortifying, using the *golay golrod*, the walking walls. Now it came down to a question of who would be reinforced first.

"What are those things and what good are they?" Tim looked up at the badly accented Russian. It was the sergeant from the mercenaries. Ivan—no, John was the English form—John Charles Hampstead. He must not have been near Moscow during the testing. The army had been encamped around Rzhev for about five days when they arrived.

The mercenaries of Captain Boyce's company had done a decent, if not spectacular job. "*Golay golrod*. Walking walls, you might say, or walking forts."

Hampstead said, "Fine. That's what they are. What good are they?"

A group of peasant draftees were pushing one of the *golay golrod* into position. Tim pointed at them. "They are made of heavy ply-wood. They let us build fortifications very quickly. In winter we can even put them on skis for ease of movement. Right now, of course, they're on wheels..." Tim's voice trailed off. He thought a moment.

It was *heavy* plywood. The panels were a good three inches thick. The wheels could even be turned a little bit. And that's what the workers were doing now. They were pushing the wall back and forth to maneuver it into a gap in the wall. Since the walls were a lot more likely to stop a bullet if it hit them at an angle, they were being set up at an angle to the city wall around Rzhev. Since the workers were filling in a gap in the wall, they were quite prudently staying behind the wall they were moving. Even if they had been in effective range of the Polish muskets—which they weren't—all the Poles would be able to see was the wall. Not that the workers seemed convinced of that. They were peasants, not soldiers of any sort. They weren't armed and weren't expected to fight, but were here to carry supplies, set up camp, and other support roles.

Tim realized that the workers were right. If they had been on the other side of the *golay golrod*, they would have been shot at and, if unlucky, hit. But the way they were doing it they were, if not perfectly safe, close to it. There was a narrow gap, less than half a foot, between the bottom of the wall and the ground. But to hit a target that size with the kind of muskets Hampstead and his men had, would take a lucky shot at ten yards.

That's when the plan began to come together. Not all at once, but in pieces. Tim could see the walls being shoved, one in front of the other...making a partial wall between their present position and Rzhev. But how would they get back? More walls. It came together in his mind. A slowly shrinking siege wall. A tightening noose around Rzhev. As the noose got tighter, the dead zone between the siege walls and the city walls would get smaller. He forgot, almost, that this was real, not a war game played at the Kremlin. Forgot, almost, that he was the most junior of aides to the general. Almost...but not quite. So it was with great humility and trepidation that he approached General Izmailov.

The general listened. Why not? It was a siege and he had nothing else to do at the moment except for smoothing over disputes of precedence or paperwork that his secretary could do better. After due consideration, he decided that it was the beginnings of a possibly very good plan. They would have to take into account that the *golay golrod* were less than completely effective when hit face-on by enemy fire. So rather than a tightening noose, it would be more like a spiked collar with the spikes on the inside.

Back in Moscow, things were not going well. The same people who would have wanted General Izmailov's head for denying Colonel Khilhov the opportunity to rid Russia of the Polish invaders now wanted his head for "ordering" it. Calls for his removal were brought up in both the *Zemsky Sobor* and the *Boyar Duma*. Others were afraid of offending the Poles and bringing about a repeat of the events of the up-time Smolensk War by squandering resources. Still others pointed out that the size of the invasion had been grossly overestimated. The close to ten thousand men that General Izmailov had should be plenty. Between the three factions, they blocked any attempt to send reinforcements. And almost blocked resupply.

Chapter 58

Crack!

Janusz Radziwill ducked behind the Rzhev city wall, cursing the Russian forces. He wasn't happy that the Russian guns could reach farther than his. He didn't like that the *golay golrod* seemed to be being used in a brand new way. Most of all he detested the flying thing.

"I hate that cursed thing. Every time it's up there, it's watching every move we make and telling the Russkies just what we're doing."

Colonel Millerov looked up and nodded. "I'm none too happy with it myself. I feel like I'm being watched every minute of the day. But—" He pointed. "I'm just as worried about the walls they're pushing inwards. And what's going to happen if the Rus get here and get in before our reinforcements get here."

"Help should be on his way from Smolensk." The last messenger had arrived just days ago. He had to swim down the Volga at night and sneak up the bank. But he had reported that the Smolensk garrison was coming.

"They need to move faster," Millerov said. "Once those forces get here, we'll have them between us and the relief. And there's no way out for them." He paused. "If they get here in time, that is."

"General Izmailov, sir." Nick paused to think about his report for a moment. "A force of about eight thousand men is approaching from the southwest. From Smolensk, as near as I can tell. They'll be here in a week."

The general looked grim. "Well, we knew it was inevitable."

He began issuing orders. "Tim, now that we've tightened the noose around Rzhev, we've got plenty of wall sections. We'll use them to build our own fortifications between us and the oncoming force. Arrange it."

That wasn't a good solution but it was the best he could do with what he had. One thing he didn't want to allow was a relief of the siege of Rzhev. Instead his force would be both besiegers and besieged.

"Yes, sir." The young lieutenant—who was looking older by the day—took off toward the peasants and soldiers who were used to move the walls.

Work on tightening the noose around Rzhev was halted while the Russians set about making their own defensive wall. To General Izmailov this was looking more and more like a carefully laid plan where someone had jumped the gun. Tim was right about the Volga, or at least he might be. If the Poles got a base on the upper Volga, they would be in a much better position to press Wladislaw's claim to the czar's throne. If the enemy got Rzhev and Tver and held them for a while, they could build up supplies and equipment to make a rapid advance by way of the Volga. They wouldn't need to take Moscow, just cut it off from the rest of Russia. Besides, if they held the Volga to Nizhny Novgorod, they held the mouth of the Muscovy River. Apparently, someone in Poland had realized that Moscow was a false key to Russia.

It was the rivers that gave someone control of Russia, not Moscow. Especially if the Poles got their own up-timer somewhere to make them steam-powered riverboats. Russia now had some steamboats running up the Volga bringing supplies. What they weren't bringing were reinforcements. Izmailov wondered if the people back in Moscow were crazy.

Meanwhile, everyone was working to get a second wall up about fifty feet outside the first and to get all their supplies between the two walls. That would give them a corridor that would stretch from the river on one side of Rzhev to the river on the other side. Rzhev was located on both sides of the Volga, but a bluff on the north side of the river commanded the lower city on the south side. For now, Izmailov would cede the lower city to the Poles. He could take it back easily enough once they had the upper city in their hands. There had been a ferry between the two, but that was easily dealt with. The Volga here was a bit over a hundred yards wide, making it impossible to occupy both sides of the river without dividing his force. The good news was the volley guns and small cannons placed at either end of the corridor could prevent the Poles from resupplying Upper Rzhev by crossing the Volga. That same bluff gave the Russian guns an advantage when protecting their resupply.

"All right, Nick. From now on you base out of Staritsa. I want you well away from Cossack patrols." Starista was about thirty miles as the crow—or *Testbed*—flew, a bit over fifty miles along the river. And it had enough defenses to keep *Testbed* safe. "Do you really think the blinker lamps will work in daylight?"

"They should, General. The lamp on *Testbed* is located in shadow, so as long as we stay out of the sun, you should be able to see the flashes. You have the grid map and we got a good enough look at their army to give a good read on their units. They have been designated A through K. We'll send an offset for the code wheels at the beginning and end of each message."

"What about us sending you messages?"

"Should work about the same. Blink at us from a shaded spot." Nick said. "What really worries me, General, is . . . well, they will know that we are telling you their locations. And we can't stay up all that long. They can just wait for us to leave, then move their units and attack where you're not expecting it."

"Pity about that," Aleksander Korwin Gosiewski said. In general, Gosiewski was quite pleased with the way things had gone since his forces left Smolensk. He wouldn't have done what Janusz Radziwill had, but since Janusz had opened the way, Gosiewski was fairly sure that he was safe from the political repercussions. And if it increased the size and power of Lithuania within the Polish-Lithuanian Commonwealth, that was all to the good.

"Our eight thousand and three thousand in Rzhev . . ." He felt confident that he could rout the Russians. His force was a modern army, six thousand infantry, two thousand cavalry. "But I would have liked to capture that balloon. I doubt it will return; I suspect the Rus commander has sent it away to keep it out of our hands."

He nodded to his subordinates. "But it doesn't matter that much. There is a time for subtlety, gentlemen, and a time for more direct means. This is the latter."

"Sir!" Colonel Bortnowski said.

"As soon as their balloon is out of sight, Colonel, you will take the German dragoons..." Gosiewski continued with a list of units designated to attack the east downriver edge of the wall. "We will hold here until the artillery has produced a breach in their *golay golrod*. You will then advance. Our situation is simple. Once we get within their outer wall, at any point, they are done and we can roll them up. The Russian soldiers don't have the stomach for a standup fight. They carry walls with them so they'll have something to hide behind. Take that away and they're like sheep among wolves."

It took another hour to work out all the various details, including a skirmish against the upriver edge of the wall to pull the defenders away from the planned breach point.

Chapter 59

"General, the Poles are moving," Tim said as he entered the tent.

"What?" the general had been taking a nap. He sat up on his cot. "Their cannon?"

"Not yet, sir."

"Very well. Give me ten minutes."

By the time General Izmailov got to the walls, the Russian corridor was acting like a disturbed ant bed. Izmailov didn't rush. He strolled. Exhibiting no hurry, he listened to reports as he went, stopped and greeted people. And, to an extent, the ant bed calmed. Actions became less frantic and more purposeful. When it was reported that the Polish cannon were moving into position, he quickened his pace and started giving orders.

"Get those guns in place!" The small rifled cannon of the Russians were moved into position, set up and loaded behind sections of wall. Ropes were attached to those wall sections so that they could be quickly moved out of the way.

"We'll give it to them now, boys," General Izmailov shouted. "Before they realize what hits them!"

The order was given while the Polish cannon were still out of effective range. *Their* effective range—not the effective range of the rifled breech-loading Russian guns.

The men on the ropes strained and the walls moved out of the way.

"Aim them! Don't just point them randomly!"

The gunners took a moment to refine their aim.

"Fire!"

Boomcrack! Boomcrack! Boomcrack!

The small cannons sounded like they couldn't make up their mind whether they were cannon or rifles. The rounds they fired were small, just under an inch across and three inches long. But they exited the Russian guns in a flat trajectory and hit very close to where their gunners aimed them. Two rounds struck the outer wagon of the Polish gun train. The third missed, but hit a wagon wheel which it shattered. Pointlessly, though, since the exploding powder wagons would have destroyed it a tenth of a second later anyway.

A Polish gunner lay on the ground, blown off his feet but otherwise uninjured, shaking his head less to clear it than in confusion. The Russian guns were half again out of a cannon's effective range. But even as he lay there, he heard another *boomcrack* and the gun carriage of one of the six Polish nine-pound sakers was struck and damaged by another Russian round. The gunner, after due consideration, decided that where he was, was a rather good place to be. Much better than standing up next to the guns.

Aleksander Korwin Gosiewski was not so sanguine. In the midst of disaster, he saw what he wanted to see. The Russians had opened a breech in their wall to allow their cannons to fire. He decided that if he moved fast enough he could exploit the breach. He rapped out orders to Colonel Bortnowski and sent off the messenger. "Attack now. Go for the breach. Charge, curse you! Charge!"

Much against his better judgment, Colonel Bortnowski charged. In a manner of speaking: the charge of a pike unit is rather akin to the charge of a turtle. Slow and steady. Which may win the race and may even win a battle when it's charging another pike unit. But when charging a wall two hundred fifty yards away and when that wall is manned by troops with rifled chamber-loading AK3's that can be fired, have the chamber switched, then fired again several times, the charge of a pike unit becomes an organized form of suicide. Eventually, of course, the pikes broke. But not nearly soon enough. Their casualties were much worse than the casualties the Russian cavalry units had suffered just weeks before.

Colonel Bortnowski was among the dead. They really should have used the Cossack cavalry, but it was in the wrong place.

The Polish force withdrew, but it was only temporary, as General Izmailov knew quite well.

"Gentlemen, our situation is untenable as it stands," General Izmailov said. "We must take Rzhev and soon. Tim, I want you to coordinate with the unit commanders, start tightening the collar again. Get us salients as close to the to the walls of Rzhev as you can..."

The general described what he wanted and work began again. The plan was to get several points right up against the walls of Rzhev. That would still leave the problem of defending against a potential attack by the Polish relief force while using most of his force to breach the defenses of Rzhev. To attack effectively—and just as important, quickly—they would need overwhelming force against the troops occupying the town. To get that, they were going to have to virtually strip the outer *golay golrod* of fighting men. And like any fortification, no matter how temporary or permanent, the walking walls needed to be manned be effective.

Two weeks later they were in position and as ready as they were going to get. At the closest point the inner *golay golrod* was only twenty feet from the makeshift walls around Rzhev and there were five points where they were within fifty feet.

Nick gave a bit more steam to the right side engine to turn *Testbed* left. The winds were gusty. He had gotten word a week before that they would be making the attack on Rzhev today. His job was especially vital because to make it look real they had to know where the Polish forces were attacking long before it happened. He looked out and noted the position of a Polish cavalry unit.

Rrrrriiiipppppp!

Nick looked up and swore.

The gas bladders on *Testbed* were made of goldbeater skin. Those were made from the outer membranes of the intestines of large animals, usually though not always calves. Goldsmiths used them to beat out gold leaf. For goldbeater skin, the intestines were cut open and glued together a couple of layers thick. The sheets of goldbeater skin were mostly self-adhesive and formed into short, fat sausage shapes rather than round balloons. It had never occurred to anyone to wonder what would happen if you applied steam.

Granted, by the time the steam reached the steam bladder it had cooled quite a bit. On the other hand, the steam bladder on *Testbed* had by now been slow-cooking for several weeks. A little bit of extra steam pressure was all it took. Of course, it gave along the seams. As soon as the rip happened, the steam spread out still further and turned into mist, then started condensing onto the other gas bags in *Testbed*, where it did comparatively little harm. But the steam cell was gone; its lift was gone.

The gondola lurched. Nick swore again and reached for a lever to angle the thrust that remained to him.

The steam bladder, when filled and functioning properly, provided about five hundred pounds of lift to *Testbed*. The semi-rigid airship had just gone from neutral buoyancy to five hundred pounds *negative* buoyancy. Which didn't mean it dropped like a five-hundred-pound lead weight. It was more like a five-hundred-pound feather. The steam bladder was located three-quarters of the way to the front of *Testbed*, just above the gondola, so naturally it nosed down. Which meant that the engines were pushing down as well. Airships dive like they do every other maneuver. Slowly. A similar disaster in an airplane would have given the pilot less than two minutes to fix the problem, as the plane nosed over and accelerated to over a hundred miles an hour straight down. Nick had a good five minutes before he would hit the ground.

First, reverse thrust on the steam engines. Nick shifted a couple of levers. Then, angling the thrust—he shifted more levers as he continued to lose altitude. Shift the trim weight. More work. He had to crank it back to the tail of *Testbed*. In doing these things, Nick lost about two thousand feet of altitude.

"It's coming right at us!" one man screamed.

The big balloon looked to the Polish troops on the ground like it was making a slow-motion dive-bombing run—not that they had ever seen a dive-bombing run of any sort. The nose of *Testbed* was pointing straight at them and it was billowing white smoke. Steam, actually, but they didn't know that.

"Fire, you bastards! Fire!"

Chaos reigned for minutes. Some of the men decided to be

elsewhere, but a surprising number stood their ground and started shooting.

Testbed was still out of what could reasonably be considered effective range of a seventeenth-century musket. At that range a seventeenth-century musket couldn't hit the broad side of a barn. But *Testbed* was significantly bigger than the broad side of a barn. Even a big barn. Inevitably, it got hit several times. Bladders filled with hydrogen were struck by musket balls. And nothing much happened. To get hydrogen to explode takes three things, hydrogen, oxygen and a spark. The hydrogen and oxygen need to be mixed together fairly well to get any kind of significant flame. But the crucial issue here was the lack of a spark. The lead shot back from the muskets was indeed still quite hot, but not that hot. Besides, there was all that steam condensation on the bladders and the skin of *Testbed*.

"Nothing's happening! It's still coming!"

By the time Nick had *Testbed* leveled out, it had a couple of dozen holes poked in the skin and three of its four hydrogen bladders had been punctured. But it took a long time for the hydrogen to leak out of a balloon forty feet across. *Testbed* continued on, as best anyone on the ground could tell, totally unaffected by the shots fired at it.

As best anyone on the ground could tell.

"Stupid fools," Nick said. *Testbed* was losing lifting gas and was already negatively buoyant. Further, it was not recovering any of the steam it was using to run the engines. So while Nick had hours of fuel left, he had five or ten minutes of water and when that ran out, he would lose power. Nick headed for base.

He didn't make it. He literally ran out of steam just over halfway there. Absent the engines that had been holding him up, he started to sink, fairly slowly, to the ground. Nose first.

Back at the battle, Gosiewski saw his opportunity but had some difficulty exploiting it. After the disastrous attack of the first day there wasn't a lot of enthusiasm for frontal attacks on the *golay golrod*. It took a while to get things organized.

Chapter 60

Sergeant John Hampstead looked over at his captain. "They'll be coming, sir. Now that the balloon is gone."

"I know." The captain nodded. "But where?"

Hampstead shrugged. "Maybe on the left. There are some gaps on that side. Sure as hell, we can't be everywhere." Their unit had been left on the outer wall to stiffen the peasant levies which were unarmed, just there to make it look like the wall was manned. The peasants had sticks painted to look like rifles and muskets, because the Russian government wasn't keen on arming peasants. Armed peasants tended to turn into Cossacks or bandits. Not that there was much difference between the two.

So Sergeant Hampstead and Captain Boyce had been assigned to go to wherever the Poles attacked and shoot so that it looked like the whole wall was manned by armed troops.

Captain Boyce nodded again. "It's as good a place as any, John. Start shifting the men." They could hear shooting from behind them. The Russians were in Rzhev and would be occupied for hours cleaning out the Polish troops in the town. If the outer wall was to hold, it would be them that held it.

"Form the men just inside the wall! We're going to wait right there."

"What about the firing ports, Captain?"

"I'm getting sneaky, John," Captain Boyce told his sergeant. "As important as holding this part of the wall is, convincing the Poles that we are just one of the units manning them is just as important. We need to give them a reason why the other parts of the wall aren't shooting." Then he turned to the peasant levies. "Who's in charge here?"

Having identified the man, Boyce explained what he wanted. "Tie ropes onto the *golay golrod*. When I give you the word I want you to pull these two sections apart. As quickly as you can. Then when I tell you, push them closed again."

Then man nodded and started giving orders. It would give them a roughly twenty-foot front. "John, two ranks only and keep the pike men in reserve. Have the men fire as the *golay golrod* clear the breach. Then fall back as soon as they have fired. Reload and reform as the walls come back together."

It didn't go like clockwork. Unless you were talking about a clock with a busted arrester gear.

"Open!" The walls started coming back with dozens of men pulling each wall. The troops started firing. *Blam Blam, Blam Blam*, and the walls retreated. And they did a credible job at first of retreating behind the *golay golrod* but then things went awry. Some men kept going, others stopped too soon and the walls caught up and passed them, leaving them exposed to enemy fire. Almost no one had time to reload because they were too busy moving. Then there were the Polish troops—who had been taking sniper fire from those walls for weeks. As best Boyce could tell, no one gave the order but the Polish formation went into a charge as the walls opened. They took casualties, lots of them, since Boyce's troops were firing from pointblank range. But the Poles saw the breach and ran right over their fallen to get to it.

Boyce ordered the wall to close before it was all the way opened. But it wasn't soon enough. The walls didn't close all the way; they were blocked by Polish troops.

Boyce on one side and Hampstead on the other, they struggled to reform the men and close the breach. They weren't alone. The Russian peasants, armed with whatever was handy, were right there with them.

Ivan didn't really know why he'd been assigned to this wall section, or even why he'd been pulled away from his farm. But

one thing he did know was that Polish forces loose in Russia
were a bad thing. He'd been hearing the stories all his life, how
the Poles had decimated his village and killed his grandfather.

He didn't have one of the fancy guns the soldiers had, but
he did have an ax he used to cut wood for the walking wall. If
nothing else, he and his peers could use their axes against the
Poles. And they would, he knew. Nobody wanted the Poles in
charge again. The boyars were bad enough.

So he stood in the shadow of the wall, waiting for the inevitable rush of men trying to get inside. Then he swung the ax,
the blade flat because he didn't want it to get stuck in bone or
armor. The Pole dropped to the ground and Ivan swung at the
next one. Misha was swinging just as frequently. Some of the Poles
got past, of course. An ax doesn't have much chance against a
sword, a pike, or even a flintlock pistol.

Still, they kept swinging.

"Get a message to Izmailov," Boyce shouted across the breach.
"Send a man, now!"

Hampstead grabbed the nearest man and sent him inside Rzhev.
"Tell the general we need more men. And we need them now, if
he doesn't want the Poles up his backside!"

In a sense, Boyce's trick had worked.

To the Poles it did look like one more weird Russian maneuver
using the *golay golrod*, but their commander thought that this one
had backfired. It was clearly poorly planned and not drilled nearly
enough. At least, not at the place the Polish force had attacked. It
might work better at other points along the line, but that didn't
really matter. They had a breach and poured everything they could
into it. The unsupported peasants at other places along the wall
were not attacked. And the maneuvering to bring forces to the
breach cost the Poles time.

"Back to the walls," Izmailov roared. "These pigs are well stuck."

Janusz Radziwill was dead, and most of his officers. The remain-
ing force inside Rzhev were rounded up and under guard. "Back
to the walls," Izmailov roared again. Tim gathered the men he'd
been leading and headed back to the breach in Rzhev's walls.

✧   ✧   ✧

"There's nothing there but peasants and sticks," Gosiewski shouted. "You're not turning back from peasants, are you?"

The Polish forces pushed toward the breach again.

"Here they come!" Tim's voice cracked on "come."

But it didn't matter that he was only seventeen. The men followed him readily. Nor were they the only group. Russian troops were turning over their prisoners to anyone handy and heading back to the walls. Unit cohesion ceased to exist. But by then most of the Poles in Rzhev were unarmed and most of the citizens of Rzhev weren't.

Suddenly Tim stopped dead in his tracks. They had reached the outer wall but the Poles weren't actually coming at them. They were nowhere near the breach. The Poles were crossing in front of them, not preparing to attack. He looked around trying to make sense out of the confusion and chaos that was battle.

Rzhev had been retaken. The volley guns and cannon that had been preventing resupply were no longer needed in that role. They hadn't been moved in preparation for the battle because the general didn't want the Poles across the Volga making a dash to reinforce Rzhev while the assault was still going on. But now, what purpose were the volley guns serving? He turned to find a man with an AK3 near him.

"Can you hold here with what you have?"

"I should be able to. Besides, more men are coming all the time. What you have in mind?"

What Tim had in mind was far above his authority. "Never mind. You men! Stay here." Then Tim ran. By going inside the inner wall, he shortened the distance he had to travel considerably. It still took him ten minutes to reach the volley guns. And considerable shouting to get them to pull away the wall section. "The general's orders! Bring the volley guns and follow me."

Of course, they weren't the general's orders; they were Tim's orders. And if the general decided to make an issue of it, Tim was going to be in a great deal of trouble. But somewhere during the battle the career of Lieutenant Boris Lebedev had decreased in importance. What was vitally important was getting the volley guns where they were needed.

Tim stood on the volley gun platform, which was being pulled by two steppe ponies. It wasn't a grand gesture; he needed the height to see over the wall to locate the breach. "That way!" He pointed. "Another hundred yards."

Tim and the gun crew were inside the inner walking wall. Just on the other side of it was a mob scene, packed with Poles slowly pushing back. The Russian defenders were spread along the wooden trench made by the two walls. Carefully, they lined up the volley guns at points where wall sections met.

That was when Tim realized the flaw in his magnificent plan. The *golay golrod* were made up of wall sections that could be latched together. But the latches here and now were on the other side. They couldn't open the walls. They knew where the latches were; there was one near the top one and near the bottom. Tim cursed himself for a fool. "We'll have to move the volley guns to where we control the walls." He climbed back up on the gun platform and looked over the wall again, almost getting shot for his trouble. "Over there." He pointed back the way they'd come. "Three wall sections."

When they got to a section that the Russians mostly controlled, Tim used the volley gun platform and scaled the wall. This time he almost got chopped up by a Russian peasant with a bloody ax and covered with gore. "Open the walls! Open the latches! Let the volley guns through!" And, surprisingly enough, that's just what they did.

The Russian version of the volley gun was an outgrowth of the same technology used in the AK3. The plates were loaded with AK3 firing chambers and were ignited by a quick fuse. They were slower firing than the ones in the west, but Russia was still having trouble with primers. They had twenty-four barrels arranged in three rows of eight. If all went well, the preparatory work was done on the chamber plates before the battle started, so all that was needed to reload was to pull a chamber plate and replace it with another before lighting the fuse. They were cranked, but only for traversing.

The last Russian slipped from in front of the volley gun. The gunner lit the fuse and started cranking. *Crack Crack Crack Crack...* twenty-four barrels in order. Then the gunner pulled the plate, inserted another and did it again. The gunners for the volley guns were big men. The plates weighed upwards of thirty pounds.

The volley guns wouldn't have been enough by themselves, but they took the pressure off the Russian troops long enough for a semblance of organization to occur. Unarmed peasants retreated to be replaced by armed *Streltzi* carrying AK3's, and the weight of fire shifted. The battle for Rzhev was effectively over.

Chapter 61

"Lieutenant, you are to report to the general's quarters."

Two weeks after the battle, things had stabilized. Rzhev was surrounded by three walls, one inside the other. The Rzhev wall that had been built in a somewhat haphazard manner by the Poles and the two layers of *golay golrod* together constituted a fairly formidable defensive network. Starving the victorious Russians out would take time. Meanwhile, the walls were bolstered by sand bags and firing platforms. Neither Tim nor General Izmailov had yet had occasion to mention Tim's orders to the volley guns, given in the general's name. Tim had been starting to hope—against his better judgment—that the general was going to let the whole thing pass.

"What am I going to do with you, Lieutenant?" General Izmailov sighed rather theatrically. "I have been reading a translation of an up-time book on a French general who had an elegant solution for this situation. He was dealing with a general, not a lieutenant, who acted on his own authority. At their base, the situations are quite similar. Bonaparte's elegant solution was to give the general a medal to acknowledge his achievement." There was a short pause but Tim knew he was far from out of the woods.

General Izmailov continued, "Then, to maintain good order and discipline in the army, he had the man shot for disobeying orders." General Izmailov paused again and waited. Tim remained silent.

"What do you think of Bonaparte's solution, Lieutenant? I could have you a medal by sunset."

Tim hesitated, looking for the right words. "I can't say it appeals to me, sir. But I grant that the solution has a certain, ah, symmetry." He stopped. Tim really wanted, right then, to bring up the political consequences to the general should he find it necessary to execute a member of a family of such political prominence, even a minor member of a cadet branch. He didn't, though, partly because it would sound like a threat—probably not a good tactic against someone like Izmailov—but mostly because Tim understood that while what he had done was the right thing for that battle, it was the wrong thing for the army. He had sat in *Testbed* and watched as Colonel Khilkov used his family position to destroy a couple of Russian cavalry regiments. He knew as well as General Izmailov that if word got out, his example would be used to justify every harebrained glory-hound for the next hundred years. Who knew how many people that would kill? Tim had known when he was doing it that it would cost him, but not how much.

"For political reasons I can't use Bonaparte's elegant symmetry. You will get neither the medal nor the firing squad. Those political reasons are only partly to do with your family." General Izmailov gave Tim a sardonic smile. "I will take the credit for your brilliant move and it may save my life when I must explain to the *Boyar Duma* my acquiescence to Colonel Khilkov's less-than-brilliant actions. We will say that it was a contingency plan. You will get a promotion, then you will receive the worst jobs I can come up with for some time to come. You will accept those jobs without complaint! Understand me, Lieutenant. You deserve the medal you will never get, but you also deserve the firing squad that you won't face this time. Don't make the same mistake again."

Tim was still doing latrine duty when Moscow finally decided to send reinforcements. At that point the ranking Polish officer withdrew his army. The Lithuanian magnate's campaign had not been sanctioned by either King Wladyslaw or the Sejm. Such private adventures by the great magnates of the Polish-Lithuanian Commonwealth were not particularly unusual—and if successful, got after-the-fact backing. But if they failed disastrously, the magnate could face severe repercussions. If nothing else, he'd be in such a weakened state that other great magnates—they all maintained large private armies—would be tempted to attack him.

As for Third Lieutenant Boris Timofeyevich Lebedev, he continued to receive unpleasant assignments for the next six months, much to the irritation of his father. But Tim never complained.

Chapter 62

September 1634

"So how was the wedding, Colonel?" Boyar Fedor Ivanovich Sheremetev asked.

"I found it quite interesting, sir," said Colonel Leontii Shuvalov. "Though I will admit I was a bit disappointed to find that the Poles had held a war while I was gone and I wasn't invited."

"Rzhev made things much more difficult," Sheremetev said. "Filaret is making noise about invading Poland again. And without Shein, we probably couldn't hold him back. Shein figures we are getting stronger, faster, so time is on our side for now. But he will switch back as soon as he figures we're ready." Sheremetev shook his head in disgust. "None of them can see that Poland is not the real enemy. The real enemy is Gustav Adolf and his new USE. So tell me about the USE, Leontii."

Leontii made his report. That the USE was rich and powerful and becoming more so every day was beyond question. He had seen several different kinds of airplanes. The largest of which was dwarfed by *Testbed*, but the slowest of which made the balloon seem a snail by comparison. But the real danger was the factories, which turned out hundreds of items in the time it would take a craftsman to make just one.

Yet Russia had factories, too. "While we are behind, we aren't that far behind. I took a steamer from Rybinsk, one of the ones that they were using to resupply Rzhev. I was amazed by the factories along the Volga."

Sheremetev grunted. "As new items come out of the Dacha, Princess Natalia doles them out to her friends at court. And they start hiring workmen and setting up 'factories,' as they call them. They are merely workshops."

Leontii looked at his patron questioningly and Sheremetev grunted again. "Granted, they have a lot of serfs working in them except during planting and harvest. And I'll even grant that the czar's paper money has increased trade. But I don't trust it. All these changes. It's too much, too fast."

"As you say, my lord," Leontii said. "But it's nothing compared to what they are doing in Germany." Leontii went on to acknowledge the corrupting influence of the up-timers, but pointed out that Vladimir and the Dacha were proving incredibly valuable and were probably essential. "Sooner or later—not even Poles are *that* dumb— King Wladyslaw or some of the magnates will recruit up-timers of their own. By the way, how are they taking the events at Rzhev?"

"The *Sejm* seems very upset at the outcome. More upset than cautioned, unfortunately. It must be our fault and we must have somehow cheated, they think." Sheremetev shrugged, acknowledging that they might have a point. "Made a deal with the devil, something, anything, other than that they attacked us and we outfought them. They seem especially worried that we had such things as breech-loading cannon and that the walking forts proved so effective.

"It hasn't made things any easier on the diplomatic front. About the only thing keeping them from a full-scale invasion is Gustav Adolf's presence on their western border. The Truce of Altmark expires next year, and the way that Sweden and the USE have been going, Poland simply can't afford to be involved in a war with us when Gustav Adolf gets around to them. What concerns me is I don't see any particular reason for the Swede to stop at the Russian border."

Through the fall and winter of 1634, the *Boyar Duma* debated. And talks with the Polish-Lithuanian Commonwealth went nowhere. In the winter of 1634, Patriarch Filaret became ill and much of the heart went out of the faction that advocated an attack on Poland.

Meanwhile more factories came on line. most of them using forced peasant labor. This upset the peasants because winter was their traditional light time. It also upset the great families because they couldn't hire the peasants without their landlords' permission.

Since the Ring of Fire, the anti-serfdom movement in Russia had slowly grown from two directions, top down and bottom up, with the service nobility caught in the middle. The top down part was a mix of morality and self-interest. It was fairly small, because the top of the Russian pyramid was small. There were fourteen to twenty great families, depending on how you counted, and a similar number of really large monasteries. A few hundred people in the great families and no more than a few thousand in the monasteries. Still, they were the most powerful people in Russia.

On the other hand, there were over thirty thousand members of the service, or bureaucratic, nobility—people whose livelihood depended on serf labor. And they were the people holding down the vital mid-level military and civilian posts. They were the tax collectors, the construction supervisors and the managers. In the Russian army, they were the captains and the colonels, but rarely the generals. It was the service nobility, bureaucrats and soldiers alike, that had kept Russia from collapsing into chaos during the Time of Troubles. They had stayed on the job and mostly out of politics, serving whichever czar was in power, and kept the wheels from coming completely off. They were generally nonpolitical, but threatening to take away their serfs would change that in a hurry. As had been shown in 1605, the last year when peasants leaving the land hadn't been forbidden.

Then there were the serfs themselves, by far the largest proportion of the Russian population. While many, perhaps most, resented their status as serfs, few of them objected to the institution as such. It wasn't that they found the social order objectionable—just their place in it. They ran to the wild east, they ran south to the Cossack lands, they even ran west into Poland, hoping for a better deal. What they didn't do was stand where they were and say "This is wrong!"

It was a subtle but important distinction. There was no Harriet Tubman sneaking back into the Moscow province to smuggle other serfs out to the Cossack territories where they could be free. No Russian Frederick Douglass standing proudly and articulately to decry not just his serfdom, but *all* serfdom. At least, they hadn't done so before the Ring of Fire.

The Ring of Fire was changing all that, though it took a while for the change to take root. But ... not that long a while. Rumors fly on the wings of eagles, they say. They fly even faster on wings made of mimeographed paper, and the more radically inclined of the boyar class could afford lots of paper. Russia might not have had its own Tom Paine, at least at first. But the writings of the original made their way into Russia and into Russian. And they resonated. Resonated like jungle drums, like liberty bells. Soon enough, Committees of Correspondence sprang up in a number of the larger cities and towns. Small ones, true, but they were able to begin articulating the rebellious thoughts and anger of Russian serfs.

Russia was still not a country anyone would describe as a powder keg. The population was mostly illiterate and mostly rural—and diffuse, at that. And while some elements of the upper classes were becoming radicalized, no one wanted a return to the Time of Troubles. No one wanted Polish troops flooding into Moscow again.

Then there was Rzhev. In military terms, Rzhev wasn't very significant at all. But in emotional terms it was. In Rzhev Russia defeated the Poles. And the army that did it had a good number of serfs in it, with a lot of them involved in the fighting. In Rzhev, the Russians showed themselves to be technologically superior to the Poles. Rzhev brought a new feeling of confidence to Russia, and a great deal of political capital to the czar.

Patriarch Filaret wanted to spend that capital invading Poland and retaking Smolensk. But Czar Mikhail Fedorovich was beginning to consider other ideas. He'd now had three years to read about the history of what would become the Russia of the Romanov dynasty in another universe. Three fairly easy years, too. Despite his formal prestige, no one really demanded much of the czar, not even his father, so he had plenty of time to think about what he'd learned.

By the end of the year 1634, he'd come to accept the condemnation spoken so many times and so harshly in the speeches of Mike Stearns, the USE's prime minister. Serfdom had to go. Or, sooner or later, just as it had in another world, it would bring down the Romanov dynasty. Czar Mikhail had no desire to see himself—or even one of his descendants a century or two from now—being shot along with his whole family in a cellar somewhere.

In that other universe, one of his descendants—Czar Alexander II—had attempted to reform serfdom. Had even succeeded, to a degree. Not enough and certainly not soon enough—but that was no excuse for inaction on Mikhail's part. Alexander's attempt had happened in 1861, almost a quarter of a millennium in the future.

Two centuries and twenty-seven years was a long time. Still, it was best to get started. Not even Mikhail Romanov was that much of a procrastinator.

Part Five

The year 1635

Chapter 63

February 1635

Fedor read the newsletter again, his jaws tight.

> *In an unprecedented move, today Czar Mikhail decreed that "Forbidden Years" are now limited, with some qualifications. Anyone who wants to buy out and leave his current lord may do so, provided he is willing to move to Siberia and look for gold or other metals and resources that are now known to exist.*
>
> **Treasure Maps For Sale Here! Up-time sources used! Mine for GOLD, SILVER, COPPER! Find OIL!**

Angrily, he shoved the paper back at Stepen. "And what are we going to use for labor now, Stepen? The czar has betrayed us!"

"Shhh!" Stepen hissed. "You want to get us killed!"

"I'm as loyal as any man," Fedor insisted, though more quietly. "But that doesn't get the crops in. Without our serfs my family will starve...and so will yours."

Stepen thought that was overstating the case, but it was true that members of the service nobility, like himself and Fedor, needed their serfs. There was never enough labor. "They claim that the new machines will take care of the labor problem," Stepen said, still trying to calm his friend.

"They claim! If we could get them. You know how long the waiting list is and you know the boyars will all have them before we even see one. Which is probably a good thing, because who knows if they will work?"

Stepen considered bringing up the increase in pay, but he was very much afraid that Fedor would start yelling again. Fedor had already made his opinions on the new paper money quite clear, many times. And honestly, Stepen tended to agree with him. How could a piece of paper with printing on it have value? It just didn't make sense. Whenever he could, Stepen spent the paper as quickly as he could and saved the silver. He wasn't the only one. By this time a silver ruble, which nominally had the same value as a paper ruble, was buying three times as much. It didn't occur to Stepen that the new paper rubles were worth three-quarters as much as the silver rubles had been before the paper rubles were introduced. Silver rubles were disappearing into holes and hidden compartments all over Russia, in a classic example of Gresham's Law.

Stepen and Fedor had recently been transferred to Moscow to appointments within the Bureau of Roads, because the Bureau of Roads was expanding with the introduction of the Dacha scrapers. They had both gotten raises, but those raises hadn't been in the form of more lands as had been usual. The raise had been more of the new paper money.

They didn't see Pavel Borisovich sitting in the next cubicle with a friend.

"Papa, have you heard about the new proclamation?" Pavel asked Boris. "I was having lunch with Petr Ivanovich over at the bureau of roads and a couple of the new hires were talking. They seemed pretty upset."

"Yes. I imagine they were."

"How bad is it?" Pavel asked.

"It probably won't be too bad for us. We have new plows, a seeder, a reaper and a thresher. But it will ruin a lot of the lower nobility. How many are ruined depends on how many of the serfs can buy out and how many decide now is a good time to run." Serfs running away had been a major problem for years. They were often aided and abetted by the boyars and the church, who always needed more labor.

Russia had had a well-developed bureaucracy for many years. What Russia hadn't had when it was developing that bureaucracy, though, was the money to pay the bureaucrats. So whether it was a clerk in Nizhny Novgorodi, a manager in the bureau of roads, the *Konyushenny Prikaz*, or a cavalry trooper, most of the pay for his service was in the form of land granted on a semi-permanent basis by the czar.

Even at this late date the knots of law and custom that turned a free man into a serf weren't quite absolute. If you could escape and stay gone for five years, you were free. And the government wouldn't hunt you; that was up to the person who held the land you were tied to. Also, in theory, there were times when you could buy your way out of your chains. In theory. The last thirty or so years had been "Forbidden Years," during which even if you could come up with the cash, you weren't allowed to change your status.

Boris continued. "Politically, it's hard to say. The czar may gain enough from the high families and with the general population to offset what he's going to lose with the *dvoryane* and *deti boyars*." Czar Mikhail had been, at least on the surface, quite clever in how he had implemented the new "Limited Year," but Boris wasn't at all sure he had been clever enough.

"It's a big step forward," Bernie Zeppi said. "A really big step."

"It's a disaster," said Filip Pavlovich, Bernie's sometime tutor. "The czar's gone mad. Labor, Bernie. There's not enough. There's never been enough. Look, Bernie. I know that serfdom is wrong. You've convinced me. You and Anya. But the service nobility will not stand for this."

"Freedom, Filip," Bernie said back. "Why don't people get that people will work harder and produce more if they're doing it for themselves?"

"Because it isn't true," Filip told him bluntly. "Oh. People probably will work harder if they're paid. But not enough harder to make up for the cost of paying them. Besides, what is the service nobility going to pay them with?"

Natasha felt like burying her head in her hands. Or possibly screaming at the top of her lungs. Instead, she took a deep breath, and said, "Gentlemen, this isn't a productive conversation. Can we get back on topic, please?"

"It will make Czar Mikhail even more popular than the win at Rzhev," Anya pointed out.

The presence at the meeting of Bernie's former leman—or, rather, Anya's ease at speaking in the meeting—was an indication of just how much Bernie's presence had affected the Dacha. Bernie was blind to class and it was rubbing off. It had been rubbing off now for three years—on Natasha herself most of all, she sometimes thought.

Anya had started off as a cook's assistant and with help from Bernie had become the Dacha's household accountant. In the process she had become involved in the development of the EMCM, Electro-Mechanical Calculating Machine.

"Popular with whom?" Filip asked. "Serfs don't have weapons, unless you count an ax as a weapon. The service nobility does. And so does the *Streltzi*. And it's they who will be most affected. When your Czar Lincoln talked about limiting slavery, not abolishing it, it caused a revolution and that was in a country where only a third of it had slavery in the first place. In Russia, serfs are everywhere. I'm not saying serfdom is a good thing, Anya. But it's too soon to do this."

"More money for Vladimir," Bernie said. "Reapers and threshers are going like hotcakes. What's weird to me is that you—" He pointed at Natasha. "—aren't freaking out about losing serfs. You've got all these lands to take care of."

"I," Natasha said, "can afford to hire help. And people want to work for us, because we can afford to take a smaller cut, because we have more people. Most of the truly wealthy are the same way, you know. As is the church. We can make a deal, attract more of the labor force. It's the service nobility, people like Boris and Filip, who need the serfs tied to the land. That's what concerns Patriarch Filaret. Ill as he is, he counseled the czar against this move. And Czarina Evdokia is very, very worried. But the boyars and *Duma* men are all for it. It will make it much easier for us to poach serfs from the service nobility. There's a lot of nervousness in Moscow right now."

"And it won't take much to start a firestorm," Filip said. "It's not like we haven't had them before. Or wouldn't have them in the future. Remember Peter the Great. For that matter, remember

1917. That's why I said it's too soon, Bernie. There aren't enough plows and reapers yet to make much of a difference in overall production. And members of the service nobility like me mostly don't have them."

Anya sighed. "I understand your point, Filip. But already serfs are being put to work in factories. Rented out, or close enough to make no difference, to make their lord extra money. It will never be the right time! Slavery and serfdom don't just fade away. No oppression does. It takes people standing up and saying 'enough, no more!' And making it stick."

Natasha knew that was true. Evdokia had discussed it with Mikhail. Bernie was wrong. It was probably true enough that people worked harder when they were working for themselves. And the evidence was pretty clear that societies without serfs were, over all, more productive than those with serfs. But that extra productivity didn't go into the pockets of the lord. It went to buy the former serf a new suit of clothes or an extra room of the house, maybe some toys for their kids. Which worked just fine for society as a whole, but very badly so far as the lord was concerned, since he now had to pay for labor that he used to get for nothing or at least a lot less.

Meanwhile, Bernie was grinning. Natasha raised an eyebrow in question.

"It's just that it's the downtrodden middle-class getting squeezed between the rich liberals and the poor, just like back in the twentieth century."

Anya shook her head. "Yes, but your middle-class didn't keep slaves, Bernie."

Chapter 64

Grantville
March 1635

"What's up, dude?" Brandy asked. Calling Vladimir "dude" in her empty-headed surfer girl voice usually got a laugh and sometimes led to other things.

"Huh? What?"

But not this time apparently. "What's wrong, Vladimir?"

Vlad sat down heavily. "I'm worried. There's bad news from Moscow, but I'm not sure how bad it really is. Boris is being reticent. It could just be that he's busy I guess . . . but it could also be that he's distancing himself from the family. Father Gavril showed me some letters from his family which indicate that the *dvoriane* in the military are badly upset with Czar Mikhail and increasingly concerned with foreign influences on him."

"Kseniya, could you puh-leeze explain all this to me?" Brandy ruffled her hair, looking like she was about to start tearing it out at the roots. "What's going on in Moscow? Vladimir's worried sick about Natasha, and Natasha is worried sick about, well, everything. But at the same time, Natasha says that the income from the lands is fine, higher than ever. And from sales of the farm equipment. That's got to be helping."

Home, Kseniya thought, was difficult to explain to an up-timer. They were so rich. They just had their brains in the wrong... no, that wasn't right...they had their brains in a *different* place.

She held back the sigh, then said, "In the last years...so many changes. It's hard to adjust to so many changes. You know, my father is *Streltzi*, right?"

Brandy nodded.

"*Streltzi* means shooter. Mostly we are city guards, but we also guard caravans and when war comes the *Streltzi* are the infantry. But it is usually not war and being the city guards doesn't take up all of our time. So most *Streltzi* have another job: merchant, baker, leatherworker or silversmith, something. My father is... like a sergeant major, but my family also owns a tannery. We're *Streltzi*, but upper *Streltzi*. But, my father-in-law is *dvoriane*. The *dvoriane* are court nobles and army officers, sometimes bureaucrats, depending on what job is assigned. In fact, my father-in-law is an officer in my father's regiment. But my father-in-law's family is not as wealthy as my family. They receive thirty-five rubles a year and a...I don't know a German word that fits *pomestie*. *Pomestie* is land given, or perhaps loaned, to the *dvoriane* as part, usually the larger part, of the payment for their service to the crown. The *dvoriane* get to collect the rent on the *pomestie*. But while my father-in-law receives *pomestie* lands enough to make him richer than my father, he doesn't have enough tenants, ah, serfs, for more than half the lands and you can't collect rent from serfs who aren't there because they ran off to work for a monastery or high boyar."

"Why do the serfs do that?" Brandy asked. "It seems it would just be trading one master for another. You would think that the small holders would be, ah, the good guys, here. That they would be the allies of other men, those who have even less."

"They can't afford to be," Kseniya insisted. "Remember the expenses. They don't have labor-saving devices. They need the serfs."

"I bet there are a lot more of these small holders than there are high boyars and churchmen, aren't there?" Kseniya nodded and Brandy thanked her and went off to do some thinking.

She remembered things said about the *dvoriane* in other conversations. And a quote from somewhere: "Never trust a banker." There was more to that quote, but she couldn't remember it. The thing was, the *dvoriane* sort of felt like the bankers from the quote. People who would cover themselves first, last and always. Who wouldn't take sides, or would change sides as the wind shifted. Yes, she understood the predicament of the bureau men and soldiers of the service nobility. But that didn't make serfdom right. She also remembered that Boris was *dvoriane*. And that letters written to Natasha went through the Grantville Section.

Brandy realized that Vladimir needed a way to get messages to Natasha that the Grantville Section wouldn't see. *A file baked in a cake.* Brandy giggled. *Everything old is new again.*

Some days later, a serf named Yuri laid a bar of white-hot steel in the slot of a drop forge and waved. Another serf from his village pulled the lever and the hammer came down. The bar weighed fifteen pounds and the hammer, which had to be lifted by means of a crank, weighed over a ton. The force of the blow transmitted through the bar and the tongs hammered his arms. It was hard work. Not the sort of work Yuri enjoyed. It was hot and it was bloody dangerous. It wasn't the sort of job that Yuri would have chosen. But Yuri was a serf. He wasn't given a choice.

It was also, in Yuri's opinion, stupid. There were a lot of things that needed doing in the village before spring planting. Instead, he was here making extra money for the lord and he knew perfectly well that neither he nor anyone in the village would see a kopek's worth of the money. No. The money would go to the lord to pay the village's debt and there would be more fees to make sure that the village never got out of debt. He wasn't going to be able to buy off his ties to the land. He wasn't even working in his home village. The foundry was fifteen miles away from home and he was being charged rent as well as everything else. There are limits to all things and Yuri had just about reached his.

Since he couldn't hope to buy out, he'd just have to run. He didn't want to, because it would stick the rest of the village with his debt. But he'd had enough. Yuri began to plan. He couldn't tell his fellow villagers what he was planning; they would report him rather than being stuck with his debt. He'd need food, an extra set of clothing, one of those gold-mining maps.

Yuri didn't particularly want to mine gold, but it would give him a direction to run to and even a reason for being on the road. Yuri pulled another bar from the fire and continued to plan.

Chapter 65

"We need more reapers," Anya said.

"Well, we don't have them," Natasha told her. "And we aren't going to have them before the harvest is in."

"What about renting yours out after you have your crops in? With the serfs that have headed for the gold fields, there are a lot of people, even some of the boyars, who still won't have their crops in by that time. We could probably rent them for near the cost of buying one and still not have enough to supply the demand."

It was a good plan. It probably would have worked except...

It was mid-afternoon when Peter Boglonovich plotted his measurements. The thermometer was dropping and the barometer was rising; the winds were from the northwest and strong. The front had passed through and was on its way south. And Peter couldn't tell anyone. Peter had an excellent clock and a small wind-powered generator to power his equipment and provide some creature comforts. What he didn't have was a radio. He had maps—good ones—and he knew how to use them, having been trained at the Dacha. He received weather data to plot on those maps from other stations once a week and sent his data off with the same messenger. The messenger was due in two days and Peter figured that the cold front would be halfway to Moscow by then.

"What's the use of a weather station if it doesn't have a radio?"

Peter muttered. He knew the answer. He was up here to provide a plot, a record of weather conditions, that could be used to make the predictions more accurate when they got the radios installed and could do real-time prediction. Establishing a baseline was all well and good, but if Peter's calculations were right, real-time weather prediction was going to come too late. This storm was going to sweep over Russia, depositing sleet on fields and those crops that hadn't been harvested were going to get pounded.

Ivan looked out at his fields and saw death. Death for crops under a sheet of ice and sleet. Death for his family this winter as they ran out of food. Ivan lived on a farm forty miles northeast of Moscow and the storm still raged, beating down the stalks and turning the ripe grain to mush. He wasn't the only one by any means. The storm ripped through Russia's heart, ruining a full quarter of the expected grain crop for the year—and it could have been much worse.

On a farm thirty miles to the east of Ivan's, Misha went to the family altar, knelt down in front of the icons and thanked God and his ancestors that he had spent the money to use the reaper, in spite of his wife's complaint of his spendthrift ways. His crop was in the barn. All of the village crops were in the barn, safe from the storm.

For Misha the storm was good news. Amazingly good news. It meant that the price he could get for his crop would be considerably higher. Even after the taxes and tithes were paid, which would take more than half his crop, he would have grain to sell for the new paper rubles. Perhaps enough to pay off his debt, which would allow him to leave. At least if he promised to go to the gold fields.

Other farms had been missed by the storm or hit only by the edges. Then there were the potato fields. It wasn't just the potatoes from the Ring of Fire. The patriarch and czar had both read the histories and put in a large order for potatoes with English merchants. It had taken a while, but the merchants had delivered. A ship load of potatoes had arrived in the spring of 1635.

The peasants who had been assigned to grow them had not been pleased. But with the government promising to buy the potatoes at a fixed price per pound, and threats about what would happen if they failed to follow instructions, they had grown them. The peasants were going to be displeased again. Fixed prices worked both ways.

Still, it wasn't enough. Not with the number of peasants who had managed to buy out or simply run off. That move had delayed the harvest in a number of places and that delay had been crucial. It had destroyed millions of rubles worth of crops. The bureaucratic service nobility placed the blame for the disaster at the feet of the czar. And though they were unlikely to actually starve because of it, hundreds, perhaps thousands, of them had been ruined.

"There is grain aplenty in Poland. The storm missed them and they got their harvest in with little damage," Patriarch Filaret said. The Little Duma, Privy Council, was meeting to discuss the response to the storm and its effect on the price of grain.

"We don't have the money to buy Polish grain," Fedor Ivanovich Sheremetev countered.

"After what they did to us during the Time of Troubles, they owe us a little grain and Rzhev showed we have the might to take it."

Mikhail wished he could be somewhere else. The meeting had been going on for hours, mostly in a deadlock between his father and his cousin. Sheremetev wanted to stop the contributions to Gustav Adolf and try for a closer alliance with Poland. The patriarch wanted to keep relations with Sweden good and coordinate with them in attacking Poland from two fronts at once. Mikhail was leaning toward his father's side, mostly, because he agreed with Sheremetev that Gustav Adolf was, in the long run, the greater danger. But to Mikhail that meant that Gustav Adolf was the one who needed to be wooed, not the one to attack.

Let the Swedish king rule western Europe. He'd earned it. Russia would expand to the east, into territory that they already tacitly owned. A transcontinental railroad from Moscow to the Pacific would give Russia half a continent of growing room. In spite of his respect for the charismatic Emperor Gustav Adolf, Mikhail thought he would prefer to be remembered as a builder rather than a conqueror.

"Given the effects of the storm, we will have to, at least for now, curtail the shipments of grain to the Swedes. But General Shein will prepare the army for the possibility of action between our realm and Poland." Mikhail raised a hand as Sheremetev started to speak. "Just in case."

If this were a story they would all shut up now that he had made his royal ruling. But, of course, they didn't shut up. They kept right on arguing back and forth for another hour. Eventually, after they had forgotten who had suggested it, they agreed on Mikhail's plan of action. Mikhail would have liked to be satisfied with that, but he wasn't. His power over the boyars and church were both getting weaker, not stronger, as time went on. When the meeting finally broke up, he happened to see Sheremetev's expression. It worried him.

This was a disaster, Sheremetev thought as he left the chamber where the Little Duma met. War with Poland would be a disaster for both countries, no matter who won. It would be a disaster for the Sheremetev lands and for both nations, leaving them open to the ravages of the Swede. Russia needed Poland as a buffer against the west. It needed a Poland strong enough to fight off the threats from central and western Europe. And the patriarch was going to destroy that buffer even if he won. There was no other choice. *Filaret has to go.*

"Natasha, you see Czarina Evdokia often, do you not?" Boris asked.

Natasha, hearing the tone of his voice, took a long look at him. Boris was always a bit pasty-faced, but these days he was dreadfully pale. And had dark circles under his eyes. Which, oddly for the current situation, almost made her laugh. He looked so much like Bernie's cartoon. "Yes, I do, Boris. Why?"

"I'm worried," Boris said. "I know there's something going on. Something bad. But I'm excluded. The word is out that I'm too close to the Dacha to trust." He sighed. "It's to be expected, of course. Nevertheless, I do hear rumors. One is that the *strelzi* are angry, and are making alliances with a number of men in Moscow."

"What do you want me to tell Evdokia?" Natasha asked.

"To be careful. Very careful. Even to get out of Moscow, if they can."

Chapter 66

September 1635

"Zeppi seems to think so, but our research has shown that you spend much more in fuel for moving the same weight with heavier than air craft," Gregorii Mikhailovich explained rather more fully than Colonel Shuvalov thought was really necessary.

"Zeppi?" Lufti Pasha asked.

"A member of our staff hired from, ah, central Germany," Colonel Shuvalov said. The Ottoman sultan, Murad IV, insisted on maintaining the pretense that the Ring of Fire was a hoax and that up-timers didn't exist—while he sent his agents everywhere to learn whatever they could from that nonexistent future lore.

"I understand." Lufti Pasha smiled at Colonel Shuvalov. Clearly a man who knew how to play the game. "We will not be meeting him, I take it?"

"I am afraid not," Colonel Shuvalov said. "He is supervising an installation in Dedovsk."

The installation in question was a prototype telephone system, about which Bernie said he knew almost nothing and was skeptical it would succeed. He was not even there. The project was being carried out entirely by Russians working for Director Sheremetev, who was hoping to be able to dispense eventually with the up-time advisers; both of whom, for different reasons, were obstreperous.

But there was no reason to get into that with the Ottomans. Politely, the colonel gestured toward a corridor leading off from the salon. "Now, if you will come this way, we will show you the chemistry labs, where we make dyes and medicines—and if we can get better access to your naphtha, we will be making fuels and plastic materials."

Shuvalov took the visiting Turks off with him, discussing Russia selling them manufactured goods and buying oil and gold. The Turks seemed rather more willing to part with oil than with gold. Natasha thought that would change over time.

"We have very little choice, Papa," Pavel said. "A thousand AK3's to the Turks, due very soon, with more to follow. From what they're saying, a lot more."

Boris nodded. He thought selling the new weapons to the Ottoman empire was probably short-sighted, but...

It was hard to say. The war raging between the USE and Poland could produce any number of outcomes. In some of those outcomes, having a well-armed Turkish neighbor could be to Russia's advantage.

Besides, it was probably all a moot point. The AK3 was a simple weapon to make, when all was said and done. Selling one to the Ottoman Empire or the Poles or anyone else was not much different from selling a million of them since there was no way that they could keep the Ottoman Empire or the Poles—or the Swedes, for that matter—from getting hold of an example rifle. So they might as well sell as many as they could. At least they weren't selling the Ottomans the breech-loading cannon. Yet, anyway.

And, otherwise, things were getting better...mostly. Not so much for the bureau men as for Russia in general. Oil and silver were arriving from the Ottoman Empire, even some food from their Balkan provinces. Wheat was expensive in Moscow, but not yet too expensive. Steam engines, rifles and other things were going south in exchange.

"And so, certain boyars gain more silver and gold from the, ah, southern trade," Boris said. "But at least they haven't shorted the grain supply...much."

"And our people are prepared." Pavel smiled. Potatoes had become incredibly popular among the peasants. You could hide a plot of potatoes from the taxman, or at least hide how many there were. There was considerable upset among the bureau men about the amount of farming equipment that was going south. But it was quiet, underground resentment. "Three of our people have paid off their debt and gone to work for the railroad."

"Signing loan from the railroad?" Boris asked and Pavel nodded. Even with the economy expanding and with inflation, enough rubles for a peasant to pay his way out of debt were hard to come by. So companies that had the money had started using signing loans to clear the peasant's debt, or, more accurately, transfer it to the company. Since the railroad was owned by the Sheremetev family, it had plenty of money for signing loans.

Except for its habit of nicking other peoples' serfs, the railroad from Moscow to Smolensk was a project that Boris strongly approved of. It used wooden rails, which would require constant maintenance. But Russia was well-supplied with wood, whereas iron and steel were far too expensive for such a massive project.

Boris wondered about the railroad. Fedor Ivanovich Sheremetev was one of the leaders of the pro-Polish—it might be better to say, less-anti-Polish—faction in the *Boyar Duma*. The railroad could serve to facilitate trade with Poland, and through Poland with Austria-Hungary, but it could also be used as logistical support for an attack on Poland. Boris wondered which the director-general had in mind. Probably both.

Meanwhile the industrial base along the Volga was producing more and more goods. Mostly simple stuff. The stuff that didn't need that much infrastructure. But it was surprising how much fell into that category, when it wasn't competing with established products.

"And our factory?" Boris waited for his son to find the figures, then said, "Excellent. Absolutely excellent."

Freeze drying is expensive and time consuming when compared to canning...if you already have the infrastructure for a canning industry. It's much less so when it's competing against small-scale canning and down-time preservation methods. Once you had the foods freeze-dried, they were lightweight and stayed good for a long time. Which made them highly prized, both by the military and the civilian population. Boris' family and some partners from the Grantville Section had put together a small freeze-drying plant near the family's lands and added a lot of gardening. Carrots, onions, peas, cabbage, beets, even berries, were all being diced up and freeze-dried, then sealed in waxed paper pouches and stored in crates. Quite a bit of it was sold to the army and more in Moscow. Aside from the extra income, it meant that they had fresh (or the next thing to it) fruits and vegetables even in late winter and early spring. Which did good things for the health of his family and his serfs.

The new farming equipment meant that he needed a lot less labor in the fields most of the time, which had given the serfs time for the gardening. Boris, with his connection to the Dacha and the information from Grantville and the Ring of Fire, was running a year or more ahead of his neighbors, which meant that his family was doing a lot better than others of the same rank. Which was a good thing because there was considerable inflation of paper money, and silver was increasingly hard to come by. A paper ruble was—by law—worth the same as a silver ruble, but—in fact—worth less. How much less? No one knew. Gresham's Law was working at full force in Russia where the ruble was legally the same whether silver or paper, but not in Grantville where American dollars weren't tied to silver. Boris was, of course, paid in paper rubles—so the farm income was especially important.

Boris went back to his paperwork, wondering how things were going at the Dacha.

Chapter 67

October 1635

Father Nikon walked down the hallway of the patriarch's palace as though he had every right to be there. He didn't. At least not officially. The person who occupied the patriarch's seat would have said he didn't, but he had God's permission to be here, so he didn't much care what Filaret thought. The monastery he was from wasn't the one his papers said he was from, or he would have had guards escorting him everywhere. Father Nikon was here because Filaret feared the up-time wisdom and wanted to keep it all to himself. But God had provided that wisdom to the entire world and Filaret was serving the devil in attempting to restrict it.

Archbishop Joseph Kurtsevich and Father Nikon had discussed the matter several times and both the wealth and the new spiritual wisdom that God had sent from that other future had demonstrated that Filaret didn't hold God's favor. Control of the God-provided wealth of knowledge from the future didn't belong in the hands of a man who was so stingy with its benefits.

Filaret was holding back the religious truth revealed by the up-timers. God had passed a great new miracle by bringing forth an entire new town from the future. Possessing new truths, practical as well as spiritual. But the false patriarch, Filaret, was suppressing the truth in order to maintain his personal power. He was rejecting the spiritual aspects of that new truth, considering only those dribbles that might seem useful to him at the moment.

So Father Nikon had been told. So Father Nikon believed.

He would remove the impediment and God's Grace and the up-timer's knowledge would flow into Holy Rus as a great flood of cleansing.

Here in the patriarch's palace, priests' robes were not the least bit uncommon. And three additional priests wouldn't be noticed in any way, so long as they kept their six-shooters hidden. Father Nikon was proud of his. It would be the instrument of God's will. There were privileges that went with devotion to God. Father Nikon was confident that he would receive them in this world or the next.

The door to the patriarch's private quarters were guarded but that was expected. Father Nikon walked by them and then turned to face the guard as though just remembering something. The guard turned to look at him and Father Simon grabbed him by the throat and stuck a knife in his back. But the man didn't die quietly. He jerked and tried to scream and banged a fist on the door to the patriarch's rooms.

Filaret looked up when the pounding on the door began, annoyed. "What is that noise?" he grumbled. "Go out there and stop it."

The guard, obeying his instructions, opened the door only to be flung back into the room as the door was slammed inward. Filaret stood, in shock, as the men rushed into the room.

Almost before Filaret consciously realized what was happening, he ducked behind his desk and started scrambling to get the drawer open. Filaret, too, had one of the Gun Shop's six-shooters that had been introduced by Cass Lowry.

Filaret's guardsman started to shout, then there was a loud bang. Filaret never reached his six-shooter. The men ran around his desk and three shots were fired.

The noise brought more guards, as Father Nikon had expected. What he hadn't expected was the bullet that entered his heart. Because he'd been assured that, once the false patriarch was dead, he would be safe and protected.

Father Simon was killed next, then Father Petr joined him.

✧　　　✧　　　✧

"What's going on here?" Fedor Ivanovich Sheremetev shouted. "Where is my cousin? We have an appointment."

"The patriarch has been murdered."

"How did you allow this to happen? Where are the assassins?"

"I don't know, sir. The two guards that were here are dead. We had to kill the assassins. They were armed with up-time weapons. Could they have been sent by the Swede?"

"Oh, my God. My cousin! The patriarch and I disagreed on many things, but Russia is a poorer place without him. For now we must see to protecting the czar and the royal family. Come with me, Captain."

Over the next few hours, Fedor Ivanovich Sheremetev went about protecting the realm from the unknown threat. Just as he'd intended. He spirited Czar Mikhail and his family out of Moscow, and then called an emergency meeting of the *Boyar Duma*.

The rumors started spreading before the meeting started, for Fedor Ivanovich Sheremetev had seeded the ground.

The primary rumor was that the czar and the patriarch had had a major argument over Czar Mikhail's plan to allow all serfs who could afford to buy out of their bondage to the land to do so. In the course of that argument, it was said, Filaret had suffered a heart attack.

A secondary rumor was that Czar Mikhail had shot his father.

Another was that he collapsed, weeping hysterically, when he heard the news.

But, consistent among them all, was that without Filaret's influence, the czar would allow the serfs to run free.

Moscow was packed with service nobility, whose estates would be left worthless by such an act.

Chapter 68

"Back," Boris said softly. "Get back."

Pavel pulled his head away from the alley's mouth. "We can't go that way, Papa."

"Then we'll turn back and try another. We've got to get home to your mother and get her out of here."

Boris and Pavel had rushed home, taking as many back ways as possible. There was danger on the major streets of Moscow, and it wasn't just the burning buildings. Gunshots were frequent.

When they reached the house, Mariya had already packed. An old Moscow hand, she'd smelled the smoke and heard the shots. Fire was never a good thing in wooden Moscow, which had burned and arisen from its own ashes numerous times.

"What started it this time?" Mariya asked.

"The patriarch is dead and there are crazy rumors making the rounds," Boris said. "But they all seem to agree that the czar is planning to free the serfs."

"He'd never do it," Mariya said.

"I don't know," Boris said. "He's been influenced a lot by the up-timers and the way they feel about serfdom is totally unreasonable." Boris shook his head. "But it doesn't matter now. Get the bags out to the carriage."

"Where are we going, Papa?"

"You and your mother are going home to the village. On your way, stop by the Dacha and pick up Ivan."

"You think it's that bad?" Mariya asked.

"Yes. This isn't just a riot. This is politics," Boris said.

"I don't understand," Pavel said, somewhat apologetically.

"That's because you don't remember the Time of Troubles," his mother explained. "*Dvoriane* serve Russia and stay out of politics. Especially at times like these."

"But surely not this time. This time the *dvoriane* are involved and the boyars' sons as well. This is about the serfs and the limited year. Our friends and our neighbors are involved. Many of them could lose everything if their serfs run off looking for gold—"

Suddenly Pavel found himself against the wall with his father's hand around his throat. Pavel was a fairly tall young man, taking more after his mother than his father. He was also fairly quick, but he had been looking right at Papa and hadn't even seen him move.

"Yes," Boris said. "And whoever wins, a lot of them are going to die in the next few days and weeks. The ones who have made too much noise. Someone is giving the *dvoriane* enough rope to hang ourselves. The bureaus are going to be purged. That includes friends of ours, people we have known for years. But it's not going to include your mother or your brothers or you. Not if I can help it. We don't stay out of politics because we don't care, boy. We stay out of politics to stay alive. And I'll tell you something else. Whoever wins, it won't be the serfs and it won't be the *dvoriane,* the boyars' sons or the *Streltzi.* It will be a faction of the high families. And any *dvoriane* who gets involved will lose...even if they are on the winning side this time."

Pavel looked at his mother but she was looking back at him just as hard-eyed as his father. "You don't remember what it was like when we had three czars in as many weeks, Pavel. But I do and your papa does."

"Now, are you going to do what I tell you to?" Boris asked and Pavel felt his father's fingers tighten around his throat. Pavel nodded.

Then his father released him and went on as though nothing had happened. "On the way, you pick up Ivan. Thank God that two of your brothers are in Germany already. If Natasha asks what's happening, tell her but don't dally to do it. I wouldn't be surprised if the Dacha is targeted in the next few days."

Boris' estimate was off. When Pavel and Mariya passed the

Dacha there were troops already there. In fact, there were troops at the Dacha before the riot was well started.

After seeing his wife and son off, Boris went back to the office. This was a time to be precisely where you were supposed to be and easy to find—so people wouldn't think you were somewhere you weren't supposed to be, doing something you shouldn't.

By the time he got to the office, several of his more experienced people were already there. "Gregori, I need you to sanitize our records."

"You think we're going to get inspected?" Gregori asked, then blushed for such a silly question.

"Of course we will. Every bureau in Russia is going to get inspected after this. Oh . . . and Gregori . . . not too sanitized."

Gregori smiled. It was still a rather nervous smile, but at least it was the smile of a man who knew what he had to do. The way these things went, the inspectors would keep looking until they found something. It was best to leave them something minor to find.

"I'm sorry," Colonel Shuvalov said politely. "But I have my orders from the *Boyar Duma*."

From the *Boyar Duma*, Natasha noted. Not from the czar or from the Assembly of the Land. Just the *Boyar Duma*. The cabinet and the bureau heads had taken over the government. The troops, she was told, were there for the protection of the Dacha. Natasha also noted that the colonel was a member of the Sheremetev faction at court. Which wasn't good news. The takeover of the Dacha was amazingly anticlimactic, certainly for most of the people living and working there. From the start, the majority of the workers and researchers had been from the *dvoriane* and the *deti boyars*. Including a couple of boyars' sons. Oh, there were a few peasants who had, through talent and work, made a place for themselves among the researchers. Anya and a few others. And more *Streltzi*, especially where craftsmanship was needed. But the cultural outlook of the Dacha was that of the *dvoriane*: do your job and stay away from politics. At least court politics . . . the bureaus had their own.

Unfortunately, that option wasn't really available to Natasha. What protected her was the value of the Dacha itself. That, and keeping her silence. Changes were happening all over. The winners were moving their family members into positions of greater influence.

Chapter 69

December 1635

"Where are you headed, Tim?" Ivan Maslov asked, looking over Lieutenant Boris "Tim" Timofeyevich Lebedev's new uniform—complete with the new lieutenant's insignia—with more than a touch of envy. Then he grinned. Tim was finally back in Moscow having—lucky fellow—missed Sheremetev's takeover in his absence. Tim was still not as good as Ivan was at war games but was getting better. More importantly he was a friend, and Ivan was pragmatic enough to realize that Tim's friendship was even more important now than it had been before the coup.

Tim shuddered. "My uncle...he requires my report."

"But you did well at Rzhev! At least officially." Ivan envied the status his friend's family provided but didn't envy Tim his great uncle at all. He had met the old monster once and that was more than enough. Tim's great uncle was, by good fortune, a supporter of the Sheremetev faction, which now controlled the *Boyar Duma*. General Shein, on the other hand, was now in charge of one section of the Siberian frontier, demoted and sent as far from Moscow as you could get and still be in Russia. From what Ivan had heard, General Shein had missed execution by a hair's breadth.

"My uncle is not limited to official channels," Tim said. "I'm to have a chat with him. Which translates to giving him a full report on everything that happened. It will take hours, I promise you. Hours! I won't be able to gloss over anything."

Ivan knew that Tim would much rather downplay parts of what happened in Rzhev. More for Izmailov's sake than his own. Which was a pretty positive response to someone who had you cleaning out latrines.

Tim's great uncle was no one's fool and ten times as politically astute as Tim ever wanted to be. It had taken him all of a minute and a half to get through the fiction of the contingency plan. He had laughed at General Izmailov's notion of giving Tim a medal and then having him shot. A rough, cackling laugh, that seemed to come from the depths of hell. "A good plan," his uncle said when he finished laughing. "But he was wise not to carry it through. I would have regretted having a man of such wit put to death."

Tim waited. Silent. At attention.

"Well?" his uncle barked.

"Yes, sir. General Izmailov is a great general and a great asset to Russia."

"But a friend of Shein's—one of his protégés, in fact. Keep your distance from him, boy. Sheremetev's not fond of Shein. The war party didn't do well in this last shake up. I'll try to keep your general alive for you, but not to the point of risking the family. Now tell me about Khilkov. What went on? And why did Izmailov let him do it?"

Tim told him. It wasn't like General Izmailov had much choice, considering Khilkov's family connections. Then they went on to the situation in Rzhev and the Polish border in general.

"Rzhev was a mistake, sir," Tim said. "They didn't have the steam ships to take advantage of it, even if they had held the town. It really was one of the magnates going off on his own."

"I don't doubt it, boy. That's what started that business with the false Dmitris, back at the beginning of the Time of Troubles. Poland uses its magnates to test the waters."

"Yes, sir. But they didn't have the logistic train to support it even if it had worked."

"You seem pretty sure of that, boy. The Poles are cavalry. They need their horses but can steal the rest."

Tim hesitated. He was in fact quite sure that cavalry would be trashed if it lacked infantry support and Russia controlled the rivers for troop transport. But his great uncle was a boyar of the *Duma* and ruled the family with an iron hand. "Not with us controlling the river with steam barges. War horses need grain, horseshoes, and so on. Cavalrymen need food and equipment—which breaks in the field—and gunpowder. They would do damage but with the steam barges to put troops in front of them and the walking walls and cannon...especially with the AK3's...they are going to run out of cavalry long before we run out of bullets. Over the course of an hour cavalry can outrun a steam barge, but over a day they can't keep up. With the dirigible to locate them..." Tim shook his head. "They wouldn't last a week."

"Tell me about the flying ship."

"It told us where they were. That was important in Rzhev, but would have been even more important if the Poles had tried to push farther in. It would have let us see where they were going and get there first. They would have been forced from one trap to another, until they were utterly destroyed. Cavalry is doing well to cover thirty miles a day; a dirigible can cover that in an hour or two, if the wind is good. Then go home and tell the infantry and mobile artillery where the cavalry is headed. Cavalry's day is over except as support troops. If that." Which was a risky thing to say because his great uncle had been a cavalry commander under Ivan the Terrible.

All in all, it was a grueling interview and Tim was happy to get back to the Kremlin. Though Tim didn't know it, the interview had a strong effect on the policies of the *Boyar Duma*. Cavalry, which had always been the province of the service nobility, was downgraded in importance and so was the service nobility. Instead, the *Streltzi* class with its rifle companies would be given more support and respect. It wouldn't happen in a year or even a decade, but between the destruction of Khilkov's cavalry and the many reports, both official and unofficial, the writing was on the wall. Eventually, because the service nobility was the class that produced the bureaucrats and the *Streltzi* class was the class that produced the merchants, the private sector would gain—a bit at a time—the ear of the government and the public sector would be heeded a bit less. The years of limited mobility would not be allowed to lapse. With inflation, that would mean that more and more of the peasants would be able to pay off their debts to the lesser nobility and seek factory jobs.

Totally by accident and without ever knowing it, Tim had struck a blow for freedom. A small blow. Even a tiny one. But enough such tiny blows and even the massive edifice of Russian serfdom might eventually fall.

Tim had a week in Moscow to get all the new uniforms made, then he got sent as executive officer to a cousin who was leading a contingent of cavalry to the city of Murom. It was too late in the year, unfortunately, to use one of the new steam barges for the purpose. The rivers were already freezing over. Tim had hoped to ride on one of them.

"How is it, my friend," Ivan asked Tim, grinning evilly, "that you have all the connections, the rank and a letter of thanks from the czar and I get the plum assignment?"

It was, Tim thought morosely, an excellent question. Of course, Ivan's grin made it even worse. "I told you I wouldn't be able to leave anything out," Tim said, referring to the meeting with his uncle. "I'm being reminded I need to learn to follow orders. So while you become the aide of Captain Ruslan Andreyivich Shuvalov, new commander of the dirigible *Czarina Evdokia*, I become the Executive Officer of Cousin Ivan Borisovich Lebedev. Which means I get to do all his work while he gets drunk and bothers the local girls."

"Your cousin who is also a captain and the new commander of the Murom *Streltzi*. Murom being the family seat of the newly famous Gorchakov family. So the whole town is supposed to be full of electricity and every peasant's hovel has indoor plumbing."

"While you get to go flying in the newest and biggest airship in the world. At least, I think the *Czarina* is going to be bigger than any other so far built. In a just world, you would be stuck as Cousin Ivan Borisovich's aide in Murom with its electricity, and plumbing—which I bet is not as good as rumor says—and its small force of *Streltzi*. While Nick would be the captain of the *Czarina* and I would be his executive officer, running test flights over Bor."

"That would be illegal and you know it. You're great house and Nikita Ivanovich Slavenitsky is *deti boyar*. They can't place someone of your family rank under someone of his."

"Fine, so leave Nick as captain and let you be his aide and Ruslan Andreyivich Shuvalov be his executive officer. Not the other way around."

Ivan sighed histrionically and Tim wanted to hit him, mostly because he knew his friend was right and he was being silly. Then Ivan continued, "Sheremetev's faction won in the latest shakeup. With the death of the patriarch and the purges in the bureaus, the Gorchakov clan—while not in disgrace—didn't exactly come out of it smelling of roses. Besides, you know as well as I do that the Sheremetev family outranks the Gorchakov family. If the Gorchakovs were in better odor at court then Captain Slavenitsky might have gotten the slot but Ruslan Andreyavich Shuvalov wouldn't have been put under his command even then.

"With the shake up, the riots, the patriarch's death, Sheremetev has been declared Director-General by the *Boyar Duma*. He is the effective ruler of Russia and he is going to do everything he can to shift any of the glory that comes out of the up-timer knowledge to the Sheremetev clan. That's why his up-timer Cass Lowry is to be put in charge of the Dacha. And they couldn't put you under the command of Captain Ruslan Andreyavich Shuvalov any more than they could put you under the command of your friend Captain Nikita Ivanovich Slavenitsky. That's the drawback of being of a great house. The only way they could make you the executive officer of the *Czarina* would be to put your cousin in command of her."

"Anything but that." Tim shuddered.

"See!" Ivan said. "And Captain Shuvalov is a capable man, if a bit of a cold fish. So, since you're guarding the Gorchakov family seat, what's happening at the Gorchakov Dacha?"

Part Six

The year 1636

Chapter 70

February 1636

Cass rode up to the Dacha with a mixture of trepidation and glee. He was finally going to get his own back from that traitor Bernie and his bitch Natasha. And he planned to have a little fun with that Anya chick, too. At the same time, Cass knew he had to be careful. Sheremetev and his gang weren't the sort of people you crossed. But sooner or later, they'd get bored and leave the place fully in Cass' control. Then he'd have the run of the place.

For several weeks things went along pretty much as they had before. The Dacha's contacts with the outside world had always been limited; now they were the next best thing to nonexistent. Even contact with associated projects like the *Czarina Evdokia*, the large dirigible being built in Bor just across the Volga from Nizhny Novgorodi, or the foundry and gun shop located in Podol just a few miles away from the Dacha, were difficult and sporadic.

"I'd kind of like to know what Cass is doing here," Bernie said. "And do we know anything about why Tami Simmons came to Moscow also, and with her whole family? She's the American nurse."

"The czar and czarina were so impressed with the spring typhoid reductions they decided to bring in a real up-time medical expert. Do you know her?"

Bernie shrugged. "In passing, the way people in a small town more or less know anyone else in the town. She's from Kentucky, originally, and she's a lot older than me. I know her husband Gerry a little better, but still not very well."

Bernie looked around the room at the tense, worried faces, then back at Natasha. She was pale enough that she wouldn't need the kabuki makeup women wore in Russia in the here and now. Bernie tried for something vague and unthreatening. "That Shuvalov dude seems like a pretty good guy. Do you think he'd let me send a message home?"

He hadn't thought it was possible, but Natasha went even whiter. "Don't try it right now, Bernie," she said. "Just leave it for a bit."

"Are you going to tell me what's wrong, Natasha? I know there's something I'm missing here. Besides the armed soldiers, of course. And not seeing Boris for weeks. And the fact that everyone is tiptoeing around like ghosts while Cass is acting like Cass Squared."

"Colonel Shuvalov is a *deti boyar*, a retainer of the Sheremetev family, Bernie. Rather like Nikita Ivanovich Slavenitsky is to my family."

"Yeah. He's pretty polite. Nice guy," Bernie said. Not getting what this had to do with the price of beets.

"He goes out of his way to be cordial," Natasha admitted. Her face got pinched. "But stop and think, Bernie. Colonel Shuvalov doesn't push it, as you would say. But . . . he's here for more than one purpose. My family, the Gorchakov family, were once independent princes. We retain the titles and are very wealthy. We're just not as politically well-connected as some of the other great families. At least we hadn't been. With the Dacha we were starting to become so. So Colonel Shuvalov has been selected . . ."

"*He's after you?*" Now Bernie got it and he didn't like it. He *really* didn't like it. This sort of thing was bad enough when applied to some ordinary down-timer but applied to Natasha . . . ?

Somewhere in a part of his mind that he usually tried to avoid, Bernie understood that his feelings for Natasha had gelled in a certain way. Quite a while ago, in fact. But he still had no idea what to do about it, Russian noble society being what it was—and now *this* just got dumped on him!

"That's slavery . . . or something. Like something out of a book! One of my sister's stupid romance novels."

Natasha laughed bitterly. "Romance has very little to do with it. Through me, my family and its fortune will serve Shuvalov's ambitions. Our . . . sons . . . will be boyars, great family boyars."

"That stinks!"

"Calm down, Bernie. Don't lose your temper," Natasha said. "As long as we're quiet and don't make a fuss, Colonel Shuvalov will remain polite. He would much prefer to have a . . . mutually supportive relationship. But the relationship itself is in no way optional. Not on my part and not really on his. The basic motivation behind the match is to move my family's wealth into the Sheremetev family's control. It's politics, Bernie. International politics as much as internal. Sheremetev is pro-Polish, anti-Swedish. The patriarch was anti-Polish, and so favored the Swede."

"And Director-General Sheremetev has a reasonable point," Filip said. "I like the concepts you up-timers bring, but Gustav Adolf is just another would-be emperor of the world. Not that different from Genghis Kahn or your Napoleon or Hitler."

"Oh, come on. Gustav Adolf isn't anything like Hitler," Bernie said.

"And how is Gustav Adolf different from Adolf Hitler, in the up-timer histories?" Misha asked.

"He's Swedish, not German." Nikolai laughed.

"Hitler was . . . would have been . . . Austrian, not German. Gustav Adolf made himself emperor of Germany the same way Hitler did in that other history, and is at war with a lot of the same people. France, England, Poland."

"Which is just fine with me." Nikolai wasn't laughing now. "Useless Poles! With their false Dmitris, murder and looting. At least we taught them a lesson at Rzhev."

"And after that?" Misha asked. "How long before Gustav Adolf's Operation Barbarossa?"

"He's too canny for that. After all, the histories make it quite clear how it turned out. Besides, the reports are that he's out of commission because of the wounds he got at that battle last fall."

Misha shrugged. "He may well recover. And if he doesn't, we will have to deal with Oxenstierna, who is no better. Hitler was a lousy general and didn't understand Russian winters. Gustav

Adolf and Oxenstierna are very good generals and do understand
Russian winters. That makes them more dangerous than Hitler,
the way I see it."

For a while Bernie let the conversation roll over him. He had
been paying a bit more attention to politics since the coup, and
he was having a lot of trouble making sense of it all. He appreci-
ated that Gustav Adolf had ridden to the rescue of Grantville in
the Croat raid, but he didn't approve of the USE having a king
or the New U.S. being reduced to just another state. It seemed
like Mike Stearns had given up too much of what America had
been up-time. Maybe he had no choice, but that didn't make
Bernie any more loyal to some Swedish king and his German
prime minister.

Bernie came to another realization, at that point. The Ring of
Fire had happened almost five years ago—and he'd spent more
than four of those years in Russia. By now, Bernie had more
friends in Russia than he did in Grantville. His Russian was fluent and idiomatic, even if he'd always have a fairly pronounced
accent. So Natasha told him, anyway.

For that matter, the American he was probably closest to,
Brandy, had gone and married a Russian herself. He had to face
it. The America he knew—had been born in, raised in—was just
gone. Gone forever. The USE that had sort of replaced it in this
universe didn't really mean much to him.

The truth was, the USE seemed just like another down-time
nation. From where Bernie was sitting, there wasn't really that
much difference between Czar Mikhail with Sheremetev and King
Gustav Adolf with Wettin. At this point, Bernie just hoped that
the kings, emperors and czars of the world didn't start a war that
had up-timer fighting up-timer. He honestly didn't know what he
would do if that happened.

It wasn't that Bernie had any love for the Russian government,
because he didn't. The czar himself seemed like a pretty decent
guy but he wasn't running the show—and serfdom just plain stank.

But that didn't really matter. For good or ill, better or worse,
Russia was his country now. It was where he lived, worked, and . . .
had fallen in love, really for the first time in his life. It was the
country where he'd healed himself, at least as well as he could.
He owed Russia for that, if nothing else.

In for a penny, in for a pound, as the old saying went. He

had no idea what to do, but he did know where he'd be doing whatever he did. Right here. In—ha! who would've guessed?—Mother Russia.

Natasha was still talking. "They don't intend to take the family's wealth away—just control of it. They consider it necessary, since while the Gorchakovs aren't really one of the great families—we are one of the twenty but not one of the fourteen—we have acquired a degree of wealth and a set of connections that makes the family potentially disruptive if not brought to heel. Reined in, as it were.

"It could be a lot worse, Bernie," Natasha pointed out. "Colonel Shuvalov is bright, charming, and a decent sort. He's not . . . one of the worst. Not old. Not gross. More modern than some."

Bernie didn't really agree with Natasha's assessment, even leaving aside his own desire for the woman. Shuvalov was also, unfortunately, completely loyal to his patron. He was aware of Sheremetev's ambitions but didn't feel that those ambitions absolved him of his duty. And if the ambition didn't, neither did the greed that the Sheremetev family was famous for.

"He's like . . . I dunno . . . some kind of samurai about duty and honor," Bernie said. "And I kind of like him. But we can't trust him because his loyalty will always come before his honor. If his boss tells him to feed us all to the pigs, that's what he'll do. I don't see how we can get out of this mess. We don't have enough men to do anything, and not enough weapons, either."

"So we keep our mouths shut," Natasha said. "We wait and we don't cause trouble. For now, Director-General Sheremetev is busy making sure his position is consolidated. Shuvalov isn't the worst. Let's hope he's left in charge here."

The worst, as Anya well knew, certainly wasn't Colonel Shuvalov. In her opinion, the worst was Cass. She didn't like the way he looked at her, not at all. And she didn't like the way he was treating the other girls at the Dacha.

And she dreaded the day Colonel Shuvalov left. Cass would have no restraints. More and more, Anya was convinced that they would have to escape.

Well, she'd done that before. But never with a princess in tow, much less an up-timer.

✧   ✧   ✧

"He's not the worst," Aunt Sofia pointed out.

"He's not the worst, he's not the worst, he's not the worst!" Natasha chanted and threw her hands in the air. "I know perfectly well that he's not the worst, dammit."

"You've been around Bernie too long," Sofia said. "Stop using that word, even in English."

Natasha turned a stone face to her. "He's not the worst. But he's not what I want."

"What do you want, child?"

"I don't know yet. I haven't had a chance to learn what *I* want."

That wasn't really true. She knew it—and judging by the expression on her face, her aunt Sofia knew it too. What Natasha wanted was Bernie, but that seemed as remote as the moon.

She paused a moment. "I want Vladimir. I wish I could talk to my brother."

"Damn their eyes!"

For a moment, Brandy thought Vladimir was quoting another book. Then she realized that he was angrier than she'd ever seen him.

They were in the salon. She was reading a book and Vladimir was trying to catch up on the endless paperwork. He'd just opened the latest dispatch bag from Moscow. "What's wrong?"

"You know that delayed mica shipment?" Vladimir leaped out of his chair and began pacing. "It wasn't delayed because of weather or bandits. Well, not real bandits. The *Boyar Duma* delayed it. On purpose. They've also taken Czar Mikhail and his family hostage, along with that nurse and her family." He thrust the letter toward her. "Look at this! Just look at it!"

Brandy was forced to push the papers away from her face. "Calm down, Vladimir. And talk sensibly. What else has happened?"

He pulled the papers back, then read from them. "Because of its vital importance to the state, the Dacha has been placed under guard." Vladimir threw the paper onto the table. "That means they've got Natasha. And Bernie."

Over the next few days, after Vladimir had calmed down a bit more, Brandy was able to read a translation of the offending papers.

Czar Mikhail and his family were safe, if being held hostage was safe. Not that they were officially being held hostage. They had "been moved out of Moscow to ensure the czar's safety." The up-time nurse Tami Simmons and her family were being held in the same place as the czar, so, again, they were safe. The manager at the mica mine, while nothing had yet been done to him, was being held under suspicion of "involvement in the recent unpleasantness." Accusations of corruption had been laid against the manager . . . and against Vladimir himself.

No shipments of anything would be sent from Moscow or from Vladimir's own lands. He was, effectively, broke.

Bernie and Natasha, along with the rest of the Dacha staff, were in "protective custody."

Chapter 71

March 1636

"We will be having guests," Colonel Shuvalov said.

Natasha looked up at his comment. "Guests?"

"Yes. Representatives from the Ottoman Empire. They have been looking at factories on the Don and Volga rivers and we have been told to be circumspect in what we show them."

Natasha hated to ask Shuvalov, but she needed to know. "What is going on?"

"The government is looking for new allies in case Gustav Adolf and the USE decide to look east for new lands to conquer."

"Insanity!"

"Actually, it's not," Shuvalov said, with what sounded like real regret. "You know that Sweden is perfectly willing to bite off pieces of Russia. Our access to the Baltic is now Swedish Ingria and we pay taxes to Sweden on every cargo that sails from Nyen. The USE is rapidly becoming the richest, most industralized, nation in Europe... Yet the Swedes still complain about our holding back the grain shipments when they know we lost a quarter of this year's crop to the early storm."

"But the up-timers would never let..."

"Let? 'Let' is not a word used with kings, Princess Natalia. Besides, Michael Stearns lost their election. He is no longer the prime minister—for that matter, unless he recovers from his battle injuries, Gustav Adolf is no longer the emperor."

"You really don't care about anything, do you?" Natasha spat. "Whatever your master says, you parrot him!"

Shuvalov looked at her and Natasha realized that she might have gone too far. Shuvalov was Sheremetev's man and Director-General Sheremetev was the most powerful man in Russia. Since Sheremetev had taken power there had been a purge of the bureaus the like of which hadn't been seen since Ivan the Terrible. The Dacha and the Grantville Section had gotten off fairly lightly—in large part because between them they were the goose that was laying the golden eggs. But even they weren't untouched. Boris had lost several people who were considered politically questionable and the Dacha remained under guard.

"Director-General Sheremetev is a great man. He is not perfect. No one is, even those touched by God. He's right about where the threat comes from. The Limited Year hasn't been repealed and the bureau men aren't screaming about it anymore. They're too busy covering their asses by kissing his. The purge in the bureaus has been extreme, but it hasn't been entirely political. A lot of the deadwood has been removed and there is greater opportunity for those with more talent and fewer family connections. Peasants aren't just going to look for gold in the mountains, they are finding factory jobs all along the Volga. The jobs aren't wonderful, but they are better than being a farmer.

"As to the director-general's foreign policy... However noble of character the up-timers may be, they aren't in control of the USE. They have influence out of proportion to their numbers, but those numbers are minuscule. Poland is probably less of a threat to us than the axis of Sweden and the USE. From where we sit, the biggest difference between Napoleon or Hitler and Gustav Adolf is that his army would probably do quite well in a winter war in Russia. He was born and raised in Sweden, after all. If he should decide to take Poland and keep coming east, we will be facing a force that outnumbers us and outguns us, led by a man who is quite possibly the greatest general of our time. We will need allies. All of them we can get.

"Natalia Petrovna," Shuvalov said, "I take no joy in the thought of war with the up-timers. But I learned at an early age that what I want doesn't control what happens."

❖   ❖   ❖

Director-General Fedor Ivanovich Sheremetev rode his horse up to the gates of the Dacha compound at the head of a troop of personal cavalry. He had still not made up his mind what to do about the Dacha. His cousin, Ivan Petrovich, wanted it. Wanted it badly. And Ivan Petrovich, corrupt as he was, had support within the family and the *Boyar Duma*. Also, Fedor could rely on Ivan to crack down on the Dacha staff.

Which was, in a way, the problem. Ivan Petrovich would squeeze the golden goose all right—but he just might choke it to death. And the Dacha had been laying right well over the last couple of years. Among other things, it had laid the logistics for the dust-up with Poland. Which had put Russia in a better position than it had been for twenty years.

A lot depended on how well Leontii Shuvalov's suit was progressing. If the Gorchakov heiress, Natalia, was proving difficult, Fedor might have to go with Ivan Petrovich because he could not afford to have the Dacha or the Gun Shop running loose. He got down from his horse with difficulty and shook Leontii's hand. "How goes your suit?"

"Reasonably well, Director-General," Leontii said. "Princess Natalia understands the situation. I won't say she is thrilled, but I doubt she will fight it."

"And how do . . ." Fedor paused as the lady in question arrived. "We'll talk later."

"The letters have gone out to Poland, what's left of the Holy Roman Empire and the Turks," Director-General Sheremetev said. "I'm not sure of the Polish-Lithuanian Commonwealth, mostly because Wladyslaw can't seem to get over the notion that he should be czar of Russia, but who knows? I expect to have better luck with Murad. I don't know which way Ferdinand will jump."

"And the riots?" Leontii asked.

"Worked quite well at distracting Mikhail's adherents and added enough between him and the bureau men to cut off most of his information flow. They have also provided more than ample justification for cracking down on the bureaus. I think we have them put in their place for now." Sheremetev snorted. "Button clerks, the lot of them. Self-important button clerks who have been getting above themselves since the Time of Troubles. They needed to be shown the stick. We'll wait a few more weeks before we show them the carrot." Sheremetev was talking about a plan to put enforcement of the ties to the land in the hands of the government.

"Anyway, you will have heard the reports by now. So what do you think of Cass?"

Shuvalov said, "He does know and understand up-timer technology. But I'm deeply concerned about his effect on the atmosphere here. I had visited the Dacha a couple of times when Bernie and Princess Natalia were in charge, and there was an openness to it. It's hard to explain. Everyone cared about the work. Everyone, from the maids with the chamber pots to Natalia herself. All the way up and down the line, everyone was concerned with making a contribution. I've tried to maintain that attitude, but with Cass it's almost impossible. He demeans everyone."

Director-General Sheremetev laughed at the colonel. "Leontii, my boy, the up-timers would call you a boy scout. I saw the same thing you saw, my friend. But it was too free. Believe me, the Dacha will produce more with a bit more of the whip and less of the carrot."

"Very well, sir. But I still despise that bastard. And I don't care at all for the way he looks at Princess Natalia."

"Is the princess interested in the up-timer?" Sheremetev gave Leontii a sharp look.

"No." Leontii laughed. "She despises Cass even more than I do. She might be interested in Bernie, though. She's young and inexperienced. I don't believe she really knows her own mind."

"And that could be dangerous." Sheremetev nodded. "I'll look into it."

Director-General Sheremetev did indeed look into it. He interviewed both Bernie and Natasha and came away from those interviews uncertain. Bernie really was too valuable an asset to dispose of casually. He understood what was being built in the Dacha better than any other single person. That very knowledge made him more dangerous.

That night at dinner, Natasha asked the question that they had all been wondering about. "What is the situation in Moscow?"

The director-general looked at her then turned to Bernie. "Are you familiar with the Tokugawa shogunate of Japan?"

Natasha knew that before Bernie had come to the Dacha he would have been, at best, vaguely familiar with the history of Japan or the rule of the shoguns. However, while most of his education as a consultant at the Dacha was technical, some of it was historical, especially for what was now current history. And Bernie had ended up translating or helping to translate quite a bit of history.

"Yes, a bit, Director-General Sheremetev. The emperor is mostly a religious figurehead. He reigns, but he doesn't rule. It's the shogun who has the real political power."

Sheremetev nodded. "Yes, that's basically correct. I believe we need a similar system here in Russia, given all the problems we've had with our czars. I believe Russia needs a strong hand at the reins, but doesn't need—certainly can't afford—the sort of, ah, disruption that a dynastic squabble would produce. To provide the first while avoiding the second, I have taken on a role analogous to that of shogun. Mikhail never really wanted the power of the throne, anyway. This way Mikhail will remain safe, comfortable and secure . . . as long as there is no trouble." He smiled.

It was, Natasha thought, an extremely cold smile.

"Mikhail's limited year was a good plan, poorly executed," he continued. "We do need more gold and silver to augment the paper money and to use in foreign trade. However, the way he did it, without properly preparing the ground, almost led to a revolution."

Natasha didn't snort, not even under her breath, but she wanted to. Yes, the *dvoriane* were upset, but they never would have rioted unless they believed that they had support in the *Boyar Duma*.

"He had no means in place to ensure the loyalty of the service nobility," Sheremetev continued. "That is why I have created the post of political officer. Russia had them up-time under Stalin's rule. They watched the service nobility, even if they called it something else in the twentieth century. Political officers will be mostly, but not entirely, *deti boyar*, whose job is to make sure that their charges don't do anything stupid. I thought of using the church, but people get really upset about things like that."

Suddenly everyone was looking at Colonel Leontii Shuvalov.

Director-General Sheremetev noticed and laughed. "Oh, not at all. Leontii is a fine man, but not nearly the right man for this. The new political officer for the Dacha is . . . Cass Lowry."

Chapter 72

A hunting lodge just west of Tatarovo

Mikhail Romanov, Czar of all the Rus, bounced his daughter on his knee with a mixture of relief and profound loss. The relief was because he and his family were safe—at least for the moment. The loss was not for the loss of power, but for the loss of his father.

Mikhail had been told that his father had died of a stroke and that was entirely possible. Filaret, Patriarch of Russia, had in fact had a series of minor strokes. And, considering the rumors about the limited year and the peasants, the riots were a natural response to his father's death.

Still, the timing was suggestive, and Fedor Ivanovich had been awfully quick to respond. Filaret would never have gone along with Sheremetev's takeover and he had the connections to fight back. Mikhail couldn't help the belief that one of Sheremetev's agents had managed to get close enough to the patriarch to help the stroke along. The possibility that Filaret was still alive was no more than a fantasy.

Mikhail knew that he should be fighting "Director-General" Sheremetev because of those suspicions and for the good of Russia. But he wasn't. He knew virtually nothing of what was going on in the wider world. He had no basis to plan and, for now at least, he and his family were being treated quite well. Also, from what he did know, Sheremetev's plan depended on his continued safety.

Life was full of strange twists of fate and even more so when you were living in a time of miracles. The Ring of Fire had seemed a wild rumor when they had first heard of it. Sending Vladimir to confirm it—or rather, disprove it, which was the outcome they'd expected—had just been a precautionary measure. But it had all proved to be true. Vladimir had stayed in Grantville to learn the secrets of the up-timers and Boris had brought an up-timer back with him. Bernie Zeppi had started out as little more than a dictionary of up-timer English on legs. But being used as a dictionary has side effects. Poor Bernie had found himself in school. Mikhail laughed a little at that thought. One student and hundreds of anxious teachers, each insisting that he learn enough to explain some other artifact of a language that was foreign even to those who spoke seventeenth-century English. Mikhail could sympathize with Bernie's predicament; he wasn't a scholar by choice, either.

And he, like Bernie, had been forced by circumstances into a role he wasn't well prepared for when he had been dragooned into becoming czar of Russia.

Come to that, Vladimir wasn't a trained spy. Still, the young prince was doing an excellent job—aided and abetted by the up-timers' free way with their knowledge. He and Boris had kept Russia from the Smolensk War, even before Boris brought Bernie to Russia. Vladimir had married a up-timer girl and was well situated in their community. And quite openly, for the most part, sending tons of copied books to Moscow, along with information on innovations made since the Ring of Fire as down-time craftsmanship had combined with up-time knowledge. That part was harder, from what Mikhail understood, because some of the new businesses were much more secretive than the State Library of Thuringia-Franconia. Still, Boris had left Vladimir a good core organization and Vladimir had expanded it. So the Dacha and the Gun Shop, Russia's industrial and military research and development shops, were well supplied with up-timer knowledge.

That knowledge, combined with Russian ingenuity and a willingness to go with simple, workable solutions rather than slavishly copy everything the up-timers were doing, plus a brute force approach that involved putting lots of people to work on projects that the up-timers could probably do with a lot less, had stood Russia in very good stead. Both industrially and in the recent battle over Rzhev. Russia had the beginnings of an electronics industry at the price of several people accidentally electrocuted. Telegraphs and telephones in the Kremlin and spark gap radios. And they were experimenting with tubes and transistors, Mikhail was told, although so far unsuccessfully. A test dirigible built and used at Rzhev and a much larger one under construction. Plumbing at the Dacha and starting to appear other places, including parts of Moscow. New rifled muskets with replaceable chambers for the army and a few new breech-loading cannon as well. New pumps for clearing mines of water and for creating vacuums. Which apparently had a myriad of uses. Improved roads, steam engines... the list went on and on. Sucking up labor almost as fast as the new plows and reapers freed it, perhaps faster. The free peasantry—what was left of it—had been among the first to go to the factories and set up their own, along with the *Streltzi* who were Russia's traditional merchant class.

Mikhail was less happy about some of the policy changes that Sheremetev had come up with. Selling to the Turks especially bothered him.

Moscow, the Grantville Section

Boris filled out paperwork and tried not to think about what was happening. "Director-General" Sheremetev was an idiot who had no concept of how to treat people to get the best work out of them. He couldn't inspire or motivate, save through threats. But, for now at least, the threats seemed to be working. Sheremetev had complete control of the *Boyar Duma* through a combination of bribes and coercion. Worse, he was what the up-timers called a micromanager, and his decisions were wrong more often than not.

It wasn't that Boris disagreed with Sheremetev's assessment of the general situation in Europe. The Swede was much more dangerous than the Pole. That had to be clear to anyone except an idiot. Boris had studied the history of the world on the other side of the Ring of Fire and one thing was clear: Poland had always been a nuisance to Russia and usually an antagonist, but never a mortal threat. Only twice since the Mongol yoke was thrown off had foreign powers come close to destroying Russia. First, the French; then the Germans. Never the Poles.

The key was economic development. The Poles had been too

backward themselves to pose more than a middling danger. The real peril came from western and central Europe, not eastern Europe.

But economic development presupposed financial reform, and Boris didn't think Sheremetev really understood paper money. Boris didn't really understand it himself that well, but he'd seen it work in Grantville and knew it was the way forward. True enough, Sheremetev was supporting the new currency, at least officially. But where Czar Mikhail's support had been genuine, Boris figured that Sheremetev was just using it to lure people into giving him gold and working for nothing.

The end result was likely to discredit the new money altogether, and so Russia would remain mired in poverty and ignorance. Sheremetev understood the threat from western Europe—but was making it worse, not better.

Grantville

"The"—Vladimir held up his hands and made quote marks in the air—"'Director-General' is teaching us a lesson," Vladimir explained. "He's also tempting us, putting pressure on to see if we will defect. Well, if *I* will defect. You hold dual citizenship."

"What lesson?" Brandy asked.

"Don't try to hold up the Russian government. Or, more accurately, don't fail to cut him in on it."

"So how bad is it?"

"Bad! For us here it's the advances." The ruble, now a paper currency, with the image of Czar Mikhail and the double-headed eagle on the face and the Moscow Kremlin and a Russian bear on the back, was valued at less than half the value of the Dutch guilder in spite of the fact that it was supposed to be equivalent to the silver ruble coin that had twice the silver of the Dutch guilder. Partly that was because the czar and *Boyar Duma* had issued rather more rubles than they really should have. But mostly it was because the Dutch merchants resented the paper ruble. The new currency had changed the whole trading landscape in Russia. Dutch merchants had gone from absolutely vital to convenient. And the price they paid at Arkhangelsk for grain, cordage, lumber, and other Russian goods had more than doubled.

So, the Dutch wouldn't deal in Russian paper money or money of account based on Russian money. They would still accept Russian coins, but their refusal to deal in Russian paper had its effect. "If the canny Dutch merchants wouldn't take paper rubles, there must be something wrong with them. Right?" So rubles traded in Grantville, Venice and Vienna at less than a quarter of face value. And that was if you were basing face value on the amount of silver in a ruble coin. If you figured it in the price of a bushel of grain at Arkhangelsk versus the same bushel at Amsterdam, it traded at less than a tenth of its face value.

It was hard to make a profit when you were losing more than nine-tenths of your money to arbitrage. Vladimir spent his rubles where they would buy something, then shipped the goods to the USE for resale, just as he had been doing from the beginning. And, like any good man of business, he tried to find buyers in advance rather than shipping the goods on spec. What Sheremetev objected to was how much of the money Vladimir was investing in Grantville and the USE. Sheremetev wanted Vladimir to buy silver and gold and send it back to Moscow. Which made no sense at all. If Vladimir was going to do anything along those lines, he would be buying paper rubles in Grantville with silver where he could get a lot of them, then shipping the rubles back to Moscow where they would buy more.

Vladimir had contracts to sell five thousand stacked-plate mica capacitors, plus several tons of other mica products. But what he didn't have was this quarter's shipment of mica and mica-based components. Also missing were a couple of hundred miles of cordage, several tons of Russian hardwoods, plus sundry other goods. In other words, several million American dollars worth of goods, which he was morally and legally obligated to provide. And about half of it had been paid for in advance. He was insured against loss at sea. With Swedish control of the Baltic, the insurance hadn't been all that expensive.

What he wasn't insured against was Sheremetev and the *Boyar Duma* preventing him from bringing out the goods. Goods that had never sailed from Nyen—St. Petersburg it would have become in that other history. Goods that had never even reached Swedish Ingria. It wasn't just that money wasn't coming in—money that had already come would have to be paid back with penalties for nondelivery.

Vladimir wasn't broke exactly. He was now deeply in debt. In some ways that was better than being broke, but in others much worse. Partly to gain access to the developing tech and partly just because it was good long-term financial strategy, he had invested in some of the more long-term projects. He was, for instance, fairly heavily invested in three of the companies that were working on down-time manufacture of automobiles. And he was the major investor in a group that was working on the tubes for microwaves. They didn't expect results for years, but they were working on it and Vladimir was the primary backer of the research. Microwave tech was just too useful to ignore because it was hard to do.

"It's bad for us here but what I'm really worried about is Natasha. Sheremetev can make me go out and get a real job, but that's not much of a threat. The real threat is that he can kill my sister. What I would like to do is get Natasha out of Russia. But I don't see any way to do it."

"How much time do we have?"

"I don't know."

"Well, I can send a fruitcake," Brandy said, "You know the kind with a saw in it. A metaphoric saw in this case. Instructions about how to arrange an unauthorized immigration."

"It's a worthy thought," Vladimir agreed, "but I don't think she'd come. Aside from everything else, Sheremetev needs me as much or more than I need him. If he didn't have Natasha I'd be able to tell him to shove it."

Chapter 73

April 1636

"So how are they doing out there?" Natasha asked as Anya came in.

Anya had taken to sleeping in Natasha's room. Partly that was because neither Natasha nor Filip liked it when she slept in Bernie's room and Anya had discovered that she cared about that in more than purely practical terms. She still didn't know what if anything would develop with Filip, but her friendship with Natasha was genuine and mattered to her.

Bernie was no longer comfortable with their old relationship anyway. That much was obvious even if he never said anything. Anya figured his discomfort came from the fact that he knew it bothered Natasha—not that Bernie would ever admit to his feelings about the princess, or probably even understand them well in the first place. From the future or not, men were still men. Stupid, when it came to such matters.

But the main reason Anya had moved into Natasha's quarters was that she was better protection against Cass Lowry than Bernie was. Bernie was too likely to lose his temper and attack Cass, which would just make the situation worse. Natasha was a Gorchakov princess and Cass had learned the hard way that it was dangerous to cross her.

"Not well," she said in response to Natasha's question. "Mr.

345

Lowry insists that the Dacha should limit itself to strictly practical applications."

Natasha snorted. "What *he* calls practical. He wants fixed-wing aircraft! How is that practical?"

After they'd talked about the Dacha and the scientific future of Russia for a bit—bad and getting worse by the day—they switched over to more personal matters.

"So Filip seems interested in you?" Natasha asked.

"Which might have meant something if this were still the Dacha," Anya said glumly. "I mean your and Bernie's Dacha, not Sheremetev and Cass's Dacha. You know what I mean. Anything seemed possible then. We were all working to change the world. It made anything seem possible."

Anya saw Natasha's nod of agreement and understanding. "Before Bernie I was a caged pet," Natasha said. "Then Bernie arrived and there was the Dacha . . . a place to work, to read, full of people who understood. Who wanted to understand. Who thought about how things worked and how they might be made to work better. All because of Bernie. Almost by existing, he made the world bloom. For four years we had a scholar's paradise. They've been the best years of my life."

She was a young woman but in that moment sounded very old, as if she were talking about a time long ago.

"Can you imagine what it would have been like if it were Cass instead of Bernie?" Anya said.

When Natasha didn't answer Anya looked over and saw her thinking. Then Natasha spoke. "Yes, I can. I hadn't before now, but I can and the frightening thing about it is that if we didn't have Bernie to compare him to, Cass probably would have seemed quite acceptable. The Dacha would still be here. Cass would have insisted that we concentrate on fixed wings so *Testbed* wouldn't have been built and *Czarina Evdokia* wouldn't be nearly finished. But we might have a couple of working one- or two-person airplanes with hand-built engines. The real difference, though, would be the sense of the place. Less freedom, academic or otherwise. Less trying to get the job done and more, as Bernie would say, trying to cover their asses. And we wouldn't even notice what was missing. We wouldn't realize what we might have had and Cass Lowry would seem quite a useful, if obnoxious, foreign employee. Without Bernie, the Dacha would still be of benefit to Holy Mother Russia. But it would have been just technical benefit. The subtle torch of freedom that Bernie lit in all of us just by being Bernie would be gone."

Anya nodded, remembering a night when Bernie, Filip, and she had talked about freedom, slavery and serfdom. How many conversations like that had there been? How many quiet words and beliefs had Bernie Zeppi dropped like seeds into fallow ground, not because he intended to create a revolution but simply because of who he was.

And what would Cass Lowry have dropped in place of those seeds? The man might be an up-timer in his origins, but he thought like a nobleman. Lowry believed, deep inside, that he deserved more and better than anyone else. From what Bernie had said, that had been true of him even when he was a teenager with no greater title than that of an athlete.

"You're right. Cass Lowry would have fit right in with the service nobility, and we never would have seen that there was a better way."

"That's what bothers me the most. How quickly the people here are giving up on that better way. How fast ivory towers can come down. Exchange Bernie for Cass Lowry, Mikhail for Sheremetev, and heaven is whisked away, with only memory of it making what we have now seem an annex of hell. My knight in shining armor arrived four years ago and by the time I noticed he was here, it was too late," Natasha said.

"We could run, you know," Anya said. "I've done it before. We could go east to the wild lands. Russia doesn't really control Siberia. No one does."

"You ran away to Siberia?" Natasha blinked her eyes in astonishment.

"No. I ran away to Moscow," Anya said. "I wasn't even a serf. I was a slave. I ran and got lost in Moscow, found any work I could, anywhere I could. My point is we're a lot better situated now. We have money and can get or forge travel papers. On the other hand, you're an important person. I just had one slave owner looking for me. We'd have the whole government looking for us. We'd have to go farther."

"What about everyone else? What about Bernie and Filip?"

"We could take Filip and Bernie!"

"And everyone else? We could run. We could even take Bernie

and Filip, perhaps a few others. But what about the staff of the Dacha? We can't all run. Not everyone would even want to."

"I know." Anya looked down at the bed they were sitting on. "But we may not have a choice. I don't think Cass Lowry will change and I don't think Boyar Sheremetev will back away from supporting him, certainly not for me and probably not for you. It may be run or submit to Cass. And I'm not sure I could do that, not anymore."

Natasha knew that Anya was preparing to run, but took no action either to aid her or prevent her. Natasha couldn't make up her mind. In a way the Dacha was a very effective cage. Its bars were of duty stronger than high carbon steel. She couldn't abandon her scientists to Cass Lowry and Sheremetev. They had come here to work for Russia and all its people, to do good with their minds. Natasha knew that view was a bit simplistic, but it was true enough when it came down to it. So she stayed and worked and tried to protect the eggheads and the cooks. The philosophers and the gardeners. And died a bit as the dream she hadn't even known she was dreaming died around her.

As punishments for idle comments, "wasting time on unprofit-able hobbies," or lack of progress on one of Cass or Sheremetev's pet projects came down, she tried to act as a buffer between her people and their new masters. But it wasn't working. Four years can be long enough to learn freedom, but it's not always long enough for the lesson to stick. More and more the Dacha was reverting to the dog-eat-dog informer culture of the bureaus.

More and more Cass Lowry felt empowered and Natasha had to restrain Bernie and her armsmen several times. Even so, the only thing that kept Bernie alive was that Sheremetev wanted two up-timers at the Dacha. He had told Cass in no uncertain terms that Bernie was off limits. Cass had also been told that Natasha was off limits and that protection was effectively extended to Anya as long as she stayed with Natasha. The only way she had kept her armsmen alive was by ordering more and more of them out of the Dacha.

Chapter 74

June 1636

Cass Lowry was drunk again, Father Kiril noted with concern. So the Dacha, even the guards placed by Sheremetev, walked carefully. Lowry had poor control over his impulses even when sober. He had virtually none once he got drunk—and, unfortunately, he was a mean rather than cheerful drunk.

With someone else Father Kiril might have tried to restrain the drinking, but Cass Lowry had made his contempt for the Russian Orthodox Church quite plain. Lowry seemed to consider himself above any church. All of which meant that when the American went on a drunken rampage, all Father Kiril could do was watch. So he watched and became even more concerned as Cass headed for the apartments of Princess Natalia.

There was no warning at all. The door burst open and Cass came in, a bottle in one hand and a leer on his face. "Get out of here," Natasha ordered. "You're drunk."

"I sure as hell am. I'm also the boss and you've been forgetting the new order. Interfering with my administration of the Moscow Institute of Technology. That's a better name than just calling it the country house."

Not a bad translation of the Dacha's up-time usage, skittered

349

through the back of Natasha's mind, while the part of her mind that was supposed to be figuring out how to head off the disaster that was Cass Lowry was blank as a new sheet of paper.

Her rooms were being guarded by Sheremetev's troops tonight. She'd had to send too many of her own away from the Dacha to maintain a loyal guard all the time. They might restrain Cass if she called on them but the fact that he was here at all argued against it. She moved in front of Anya and Cass smiled. That was the moment she realized that Cass wasn't here for Anya. He was here for her.

Her brain froze, not so much from fear as from simple confusion. He couldn't possibly get away with it, valuable up-timer or not, touched by God or not. Not in Russia, not even in Germany. Raping Anya or any of the servant girls, even killing one of them, he could get away with. But a princess of Russia? Even Sheremetev, perhaps especially Sheremetev, would have him drawn and quartered for the offense against all the nobility of Russia.

Then he grabbed her arm and all doubt fled. "Stupid downtimer bitch. You think there's any real difference between you and any of the other whores in Russia? You're all down-timers, whatever silly-ass titles you give yourselves." With his other hand he ripped open her dressing gown. "Time for you to learn your place, *Princess*, after what your guardsmen did to me when I first got here."

Now he had a hand on her breast and she tried to shove him away. For just a split second it seemed like she had succeeded, at least in part. His hand left her breast and there was space between their bodies.

Then his fist hit the side of her face. She hadn't seen it coming and it didn't exactly hurt, not yet, though it would later. For now it simply stunned her. She couldn't move, couldn't react when that same hand reached down and grabbed her down there.

Anya had expected Cass to come after her too, but she had been ignored as he went after the princess. Anya was a small woman, but she grabbed Cass' arm and got flung across the room for her trouble. Cass Lowry was a physically strong man, whatever else might be said about him. Anya had no more faith in the guards outside the door than Natasha did. Instead she went for the pistol in Natasha's bed stand.

Even with a willingness to sacrifice some serfs to the project, Russia didn't have nearly enough fulminate of mercury to supply an army and the newer, safer primer that had been developed later had only reached Russia after it had reached the USE. So production was still quite limited. Limited, that is, when you're talking about providing percussion caps for an army. Not the least bit limited when it came to providing caps for a few hundred of the privileged of Russia. The Dacha had plenty of guns. Natasha's had been made by the czar's own gunsmith. It was a .36 caliber cap-and-ball revolver. By the time Anya had it in her hands, Cass Lowry had Natasha on her bed, completely exposed and was pulling his pants down.

Anya pointed and shot. And missed at less than six feet. She was a good shot and practiced twice a week at the Dacha's firing range. But she was now learning how easy it was for even a marksman to miss a target in a real fight.

For a moment she just stared as Cass Lowry turned and looked at her, an expression of surprise on his face.

There were still five rounds left in the revolver. She aimed again, more carefully, taking that extra split-second to steady herself. At the chest, the best target.

She fired. Lowry staggered, as he tried to rise. Anya cocked the hammer, bringing another chamber in line. Fired. Lowry fell back on his buttocks, then leaned to one side, resting on his hip.

Blood was spreading across his chest. His eyes were open but no longer staring at her. They were staring at the nearby dresser. Or possibly at nothing at all, any longer.

Three shots left. Anya stepped forward two paces, brought the muzzle within six inches of Lowry's skull, cocked, and fired again. Blood, bone and brains splattered the wall behind him.

Two shots left. Amazingly, the man was not down; still lying on his hip, propped up on an elbow. His eyes were still wide open. Yet he had to be dead!

She cocked and aimed again.

Then the guards came rushing in. Sheremetev's men looked at Anya holding the gun, Cass on the floor, and began bringing up their own guns. Big and clumsy old-fashioned snaphaunce muskets, though. Their employer was something of a miser.

Anya turned and fired at the nearest of the two men. She was getting better at this. He went down with a bullet in his chest.

She turned to the other guard and fired her last shot. He went down too, although she had missed her actual target. She'd been aiming for his chest also but the shot had been hurried and struck him in the throat instead.

No matter, he was dead or dying. She glanced back at Lowry. The American had finally collapsed on the floor and was now obviously dead—even though his eyes were still open.

Anya heard a little choking sound and turned to Natasha, who was looking around in shock. Anya didn't blame her. It had all happened so fast.

Father Kiril jumped at the sound of the first shot, then rushed to Princess Natalia's private wing. He was joined on the way by the princess' aunt Sofia.

"I knew it would happen," Sofia gasped. "That, that...cretin!"

Kiril knew who she was talking about. Although cretin might be a bit tame, in his opinion. "He was drunk earlier, but I didn't expect him to actually come here."

They stopped and looked around the princess' room at the same time. Natasha was cramming jewelry and papers into a bag, urging Anya to hurry.

Sofia gasped. Natasha's face was reddened, as though she'd been punched and her dressing gown was in tatters. "Natasha!"

"Cass tried to rape her. And I shot him." Anya pointed at the limp form of Sheremetev's prize up-timer. "Then they came in and tried to draw on me with a gun in my hand, and I shot them." She pointed at the guards.

Sofia's face paled and Kiril couldn't quite tell if it was the news about Cass or that Anya, a peasant, had been shooting up members of the service nobility. That didn't matter now. It was obvious that Princess Natalia was in shock. Anya seemed to be doing better but Anya had previous experience with violence.

"We have to get you out of here," Kiril said. "And we have to do it now. There's not much time. It's only pure luck that none of the other guards were near the house."

"We'll need horses," Princess Natasha said. "Anya and I can... can..."

"Don't be ridiculous," Sofia said sharply. "You and Anya are leaving, yes. But not on horses."

"But, but..."

"I've heard Bernie's car roaring around this place for weeks," Sofia said. "You'll take it."

"But, but..."

"Neither of us know how to drive," Anya pointed out.

"So we wake up Bernie!"

"We can't take Bernie!" Natasha insisted. "He'll be safe, if we can get away. Sheremetev won't hurt him. He needs an up-timer." She pointed at Cass on the floor.

"Bernie would follow you anyway," Sofia snapped. "So stop being silly."

Kiril's mind was racing. "And Filip. You'll want Filip."

"Why Filip?" Anya said, then almost dragging the words out. "He has a secure position here. It would be better if he stayed here where it's safe."

Father Kiril smiled. "For the same reason that we're going to send Bernie. He would follow you anyway. Besides, who do you think has been writing the Flying Squirrel pamphlets? Filip isn't safe here, not with the heat that will be coming down."

Anya nodded, accepting Father Kiril's logic "And Gregorii," Anya said. "He's been working on our papers, just in case."

"And you, Father," Sofia said. "All these children need an adult around."

Chapter 75

"Wake up! Wake up!"

Bernie was never at his best when shaken out of sleep. "Wha... Who...?"

"Bernie, wake up," Natasha said. "We have to go."

"Go where?"

"Anywhere away from here."

That last comment woke Bernie up fully. "Natasha, what happened?"

"Quickly, Bernie. Quickly. I'll tell you on the way." He was half out of his room before his mind caught up with his body. "All right, everyone stop. What's going on?"

"We don't have time for this!" Natasha said exasperated.

"We don't have time to skip this part," Bernie said. After four years of the enthusiasms of geniuses he knew well how easy it was for them to get excited and forget minor details like, say, shoes in a snow storm. "What are we trying to accomplish? What can we do that will make it safer and more likely to work? What must we do that will prevent it from working?"

"We're trying to escape! We can move quic—"

Bernie held up a hand. "Escape to where? For how long? From who?"

And that brought everyone up short.

Father Kiril quickly and concisely filled Bernie in on what had happened.

"Anya," Natasha added, "had been working on just-in-case plans to escape to the east."

"Good thinking, kid," Bernie said. "I figured on running west myself, but all the forces that would be hunting us are in that direction and that's the direction they would expect. So we escape to the east long enough to get away and figure out what to do next?"

There were nods.

"We're escaping from the present government of Russia, not just Sheremetev and his goons since he's running things now. Which means we need to be as far and as long gone as we can before he realizes we've left. What about the radio?"

"What about it?" Sofia asked. But Natasha was nodding.

"We'll have to break it and in a way that will be hard to fix quickly," Natasha said, cringing a bit at the thought of destroying the best radio in Russia. "Otherwise they will be able to tell Moscow what has happened in seconds instead of hours."

"But Moscow has its own radio," Anya said. "We can't break that one."

They continued to talk as Bernie grabbed up two guns, a spare pair of pants and shirt, and a heavy jacket. "I'll get the cash. All the money in the Dacha safe. Paper and coins both," Sofia said. "Money is money."

Bernie went to check on the car while Sofia headed back to Natasha's rooms and the Dacha safe. Anya and Natasha went to get Filip and Gregorii and they all met back at Natasha's office, which had been soundproofed two years ago to keep the occasional booms, bangs and clangs of experiments from aggravating the boss. And which, just incidentally, had kept the rest of the Dacha from hearing Anya shoot holes in Cass and two of Sheremetev's guardsmen.

"So how do we take the radio shack?" Filip asked. It was more than a shack, though not much more. It had two rooms—the radio room and a toilet. And there was someone always on duty in case there was a message from Moscow. There were six radio men at the Dacha, but only one was on duty at this time of night.

"Keep it simple!" Anya said. "Walk in, point a gun at him, tie him up and gag him, then bust the radio and leave."

Which is what they did. The guard didn't resist and they tied him up as much for his protection as theirs. They told him what had happened in Natasha's rooms and mentioned making a run for Poland and the USE. Between Filip and Bernie, they knew which bits to break that would take the longest time to fix. There were a couple of pieces from up-time that Vladimir had sent from Grantville; those they took with them. For the rest they took pieces and spares and hid them under junk in Bernie's garage. They really didn't want to break the stuff, just take it out of commission for a little while.

Sofia elected to stay behind. The final tally of those going were Natasha, Bernie, Anya, Filip, Father Kiril and Gregorii. They would take the car. After they left Sofia would tell a list of people to run if they wanted to and to go to Natasha's estates, not to try to follow them to the USE. That way, if their judgment was wrong and some of the people were working for Sheremetev, they would lead the search west.

They hoped, anyway. Bernie was skeptical, since no matter what anyone told Sheremetev's people, the car was bound to leave tracks in the road at least in places. But maybe seventeenth-century Russian secret policemen were just as prone as the authorities he'd known back up-time to believe what they were told instead of their own lying eyes.

The first graying of dawn was in the sky when Bernie turned the key and the old Dodge started up. When they drove out the gate of the Dacha, the trunk was filled with money, weapons, ammunition and bits of irreplaceable tech. Bernie had also taken the time to hitch up a small trailer on which they were towing as many five-gallon cans of gasoline as they'd been able to fill.

He could only hope the jury-rigged hitch would hold, but he thought they'd probably need that extra gasoline. Bernie was more worried about the condition of the roads. The *rasputitsa* was over, the notorious muddy season that made travel extremely difficult or even impossible on Russian roads for weeks during the spring and fall. But "over" didn't preclude running into some still-bad stretches if their luck turned sour. If they did run into such a muddy stretch, they'd lose the fuel trailer for sure and might get bogged down altogether.

On a more positive note, any pursuers would have the same problem. Mud wasn't any friendlier to horses than it was to wheeled vehicles.

The Dacha had started four years earlier as a largish house with a hunting park behind it and a tiny village in front. That had changed. Fencing and walls had been added, a canal had been dug that connected the Dacha to the Moskva River. The Moskva fed into the Oka, which fed into the Volga; which allowed goods to travel to the Dacha from all of Russia by river and canal. More buildings to house researchers and research had been added. The gate going from the Dacha proper to the villages was manned but not closed. As the Dodge approached, the guards waved for it to stop but Bernie didn't slow down at all. The car kept right on going and the guard who had been blocking its path was a bit slow in jumping aside. He was used to the speed of horses, not of cars.

Bernie winced as he felt the thump of car striking flesh. The guard was knocked aside and slid into the canal that flowed past the gate where he came to rest, his lower body in the water. Hopefully he was just injured. Bernie didn't have anything against the man personally. He was just doing his job.

Then they were speeding through the village that provided support for the Dacha. The peasant inhabitants were just starting to wake up. Once through the village they were on one of the roads built by the scrapers over the last three years. Roads that led to Moscow to the west, to Murom and the Gorchakov estates to the east, to Ivanovo to the north and many other places. The road they were taking, as it happened, was the road to Murom and the Gorchakov estates. They could have carried more if they had taken a steam barge, but a steam barge would have had to travel either to Moscow or to Murom, which would have told Sheremetev where they were simply by knowing where they weren't.

Bernie, of course, was in the driver's seat, Natasha in the front passenger seat. Father Kiril and Gregorii were squeezed into the back seat along with Filip, and Anya was seated on Filip's lap. Given Natasha's slenderness, that probably wasn't the most efficient placement. But even in the Dacha community, squeezing the princess into the back seat just because Father Kiril had a fatter ass wasn't going to happen.

By four hours later, they'd gotten a hundred miles away. So the odometer said, anyway. That was far enough to stop and rest for a bit, while they considered their plans. Up till now, their "plan" could pretty much be summed up as *get the hell out of Dodge.*

In a Dodge. Bernie started laughing.

"What is so funny?" Natasha demanded, a bit crossly. There were disadvantages to having a slim build while riding in a car crossing bumpy roads and driven by a lunatic up-timer. Less padding.

Bernie shook his head. "Ah . . . never mind." Even for Natasha, the cultural references were too complicated to explain under the circumstances. "What do we do now? You realize we can't pass any guard checks."

While their artist, Gregorii, had made himself a set of papers for travel when Anya requested a set for herself and Natasha, none of them had considered that Bernie, Filip, or especially Father Kiril, would have to run.

"Where do we ditch the car?" Bernie asked. "It's the only one in Russia, so there's no way it's not going to get noticed."

"The car will get us to my estates faster than any other possibility," Natasha said. "Certainly faster than any pursuit. We'll pick up armsmen and decide where to go and what to do from there."

"You know what I'd really like?" Bernie asked.

"No. What?"

"I'd like to break out the czar."

"Impossible!"

"We can't!"

"Are you mad?"

The uproar that caused just about caved Bernie's head in.

"Stop and think. Why is it impossible?"

"It is."

"Too many armsmen."

"We don't even know where they are."

"*Stop!*" Bernie shouted. "Think, dammit. One at a time."

Natasha, being the person who outranked everyone else, said, "We don't know where they are."

"How many places can they be?" Bernie asked.

"Hm. Not all that many," Father Kiril said.

"So we get to your place," Bernie said, "we call around on the radio and try to figure out where the czar is likely to be."

"Are we sure the czar wants to be rescued?" Father Kiril asked. "At the very least, he and his family are safe where they are."

"Are they really?" Anya asked. "Does Sheremetev really need

them? Remember the Time of Troubles. No one worried about the various czars then, did they?"

They spent the rest of the trip talking about how and whether they should attempt to rescue the czar.

Bernie had been to Natasha's home before. It was more a palace than a castle, though some of the older parts had a significant castle influence. It was a large, walled compound on the south side of Murom. And it was quite improved over the last four years. It had indoor plumbing of a sort, at least in a few places. It had a water-wheel generator that kept charged a fairly large room full of lead-acid batteries. There were a few light bulbs, though they were neither all that bright nor all that long-lasting. Mostly the electricity was used for heating elements. Heating elements that could be turned off and on quickly and efficiently, for cooking and the heating of rooms while using little wood and producing less smoke. Still, it was an example of conspicuous consumption but about the least that a princess who was also the head of the Dacha could get away with.

Even the Dodge had been there before. Once. To show off its existence to the citizens of Murom, with weeks of preparation and hoopla leading up to the visit. Now, about two-thirty in the late fall afternoon, the Dodge came roaring up the road, raising enough dust for a company of horse. If a company of horse could possibly move that fast, which it couldn't.

Chapter 76

Lieutenant Boris Timofeyevich Lebedev, as it happened, was on the city wall inspecting the guard when he saw the dust cloud in the distance. One of the city *Streltzi* whom he was inspecting told him what it was.

"It's a dodge," the man said. Then, seeing Tim's confusion continued, "The magic vehicles that come from the future and eat burning naptha, they're called dodges. That must be the princess' dodge. Well, it's officially owned by the outlander from the future, but he works at the Dacha, so I figure it's hers anyway."

Whatever it was and whoever it belonged to, it was raising a lot of dust and coming awfully fast. Besides, they had received no word that Princess Natasha was coming and they should have. "Inform Captain Lebedev that we have a dodge approaching Royal Gate."

As fast as it moved, Captain Ivan Borisovich Lebedev reached the gate before the dodge did. But it didn't give the captain all that much time to consider what to do. In Tim's experience if the thing approaching was something other than a drink or a young girl, his cousin took considerable time deciding what to do about it. But woe be to the subordinate who acted in advance of those decisions. This time, as it had so many others, the thing approaching passed before the captain made up his mind. It slowed. Two people in the front seats waved at the gate guard and it kept right on going, just as if it had every right to be here, not at the Dacha where it was supposed to be.

The captain, having failed to act in time to stop it, now followed after it, Tim following in his turn. By the time they got down off the walls, it was turning into the Gorchakov palace—again just as if it had every right to. As it happened, the Murom radio was located in the Gorchakov palace. Why not? It was provided by the Dacha and the batteries to run it were in the palace. Until quite recently all the operators of it had been Gorchakov retainers. Where else would it be?

In the city hall seemed a good place to Tim, but moving it there was another thing his cousin Ivan Borisovich hadn't decided on yet. So it had stayed in the palace. They had put their own radioman in charge of all the other radiomen in the radio room.

Tim wondered if that worthy happened to be on duty at the moment as he followed his cousin toward the palace gates.

The palace gates that had opened so easily to admit the Dodge failed, for the first time, to admit Tim and his cousin. They were informed that the princess was now in residence and they could not be admitted without her consent. That was especially inconvenient since they had been living there since they had arrived in Murom. By tradition, the captain of the Murom *Streltzi* was a boyar's son, a retainer of the Gorchakov clan. Being a retainer, he lived in their palace.

When the *Boyar Duma* had made cousin Ivan Borisovich captain of the Murom city guard, they had not specified quarters. So when Tim and Ivan Borisovich had gotten here, the Gorchakov's captain, one Vladislav Vasl'yevich, had been unceremoniously ejected from his rooms and sent to stay with the guards. Just one of so many things Tim's cousin had done to make himself popular with his new subordinates. Tim knew this was an unimportant post. Was supposed to be an unimportant post. But just at the moment, this post was starting to look pretty important.

While Captain Ivan Borisovich Lebedev was still fuming and threatening, word reached the gate that the captain was to be admitted. And was to report to the princess post haste. So off they went, Tim trailing his cousin and both of them surrounded by Murom *Streltzi* who were not hiding their grins at all well.

✧   ✧   ✧

Princess Natalia Gorchakovna looked stone-cold and somewhat miffed. Tim suspected that she was actually in a rage, but she was doing an admirable job of hiding just how much of a rage. Which was quite understandable given the recent events in terms of control of the Gorchakov estates. With Prince Vladimir in Grantville and Princess Natasha sequestered in the Dacha, control of the estates had fallen to estate managers who had proved less strong in their loyalty than might be hoped. Through bribes and coercion, actual control had shifted to the Sheremetev clan.

"Who, precisely, are you people?" the princess demanded.

Ivan Borisovich, as was his nature, began to bluster. And Tim cringed internally. Tim had never had great respect for his older cousin and his time in Cousin Ivan's command had only made his opinion worse. The man was an embarrassment to the family.

"Captain Lebedev. My executive officer, Lieutenant Lebedev," Ivan Borisovich said. "We were sent by Director-General Sheremetev and the *Boyar Duma* to reassert government control over Murom and the Gorchakov estates. How *dare* you have us held at the gates? We are Great House."

"The proper form of that question is," Princess Natalia said coldly, "how *dare* you have us held at the gates, Princess? Your family may be great house, but apparently they didn't teach you manners. But see, the answer appears magically when you ask the question correctly. *Princess* is how I dare! These are my lands, Captain. My city. My house. My people. The real question is what are *you* doing here in my home?"

"Who are you to question me?" Ivan Borisovich said. "You're supposed to be in your dacha."

"Arrest him," the princess said. "And the other one, while you're at it."

The princess' men immediately leveled their guns at Tim and his cousin.

Ivan Borisovich was an idiot when times were good. He was an even greater idiot when times were bad. Tim was grateful that he was being held in a separate cell, even though he could still hear his cousin's blustering, if dimly.

Unlike Ivan Borisovich, Tim was a popular young man. Due to his actions at Rzhev, for one thing, and his much nicer nature, for another. So Tim wasn't entirely surprised when the young

Streltzi of Murom, Pavel, brought him some food and stayed for a bit to talk. He'd had long talks with Pavel before, while they were pulling guard duty.

"It's a terrible thing that happened to the princess," Pavel said.

"She seemed fine when she had me arrested," Tim pointed out.

"She barely escaped! That outlander—the other one, not Bernie—he attacked her! In her own bedroom!"

Tim found himself interested, as the story continued to pour out of Pavel. Pavel wondered what Director-General Sheremetev was thinking putting a man like Cass Lowry in charge of the Dacha. Especially when it was doing so much for Russia under Princess Natalia.

Tim knew precisely what Director-General Sheremetev was thinking. His great uncle had told him. The Gorchakov family was becoming dangerous. Princess Natalia Gorchakovna had been using her position in the Dacha to garner support among the great houses. After four years, she had garnered quite a lot. Cass Lowry was the Sheremetev family's way of saying to the other great houses "If you want high tech in the future, you apply to the Sheremetev family not the Gorchakov family." At the same time, Tim had met Lowry and didn't like the man. Pavel's description of the attempted rape of a princess seemed quite believable.

"How can you work for Director-General Sheremetev," Pavel asked, "when he's doing what he's doing? Putting people in prison right and left? Killing all those people in Moscow in his purges?"

Tim had begun to wonder about that himself.

"And what about Czar Mikhail? Taken out of Moscow! What kind of man does that, imprison the czar?"

"No one is imprisoned. The czar and his family are just at a hunting lodge, to get away from the troubles in Moscow. He even took his up-time nurse and her family with him," Tim said.

"How do you know that?" Pavel sneered.

"We get radio messages from him," Tim said. "The hunting lodge he's at isn't on the normal network, so they radio through here."

Russia had set up radio stations just within range of one another. Each one had a high antenna placed on a high hill or at the top of a tall building. There were normally two or three radio stations within range of each antenna, not that there were all that many yet. When a message was sent, it would be tapped out in the Russian version of Morse code and would be heard by the station the transmitter was tuned to. That station would then resend the same message up the line. This would repeat until the message arrived at the proper place. So the fact that they were getting messages directly from the hunting lodge meant that the czar had to be somewhere within twenty-five or thirty miles. Tim knew all that, but he didn't think about it when he told his friend Pavel that the czar's messages traveled through Murom.

"So, he has to be somewhere near," Pavel told his boss. His boss, in turn, told the princess. And the princess, of course, told Bernie and her other friends.

"But Sheremetev doesn't have any lands within thirty miles of here," Natasha said. "Not one village, not one house. Nothing."

"Do *you* have a hunting lodge within thirty miles of here?" Filip asked.

"Yes, just west of Tatarovo." Natasha stopped. "You don't suppose..."

"So we go get him?" Bernie asked.

Vladislav Vasl'yevich, restored for now to his post of captain of the Murom *Streltzi*, said, "Not the princess." Then looking at Natasha, "You should stay here where it's safe."

"No, my good and loyal Captain," Natasha said. "I must go because it will fall to me to decide what to do if the czar is not, in fact, being held against his will."

Chapter 77

An exhausted trooper rode into Moscow and made his way to the Kremlin. After a couple of misdirections, he reached Director-General Sheremetev and reported that Princess Natalia Petrovna had escaped in the Dodge with Bernie Zeppi, and some others. Cass Lowry had been killed, apparently by either the princess herself or one of her chambermaids. One of the guards had been killed and the other badly wounded. He'd been shot in the chest but the bullet had missed his heart. His survival now seemed likely, but so far he hadn't told them anything very coherent.

Director-General Sheremetev and a troop of his men left immediately for the Dacha.

Sofia smiled to herself when she heard the uproar outside her quarters. She never had liked that Sheremetev brat, all puffed up and strutting the way he did. She sat quietly, waiting, knowing what was about to happen. She'd grown up in Russian politics, after all.

As she expected, there was no polite knock. Her door burst open, armed men stormed in, searched her room for what hidden dangers they imagined, then the man himself strutted in. Richly dressed, overbearing, and much too old to be doing this. Even if he succeeded, the stupid man would die, probably within a few years, as the next Time of Troubles began.

"Where is Princess Natalia?" he growled.

"That's none of your business," Sofia answered calmly. "Princess Natalia is Great House. You have no authority over her."

"I'm the Director-General. I speak for the *Boyar Duma*," Sheremetev said.

"The *Duma* has no authority over Princess Natalia," Sofia pointed out.

"The *Duma* speaks for the czar."

"Let the czar speak for himself, then."

Balked, Sheremetev stepped back and, somewhat more politely, asked, "What happened here?"

Sofia told him of the attempted rape and of Anya coming to Natasha's defense.

"A household servant killed two of my men!" Sheremetev was outraged and deeply offended. More by the manner of his men's death, than the fact that they were dead. To die at the hands of a menial! It was desecration. He turned to one of his guards. "Find that woman and bring her here."

Sofia tinkled a little laugh. "Be my guest. If you can find her."

"Are you saying Princess Natalia took a murderess with her?"

"She took her servant with her, yes. *We* are loyal to those who are loyal to us," Sofia said, "unlike some people."

"Take her away," Sheremetev told his guards. "I'll decide what to do with her later. For the moment, take me to the radio room. I need to send a message."

Sofia started laughing.

"What do you mean you can't fix it?" Sheremetev demanded.

"We *can* fix it, sir," the technician said. "But not quickly. We will have to make new parts, which will take a couple of days."

Sheremetev was tempted to have the man punished, but the technician was the nephew of one of his supporters. He couldn't have him beaten with a knout like a serf. Yet.

"Back to Moscow!" Sheremetev shouted. "That's the closest radio."

At last, and several hours later, Director-General Sheremetev strode into the radio room in the Kremlin and ordered that a demand for Princess Natalia's arrest be sent to all stations. The message went out, but because of the many stations it would be transmitted through, it would take still more time.

Chapter 78

As Natasha, Bernie and the rescue team were driving away from the palace at Murom, a radio message came in.

> PRINCESS NATALIA GORCHAKOVNA WANTED IN CONNECTION WITH DEATH OF TWO MEN AT ARMS AND THE SEVERE WOUNDING OF CASS LOWRY. REPORT SIGHTINGS TO MOSCOW AND DETAIN. BY ORDER OF THE BOYAR DUMA AND THE DIRECTOR-GENERAL FOR CZAR MIKHAIL. END MESSAGE.

The radio operator was one of Natasha's loyal men. Alas, his boss wasn't.

Partly out of fear, and partly out of greed, Petr Timofeyivich used the order from the *Boyar Duma* and the czar to release Captain Ivan Borisovich Lebedev and his men.

Control of Murom passed quickly—but not firmly—back into the hands of Sheremetev loyalists. This had very little effect on anything. Most of the people in Murom were keeping their heads down and staying just as far from politics as they could manage.

A radio message was sent to Moscow telling that the princess had been spotted, but had left before the message ordering her detention had arrived.

For the next several hours, things were very tense in the halls of government in Murom. Captain Lebedev didn't even attempt to keep the lid on, raging around the palace. Lieutenant Lebedev, however, had made friends with the *Streltzi* and urged them to wait and remain calm.

The Dodge traveled slowly, pulling a down-time made trailer behind it. The trailer carried some twenty of Natasha's men at arms led by Vladislav Vasl'yevich. In order to avoid jarring the men too much, Bernie kept the speed down to around twenty miles per hour, and often much less than that. The thirty-two mile trip to the hunting lodge took three hours. It was evening when they approached the hunting lodge.

"You need to warn me before we get there, Natasha," Bernie said. "We need to stop the car a mile or so away from the lodge and let the boys in back out of the trailer."

A few minutes later Natasha told Bernie to stop. "The path goes forward, then turns right. After the turn, you can see the lodge."

Bernie consulted with the armsmen, including one of her huntsmen who was very familiar with this particular lodge. "How close can you get before you're spotted?"

"It depends on who's doing the spotting," the huntsman said. "If it was you I could tap you on the shoulder before you knew I was there."

"Maybe you better go scout for us then."

"I can do that."

The wait seemed to last forever, but it wasn't really that long before the huntsman came up behind Bernie and said "Boo." Bernie grinned and turned to face the man. He'd spotted him well before time. The huntsman grimaced. "So what did you see, Boo?" Bernie asked.

"About a hundred yards east of the lodge, there are several tents and a paddock with maybe twenty horses. Considering the size of the lodge, I don't see how there can be more than thirty or so men, at most."

"All right," Bernie said. "You and the men infiltrate. Natasha and I will drive in just like we own the place."

Vladislav Vasl'yevich started to object but was interrupted.

"I do own the place," Natasha said.

"Fine. We're the distraction, Natasha. Ride in like the queen of England, order them off your property. And while they're

arresting us, the rest of these guys will get the drop on them."
Bernie didn't have to explain "get the drop on them." He'd already
done that. Many times.

And, in essence, that's what they did.

Bernie drove up to the house, with the horn blaring. Most of
the horses in the area panicked. Half a dozen men came out of
the tents and one man came out of the house itself.

Natasha emerged from the car, using her most regal manner.
"What are you people doing at my lodge? You're trespassing. Get
out at once!" Then, apparently seeing Czar Mikhail for the first
time, she added, "Except, of course, for Your Majesty. You are
always welcome on my lands."

The czar was looking as shocked as anyone. But it wasn't he
who spoke. It was a man Natasha had never seen before, who was
dressed in a black fur coat with a silver dog's head clasp. Sixty
years before, Ivan the Terrible had created a band of enforcers
called the *Oprichniki* who were recognized by their black fur coats
and the severed dog's heads they carried. Later Ivan had outlawed
them and made it a crime to even say the word *Oprichniki*.

This man and the six he had with him, also wearing the clasp,
weren't the same *Oprichniki* as Ivan had had. A silver dog's head
wasn't the same as the severed head of a real dog. Still, the sym-
bolism was unmistakable.

"You are under arrest!" the latter-day *Oprichniki* said.

Feeling more than a little pale herself, Natasha turned to the
czar and waved at the man in black. "Did you authorize this,
Your Majesty?"

She was unutterably relieved to see the little, almost uncon-
scious, shake of the czar's head.

The black coat spoke again. "Seize them!"

"Hold!" Natasha shouted. "You have no authority here and
none over me! The only one who could give you such authority
is right here and he hasn't done so."

Her arguments went unheeded and the troops kept right on
coming. Then she heard Bernie.

"Hey, Dogboy!" he shouted. "That fancy silver puppy won't
stop a bullet."

When Natasha looked, Bernie was holding a large up-time
revolver pointed at the chest of the *Oprichniki*.

"My men will kill you and the princess!" the *Oprichniki* shouted back.

"Could be," Bernie acknowledged rather more calmly than Natasha really would have preferred, "but you will still be dead."

"They will be dead before then," came another voice, as calm as Bernie's but much colder. Looking over, Natasha saw that Vladislav Vasl'yevich had come out from the gap between two of the tents, followed by several of his men. All of them had their weapons raised and ready to fire.

The czar himself was looking a bit conflicted about the rescue. The dogboy still under Bernie's gun was looking very angry. But the confrontation was over, obviously. The man could be as angry as he wanted, he had no chance against the odds he was facing.

So, Bernie turned toward Natasha and began re-holstering his gun. But she was staring past him looking at Dogboy and the czar. Then her expression changed. Bernie turned back to see Dogboy pulling out a pistol of his own and pointing it, not at him or Natasha, but the czar. The czar was looking back at Dogboy with a half-frightened, half-resigned expression on his face. As though the fate that he had been dodging all his life had caught him at last.

Then Vladislav Vasl'yevich jumped, knocking the czar out of the way.

Bernie fired, Dogboy fired. Vladislav Vasl'yevich went down, spraying the czar with his blood.

Dogboy went down, too. Wounded in the shoulder, not dead, but he'd lost his gun.

A couple of the other dogboy guards took the gunshots as a license to resume hostilities, but Vladislav Vasl'yevich's men began firing at them immediately. Numerically, the two groups were about evenly matched, but the Gorchakov guards were equipped with the brand new AK4.7 cap-lock repeaters. The .7 modification was only partly to the gun. The center fire chambers could be fitted into a clip that was shifted right to left, one chamber every time the lever-action was opened and closed so that it was fire, cock, fire, cock. The dogboys, on the other hand—with standard Sheremetev pecuniary habits—were equipped with the cheaper AK3 flintlocks.

It was a damp day, too. The only dogboy gun that came to bear squarely on its target misfired. The end result was a simple massacre. After seeing Vladislav Vasl'yevich gunned down, his men were in no mood to take prisoners—*any* prisoners, not just the two who'd raised their guns.

Two of the dogboy guards survived, but they were badly wounded. Meanwhile, another group of Natasha's guards had rescued the czarina, the nurse, her husband, and all the children.

They questioned the chief dogboy who was, as it turned out, an *Oprichniki* of the *Boyar Duma*. So this was the form that Sheremetev's *political officers* were to take. Ivan the Terrible's *Oprichniki* had been his personal secret police and ultimately had proven to be more trouble than they were worth. But they had included many people who would, in later years, prove very important—including Patriarch Filaret and Boris Godunov. So the *Boyar Duma*, also in need of a force to put down dissension, had created an updated version.

A contingent of that new organization had been given the job of guarding the czar. Their commander, the one with the dog's head clasp, was under orders to kill the czar, but only if it looked like the czar might escape. The same orders were in place for the czar's family, but only if the czar was dead first. The *Boyar Duma* didn't want Mikhail free and after revenge for a dead family. They didn't, even Dogboy insisted, want Mikhail dead. Just out of the way while they did what was needed to keep Russia safe from the corrupting influences that Mikhail and his father had allowed in. Russia needed a strong hand. The Russian people tended to become bandits and brigands if they were given too much freedom.

"Look, folks," Bernie said after a while. "This is all very interesting and I'm sure quite socially relevant, but is this really the time for a debate on political philosophy? They were going to kill you, Your Majesty. Maybe not now, but once they were sure of themselves. At best, they would keep you and your whole family prisoners for the rest of your lives. Meanwhile, the bad guys are after us and I don't want to stick around to find out what they'll do if they catch us. It's your country, Your Majesty. If you want to stay here and trust to the good offices of the *Boyar Duma*, and that fink Sheremetev, that's your choice. But we need to leave."

The nurse, Tami Simmons, spoke up. "We're going with you!

I'm sorry, Your Majesty, but I don't want my kids here when these guys' friends show up."

The czarina agreed, and then so did Mikhail. So, the czar and czarina and their kids would ride in the Dodge with Bernie and everyone else they could fit would ride in the trailer. That still left half a dozen of Natasha's guards without transport. They took the horses in the paddock. All of them. They would need remounts and didn't want to leave the dogboys with transportation. There was serious talk about killing the dogboys. And as a sort of compromise, Czar Mikhail had them swear on pain of death not to serve the *Boyar Duma* anymore.

Bernie didn't figure the oaths would last past the time it took them to get over the horizon, but he didn't really care either. Natasha's guardsmen were to make their way back to Murom as fast as they could and if Natasha wasn't there when they arrived, at the very least orders would be.

Bernie, the czar and the czarina talked as Bernie drove them slowly over the rough roads, fields, and trails back to Murom. And by the time they got there, the czar had decided.

Well, the way Bernie figured it, the czarina decided and the czar went along. Mikhail Romanov didn't strike Bernie as the forceful type. The decision was that the czar, czarina and the children would go to Bor, take possession of the dirigible *Czarina Evdokia*, and then decide where to take it.

Bernie thought about arguing for Grantville, but decided not to. The truth was, Grantville and its USE were now more of a foreign country to him than Russia was. To the extent that Bernie Zeppi felt he had a king—not much—that king was Mikhail Romanov, not Gustav Adolf.

Chapter 79

They drove up to the palace at Murom, fat and happy, totally unaware of the changes that had taken place while they were off rescuing the king of the country and his family. The guards waved them through the city gate, then others waved them through the gates of the palace compound.

Not until Bernie stepped out of the car did the guns appear.

"Oh, crap," Tim heard the up-timer say. "This couldn't just be simple."

Captain Ivan Borisovich Lebedev sneered at him. "You are all under arrest in the name of the czar."

Then Tim saw the other door of the dodge open and Czar Mikhail stepped out. Much to Tim's surprise.

"Really?" Czar Mikhail said. "I wasn't aware that I gave an order for this man's arrest."

Cousin Ivan Borisovich gaped at him. "What are you doing here? You're supposed to be at the hunting lodge."

"I got tired of hunting," Czar Mikhail said, though Tim knew very well that he hadn't been hunting.

The up-timer started grinning. Cousin Ivan looked back and forth between the up-timer and the czar. The guardsmen and *Streltzi* who had performed this ambush started looking at each other, trying to figure out what to do. Tim couldn't help but sympathize with them. The day had been a whipsaw, the Sheremetev clan in control of the city, then the Gorchakov clan, then the Sheremetev again. Then, when the Gorchakovs came back and were arrested by the Sheremetev in the name of the czar, out pops the czar himself to countermand the order. Of course, most of these men had never seen the czar, but Cousin Ivan had confirmed his identity. For that matter, Tim was starting to feel a bit whipsawed himself. He was a loyal member of his clan, but his oath was sworn to Czar Mikhail. Who was standing right here, denying that he'd ordered the arrest of the up-timer. Tim was fully aware that many of the orders that were given in the czar's name were actually given by the *Boyar Duma*, but presumably the *Boyar Duma* was acting *for* the czar.

"You are under arrest by order of the *duma!*" Cousin Ivan shouted. For once in his life, Ivan Borisovich Lebedev had made a quick decision. And it had to be one of the worst decisions that Tim had ever heard.

All of which left Tim with nothing to do but make a quick decision of his own. Who did Tim serve? The family or the czar? Clan or kingdom? And the answer surprised Tim as much as it did his cousin when Tim pulled his pistol out, stuck it in his cousin's back and said, "I don't think so."

In a strange way, the up-timers really were a corrupting influence on Russia. Before the up-timers, Russia had been, in Tim's eyes, anyway, an amalgamation of feuding clans. Now it was a nation. Becoming one, anyway. And it was that nation that Tim decided to give his loyalty to.

"Be careful, Cousin," he continued. "If you say the wrong thing here and now, you will die with my bullet in your back. You do not arrest the czar of Mother Russia. To attempt to do so is treason. I am not a traitor."

Cousin Ivan went back to not making decisions. Probably for the best.

"What do we do now, Your Majesty?" Tim asked, once all the armed troops had declared for the czar and Cousin Ivan was on his way back to the cell.

"There is a dirigible in Bor. We will take possession."

"As you command, Your Majesty," Tim said "And go where?"

"That's a more difficult question," Czar Mikhail said. "I don't want to abandon my people. And the political consequences of my leaving Russia would be extreme."

Tim nodded in understanding. Russia, in its way, was a very insular nation. Were the czar to move into exile in some other state, it would be awfully hard for him to ever come back.

"Well, that just leaves east," Filip said. "Far enough east that it will be difficult for the Sheremetev faction to get their hands on you, but not so far that you can't return when the time comes."

They started looking at maps, trying to determine the best place to go. "What about the people of Murom?" Natasha asked. "Especially the guardsmen and the *Streltzi*, but, really, all the people, the factory workers and the servants. When we leave, will they be punished for letting us go?"

Tim wished the princess had asked that question when there wasn't a mob of *Streltzi* standing around to hear it.

"Set them free and tell them to leave," Bernie said.

"Order them to leave their homes and their town?" the czarina asked.

"Leave it up to them," Bernie said. "That's all you can do. You can't order them to be free, only offer it."

Filip was nodding. Tim remembered Filip, from his two visits to the Dacha, as a sort of silly fellow, always talking math and theory. Yet here he was with the czar, the princess and the up-timer along with the blond servant girl discussing . . . Discussing what? Tim wasn't sure. The fate of Russia? The future of the world? Who were these people and how had Tim fallen in with them?

The blond servant girl, Anya, spoke up. "That's the truth of it, Majesty. Freedom can be taken or it can be offered, but it can't be forced on those not ready to embrace it."

"And is Russia ready to embrace it?" the czarina asked.

"Russia is not all one mind, Majesty," Filip said. "If offered freedom, some will accept, others will hide in their holes waiting for a new master to come along. Still others will take it as license, as the Cossacks do, and try to become those new masters. All you can do is the best you can do. But I have become convinced that the gain in liberty is worth the cost in security."

The czar was looking at Filip speculatively. "I'm not sure what it is, but what you just said reminds me of a pamphlet I read once. I think it was signed 'the Flying Squirrel.'"

Filip shrugged with a half smile. "I read a lot, Your Majesty. Perhaps I read that pamphlet."

"Perhaps," the czar agreed doubtfully.

"So," Princess Natasha interrupted, "we offer those who wish to follow us to the east a drink of freedom, and see who drinks?"

"That'll work," Bernie agreed, "as long as we can figure out where we're going. But it'll mean we have to announce where that is."

They went back to the maps.

The map they were looking at was a copy of one that had been sent to the Dacha, which was a copy of one in Grantville. They were fair copies, though. And features like rivers were clear enough. The place where the Ufa River . . .

Tim spoke up. "We have a problem, Your Majesty, and its name is steamboats. Steamboats in the last two years—but especially in the last year—have increased the goods transported on the Volga. They kept us supplied at Rzhev and by now they can move armies. Small armies, but still armies. If we go near a river, especially one that connects to the Volga, and most of them do, it will be easy to send an army after us."

"We have two problems," the up-timer said. "Contradictory problems. We want a place where those who want to can follow us and we want a place where the czar's family can be safe from pursuit."

"I wish my friend Ivan were here. He's better at this than I am," Tim said. "He's stationed at Bor where they're building the dirigibles."

"Then we'll be seeing him fairly soon," Czar Mikhail said. "As I said, it is our intent to take possession of the *Czarina Evdokia*."

"Well, then he will be able to help us. But what do we tell the people here?"

"Send them to Ufa, those who aren't going with us. There's a fort there, built by Ivan the Terrible in 1574 and a town that grew up around it. It may not be where we end up, but it's a place to gather," the czar said. "The steam barges can get there I know, because I took one to see it last year."

"Which means that Sheremetev can load an army on steamboats and take it there," Czarina Evdokia said.

"There is that, but I think we must take the chance," Czar Mikhail said. "Perhaps Tim's clever friend, the baker's son, will have a better option."

Tim just listened as much as anything, shocked by the fact that the czar knew who Ivan was.

✧　　　✧　　　✧

Natasha left them to work out the details and called for her factor, who was supposed to have been managing this part of her family estates.

"So, Pavel."

"Princess." Pavel looked uneasy, as well he should.

"You turned my estate over to the Sheremetevs. I'd like to know why. Did they pay you?"

"Your Highness, they had all the proper forms endorsed by the *Boyar Duma*. To disobey would have been treason. They threatened me," Pavel said. "And my family. What was I to do? Your brother has been gone from Russia for years and..."

Pavel hesitated and Natasha thought that he was about to complain about her not taking a husband to manage the family's wealth properly. It was a complaint he had made before, several times. Pavel was a very capable man who had been quick to adopt the innovations and new industries made possible by the Dacha, which was why he still had the job despite Natasha's annoyance at his attitude.

But instead he just said, "You were out of touch. And the work must go on. I had no instructions to the contrary."

"Very well. Give me a report on what has been happening since we last talked," Natasha said.

It was a long report and much of it wasn't very pleasant hearing. Many of the reforms that she had made under the influence of Bernie, and increasingly the influence of Anya, Filip and Father Kiril, had been reversed. The bonuses for good work and good ideas, the improved working conditions and pay, had been stopped and some of them had even been backtracked, treated as though they were loans, not payment, making greater debt that the serfs owed her. Then there was the diversions of funds, prices much too high paid to the Sheremetev clan for too little goods of too little quality and goods produced here sold to Sheremetev connections for kopecks on the ruble. "Director-General" Sheremetev and his greedy family hadn't chopped off the head of the golden goose, but they were halfway to strangling the poor bird in trying to squeeze extra eggs from it.

As she listened she was forced to a realization. She couldn't save it. The industrial base that she had been working to build here wasn't something she could defend from Sheremetev. Even the estates and lands that had been her family's for generations would be lost, at least temporarily, and the knowledge of that loss almost ripped the heart out of her. At the same time, this was strangely liberating. The family lands were gone, the serfs and other workers who made those lands productive would not be owned by her family, no matter what she did. The only question was who would get them. When it finally came, the decision to free her serfs from their ties to the land was easy. Better they should belong to themselves than Sheremetev, much better.

"Very well," Natasha said. "There is a proclamation I must make and legal documents that I need drawn up."

When the nature of those legal documents was made clear to him, Pavel had a fit. He explained that Natasha was a spoiled little girl and that no man would be so foolish, not even her idiot of a brother who married a peasant. He was, in fact, so angry that his thoughts about the innovations, at least the non-technical innovations came boiling out. That she was wasting her family's heritage was clear. That the peasants that she showered useless and expensive gifts on would work harder with a touch of the lash instead. Natasha was tempted to give Pavel a touch of the lash, but she restrained herself. She needed to hear this. She especially needed to hear who else among her factors and agents felt this way.

So she listened meekly, like a school girl taking her deserved scolding. And Pavel, in his anger and desperation, poured out quite a bit she needed to know.

Then she had him arrested.

Another clerk was called and the proclamations were drawn up. All the serfs on all the Gorchakov lands had all their debts to the Gorchakov family forgiven. They were, if they chose to be, released from their bonds to the land and were asked to join Natasha in the east where they would build together a new land of free people. Those who chose to stay on her lands were welcome to do so, but should be warned that those who would likely seize her lands were less likely to respect her decrees in regards to the serf's debts. Having had her documents written up, she took them off to be examined by the czar.

Meanwhile, the clerk who had taken down the documents took himself off to repeat their contents to anyone who would listen.

✧   ✧   ✧

The czar, the czarina, and his ad hoc *Duma* of Bernie, Anya, Filip, Kiril, and Tim, listened to her plan with varying degrees of shock. Tim was flabbergasted and honestly thought it was a horrible idea. Not without reason. The serfs would run, some to the east following Natasha sure enough, but others into banditry among the Cossacks. And as word spread of what she had done, other serfs would run, hoping to hide among hers. The nation would collapse. Anarchy would rule and Russia would burn.

"Perhaps," said Filip. "In fact, I suspect you're quite right. But it won't be better for waiting. Serfdom eats at Russia like a tape worm, sapping the nation's strength and killing its greatness unborn. And the longer we wait before seizing freedom, the less we will know how to handle it when we finally gain it."

He smiled, then. "If nothing else, Your Majesty, you can form a legitimate Cossack state." Filip waved his hand toward the east. "Somewhere out there."

Mikhail Romanov looked like he'd eaten something profoundly distasteful. Cossacks were outlaws, bandits, renegades.

On the other hand . . .

The czarina, it turned out, agreed with Natasha and Filip. So, that possible obstacle eliminated, the czar cosigned and endorsed her proclamation and did her one better. He invited all the Russians who would be free to join them in the east at the fortress at Ufa. Then, for almost the first time in his tenure as czar, Mikhail made a speech. In the speech he didn't command, didn't even implore, but simply offered. "Come with me to the east and freedom," Mikhail said. "Come with me if you dare. Take every steam engine you can find and put it on anything that will float and follow me to Ufa. Help me build a Russia free of serfdom."

It wasn't a great speech. But it was the best Mikhail could do on the spur of the moment. Then they loaded up all the troops they could on the two steam barges that happened to be in town and headed for Bor.

Chapter 80

"We forgot to destroy the radio," Anya said as the barge was steaming down the Oka toward the Volga and Bor.

"You can't think of everything. It was pretty wild in Murom when we left. It was looking like war was going to break out between those who wanted to follow us and those who didn't want to lose their homes and their businesses."

"Besides, Sheremetev knows we didn't try to go west, so he'll be coming after us and there aren't a lot of directions we can go on the river. If we ain't going upriver, we're going downriver."

"Sir, sir! We need help!"

Captain Ivan Borisovich Lebedev struggled out of his drink-sodden daze, trying to understand what this idiot was talking about. "What? Let Tim handle it."

"But he's not here. He left with Czar Mikhail and all those people. And we've got fires in the city! There's fighting."

"Fighting about what? And why aren't the *Streltzi* doing anything about it?"

"But the *Streltzi* are gone. Most of them."

"Is anybody still here?"

"Well, you are."

And that's when it finally penetrated. Ivan Borisovich Lebedev was in charge. Really, honestly, in charge. The thing he had tried to avoid his entire life had come upon him. He needed instructions. There was no one here to give them. That's when Ivan thought of the radio room.

Half an hour later, in the radio room, still hungover, with a half-dozen of what passed for the "leading figures" of Murom, all of them shouting at him to do something, Ivan told the radio man, "Just report to Moscow what has happened here."

The key started tapping. The locals kept yapping. And Ivan's head kept pounding.

"One at a time! You, what's your complaint?" Ivan said to a short, balding man with a pot-belly.

"The servants raided my shop and ran off! I want my goods back. And my servants back! What are you going to do about it?"

"I'm going to have you thrown in the cells if you don't quiet down. Were these your servants?"

"I was renting them," pot-belly said. "From the Gorchakov clan."

"So these are some of the serfs that Princess Natalia . . . oh, my head . . . that Princess Natalia freed or whatever. What was all that about?"

An older man with graying hair said, "Yes, they were. About half the work force in this town were serfs of the Gorchakov clan that were shipped in from their estates to work in the various shops."

"So, basically, they had a perfect right to leave," Ivan pointed out.

"Of course not. We had a contract. The Gorchakov factor signed it."

About this time there was an explosion outside. Ivan went to the window and looked out on a small town in flames. "We've got bigger problems than missing serfs." He turned back to the radio operator. "What does Moscow have to say?"

The operator shrugged. "The message probably hasn't even gotten there yet. It has to go through seven stations to get there."

Back in Moscow, Director-General Sheremetev was having his own problems. He had orders out to arrest Princess Natalia and Bernie for treason, and, thanks to the new patriarch, heresy. However, even four years after the up-timer's arrival, a single station going off line could stop the word from going out. Some of the steam barges and boats on the river system had spark gap transmitters or crystal receivers, but not all of them. Not even most of them. Which meant he had no idea where they had gone once they left Murom. And he was beginning to wonder if they had gone after the czar. Meanwhile, he hadn't heard anything from Murom in the last few hours and they weren't answering their radio.

Murom was over two hundred miles from Moscow by road and almost four hundred by riverboat. Cavalry would take at least four days, more probably a week, to get there. Riverboats would be faster but would leave them stuck on the river once they got to Murom. Meanwhile, the Gorchakov girl was running around Russia, spreading disaffection.

"Meanwhile," Colonel Shuvalov suggested, "we should order the Nizhny Novgorod *Streltzi* to arrest Princess Natalia and the up-timer."

"Are they dependable?" Sheremetev asked.

"I don't know," Shuvalov admitted. "I don't know who the commander of the local *Streltzi* is and we haven't appointed a political officer to Nizhny Novgorod yet. We should have, but we've been stretched very thin. We have one in Bor just across the river, but that's because of the dirigibles. There may be some loyalty to the Gorchakov clan since the industry that is developing there comes in large part from the Dacha. How much loyalty that will buy is anyone's guess."

"Well, find out who is in command of the *Streltzi* there. That should tell us something."

It took Colonel Shuvalov a few minutes to find out and it turned out that the *Streltzi* commander at Nizhny Novgorod was a bureau man, not a *deti boyar*. Just a bureaucrat trying to keep his head down.

"Send the orders under the authority of the *Boyar Duma* and the director-general, acting for Czar Mikhail, as usual," Sheremetev said. "That should give us the far end of the pincer." Sheremetev drew a line on the map with his finger going from Nizhny Novgorod up to Kineshma then sweeping the whole hand back toward Moscow. "Meanwhile, we need to get troops on their way from here. I want you to lead the cavalry contingent. And find me somebody trustworthy to take a couple of companies of infantry by riverboat."

Sheremetev drew his finger along the map again, this time tracing the Moskva River to where it joined the Oka, and on up the Oka to Murom. "The riverboat will probably get there before your cavalry does. They will have farther to go, but steam engines don't get tired."

"I'll be on my way at first light then," Shuvalov said. "Soonest started, soonest finished."

Dawn came and the cavalry and the riverboats left, and still no word from Murom. They weren't answering their radio nor forwarding messages in any direction. That, unfortunately, wasn't that unusual. The radio telegraph links were new and didn't have nearly enough redundancy. Well, Murom did. It was the hub for its area because it had the greatest range and because it was the Gorchakov family seat. Which meant that as long as Murom was down, messages would have to go a long way around. So why was the Murom station not active? Sheremetev wondered. It made no sense. Had they gone back to Murom for some reason and if so why hadn't they been arrested?

Sheremetev didn't expect to hear from Colonel Shuvalov for four days. But, worried over the silence at Murom, he gave orders that all messages be brought to him immediately. He didn't think to mention that the *Boyar Duma* no longer needed copies of the messages. And, honestly, it probably wouldn't have made any difference if he had. Selling copies of message traffic to interested individuals was a pretty obvious supplement to a telegraph operator's pay, and in Russia of the time a telegraph operator who wasn't selling copies was more likely to get fired than one who was.

When the news came, it was from Murom. The clerk handed Sheremetev a stack of sheets that had been typed as they came in. He didn't mention the file copy or the three copies that had been sold to other interested parties. He also failed to mention that the sun was up or that there was air in the room. The obvious need not be commented on. They, the original, the file copy and the copies for sale were all typed on a special typewriter developed at the Dacha for use in the radio telegraph stations. It used the Cyrillic alphabet, but was all capital letters, because the more different code groups there were, the longer the code groups needed to be and the longer it would take to send any message. As had been explained to Sheremetev many times, but it still irritated him. However, that was a minor irritation compared to what was to come.

✧   ✧   ✧

The first radio message Sheremetev received was semi-incoherent. It talked about Princess Natalia coming back to Murom with Czar Mikhail, freeing all the serfs in Russia, and Murom burning. It made no sense. Sheremetev sent the radio man back to the radio room to call for clarification.

The clarification, when it came, wasn't very clear at all. So Sheremetev sent his own message.

> PRINCESS NATALIA GORCHAKOV IS A TRAITOR
> TO THE BOYAR DUMA AND THE CZAR IS BEING
> HELD BY HER UNDER A SPELL. SHE AND HER
> UP-TIMER ARE TO BE SHOT ON SIGHT. THE CZAR
> IS TO BE TAKEN INTO CUSTODY FOR HIS OWN
> SAFETY.

Having sent off that message, Sheremetev called in the new patriarch to endorse the fact that the czar was under a spell.

The greatly enlarged group that had left Murom on two riverboats were in ignorance of these orders till they were halfway from Murom to the confluence of the Volga and the Oka rivers. But one of their boats had a radio on it and it picked up the clackity-clack of the message being sent from one riverside station to the next.

After some discussion, they decided to stop at the next station.

They marched up to the station which was in a village on the side of the Oka river. The telegraph crew were a family of the service nobility, but the very lowest end. The village had five families and maybe twenty-five people. It supported itself by fishing and farming. The telegraph crew received the rents from the village and a small salary, which they used to support themselves. The mother, the father and the eldest daughter, as well as three of the serfs in the village, could operate the spark gap transmitter. A small steam engine ran the generator that charged the battery. When it broke down—which it did frequently—they made do with a foot-pedal.

Whether they would have attempted to arrest the czar had they been in a position to, who knows? They were in no position to arrest anyone. There were four old-fashioned guns in the whole village. Instead, the czar had them send both ways along the chain his own orders. First was a repeat of Princess Natalia's proclamation of forgiveness of debt for the serfs tied to her family's lands and his offer of freedom for any serf that chose to join him in Ufa.

"But what about my serfs?" complained the father, in dress not dissimilar to one of his serfs. "How is my family to live without the rents?"

"And yet the work of the station is done as much by your serfs as by you," Anya said. The messages went out, and with a further message. Sheremetev was not to be obeyed. Czar Mikhail revoked his authority and ordered his arrest.

"That's actually more than I have the authority to do without the concurrence of the *Boyar Duma* and the Assembly of the Land, so I don't really expect those orders to be obeyed. But they ought to muddy the waters." And they did. The telegraph stations responded on the basis of personal choice. Some passed Sheremetev's messages and not the czar's, some passed the czar's and not Sheremetev's, some passed both, and a few passed neither.

The telegraph operators talked about what was going on. Most of them had been trained at the Dacha and most of them were of the upper end of the *Streltzi* class or the lower end of the service nobility. They were free, not serfs. Not tied to the land, but they worked for a living. Their pay was a farming village or an income, depending on where the station was located. Most of them had moved to the place they now occupied because they had been assigned to it.

Unanimity was noticeable by its absence.

Chapter 81

Sheremetev was still furious over the news that the czar was with Princess Natalia and still discussing what it would cost to have the patriarch endorse his claim that Czar Mikhail was under a spell when a new telegraph message arrived.

> BY ORDER OF CZAR MIKHAIL, FEDOR IVANOVICH SHEREMETEV IS TO BE PLACED UNDER ARREST FOR TREASON AND KIDNAPPING OF CZAR MIKHAIL AND HIS ROYAL FAMILY. HE IS ALSO SUSPECTED IN THE DEATH OF PATRARCH FILARET. CZAR MIKHAIL INVITES ALL FREEDOM LOVING RUSSIANS TO JOIN HIM AT UFA WHERE NEW LANDS WILL BE GRANTED. SERFS WILL BE RELEASED FROM THEIR BONDS TO THE LAND AND THE FREEING OF HOLY MOTHER RUSSIA WILL BEGIN.

Sheremetev threw the message across the room and the new patriarch picked it up to read, while the boyar read the rest of the messages.

> BY ORDER OF PRINCESS NATALIA GORCHAKOVNA THE DEBT OF ALL SERFS ON ALL GORCHAKOV LANDS IS HEREBY FORGIVEN. ALL MY PEOPLE

ARE INVITED TO JOIN ME AND CZAR MIKHAIL
IN UFA WHERE A NEW FREE RUSSIA IS BEING
BORN. I DO NOT REQUIRE THIS OF YOU WHO
OWE ALLIEGANCE TO ME BUT OFFER IT TO YOU.

This message Sheremetev handed to Patriarch Joseph. "These
two, oh . . ." Sheremetev paused, looking for a word vile enough
to describe the two messages, then gave it up and simply said,
"documents spell the end of order in Russia. They are the death
knell of our way of life. You must support me in this, Patriarch."

"Of course, Director-General. However . . ."

Sheremetev listened as Joseph laid out the nature of the bribe
he would demand in exchange for his support.

The word was already out. Dmitri Mamstriukovich Cherakasky,
one of Filaret's long-time friends who had only abandoned the
war party since the Ring of Fire, came storming into Sheremetev's office in the Kremlin, slamming open the door. Sheremetev
would have been expecting him if he had thought about the
copies of the dispatches that had gone to other members of the
Boyar Duma, but he hadn't.

"So the czar didn't willingly retire to the hunting lodge but was
held there." Cherakasky sneered. "I suspected that, but decided to
give you your chance because war with Poland would have been a
disaster, however well we did in Rzhev. But having him and his family, you—you bumbling fool—kidnapped him, then lost him. You're
finished, Sheremetev. I'm going to the *Boyar Duma* and you'll . . ."

Bang!

The sound of the pistol was loud in the closed room. Sheremetev
swung the pistol to point at Patriarch Joseph. "Forget the bribe.
You'll support me or you'll be where he is now."

The guards rushed in and then stood there looking back and
forth between Sheremetev and his gun, and Cherakasky bleeding out from a sucking chest wound on the floor, and Patriarch
Joseph, who stood stunned.

"Petrov, who of these are trustworthy?" Sheremetev spoke quickly,
waving his gun at the other guards. The problem was that most
of the *Boyar Duma*'s guards owed their primary loyalty to the
various boyars of the Duma, not to Sheremetev.

Petrov didn't hesitate that Sheremetev noticed. Instead he simply
drew his own pistol and pointed it at the official section leader.

"I'll need your weapon, Sergeant. You'll get it back after things are settled." He then gave quick, concise orders for two other men to take the weapons of the other three men in the detail. All the while explaining that it would be better for the disarmed men if they were in no position to interfere. "No one can blame you for what happens after you're locked up, fellows."

After the guards had been restrained, Sheremetev gave orders to the rest. Three boyars were to be arrested. "Patriarch Joseph and I have a few things to talk over."

As Sheremetev was cleaning his own house in Moscow, the riverboats were carrying the czar, Natasha and Bernie to Bor.

In Bor, Captain Ruslan Andreyivich Shuvalov, commanding the dirigible *Czarina Evdokia*, got the message first and immediately ordered the arrest of his second-in-command. He privately rather liked Nick, but Nick was on the wrong side. He also ordered the arrest of the station commander of the Bor *Streltzi*, who had also been a Gorchakov appointee. A man, as it happened, who out-ranked him, according to the new order of ranks that had been introduced since the arrival of the up-timers. But the new ranks didn't mean all that much yet, when compared to the traditions of Russia. What mattered was who you owed your allegiance to. Captain Ruslan Andreyivich Shuvalov owed his to the Sheremetev family, which meant the czar was on the wrong side, too. He prepared the dirigible for flight so he could provide tracking information and force the czar back into the hands of the *Boyar Duma* where he belonged.

Ruslan Andreyivich over-rode the political officer, who wanted to have Nick and the former commander executed. He wasn't by nature a vicious man, just utterly pragmatic. Besides, after this had all settled out, he would be working with these people or their relatives. The less blood on his hands, the easier that would be.

He didn't arrest Ivan the baker's boy for two reasons. One, Ivan was too junior, and two, he was a Sheremetev connection who had gotten the post by virtue of his tie to Boris Timofeyevich Lebedev, so should be quite dependable. He considered promoting the lad to take Nick's place, but he couldn't. Ivan was, after all, the son of a baker. *Streltzi*. He couldn't be placed over members of the service nobility.

✧   ✧   ✧

"You know," Tim commented, "when you came back to Murom, you didn't realize that word had reached the town to arrest you. But we can be pretty sure that word has reached Bor. They may think that we're heading directly to Ufa, but to get to Ufa by river we have to go right by Nizhny Novgorod and Bor."

"Do you think they will be ready for us?" Bernie asked. He'd seen Tim in the war games at the Moscow Kremlin and had been impressed by the kid in Murom.

"I don't know." Tim said. "That is, I don't know how they will be ready for us. What they will have done to prepare for us. By now they know we are on the river but some of the messages we picked up when we stopped at that radio telegraph station suggested that much of the *Streltzi* from Nizhny Novgorod are out beating the woods looking for the princess. Getting the order to go into the field to the city that *Streltzi* are stationed in is easy with the radio links, but getting the order to go back home to them once they are in the field is a lot harder. Unlike the up-timer radios, the spark gap units that we are building here are not portable. Well, you can put one on a riverboat..."

"The strategic situation?" Natasha said. "Let's keep to the point."

"Sorry, Princess!" Tim blushed. "They may be able to get them back before we get to Nizhny Novgorod, but it's not that likely. So it's probably going to be about half the garrison at Nizhny Novgorod—that's maybe a hundred people and we have almost that many with us. Nizhny's *Streltzi* are pretty well-armed. I think they have the AK4's, that is the cap locks, but not the 4.7's which have the new chamber clips. So we will have a better rate of fire. That's brand new. Only the Gun Shop, the Dacha and your *Streltzi* at Murom are equipped with the 4.7's."

"And a few hundred rich nobles who have to have the newest gun no matter how much it costs," Anya added.

Tim—who was wearing the brand new six-shot revolver—was spending quite a bit of time pink, to the amusement of the ladies.

"Anyway, we should have a better rate of fire for the first few minutes of battle if it comes to that," Bernie said. "Got it."

"Yes, but I don't think it will come to that unless we actually stop in Nizhny. I think they will look at the boats and the guns and the fact that the czar is aboard and not shoot if we don't. Maybe."

"What about Bor?"

"The same. If we don't bother them, they won't bother us."

"But we are going to bother them. We are going to go in there and take my dirigible," Czarina Evdokia said. Since it was named after her, she took a proprietary interest in the giant airship. "It's completed most of its trials and we are going to need it."

Tim nodded respectfully. He agreed with her because it was the solution to one of the biggest problems facing them. The czar, or at least the czar's family, must be protected, out of reach of the *Boyar Duma*. But at the same time, they needed a place where people could come join them until enough had joined them to take the fight to the boyars. The dirigible would let the czar reach the hoped-for followers without falling into the hands of the *Boyar Duma*. They had the place to meet, but it was too easy for the *Boyar Duma's* troops to reach by riverboat. The dirigible, which the czarina wanted for emotional and prestige reasons, Tim wanted for tactical reasons. Which meant they had to get it.

"Captain Ruslan Andreyivich Shuvalov is a skilled commander, if not overly imaginative. He knows that the dirigible is of considerable military value. He discussed it with me and Ivan on the boat that took me to Murom. He understands its scouting value but doubts its value as a cargo or passenger craft. He'll be preparing to use it to track us for the *Boyar Duma* but he won't think of us wanting it. At least, I don't think he will. Ivan, though. Ivan might consider things like the prestige having it will give us and he will certainly see the strategic value of being able to get effectively out of the boyars' range while still able to come in to strike them or recruit more forces. If I thought of it, Ivan has."

Tim had a tremendous advantage in that he knew the players. He knew Captain Ruslan Andreyivich Shuvalov and he knew Ivan. They had the same advantage when it came to him, except they probably thought he was still in Murom with his cousin. So how would they figure Bernie would look at things and how about the czar? Ruslan Andreyivich would probably not consider Princess Natasha or the czarina. He had a bit of a blind spot where women were concerned. Ivan might, but...

"I don't think Ruslan Andreyivich will be listening to Ivan that much," Tim said out loud.

"What are you talking about, Tim?" Anya asked, and Tim realized that Ruslan Andreyivich Shuvalov certainly wouldn't be considering Anya's input.

"Ruslan Andreyivich Shuvalov is smart and capable and pretty open-minded," Tim said. "But he doesn't think of women as thinking creatures and he doesn't really think of the lower class as thinking people, either. So he's not going to consider what you, the princess or the czarina contribute to our plans. He will think about Bernie and the czar; he'll probably think about the captain of the princess' guard, not knowing about Captain Vladislav Vasl'yevich's death. So he'll figure our actions based on that. He knows that Bernie is . . ." Tim ran out of words. He wasn't at all sure of how to put what was probably going through Ruslan Andreyivich's mind.

The up-timer laughed. Well, snorted humorously. "He'll figure I'm not an absolute coward but not someone that goes looking for trouble either. And sort of the same about Czar Mikhail." The up-timer looked at the czar of Russia like a friend, not a monarch, and continued. "Sorry, Boss, but he'll think it even less likely that you will attack."

"Yes, I know," said Czar Mikhail. Not like he was offended but more like someone touched by an old pain, a very old pain that had touched him many times before. "Good but weak Czar Mikhail, of kind heart and weak will. I know how I am thought of and I often wonder if they are right. Perhaps they are. I didn't want to be czar. I didn't want to take sides in this business, either. But I was given little choice in either case. Very well, General Tim. What will Ruslan Andreyivich's beliefs about me tell him? Do not fear for my feelings. I've heard worse and we have more important things to worry about."

Tim tried. "They will assume we will avoid a fight unless it's forced upon us. That's what the princess' guard captain would have recommended." It was also what Ruslan Andreyivich would see as Bernie and the czar's natural inclination. And he wouldn't be wrong. Tim didn't think it was actual cowardice on the part of either Bernie or the czar. But they had kind hearts, perhaps even soft hearts. Not so the women. The czarina, the princess, and the servant girl sat in the royal *duma* like hungry lionesses. Worse, angry lionesses. The gentle hearts of the men might seek peaceful resolution of conflicts, but the women wanted blood.

"So," said the czarina, "we look like we are sailing on by for as long as we can, then we attack them as fast as we can."

"Yes, Your Majesty. That is what I recommend and if Ruslan Andreyivich doesn't listen to Ivan, it just might work."

❖   ❖   ❖

"No, Ivan," said Captain Ruslan Andreyivich Shuvalov. "It's a worthy thought and I thank you for it. But it's not in the czar's character nor in the up-timer's. If it was Cass Lowry with the princess, maybe. He would want to charge in, and might even convince her guard captain that it was the best move. But not Bernie and not the czar. They will be looking for a place where they can hide and negotiate. Ufa's not a bad place for that. Though, I suspect the czar has underestimated the effect of the steamboats."

Ivan wanted to argue. He was eighteen, after all. But he was a soldier and he owed much of his present position to the patronage of his friend Tim's family. The captain not only outranked him in military terms but in social terms as well. Besides, the captain had a point. Taking the dirigible would be a considerable risk. Ivan would try it if it were him, but it wasn't him making the decision. And the captain had another point. They needed everyone working on the dirigible. It would be called upon soon. Either to follow the czar and report on his whereabouts or to ferry the boyars out here. Possibly both. So he let the matter drop.

"Yes, sir," Ivan agreed. "The forward right side engine bushing replacement is going slowly, but the other three engines are fine and the propeller cowlings are providing extra force. The spark gap radio is still not working and I think we are going to need it. But..." Ivan continued his report.

Chapter 82

From Murom to the confluence of the Oka and Volga rivers is about a hundred and thirty miles. They had left Murom at about eight in the morning as the sun was coming up. They had stopped for an hour at the telegraph station. However, they were going downriver, which gave them an extra two miles per hour. So they reached Nizhny Novgorod just before sunset.

The riverboat—more of a barge actually—was flat-bottomed and most of the time carried cargo. It carried quite a bit of cargo now and Czar Mikhail stood on top of the boxes for freight and waved to the people of Nizhny Novgorod as they went by.

Not knowing what else to do, the guards on the walls waved back. There was no question of shooting. The czar's face was on every ruble note in Russia and there were a lot of notes. There were also a fair number of telescopes by now, and some of them were owned by the citizens of Nizhny Novgorod. The man standing on a box of freight and waving at them was indeed Czar Mikhail and many of the guards on the wall bowed.

The barge and the one following it rounded the bend into the Volga, turning east, and kept going, with the czar of all Russia continuing to wave. The ship was drifting to the north side of the river as it reached the tributary that led to Bor, only a mile or so away. Casually, it turned into that tributary and the czar kept waving. Now he waved to the workmen from the dirigible station. The men and women who had built the dirigible *Czarina Evdoka* now got to see the real thing, for the czarina had climbed up onto the box beside her husband in full royal regalia and was waving as well. There were even a few cheers.

Whatever silly thing they were doing, it wasn't attacking. You don't attack a place by standing in the open in plain sight and waving like a silly idiot. But sometimes you might divert attention from an attack by standing on a box and waving...if the circumstances are just right.

The barge the czar was on went right on by the dock at Bor, but the barge behind it didn't. It hit the dock a little hard and the troops aboard it were almost jarred off their feet. They would have but for the captain's warning at the last minute.

"*Move!*" came the very carrying squeak of young Lieutenant—now General—Lebedev.

Ivan had heard that squeak before. His friend's voice tended toward the falsetto when he was excited. And suddenly he knew. He knew that the czar was here to take the dirigible, that Tim for whatever reason was on the czar's side. And he knew. Knew for a certainty that he could stop him if he moved now.

And he froze.

Ivan had the vice of his virtues. General Sherman's vice. The vice of a very smart man who, when taken unaware, will tend to overthink the problem rather than act when action is what is needed. It was why, in another universe, Sherman would be Grant's subordinate, not the other way around. And that—not any silliness about good blood or bad blood, not even the accident of fate that had put Tim in the right place—was what made Tim, not Ivan, the czar's general. Whose side was Ivan supposed to be on? Tim was on the czar's, but Tim's family was on the boyars'. Ivan could see in his mind what he had to do to stop Tim's attack and what he could do to aid it and did neither. Not because he lacked courage or even moral courage. But because he needed time to think things through when they hit him out of the blue.

Captain Ruslan Andreyivich Shuvalov didn't have that flaw, but he didn't understand what was going on either.

"What the devil is he doing?" Ruslan wondered. The czar was

sailing by, waving at everyone, and most of Ruslan's people were watching him do it.

There was some minor disturbance down at the docks, but what did Czar Mikhail think he was doing?

It took Ruslan minutes he didn't have to realize . . . "Oh my God. He's the decoy! The czar of all Russia has let himself be used as a decoy!" And the decoy had succeeded. He'd locked Ruslan's attention away from where it was needed.

At that point, Ruslan raised his rifle and sighted on Czar Mikhail. Then he stopped. It wasn't because his target was the czar. At least not mostly. It was respect for the czar all right, but for the czar as a man. A man he had always thought of as good, but never until that moment thought of as brave.

Instead, finally, minutes too late, Ruslan turned to try to save his command. Grabbing a dozen men who happened to be standing near him watching the czar and the czarina wave from their barge, he shouted "Follow me!" and ran for the attackers.

"On me!" Ruslan shouted, blinking into the setting sun's glare. "Push them back onto their boat!"

And he fired into the crowd of soldiers quick-marching up the street from the dock.

"Keep moving," Ruslan heard a high, squeaking voice shout as he pulled the chamber from his AK4 and stuck it in his pocket. He pulled another chamber out, and looked up as he inserted it into the rifle. "Fire, fire!" he shouted. And his men did, all twelve of them.

Some of their rounds hit, for he saw men fall. But then that high, squeaking voice came again.

"Column halt! First rank, kneel! First and second rank, ready your weapons." And the first and second ranks, at least thirty men, leveled their rifles at his scratch troop.

"Aim!"

And Ruslan heard his men turn and start to run. Ruslan looked back, looked at the troops across the street, then followed his men. Then the high, squeaking voice again. "Fire!"

That was the last he knew.

It was the ricochet that brought Ivan out of his frozen state. He couldn't change sides this fast. He just couldn't. But he also couldn't fight his friend Tim and the Czar of Holy Mother Rus. *So what can I do?* he wondered. *I can get Nick.* Nick had been a friend since Ivan arrived, even though Ruslan had taken command on their arrival. Nick hadn't held that against Ivan. He hadn't even held it against Ruslan. And Nick was someone Ivan could talk to, so it was to Nick, not Ruslan, that Ivan went.

With ninety percent of the inhabitants of Bor still gawking at the czar and his family, mopping up took much less time than Tim had thought it would. Even with one of his men dead and three wounded, he was able to get the column moving quickly, by leaving the wounded under the command of Filip, who had a flesh wound of his own.

Once they reached the hangar, his men came to a halt without orders. Tim had heard how big the *Czarina Evdokia* was, but hearing and seeing were not the same. He spent several minutes assigning guards and trying to figure out *where* to assign guards. While he was still in the process of this, he saw Ivan and Nick approaching.

Ivan had run to the hangar because that was where Nick was being held, only to find David Sikorski, the *Oprichniki* assigned to this force, already there, getting ready to shoot Nick on the basis of "we're in trouble and the only thing to do with prisoners is to kill them." This was only one of the many obnoxious things the little man had said over the months they'd been assigned here.

Ivan talked him out of killing Nick by pulling his own pistol—a gift from Tim as it happened—and pointing it at David's head. "I find I disagree with your position on killing prisoners when in dire circumstances."

"I have my orders," David said.

"I have my gun," Ivan pointed out.

Nick started to laugh. "I think gun trumps orders." Before David could move, Nick had pulled the pistol out of his hands.

David looked at Nick, then looked at Ivan, then ran. Ivan considered shooting him, fairly seriously, but he just couldn't bring himself to shoot an unarmed man in the back. And, apparently, neither could Nick.

"So, Ivan," Nick said, "what's been happening?"

"Czar Mikhail has arrived," Ivan said. "Sort of. He's out in the middle of the channel."

"This I have to see."

"Ivan, Nick, come over here." Tim couldn't help smiling as he recognized his friends.

"Have you heard anything about Princess Natalia?" Nick asked. "I've been worried ever since they arrested me."

"She's on the barge with Czar Mikhail," Tim said. "They'll land as soon as we're secure here."

"And then what?" Ivan asked.

"That depends, Ivan. What's the status of the *Czarina Evdokia*?"

"Mostly ready to fly. Certainly it can be made ready to fly by morning."

"Very good, then. Czar Mikhail and Czarina Evdokia are going to take possession of their dirigible," Tim said. "Nick will be placed in command and you can be my assistant."

And that's how Ivan came to defect, albeit accidentally.

It took a few more minutes to settle things, and Ivan got another shock when someone referred to Tim as "General."

"That's the signal," Czar Mikhail said. The captain of the boat nodded and waved. There was a change in the sounds of the engines and the barge started backing up. It took a few more minutes and another change in direction to get the cargo barge docked.

The crowd followed the barge, and Czar Mikhail and Czarinia Evdokia continued to wave to them. As the crowd poured onto the docks, Bernie got a bit nervous. The czar was the czar, after all, and a crowd like that could have assassins sprinkled though it. Or just the random nutcase. Even if it didn't, crowds were notorious for changing moods when they didn't get precisely what they wanted. They should have had the docks guarded before they called the barge in. More poor planning. It came, Bernie knew, from lack of real experience. Unfortunately, most of the real experience was on the other side.

But the czar carried it off. He waved, he shook hands, patted people on the back, and these weren't pushy fans at a rock concert. They were working Joes, seeing their monarch mostly for the first or maybe second time in their lives. They didn't want to hurt him or the czarina. Just being noticed was a big deal. They got through the crowd and the people followed them as they walked up the dock to the shore and then up the street toward the hanger complex where the big dirigibles were built. It was a massive building, a cathedral of the air.

Impressive, but not pretty. An example of brute force and the massive investment of labor filling in the gaps of knowledge. But it stood, and it held a massive airship and the parts to make another. Finally, when they reached the hangar, the czar's forces noticed and stopped the crowd, politely but firmly explaining that the czar and czarina needed to talk to their advisers.

In the massive hangar where Czarina Evdokia met her namesake, there was quiet. Tim, Nick, Tim's friend Ivan, Filip Pavlovich, and a grizzled old *Streltzi* who had effectively become Tim's sergeant major, were standing around talking quietly. They looked over at the new arrivals and started in their direction.

That was apparently when Anya noticed that Filip had been wounded because suddenly she was gone, moving like lightning to Filip's side.

When Bernie got there, Nick and Tim were watching the scene, while Anya, oblivious to them all, fussed over the slightly wounded Filip, who was eating it up.

"I'm an astronaut or the closest thing Russia has in this century," Nick said, in a tone of profound disgust. "And a war hero."

"I'm a war hero too, and the youngest general in the history of Russia," Tim agreed. "Even if the czar only gave me the rank because he didn't have an army to give me."

"And who gets the girl?"

"The nerd!" they said together in a harmony of disgust.

"What is the world coming to?" Bernie agreed, amused.

A few hours later, with Anya still fussing over Filip, they got down to business.

"Somebody tell me, please," Nick whined, "why we're going to Ufa. It's the back of beyond."

"Because we need a place that's far enough out that it will be difficult for Sheremetev to just roll over it."

"Ufa is on a river," Ivan pointed out. "Doesn't sound safe to me."

"You're right," Tim said. "But who says we're going to stay in

Ufa? It's just a...staging area. Well, not just a staging area. Ivan the Terrible built a fort there, you know. And it's about as far upriver as you can go in one of the steam barges. You can get a little past it, yes, but it's the last fortified position out that way. If we were to stop, say, at Nizhny Novgorod, one, Sheremetev would have to come after us. And two, it would be real easy for him to get here."

Ivan nodded. "That's true. So what you want to do is use Ufa as your border with Old Russia."

"Exactly," Czar Mikhail said. "Meanwhile, we will find a place that is difficult to reach save by dirigible and build a safe haven there. So what we want to do is ship as much to Ufa as possible by boat and barge, and then from Ufa we'll take what we have to on to...whatever place we find. That's the basic outline. The details will have to be filled in as we go along. That will be Tim's job. And yours."

Chapter 83

"Because you must!" David Sikorski shouted. "The *Boyar Duma* has ordered the arrest. Director-General Sheremetev wants these people stopped!"

"One of those *people*," the commander of the Nizhny Novgorod *Streltzi* snarled, "is the czar of Holy Rus. And if he wants to go, I'm letting him go."

David pulled out his emergency pistol. "The patriarch has proclaimed that the czar is under a spell!"

"Didn't look like it to me," the commander said.

"Can you imagine Czar Mikhail standing on a barge, waving to peasants? Of course he was under a spell! Send a radio message. You'll get confirmation from Moscow." David rubbed his eyes. It had not been a good evening so far.

After making his way to the Volga River, stealing a rowboat, rowing across the river, and having to walk a mile back to Nizhny Novgorod, he had to deal with these uncultured cretins. He had bribed his way into the commander's office and had some support among the officers. Much of the service nobility was unhappy with the changes that Czar Mikhail had proclaimed since his escape from the hunting lodge. The loss of serfs would ruin some of these men and probably do some harm to all of them.

"Just listen to me," David finally got out. "What the czar is being forced to do will destroy all order in Russia. We'll be back to the

Time of Troubles. Radio Moscow. There will be great rewards for those who support me in this."

And they did. It took most of the rest of the night, but by the next morning David had his force. It was barely two hundred men, perhaps fifty of the service nobility and one hundred fifty of the *Streltzi*.

The next morning at the docks, they loaded up the ferry that ran to and from Nizhny Novgorod and Bor, and began taking men across the river.

"Don't overload her!" Nick shouted. "I know she's big, but she's not a boat!"

"Are you sure this thing is safe?" Tami Simmons muttered to Bernie. "I don't want my husband and kids, not to mention me, falling out of the sky."

"Safer than any airplane in this century," Bernie said. "And that guy over there is probably one of the most experienced dirigible pilots in the world."

"And just how much experience are we talking about?"

Bernie shrugged. "Not a lot. Maybe two hundred hours. But he's the best we've got, and that's the quickest way out."

"Maybe we ought to take the steamboat," Gerry Simmons said.

"Okay by me," Bernie said. "But you're the ones who have to talk to the czar and czarina about it."

"Well, scratch that idea," Tami sighed. "Alexsey is running a little fever."

"Troops!" someone shouted. "Troops landing!"

"Landing where?" Bernie shouted back.

"On the banks of the Volga," said Petr Kadian, one of the Gorchakov *deti boyars*. "That way!" He pointed.

Tim headed for him. "How many? What strength?"

Tim followed Petr Kadian down the street to where he could see the troops forming up down by the river, though forming up seemed rather a generous overstatement of the sort of milling mob that was down by the river. Part of that feeling was because Tim was a professional. Not a very old or experienced one, but a professional nonetheless. Part of it was that he was still very young and most of his experience was with game pieces, not men.

All of which didn't mean that Tim wasn't right. The force that

David had raised in Nizhny Novgorod was only partly *Streltzi* and not the better part of Nizhny Novgorod's *Streltzi*. They were filled out by peasants who had very little training. If they had been defending their city walls, they would have been fine. If they had been called up to fight off an invasion with time to get used to the idea, they might have done all right. But they had been drafted into a scratch force to go arrest the czar—and in one night. They weren't sure if they should be obeying this stranger, whatever the radio telegraph said. Why should they trust the radio? It was new, it was a device, not a person they knew. They had seen the czar standing on a steam barge just the day before. They liked him. He had waved to them and so had the czarina. They really wished that political officer from Bor had just, well, stayed in Bor and not bothered them.

So they milled around, argued about where to stand and who was in front and who was behind in the line of march, and hoped that they would be too late. Tim didn't know that was what was happening. He wasn't experienced enough to know what was happening just by looking, but he was bright and had the right instincts. There was something very weak-looking about the force he was facing. He didn't know what it was, but he could feel it. It was a big force. Almost twice as big as he had been expecting, something like two hundred men. But they didn't have the AK4's he'd been expecting. Two-thirds of them didn't even have AK3's; they had old match-lock muzzle-loaders. "Come on. Let's form the men up," he said to Petr Kadian.

That proved unnecessary. By the time they got back to the hangar, Ivan had the men they had brought with them from Murom formed up with the help of Princess Natasha's more experienced guardsmen.

"So what do we do, General?" Ivan asked, with a grin.

Tim thought about it. The land between the river and the town was open; muddy bank fading to grassy field to streets and buildings. His force was outnumbered, but at the same time each of these people had sat down with the czar, the czarina, and Princess Natasha. They had talked with Bernie and Filip and they were volunteers who knew what they were fighting for. They could sit in the town and fight from behind the buildings. It would work, but it would get a lot of people killed. *No, that isn't the way.*

"We'll march out to meet them."

Ivan gave him a look and Petr Kadian asked, "Why?"

"You saw them," Tim said, still trying to figure out exactly what he had noticed about the invaders.

Petr Kadian nodded.

"Well, how did they look to you?"

Petr Kadian was by no means a military genius, but he had served the Gorchakov clan as an armsman and retainer for near twenty years. He had seen armies and he had seen battles. He had seen fierce resistance to overwhelming odds and armies coming apart in the face of a light breeze. He hadn't noticed it when he was out there looking at the opposing force because it wasn't his job to notice that sort of thing. But now that the boy general brought it up, he realized that those fellows out there were... "A rout waiting to happen, sir."

That was what Tim had seen without quite knowing why.

Ivan, now that it had been explained, knew why. "We want them to see each other run."

"More importantly, we want them to see that we won't," Tim said. "We want them to see us as a real army. The czar's army. Small maybe, but real."

They marched out in two columns with sergeants counting cadence loudly. When they were a little over one hundred yards from the still-milling mob from Nizhny Novgorod, they made a right turn and the columns stretched out into lines. Finally Tim called them to halt, then shouted, "Left, face!"

"Dress ranks!" Tim carefully paid no attention to the mob from Nizhny Novgorod as he watched the men dress their ranks, then as he walked down the line, commenting on uniforms and weapons. It wasn't a bluff. Tim was quite sure these men would slaughter the mob they were facing. And it wasn't a matter of bravery. Tim wasn't sure how to put what it was. But he never would consider doing this if he were facing Sergeant Hampstead's men. Nor if he were facing the Moscow *Streltzi*, even without the walking walls. Finally, he looked over his shoulder.

The mob of Nizhny Novgorod was no longer milling around, but they weren't forming themselves into a unit either. They were just standing there, staring.

Tim shook his head. "All right, men," Tim shouted. "On the

command, the first rank will kneel and ready their rifles. Pick your targets. We want to hit as many in the first volley as possible. We will then wait till the breeze clears the smoke away before the second rank fires." Tim looked back at the men across the field then continued, in as loud and penetrating a voice as he could manage, "There will be no reason to rush."

A shot rang out. Tim didn't spin or jump; he had been half-expecting it. He turned around to see a man near the end of the sort of arching line that the Nizhny Novgorod contingent had drifted into. There was smoke drifting from a musket in his hands. "Sergeant Kadian," Tim said loudly.

"Yes, General?" Kadian asked.

"That uncultured fellow with the smoke coming from his musket is your target."

"Right, General!" Kadian sounded quite pleased. And men started edging away from the fellow who had shot his musket.

"Very well. Where was I? After the first rank has fired and the air has cleared, the second rank will, on command, advance five paces, kneel, and fire. When the air has cleared again, the first will . . ."

Bernie and Natasha were boarding the dirigible when they heard the shot. They didn't turn. It was just one shot and all it indicated was that they were in a hurry. The *Czarina Evdokia* wasn't the *Graf Zeppelin*. It was a seventeenth-century airship built by seventeenth-century craftsmen informed by late-twentieth-century knowledge. Still, it was the same basic shape as the *Graf Zeppelin*, if a bit smaller. They loaded in a dozen passengers, and Captain Nikita Ivanovich Slavenitsky, the first Russian to fly, gave the order to pull her out of the giant hangar.

Tim finished his little speech and ordered the first rank to kneel. The Nizhny Novgorod force had lost several men who just faded away, but not enough. They still outnumbered Tim's men. "Take aim! Fire!"

Blaaam! Blam! Blam!

A bit ragged, but not too bad. And certainly better than the spatter of shots that the Nizhnys had put out in response.

"Wait for it!" Tim shouted. "Let the breeze clear the smoke!" *Let the enemy see their dead and think about being elsewhere.*

The breeze was taking its time in clearing away the smoke. And when it did, the results were a bit disappointing. They were at the outside edge of the AK4.7's range. Well outside of the effective range of a musket, but Tim had hoped for better. Almost fifty men had shot and less than ten of the enemy had fallen.

"Second rank advance!" Tim moved forward with the new front rank. "Your left! Your left! Halt!

"Kneel. Ready! Aim! Fire!"

Blam! BlBlaBlaaaam! Blam! Blam!

Definitely a bit ragged. It was strange. Tim should have been scared and, in a way he was. But the effect it had on him was weird. He just noticed things. Every detail became intense and distinct. The stench of the air, not just the acrid smoke of the burned powder but the smell of the river's muddy bank, combined with the dew on the grass. The patterns the smoke made as it wafted away under the light breeze. And, most of all, the enemy across the field. It was almost as if he could see their faces. Feel the fear that was eating away at the little discipline they had. He was honestly a little amazed that they had held this long.

Then the *Czarina Evdokia* appeared over the roofs of Bor. It was massive and it was flying. It wasn't the first time these men had seen it. It had made several test flights and some of them had gone over Nizhny Novgorod. But in this case, it meant that their last reason for being here was floating away.

"Next rank! Forward five paces!"

The Nizhny Novgorod force scattered. Tim let them. Honestly, he had nothing against those men. They were following the orders they had been given by their lawful lords.

Ivan came over. "So what now, Tim?"

"We go to Ufa."

Czarina Evdokia looked out the window of the *Czarina Evdokia*, awash in conflicting emotions. Staying alive in the bear pit of Russian politics wasn't ever easy, and her habit—along with her husband's—had been to keep her head down. That hadn't worked. Apparently it had in the other timeline, but not in this one. Now they were out of position. They couldn't keep their heads down and Evdokia wasn't at all sure that Mikhail would be able to handle being his own man. Or that she would be able to handle it. What would Sheremetev and the *Boyar Duma* do now that Mikhail had escaped the relatively comfortable prison? It was safe to assume that the gloves would come off, but how? Would they declare that Mikhail was False Mikhail, like the False Dmitris? Would they depose him in favor of Sheremetev and his family?

Evdokia didn't know. All she really knew was that she was scared to death and at the same time thrilled to be alive and flying over the countryside in a dirigible named in her honor. She looked over at her friend and confidant, Natasha, and wondered what the future would bring.

Natasha didn't notice. She was holding Bernie's arm and wasn't quite sure how it had happened. Some time, while she was watching the battle of Bor probably. But she had no desire at all to let the arm go.

Nor the man it belonged to. So many other customs and attitudes were being cast aside, why should she worry about this one any longer?

And so many things would be changing for them, anyway. She thought about what Filip had said to the czar, when he compared him to a Cossack. He'd been joking, but the more Natasha pondered the matter the more profound that jest became.

Everyone knew there were noblemen out there in the Cossack bands, not just runaway serfs. One of them, the Polish-Lithuanian nobleman Aleksander Józef Lisowski, had even invaded Muscovy twenty years earlier at the head of an outlaw army. He'd besieged Bryansk, defeated two Russian armies sent against him, burned Belyov and Likhvin and taken Peremyshl, and then defeated another Russian army at Rzhev. He'd finally left at that point, but not before burning Torzhok also.

Lisowski himself had died not long afterward. But his men still remained and still considered themselves an army. The *Lisowczycy*, they called themselves; "Lisowski's men."

There were possibilities out there in the frontier lands of eastern Europe; eastward as well as to the south. People came to such lands for many reasons; usually running from something but also looking for adventure and fortune. Former serfs, former free men, former noblemen—the distinctions became blurry in the borderlands; sometimes, to the point of vanishing altogether.

What could happen in such lands, if there were a true czar to serve as a rallying point?

She didn't know, but she planned to find out.

Cast of Characters

Anya	Runaway slave
Bates, Brandy	Researcher at the National Library
Bates, Donna	Brandy's mother
Cherkasski, Ivan Borisovich	Prince; chief of Musketeer Bureau
Fedorov, Anatoly	Apothecary
Gorchakov, Natalia ("Natasha") Petrovna	A princess of Russia; Vladimir's sister
Gorchakov, Sofia Petrovna	Natalia's aunt and chaperone
Gorchakov, Vladimir Petrovich	A prince of Russia; Natasha's brother
Hampstead, John Charles	English mercenary in Russian army
Izmailov, Artemi Vasilievich	General in the Russian army
Khilkov, Ivan	Russian cavalry colonel
Korisov, Andrei	Gunsmith
Kotov, Gavril	Orthodox priest
Kotov, Kseniya	Father Gavril's wife
Lebedev, Boris Timofeyevich "Tim"	Russian junior officer
Lebedev, Ivan Borisovich	Commander at Murom; Tim's cousin
Lowry, Cass	American hired by Russians
Maslov, Ivan	Russian junior officer
Mikhailovich, Ivan ("Shorty")	Steamboat operator
Mikhailovich, Pavel ("Stinky")	Steamboat operator
Millerov, Mikhail	Commander of Cossacks
Nickovich, Petr ("Pete")	Artisan and natural philosopher

Odoevskii, Ivan Nikitich	Bureau of the Exchequer
Petrov, Boris Ivanovich	A bureaucrat of Moscow
Petrov, Ivan Borisovich	Boris' son
Petrov, Maryia	Boris' wife
Petrov, Pavel Borisovich	Boris' son
Radziwill, Janusz	Commander of Polish incursion
Repinov, Ivan	Russian spy for Polish forces
Romanov, Alexsey	Son of Czar Mikhail
Romanov, Evdokia "Doshinka"	Czarina of Russia
Romanov, Feodor Nikitich "Filaret"	Patriarch of the Russian Orthodox Church; father of Czar Mikhail
Romanov, Irinia	Daughter of Czar Mikhail
Romanov, Mikhail Fedorivich	Czar of Russia, son of Filaret
Sheremetev, Fedor Ivanovich	Russian boyar; cousin to Czar Mikhail; chief of the Bureau of Records
Shein, Mikhail Borisovich	General in the Russian army
Shuvalov, Leontii	Colonel in the Russian army
Shuvalov, Ruslan Andreyivich	Commander of dirigible unit at Bor
Sikorski, David	Political officer at Bor
Simmons, Tami	Up-time nurse hired by the czar
Slavenitsky, Nikita Ivanovich	Pilot
Smirnov, Lazar	Electronics and radio technician; fifth cousin to the czar
Stefanovich, Petr	Mechanic
Trotsky, Fedor Ivanovich	A Russian spy
Tupikov, Filip Pavlovich	Artisan and natural philosopher
Vasa, Wladyslaw IV	King of Poland
Vinnikov, Vladislav Vasl'yevich	Princess Natasha's captain of guards
Zeppi, Bernard ("Bernie")	Up-timer hired by Vladimir